WEST OF SUNSET

WEST OF SUNSET

VALERIE ANAND

SPEAKING VOLUMES, LLC
NAPLES, FLORIDA
2017

West of Sunset

ISBN 978-1-62815-413-9

For my husband, Dalip

CONTENTS

Part One
NITA AND PERRY: 1956-7

1	The Will of God: 1956	15
2	An Extraordinary Scale of Priorities: 1956	22
3	Other People's Festivals: 1956	36
4	Causes of Dispute: 1956-7	50
5	Shadows: 1957	66
6	Love Without Prospects: 1957	77
7	Positively Negative: 1957	89
8	Kaleidoscope: 1957	98
9	Drunk in Charge: 1957	108

Part Two
SHANTI: 1966-71

10	The Day of Crisis: 1966	121
11	Letter from Home: 1966	133
12	Pressures: 1969	142
13	If Only . . . : 1969	158
14	Tears at the Wedding: 1971	170
15	Desperation: 1971	187
16	The Way Out: 1971	195
17	A Place to Live: 1971	205
18	Little Hunted Hares: 1971	215
19	Alien Life: 1971	225

Part Three
RAMINDER ROSE: 1980-88

20	Journeys and Meetings: 1980	243
21	Shall We Dance?: 1981	255
22	Drama at Diwali: 1981	270
23	Dreams and Reality: 1984	286
24	The Vigil: 1984	302
25	The Nightmare: 1984	312
26	Demonstration: 1984	324
27	Polarisation: 1984	332
28	Mutual Acquaintance: 1985-87	345
29	Dreams Become Reality: 1987	359
30	A Matter of Honour: 1987	366
31	Secret: 1987	375
32	The Bruised Apple: 1987-88	385
33	Requiem: 1988	397
34	Dusk and Firelight: 1988	405

ACKNOWLEDGEMENTS

In preparing this book, I had many facts to check and did so from a variety of sources.

Chief among the works consulted were *Amritsar: Mrs Gandhi's Last Battle* by Mark Tully and Satish Jacob (Jonathan Cape) and *The Nehrus and the Gandhis, an Indian Dynasty* by Tariq Ali (Pan Books).

For information on police work and the relationship between the police and the Indian community, I am indebted to Inspector Hayes, Community Liaison Office, Wandsworth Police Station and to PC Brij Rajanwal, both of whom allowed me to interview them at length.

Above all, I am indebted to my husband who read the manuscript through for me and set me right on many details.

The Virk and Bhatia Family Trees

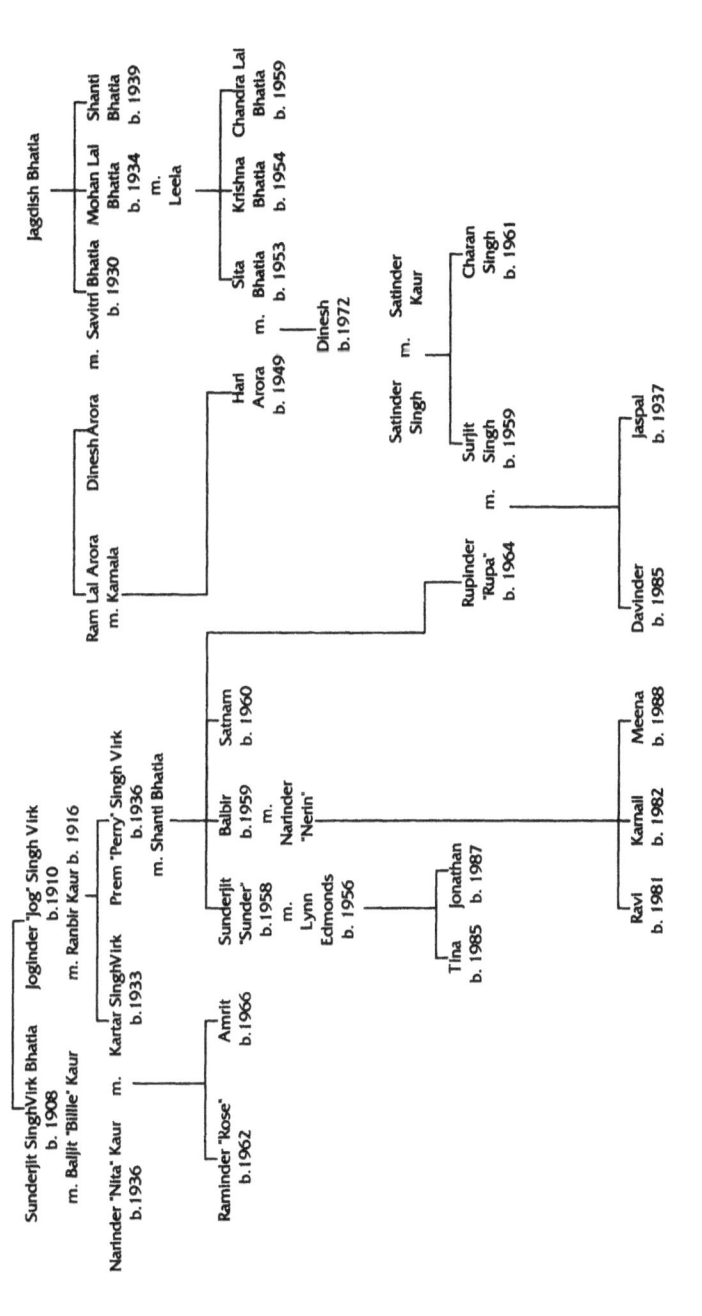

PART ONE

NITA AND PERRY

1956-7

Chapter One

The Will of God
1956

On the long, hot, crowded train journey back to Delhi from
Bombay, Ranbir did not notice the absence of her son and her
daughter-in-law too painfully. On the train she and Joginder
shared their carriage with a four-generation Hindu clan consist-
ing of a silent, white-clad great grandmother at one end, two
small and vociferous babies at the other, and a number of
chattering ladies and concentratedly card-playing males, of assorted ages, in between. There were also some children who
kept wanting to explore the train, go to the toilet and be given
things to eat.

Amid their numbers and their noise, the Virks had little
chance even to think about the parting just behind them, let
alone brood about it. By the time the train pulled into Delhi,
Ranbir had swollen ankles from sitting up all night and a headache from the din and Jog's face was lined with tiredness beneath his blue turban. He found a rickshaw and they set off for
home, half an hour's journey through the scorching dust of a
summer day already savagely hot before nine in the morning.
By the time the rickshaw-wallah had pedalled them in sight of
Safed Gardens, the block of flats where they lived, Ranbir was
preoccupied mostly with thirst.

Safed meant white, and when the flats were first built they had
been painted white accordingly. Now the paint, under constant
assault from the sun and the dust and the drips from the washing which the inhabitants hung over their balconies, had
dimmed to a faint ochre and it was peeling. As they climbed the
staircase to their second-floor apartment, Ranbir thought
crossly, and not for the first time, that whoever chose the name
should have looked ahead more carefully.

Then she followed Jog over the threshold and came, instantly, face to face with the half-open doors to the rooms where her second son Prem, whom Jog had nicknamed Perry, and her daughter-in-law Narinder, whom he called Nita, had slept. She could see the divans they had slept on, the shelf where Perry had kept his books and the recess where Nita had hung her saris. Shelf and recess alike were bare.

The emptiness hit her like a wave. She made blindly for the kitchen just as their maidservant Dina heard them and came out. Dina looked at her mistress's face and promptly embraced her.

"It is God's will, mam."

"They've gone, Dina. Both my sons now. And my dear daughter-in-law too." Ranbir hid her face in the folds of Dina's battered working sari. It was a dismal affair of cabbage-green cotton and tomorrow, Ranbir thought, she would go out and buy clothes of that colour for herself because dismal tones were all she wanted to wear for the rest of her life.

Jog's voice broke in. "Cold drinks and something to eat, Dina. Your mistress is hot and tired. We both are." He detached his wife and led her into the sitting room where Ranbir sank on to a divan and pulled her feet under her. "There, you will feel better when you have had something."

"You are not feeling it as I am feeling it," said Ranbir protestingly.

"Yes, I am." Jog switched on the ceiling fan and threw himself flat on the cool tiled floor. He closed his eyes. "But we shall get used to it. Nita should be with her husband, and young men should go out into the world and learn. Perry will come home with a business management diploma from a British college and he will get a good job and make a good match . . . "

"But Kartar already has his accountancy qualifications and he is not coming home; he is staying to work in England and that is why we have sent his wife out to him!"

"He is wanting some experience of working abroad. I have told you, I approve. They will all be back in time, and the better for their travels; you will see." He opened his eyes and sat up, hearing the slip-slap of Dina's mules. "Here's our cool drink. Come, we have not had a death in the family."

Ranbir sighed. She drank some lime juice and was pleased to hear, as Dina returned to the kitchen, the pleasant spluttering of puris being fried. She propped her back against the wall behind her. Ranbir had a straight back of which she was proud and an aquiline profile which was beginning, now that she was turned

16

forty, to look very dignified.

"You say they will come back," she said, "but Kartar's last letter was all what opportunities there are in England and if he wants Narinder" – Ranbir did not like the name Nita – "with him, that is a sign that he means to stay for a long time and . . . "

"Nita was missing her husband," said Jog mildly, shifting to an armchair. The room was shadowed and the breeze from the fan was a relief after the sweltering streets. He was beginning to feel less tired.

Ranbir sighed again, impatiently. Most people were given pet names. She had never acquired one except for a very private one which her husband used only in bed. But Joginder was usually known as Jog and only their elder boy Kartar had somehow escaped being nicknamed like his brother and his sister-in-law. She thought of it as an escape, not because she disapproved of pet names but because Jog always seemed to pick on European-sounding ones. He had indeed inflicted a much more blatant one on Ranbir's own sister, Baljit, whom he persisted in addressing as Billie, which wasn't merely European but positively colonial, with distressing associations such as hillbillies and billy-cans.

To Ranbir, whose father had agitated so passionately for Indian independence that he had landed himself with a prison sentence, this kind of thing was infuriating. She knew from experience that it was quite useless to try to explain it to the Anglophile Jog. He couldn't see it, any more than he could see why she didn't want their sons to go to England. In both matters, the small and the great, he had simply overridden her. Not because he was a bully, but because in all sincerity he couldn't understand her objections. Sometimes she felt frustrated enough to burst.

He had heard the sighs, and misinterpreted them. "They will all be all right. Nita and Perry both speak good English; they will cope."

"Yes, yes, I know." Ranbir also spoke good English but set little store by it. She had said repeatedly that she could never understand why Safed Gardens should have half its name in English. "Why can it not all be in Hindi?" It was another irritation that Jog spoke English nearly as often as he spoke Punjabi and had taught their sons to do the same, and had insisted that it was a prerequisite for Kartar's wife. "Or she won't fit in with us."

She switched to another source of anxiety. "I am still doubtful;

should we have sent those two off together? Mr Virk and Mrs Virk, and about the same age; people will think they are man and wife instead of brother and sister-in-law. There may be all sorts of confusions."

"No, there won't. Nita is very sensible, with good, traditional values. You have said that yourself, so often. That's why you have got on with her so well. Besides, she thinks of nothing but Kartar. I have said all this before." He refilled their tumblers. "And that is not what you are really worrying about. I know what is on your mind. It was why I was so determined that Kartar should be married before he went. It is a pity Perry was so obstinate about that. But he said he was not ready for marriage until he had his diploma and young men cannot be forced. Even when they are going abroad."

"Foreign girls," said Ranbir grimly. "Well, on his last night here I said to him, son, see that you don't bring some foreign stranger back as your wife. It will be bad enough if he has affairs! Things are different in the West; they are so casual there. And Perry has not always good judgment. Look how he took up with that Hindu boy from the bazaar – Mohan Lal or whatever his name was. Not that there was anything wrong with Mohan Lal but it is better that Sikhs make friends with Sikhs. He never thinks ahead . . . "

"My mother," said Jog patiently, "was a Hindu." They had had this conversation before, in varying forms.

"Yes, yes, I know, but that was then and things are different now. The two communities are separate now."

"More's the pity," said Jog. "Well, Perry is on his way now and that is that. His brother and sister-in-law will keep an eye on him. You are quite a demon sometimes, Ranbir. You want to watch over people all the time, for their own good, and push them the way you think they should go. We must not worry. We must wish them all well and trust to their upbringing and to God's will."

God's will. Ranbir, upright and unsmiling, thought that over. It seemed a peculiar choice on the part of God. India had spent a couple of centuries under British domination and had struggled out of it less than one decade ago, at the cost of bloodshed and tragedy in which her father's incarceration had been only an unimportant detail. And now, as though the absence of the English were unbearable, half the younger generation did nothing but talk wistfully of going there one day, and three of her own young people had actually gone, following the English to their homeland for all the world as though they had fallen in love with them.

Ranbir was not only worrying; Ranbir had discovered that she was exceedingly annoyed, particularly with God.

The annoyance, however, had a therapeutic effect. As Dina appeared, with puris, fruit, and more lime juice, Ranbir decided that after she had eaten, she would wash and change into her dark blue salwar kameeze which was subdued but quite smart and perhaps she wouldn't go out and buy cabbage-coloured garments after all. She would speak to Dina about the lime juice instead. It wasn't cool enough: the bottle couldn't have been standing in its cold water bath for more than half an hour. Dina should have prepared for them better.

Ranbir, in fact, had got to take her exasperation out on something or somebody.

In his certainty that there was no harm in despatching Perry and Nita to travel together, Jog was entirely right. Nita, standing beside Perry at the rail of the Italian ship *Venetian*, felt very much as though she were in charge of a younger brother and knew that her companion was slightly in awe of her.

Perry was actually the elder by two months, but to him, Nita seemed to belong more to his mother's generation than to his own. Glancing at her now, he thought that her firm, square little face was pretty but very adult in its outlines. She was wearing a sari, in which she looked alarmingly sophisticated, and somehow complete. Even in the brisk sea-wind, the sari's gold-striped loose end was not allowed to flap but hung quietly, controlled apparently by willpower. He couldn't think how she did it, and wouldn't dream of asking.

They had taken possession of their berths and in each other's company had eaten their first meal aboard but they had had little conversation. Now he said, a little awkwardly, "Does it feel strange to you, to be setting out on such a journey?"

Nita considered. "A little, yes. But Kartar is there at the other end, my husband and your brother. You will have your studies, and I will have an Indian household just as we would at home. Classrooms and kitchens and markets are much alike, anywhere."

"You're very brave," said Perry awkwardly.

"Oh, no, I don't think so. Practical, perhaps. Of course, we

19

shall miss our own society. I hope we are able to make friends of our own sort. Kartar has written me that there is a Sikh temple in London and there are even a few ladies there. It is helpful if we have some sort of community around us."

"Did Kartar write you anything about how long he thinks he will stay in England?"

"No, but I have this feeling that perhaps it will be just until you have qualified. Then maybe we will all come home together."

And she hoped and prayed that *all* would mean more than the three of them. Six months she and Kartar had been married before he went away, and there had been no child. It was a most wretched disappointment and her mother-in-law had been very sad about it. She hoped that in England, soon, she would put it right. If so, surely Kartar would want his children brought up at home in India?

Perry rested his chin on his forearms and glanced sidelong to where the ship's wake stretched out eastwards across the cerulean sea towards the hazy horizon. India lay beyond that horizon, falling further astern with each moment, dropping over the curve of the earth as he, Prem Singh Virk, sailed away to a new life and the new freedoms of the West, which he had seen in films but never tasted. In the West, if he liked, he could go out with a girl or drink openly in a pub instead of secretly in the back room of a colleague from the government office where they were clerks, using mouthwash and sucking peppermints before going home to brave his mother's sensitive nose.

He was a thin boy, only just turned twenty, not yet filled out completely. His turban still looked a little top-heavy on him. But in England, he'd become a man. He'd get his diploma and although Kartar and Nita might be making comfortable plans for them all to travel home together then, he, Perry, had other ideas. Kartar was going to work for a while in England now that he had finished studying; well, why shouldn't Perry do the same?

Why, indeed, shouldn't he, Perry, make a successful career and a permanent new life abroad?

He turned his head the other way and looked westwards, the direction in which the ship was steadily forging. The sun had swung over ahead of them and was descending towards the sea. "We're travelling west of the sunset," he said. "It's an adventure."

Nita did not reply. Calm, practical Nita had in fact been suddenly swept by panic. Kitchens and markets might well be much the same in England as they were in India, but would Kartar be the same? Three years was a long time for a man to spend away from home, among strangers. He had a steady personality, but . . .

He had once told her that she had attracted him at their first meeting because she was so serene and poised. Serene and poised, therefore, she must remain. But just at this moment, it was a facade. Her feelings went deeper, indeed, than the fear that Kartar might have changed. He still sounded like himself in his letters. The true cause of her fear was England itself, that alien, unknown destination.

Chapter Two

An Extraordinary Scale
of Priorities
1956

They were on the *Venetian* because there had been one delay after another in obtaining their passports and in the end the direct boat to England had sailed with a box of Perry's books but without either Perry or his sister-in-law.

"Bureaucracy!" snorted Jog, although he was a civil servant himself and a stickler for making sure that all forms in his department were completed in triplicate and countersigned. In the end, the *Venetian* had offered their only chance of berths in time to get Perry to England for the start of his college term. The journey involved disembarking at Naples and finishing the journey, except for the ferry across the Channel, by train.

"We shall at least see something of Europe," Nita had said. But they did not see very much, since the shipping company's representative shepherded them rapidly from boat to train and then into another train, and most of Europe passed in a blur.

The weather deteriorated as they went north. It was August but before they reached Paris it had become clear that this was no guarantee of sunshine. They crossed from Calais to Dover on a tossing grey sea under a restless grey sky and although neither of them had ever been seasick on the *Venetian*, Perry to his annoyance succumbed in the middle of the Dover Strait.

Then there were the white cliffs, clear and hard-edged in the distance, looming up like a rampart as the ship approached, and there was the slow business of disembarkation, and Immigration Control through which they slowly shuffled, presenting documents on request, with great attention being paid to the fact that they were immunised against smallpox, typhoid and cholera. They struggled through the processes of collecting their luggage and convincing Customs that they were not carrying more than the proper allowances of cigarettes and alcohol. "We haven't got anything like that!" said Nita, gesturing indignantly, her left palm facing their interrogator as if to hold him off and describing scandalised fan-shapes in the air.

Then there was another train to catch, amid the bewildering scurry and the echoing announcements of this alien English railway station. "I can hardly make out a word," said Nita disapprovingly. "It is like a duck quacking."

Their shepherd had made sure that they knew where to catch their train, but once aboard it, they were parted from him. They also seemed to have lost touch with their fellow-passengers, although many of them must be on the same train. She and Perry sat side by side, very conscious of being on their own.

The sky darkened still more as the train set off and their first glimpse of England as they crossed its south-east corner was obscured by a steady downpour. Victoria station was another grim and echoing cavern. Wearily, they hauled their cases down from the rack. "What a good thing we kept our luggage as light as we could," Perry said. "I hope my books have arrived."

"You could have bought new books in London, I am sure. There was no point in bringing them so far," said Nita. "It was too expensive. We shall have to take care with money in England. We were allowed to bring so little."

"You will be all right when Kartar is earning," said Perry gloomily. "I shall be the one who has to be careful."

His sense of adventure, which had been so strong when they sailed from Bombay, was now not only damped, he thought, but drowning. He knew, of course, that in England it rained a good deal but his experience of rain was the welcome monsoon, which relieved the breathless tension of the hot season. He hadn't thought of it before as simply depressing and cold. And this was still supposed to be summer, for goodness sake.

They had boarded the train at the wrong end and the whole length of the grimy platform stretched between them and the barrier. It was marked with the prints of muddy feet and the station's glass roof leaked in places. Because she was about to be reunited with her husband, Nita had put on an elegant red sari and she observed with regret that its embroidered hem was becoming dirtied.

They plodded along, pausing every now and then to change suitcases from one hand to the other or adjust shoulder-bags. On the other side of the barrier was a vast concourse, full of English people striding confidently here and there, completely

23

oblivious of the nervous young man and woman in the strange clothes who stood hesitating in their midst.

"We have the address," said Nita firmly. "I suppose we can ask directions or find a taxi. But Kartar said we should find him waiting as soon as we came off the platform."

"I think the train was late. Perhaps he could not wait."

"Kartar!" Nita cried.

They hadn't seen him coming because of the throng. He was simply there, all in a moment, embracing Perry, taking Nita's suitcase from her. He did not embrace his wife; that would come later and in private. But their eyes met instantly, and Nita, with a surge of thankfulness, saw in them the husband and lover she had missed. He had certainly changed a little. He looked older, for instance, more mature. But he was still, in spite of three years in this strange land, the same essential Kartar Virk.

He was taller than Perry and had his mother's aquiline profile, which could on occasion make him look fierce. Sometimes he could sound fierce, too. "Nita, you are looking beautiful, quite beautiful, but Perry, why did you not make sure she had a shawl or a coat out of her luggage; this is typical English summer weather and she will get wet!"

"Sorry," said Perry, also concluding that his brother was still the same essential Kartar, who had once bullied him so ruthlessly over doing his homework.

"Well, there is no time to open her luggage and get out something more for her; we must hurry, we have another train journey to make." Kartar began to chivvy them along.

"Another train?" asked Nita. All the way from India, she had been thinking that the sight of Kartar's face would mean journey's end. Clearly it meant nothing of the kind.

"Yes, yes, we must get out to south London, out to Clapham. We can take a train from here, it will not take long and I have got tickets for us all, but come along or we shall miss the train and have to wait another half an hour."

This train was crowded. They found seats only because, in spite of Kartar's insistence that they might miss it, they were among the first aboard. The English people who climbed into the carriage after them kept glancing at them and then looking away.

There had been plenty of oddly dressed strangers at Dover; Nita and Perry had been just two more. But this was a train for business people, going home at the end of the day. Everyone

24

seemed to be sombrely dressed, the men in grey or black, the girls in muted pastels. Perry's bright blue turban and Kartar's red one, and Nita's own crimson sari were as startling and irrelevant as gems in a coal-mine.

Kartar had seized a window seat for his wife, and Nita could see out. She glimpsed streets and houses, tightly packed and dingy-looking. There were cars, lots of cars, but like the clothes of the men, they were nearly all dark. It was still raining and there were numerous umbrellas. These were mostly black.

She caught Perry's eye, and knew that he too was depressed by their first sight of England. She thought of home, of sparkling mornings after the rains had cleared; of eating breakfast on the roof in the early sunshine with Ranbir; of golden hoopoes pecking in the red dust beside a road in a Delhi suburb; of her mother, from whom she had parted in Delhi, arriving to join herself and Ranbir for shopping expeditions in the bazaar behind Safed Gardens, and always dressed in clear bright colours: rose-pink, perhaps, or turquoise. The memory of that friendly feminine domestic routine suddenly caught at her throat. Even in Kartar's absence, she had known much calm happiness in his home. She turned her head quickly to look at Kartar's profile and found reassurance there. Home, her mother had told her long ago, was wherever one's husband was. As long as Kartar chose to stay in England, England must content her. As for Perry, she and Kartar must try to provide for him the family background which would make him, too, feel at home.

By the time they emerged from the train to tackle the half-mile trudge from the station to the house where Kartar was staying and where Nita and Perry were now to join him, it had stopped raining, but the sky was still overcast. Nita, however, had taken a grip on herself and made quietly cheerful conversation as they walked.

Perry said little. The presence of his brother and sister-in-law notwithstanding, he was already homesick enough to want to die.

Kartar lodged in a house whose landlord specialised in taking overseas students. "He's got an arrangement with London University but he takes students for local colleges too," he had explained in one of his early letters home.

The building was actually two adjoining houses, numbers thirty-eight and forty Gilmour Street, knocked into one, and since both had been rambling three-storey affairs to begin with, it was big.

"That's Mr and Mrs Houghton's private front door," Kartar said, nodding towards number forty as he led them up the steps of number thirty-eight. "This one's ours. We all have keys; you'll both be given them." The doors were identical, with stained glass panes and polished brass doorknobs. Kartar let them into a wide hallway with a black and white chequered floor, told them to leave the luggage by the wall, and showed them through an archway into a wide, light sitting room, where Nita stopped short, causing Perry to bump into her. She was wondering if they were in the right place.

The room was in a state of chaos. A dust sheet scattered with bits of plaster was spread out over the carpet, and a clutter of buckets, bottles, paint tins and paintbrushes soaking in a bowl of spirit occupied one corner. There was a table in the middle of the room and on it stood a man engaged in plastering the ceiling. Nita turned her gaze upwards and was obliged to keep it travelling for some time before it arrived at the man's face. Mr Robert Houghton, ex-sergeant major, was six foot three and a half in his socks. As he had removed his shoes in order to stand on the table, his socks were much in evidence. Her first glance had bypassed them in disbelief. Now she looked a second time and stayed riveted.

In a land where the government had apparently passed strict laws against vivid colour in any context, Mr Houghton was wearing bright green woolly socks with iridescent purple and orange swirls.

"My wife knits them for me," said a bass voice from on high. A large fresh-complexioned face with a thatch of brown hair peered down at them. "But I pick the colours and the design." Nita, feeling that she had been caught out in an impertinence, went stiff. "But she won't let me wear ties to match," said the voice. "Sorry there's such a mess; I'm trying to get this job done while I've still got a few days' holiday left. The ceiling was threatening to come down." The owner of the voice now came down himself, stepping lightly but mightily to the floor. He picked up a cloth from the table, wiped his palms carefully and said, "I'm the landlord, Mr Houghton. And you're Kartar's wife and this must be his brother. Pleased to welcome you."

Kartar confirmed the introductions, and Mr Houghton gravely shook hands with the newcomers, neither of whom had ever exchanged this occidental salute before and weren't sure whether to return Mr Houghton's large warm grip or not. They opted for caution and didn't.

"While you were gone, I shifted a second wardrobe into your room, Kartar." Mr Houghton found his slippers under a pushed-back chair and buried his spectacularly clad feet in them. "You'll need the storage space. You should be quite comfortable there until you find your own place, and there's no hurry about that. I'm not going to turf you out just because you're not officially a student any longer. Take your time. He's in number forty, at the back," he said, turning to Perry. "But you're in number thirty-eight. Nice little room in the front. You won't get traffic noise while you're studying. This is a quiet street."

Nita, getting over her momentary embarrassment, laughed. "At home, he worked with motor horns and street vendors under the window and never noticed."

"That's true. I'm not so difficult," Perry assured his host.

"Well, you won't have to put up with noise here, all the same. I'll take you all upstairs in a minute but I should think a cup of tea wouldn't come amiss first. You're the only members of the United Nations here just now . . . "

"He means all the other students. We come from all over the world so we call ourselves the United Nations," explained Kartar as they followed the landlord through a further door and into a passage. The smell of plaster which had pervaded the sitting room gave place to an agreeable aroma of cooking, mixed with something less agreeable: a curious trace of rankness.

"They're not all back from their summer vacation yet," said Mr Houghton over his shoulder, "and the ones that are here are all out somewhere. We're a thorough mixture this year. I've got Chinese, Japanese, Nigerian, Sudanese, Pakistani, West Indian, Iranian and a Frenchman and a German girl as well as you three. Inge and Jacques don't like each other but they're polite. That's one of the few rules of the house, by the way. I won't stand for trouble; quarrels and fighting and so on. My United Nations sometimes aren't as united as all that; I've often had people here who don't get along; some of them come from countries that are hereditary enemies. Well, what you do at home is your own business but while you're staying in my home, you leave your traditional quarrels in the hall along with the coats and umbrellas. You get breakfast and an evening meal

27

here, all round the table together and if someone from the country you hate most in the world asks you to pass the salt you bloody well pass it and no nonsense. Not that there'll be any problems with either of you; I know that. I know Kartar here." He paused to let Nita walk into the kitchen ahead of him and gave her a paternal but approving smile which took in her sari and accepted it in a way which induced her to smile back. "Kartar's one of the most civilised young men I've had in this house. This is the kitchen, where we also eat. Here they are, Brenda. Kartar's brought them."

The kitchen was nearly as big as the sitting room. The long centre table bore a red and white checked cloth and a tea-tray and a plate of biscuits. Brenda Houghton left a saucepan-laden stove and came to meet them, grasping a long wooden spoon. She was half her husband's size, a wiry little woman with short, rough grey hair and round dark eyes looking alertly from either side of a beaky little nose. "Hello, there! No need for introductions, you're expected. Sit down round the table." She waved the spoon to encourage them towards it. "The tea's all ready. I heard you come in. You must be Nita – glad to have you, Kartar's often talked about you – and you'll be, let me see, his younger brother and he calls you Perry. I won't ask you what your proper name is in case I can't pronounce it."

"It's only Prem, but I like being called Perry."

"Well, make yourselves at home, both of you. Seat yourselves."

Nita pulled out a chair and said, "Oh."

"Ah. Meet Hiawatha." Mr Houghton came round the table, stroked the huge black cat which was crouched on the chair with front paws folded under its chest and green eyes half closed, and then lifted it bodily off. "He's all right, Nita. He doesn't scratch. There's your chair."

"Hiawatha?" ventured Perry, as they settled themselves and accepted cups of tea.

"There's a poem about a Red Indian called Hiawatha. He was a mighty hunter. So is this fellow. Birds, mice, anything. He once killed a pigeon bigger than himself," said Houghton.

"He's one of the family," said Kartar. "Leave your door ajar tonight, Perry. Hiawatha likes to wander round the house at night and if he finds a door shut, he sits outside it miaowing and everybody wakes up."

"Good gracious," said Nita. "Really?"

Hiawatha bounded up to a wide windowsill and sat there,

regarding them enigmatically. That accounted for the rank smell, Nita thought. It was cat. In India, cats were not popular pets; they were supposed to be unlucky. Her father kept a dog and walked it every morning before he went to work, but the dog would never be allowed in the bedrooms. She had heard that in England people were different. The Houghtons clearly were, for a start.

Mrs Houghton, having handed the teacups, said, "I'd better tell you about the meals. We have a sort of international menu. You'll find something to your taste on the table every time, I hope. Kartar told us you weren't vegetarians but there often are vegetable-only dishes. There'll be a big salad this evening, and a curried chicken – not too hot – and rice, though the rice might be different from what you're used to."

"I'm quite sure it will all be delicious," said Nita politely. Across the table, Kartar was looking at her. She smiled at him, and then, with a sudden thud of the heart, recognised the insistent message in his eyes. She looked away and quickly drained her teacup. "May we go upstairs? I feel so grubby. I should like to wash and tidy myself."

"Of course, you must be exhausted." Brenda Houghton was sympathetic. "Kartar, take her up. There's more than an hour before dinner."

"I'll bring Perry up in a moment," Mr Houghton said.

They collected the luggage and she followed Kartar up a carpeted staircase and through an archway like the one downstairs. These, she realised, connected the two houses. She glimpsed a second staircase to her left. They went along a passage and then Kartar, whose hands were full, opened a door by pushing the handle down with his elbow. He led them inside, dropped the luggage on the floor and closed the door. For the first time in three years, they were alone together in a room, with the rest of the world shut out.

"My darling Nita, how I've missed you. You don't know . . . "

They came together, instantly and hungrily. The feel of him, the strong and angular bones of his body as it pressed against hers, the line of his high cheekbones under her fingers, were familiar and beloved. He smelt of clean soap and his skin was the glowing bronze which had delighted her from the day of their first shy introduction. His fingers were deep in her hair, loosening her chignon.

"Kartar! I was afraid you might have changed."

29

"I was afraid you'd have changed too. But you're just as you always were. Are you very tired?"

"I was. But not now."

Kartar laughed. "And there are other ways of dispelling tiredness, besides sleep. And it's still an hour to dinner."

At home, they had slept on separate divans, with cotton sheets and velvety rugs in winter. Here in this room, with its heavy walnut furniture, the bed was a strange English affair, wide enough for two, with unfamiliar bedclothes: thick hairy blankets and a quilted eiderdown. But the sheets were the same as in Delhi, smooth and cool, and Kartar was there to welcome her between them.

Perry found himself led into a front room which was certainly small but was very pleasing as to colour, all in tones of pale yellow. "Nice shade, isn't it?" said Houghton, as Perry put down his case and shoulder-bag and looked about him. "I redecorated this room myself, a month ago."

A narrow single bed lay along one wall and near the window was a set of empty bookshelves. Perry's box of books lay on the floor beside a basket chair.

"My books have come!"

"Yes, a week ago. Your brother got quite excited. He kept saying it was proof you were on your way. Or maybe he meant it was proof that his wife was on her way. Hard on them, being apart for three years when they were only just married – it's the sort of thing you associate with wartime. Now, you've a wash-basin of your own – all the rooms have that – and there's a bathroom next door. You share that with five others and when they're all here, you can sort out with them who uses the bathroom when. Let my wife know if you need anything; extra blankets or whatnot. Just one other thing," said Mr Houghton, helpfully heaving Perry's suitcase on to the bed. "One more of the few rules of the house. No girls in here after ten o'clock and no goings on under my roof at any time. I take it you know what I mean. What you do elsewhere is your own business. I'm not responsible for your moral welfare, only for the reputation of my establishment. You can buy anything you need at any chemist and he won't ask questions."

Perry gaped.

"It's better," said Mr Houghton matter-of-factly, "to know the ropes. Now. Breakfast seven thirty in the morning, dinner seven

thirty in the evening except Sundays. On Sundays breakfast is
eight thirty a.m. and in the evening you'll find cold food in the
fridge; help yourself. We generally go out on Sundays. You
make your own bed and keep your room clean and you'll find all
the gear in the cupboard under the stairs. See you later. Nice to
have you with us."

He went out, closing the door quietly after him. Perry sank
down on his bed beside the suitcase.

He supposed it would be all right. This room was certainly
pleasant enough. One would grow accustomed. It was just
that . . .

Just that when he started out, leaning on the rail of the
Venetian, planning a new life in a land of opportunity, he had
somehow never pictured clearly what that new life would be like.
Now it had resolved itself into wet grey skies and grimy buildings, and silently disapproving people on trains and a gigantic,
ferociously friendly landlord with a lurid taste in socks, and
although he didn't know what he'd expected, this wasn't it. He'd
never seen a western film which showed people and places like
this.

He wondered how long it would take him to get used to it.

Dinner had been eaten. Nita and Kartar had arrived a little late.
Dressed in a clean sari of pink and green cotton, her hair freshly
oiled and swept into a knot and her face made up, Nita had
taken the seat beside her husband at a table crowded with
strange faces, and tried hard to absorb the Houghtons' introductions.

She had said hello to a blonde German girl called Inge and a
thin dark French boy called Jacques; to a round-faced Chinese
who insisted that he was simply known as Chang ("It's what you
call my surname but in China we put the surname first and I've
given up trying to explain to the English"), and to a solidly built
Japanese called Senta Watanabe who had virtually no English at
all.

She had been aware that she had a bloom which did not come
from cosmetics and been slightly embarrassed all over again
because when Kartar apologised for their late arrival, Mr
Houghton had said, "Oh, it doesn't matter," in tones of candidly
indulgent understanding.

She had eaten curried chicken which tasted not unpleasant
but bore no relation whatever to curries at home. She and Perry

had grown used to the Italian food on the boat; now they must adapt their palates again.

Perry, seated opposite, had looked even more bemused than Nita felt. "I hope," she said, as for the second time that evening she and Kartar closed their bedroom door behind them, "that Perry settles down well. I have been keeping an eye on him for a month while we travelled, but in a way, he will be more on his own now."

"I will watch over him as best I can, but I hope we won't be living here too long," Kartar said. "I must first find a job and then we must get our own flat. Living like this is all very well when one is a student, but now things are different. We need a proper base. Though this may have advantages at first. Mrs Houghton will help you to find your feet, get used to the shops here and so on."

"I must ask her to show me how that gas stove of hers works. I've never seen a stove like that before."

She had found time for a little unpacking before dinner; indeed, since she wished to change her sari, this was necessary. Now she moved towards her open suitcase, intending to complete the task. But Kartar reached out and drew her to him.

"If you're worn out now, just say so. I am not selfish. But, oh Nita, I'm *famished*. I'd never have come here and left you if I'd known how it would be."

"We had married life for only six months," said Nita demurely.

"Six months is quite enough for forming a habit."

"I'm not worn out. It is all right."

"You are so beautiful. I wish I were a poet. Then I could say so properly."

"I would rather be married to an accountant. I am sure accountants make better livings than poets do."

"I sincerely hope I can make a good living. There is so much prejudice here."

"Is there?"

"I'm afraid so. Everyone isn't like the Houghtons. Oh, never mind that now; we've better things to think about just now . . . and you may as well forget about that suitcase. You can unpack it in the morning."

In the night, Nita stirred and woke. For a moment, she wondered where she was. Her head was still full of the clatter of train wheels. Then her eyes, adjusting to the dimness, made out the window and a patch of starlit sky. She was in England, and from those stars, the weather must have cleared. She had forgotten that quirk of Kartar's: that odd preference for sleeping with the curtains open. He must have got up after she was asleep and drawn them back. He had done the same thing, so often, at home in Delhi. She could remember waking on the morning after her wedding, to find the sunlight pouring into the room, and as she recalled that moment, a blessed sense of security enveloped her.

Here in England, he had also apparently set the door ajar, presumably because of Hiawatha.

In the starlight, she could make out the vertical line of the crack and when she turned her head, she could see the quietly breathing hump of Kartar's body, and the dark rounded shape of his head. She stretched out a hand, very gently, to stroke his hair.

Kartar's hair was extraordinarily soft and furry, and beneath it, his head felt pliant and . . . and *vibrant*. Nita sat up with a frightened gasp and beside her on the pillow the head said, "Mrrrow?" on an enquiring note and opened a pair of green, glittering, inhuman eyes.

Nita threw herself out of the bed, scrambling for the light switch. As the room flooded with light, Kartar emerged blearily from under the bedclothes, where he had been entirely buried, head and all, gazed at the black cat blinking lazily at him from the pillow, swore, clambered out, picked Hiawatha up and marched with him to the door. "*Out!* He does this sometimes," Kartar said, coming back to the bed. "When people are new. He seems to think he has to spend a night with newcomers. But I hoped he would go and annoy Perry instead of us."

"Please shut the door. We must keep him out. He gave me such a fright!" said Nita. "It is unlucky, such a thing happening."

"Nonsense. That is just superstition. The English have hardly been an unlucky nation and in this country one trips over cats the whole time."

"Well, it's still unhygienic, cats in the bedroom." Nita picked up the pillow and brushed Hiawatha's hairs fastidiously off it before getting back into bed. "But I am sorry I disturbed you."

"You are the one who has had the long journey," Kartar said, switching out the light and joining her. "You should have your sleep. Let us hope we have peace now . . . oh, *no!*"

33

Outside the door, Hiawatha yowled. In the deep of the night, it was an appalling noise, as penetrating as a gimlet and as pathetic as the cry of a drowning child. Kartar, with another oath, sprang up once more and opened the door. "Sssscat!"

Hiawatha, with another pleased "Mrrow!" leapt past him and jumped back on to the bed.

"Go and hunt mice, you horrible animal!" said Nita. "Or if you won't hunt, sleep on the floor!"

"At least he's on the end of the bed this time, not on the pillow," said Kartar resignedly, sliding once again between the sheets. "It's only for tonight, thank God. He only ever inflicts himself on people like this once."

"You mean we must just put up with it? Let him stay there?" Nita was horrified.

"I'm afraid so. Unless we want to waken the whole house."

They lay in silence, grimly aware of the obtuse Hiawatha turning round and round and kneading the eiderdown with destructive claws, before sinking into a heavy heap on Nita's feet.

"The Houghtons are very kind," said Nita. "But we should certainly have a flat of our own, Kartar. As soon as we can."

In the morning, Hiawatha was gone. Descending to breakfast, again a little late although this time because Nita had said that she really must finish unpacking, they discovered him sitting once more like a regal sphinx on the kitchen windowsill.

Perry, who was moodily cracking the top of a boiled egg, said, "When I woke up this morning, the cat was on my stomach."

The Houghtons looked amused.

"He was with us earlier. It is a ritual we must all go through," said Kartar bracingly.

"I have never slept with a cat before."

"None of us had," said Chang cheerfully, piling cornflakes into a bowl. "But I didn't mind. He's a nice cat."

"He's a clever fellow," said Mr Houghton. "It's amazing the way he always knows where to find people."

"He almost rules this house," said Brenda Houghton, laughing. "But then, cats do. Nita, will you have porridge or cornflakes? And would you like two boiled eggs?"

"Cornflakes, please, and one egg if I may," said Nita politely. She examined her eggcup with interest. "We do not use these cups in India. We just put eggs on the plate and peel them. This

34

is a very good idea. Kartar, when we have our own flat, we should buy some of these cups."

Answering the oblique message, Kartar said, "There is one piece of news I have not yet mentioned. I have an interview on Monday. I have my work permit and I have done one temporary job, so I have a little experience to sell. Perhaps the outcome will be good. Let us hope it will."

Chapter Three

Other People's Festivals
1956

Her mother had told her that home was where her husband was, but in her moment of secret panic on the *Venetian*, Nita had sensed England as an alien place which would not be dealt with so easily, and she had been right. The presence of Kartar, and the comfortable statements that kitchens and markets were much alike anywhere, were indeed not enough. There were, she discovered, a host of other things which went to make up her idea of home, and England was exceedingly reluctant to provide them.

In India, she had taken so much for granted. Ever since she could remember, her daily life had had a pattern which marriage had not changed very much. At home with her parents, when not at school or college, she had helped her mother every day with the shopping and cooking, and the entertaining which was a natural part of life. There was always a drift of guests in and out during the evening and at weekends. At other times, she would accompany her parents on visits. Their circle was wide, for they regularly attended a Sikh temple or Gurudwara, and knew most of the congregation.

When she married Kartar, Ranbir took the place of her own mother. She called Ranbir *Bheji*, which meant mother, and helped her instead. Otherwise, little changed. She attended the same temple as before, and had the same circle of acquaintances. Married or single, she was part of a family and of a community and this seemed so natural that she never thought about it.

In England, for the first time, she was simply Nita Virk, supported by only the minimum of family and community. She had Kartar, of course, and Perry, but they were male and at home, she had been used to a good deal of female company. Here, at first, there was only Brenda Houghton. There were of course girls among the students in the house. But the Pakistani Yasmin, though sweet and gentle, was a Moslem and for Nita, the horror of the Partition, and the fighting between Moslems on the one hand and the Hindus and Sikhs on the other, was still too near to let her make a friend of Yasmin. The West Indian Lucinda was studying medicine and scarcely spoke of anything except her studies, while Inge was stand-offish with everyone, not just with Jacques. She disliked Jacques more than the rest; that was all.

None of them could give Nita any companionship and she rarely saw them, in any case, except at mealtimes. She offered to help Brenda, who accepted, but with reservations. "After all, you're paying to be here," Brenda said.

"I am no good at doing nothing and all I do now is dust our room and wash our clothes. And it will help me, too. I must learn to manage in English shops."

"You'll do that in five minutes. Your English is better than mine," said Brenda, amused, but she did at length consent to be assisted with the marketing and to let Nita lend a hand in the kitchen and even, once or twice, cook curry for dinner.

When the lost, uprooted feeling became too strong, Nita would remind herself firmly that they would not be at the Houghtons' for ever and that she would feel different when she and Kartar had their own home. But as yet, this seemed a long way off. Kartar's interview came to nothing and subsequent interviews were equally without result.

She was glad to be with Kartar for his sake as well as her own. His need of her was very obvious and she sometimes wondered, though she did not ask, how he had managed during those three years alone. She was very grateful indeed for the existence of the Shepherd's Bush temple.

The converted house in west London, which had been a Sikh temple since before the war, was to Nita an Indian oasis in a grey occidental desert.

Kartar had taken both Nita and Perry there, only a week after their arrival. Perry managed to convey, without actually saying so, that he was only going along to please Kartar. But for a few blessed hours, the grateful Nita had found herself once again in an atmosphere she recognised. There was the canopied altar, the Holy Book on its embroidered cloth, before which she knelt to make her offering of a few coins, and there, to her relief, on the left-hand side of the white-sheeted floor, sat a handful of

37

ladies in salwar kameeze and sari, heads covered and shoes removed. There were not many of them and most were older than herself. They were mainly the wives or in some cases the mothers of the men on the other side, the majority of whom were workmen and factory hands. The women's lives were not much like her own and none of them, in any case, lived in or even near Clapham. Close friendships of the kind she was accustomed to at home were not possible. But there was something: a feeling of not being alone any more. She was glad when Kartar said they would attend regularly. After going to the Gurudwara, Nita always returned to Clapham in an animated mood.

The Houghtons had noticed. "Your temple means a lot to you, I can see that," Robert Houghton said over dinner one cold, wet December Sunday when he and Brenda had decided to stay in, and Nita had undertaken to provide a hot meal for the household. "You even took the trouble to go to your service in this weather, and when you've done so much cooking, too."

"The turbans are part of it all, aren't they?" Brenda Houghton said, handing potatoes. "Kartar's told us that much. But what exactly is their significance?"

This was an unexpected question because religion, as a rule, was discouraged as a topic of conversation at the Houghtons' table, owing to the presence of two individuals called Aziz and Mr Bharucha, both of whom hailed from Iran, but belonged to different religious communities.

Aziz was one of the three Moslems among the tenants. The others were the quiet Yasmin and a placid Sudanese called Akbar. Aziz, however, was neither quiet nor placid but regrettably stiff-necked, and seemed positively to enjoy being offended, especially by Mr Bharucha, who was older (which was why he was always known as Mr) and followed not Islam but the Zoroastrian religion. They were seated well apart at mealtimes and Mr Houghton regularly and angrily repeated the house rules to them and had once threatened to make them both leave, but they still wrangled so persistently that Robert Houghton had taken to calling a halt whenever any religion at all found its way into the conversation.

This time, however, after a sharp warning glance at the two potential sources of trouble, he said, "Yes, tell us."

"It's complicated," said Kartar. "It is not at all easy to explain, right from scratch."

Nita was frowning. "It's certainly not simple. It's like putting centuries of history into a few sentences. You see, India's more Hindu than anything else – only that's simplifying it too much because there are all sorts of religions and sects – but anyway, it'll do just for a beginning. Only, over the centuries, there were many invasions from the north by Moslem peoples and sometimes India has had Moslem rulers, although most of the people were still Hindu."

"Except those converted at sword point," said Mr Bharucha helpfully at this point.

Aziz bristled and Mr Houghton said sharply, "Shut up, you two. If you interrupt again you will leave this table. Just for once, keep quiet and listen to somebody else. Go on, Nita."

"Well, the two were – are – so different," said Nita. "The Hindus believe in many gods and have a caste system. The Moslems don't believe in caste and they worship only one god, Allah. Then in the fifteenth century, a teacher called Guru Nanak arose who tried to teach a way that would break that pattern, a way that believed in one god, but not in caste and treated women as the equals of men. That was the beginning of Sikhism."

"And the turban?" said Brenda Houghton.

"That came later." Kartar took up the story, with one eye on Aziz. "Later, there was much trouble between some Moslem conquerors, the Moghuls, and the Hindus. A Sikh leader called Gobind Singh formed the Sikhs into a kind of military sect to protect the other Hindus. And to hold them together and make them proud and make them *visible* – so that they wouldn't be tempted to go quiet and pretend they weren't there, which is very easy to do when times are dangerous – he gave them rules to keep. Sikhs mustn't cut their hair or shave off their beards, but the men must keep their hair tidy within the turban. There are other things too. A Sikh wears a steel bracelet – I've got one, see" – Kartar put his fork down for a moment and pulled back his shirt cuff to show them – "and a really traditional Sikh would carry a sword, but of course the twentieth century has made a difference to that."

"But a Sikh bridegroom carries one at his wedding," said Nita. "You had one."

"But this is fascinating!" Brenda Houghton said. "Kartar, you never told us any of this before!"

"We didn't ask," said her husband. "It's taken Nita to draw us out. We shall miss you when you leave us, Nita."

39

"Is there any news about that? How is your job-hunting going, Kartar?" Brenda asked.

Kartar sighed. "Not successfully as yet," he said.

"It will come," said Brenda comfortingly, and then, with an air of one who deliberately changes the subject, began to talk of the party which was planned for Christmas Day, which would include a Christmas tree, games, and a sing-song with the help of a guitar-playing friend of Mr Houghton.

Halfway along the corridor, Perry paused to balance his over-stuffed briefcase on a bent knee while he forced it to shut properly. Life seemed to be all study these days. He'd have precious little time to himself over the Christmas break and much of the work concerned the subjects he disliked most. He could cope with figures and graphs and he was positively talented on paperwork systems and filing techniques but when it came to company law and report writing, his mind glazed over.

At school, he had enjoyed both Punjabi and English literature but business jargon was agony in any language. He had committed himself to a two-year course, and one term had almost defeated him. He preferred not to think about the remaining five.

His fellow students streamed past, heading for the streets of south-west London, where the shops had taken him by surprise by bursting into a Yuletide brightness, with Christmas trees piled up in the entrances to open-fronted greengrocers, and tinsel festoons all over Woolworths. Some of the students called greetings to him as they passed. "Have a good Christmas, Perry!" "Don't eat too much!"

He called back similar answers. Most of those who addressed him were foreign students like himself. The English were not exactly unfriendly but they were reserved. Kartar, who had been through it all too, said that they were a haughty lot, still mentally stuck in the days of the British Raj, but Perry was inclined to think that with this younger generation at least, the problem was more like shyness. Dark skins were strange to them so that they could only approach with caution, and as far as he and Kartar were concerned, the turban bewildered them. The turban was very likely part of the reason why Kartar was finding it so difficult to obtain work.

But although he made excuses for them, he was acutely aware of them: a whole community of potential friends who wouldn't reach out a hand to him. He thought often of Delhi and of past friends now out of touch or lost altogether: the government office colleagues with whom he had drunk illicit whisky; poor Satnam Singh, his classmate, who had been visiting relatives in Lahore when the Partition rioting began and had been killed, in God alone knew what frightful circumstances; Mohan Lal, the son of the Hindu shopkeeper in the bazaar behind Safed Gardens, older than Perry but a good, cheerful friend. Kartar had known him slightly too.

Their mother had disapproved because Hindus and Sikhs didn't, these days, mix as they did when his paternal grandparents were married. When Mohan Lal for some reason left home, she was pleased. But Perry had missed him, and still did.

Snapping the briefcase shut at last, he made for the exit and found it blocked by a passionately embracing couple. He squeezed irritatedly past with a muttered "Excuse *me*," and plunged out into a steady drizzle to start the three-station Underground journey from Tooting to Clapham South. As he strode along the wet pavements, over the reflections of neon shop displays in honour of an alien festival, he recognised ruefully that the canoodling couple had annoyed him, not because they were in the way but because he was envious.

Since coming to England, he had found nothing to assuage his homesickness. He was homesick still. And he was lonely.

It was not the loneliness of solitude. He ate meals round the Houghtons' busy table and his brother and sister-in-law were still there and during the college day he was at least physically in the company of the other students.

But Kartar and Nita were largely engrossed with each other and with Kartar's efforts to find a job and Perry did not intrude on them. At college he had made no close friends even among the other foreign students and it was the same with the students at the Houghtons'. None of them were at his college; like Nita, he rarely saw them except at mealtimes. Chang had introduced him to the local pub, where Perry had discovered beer as well as whisky, but there was no depth to the acquaintanceship. And that was all.

The Houghtons had duly provided him with a key. He let himself in at the door of number thirty-eight, to be greeted by the characteristic smell of the Houghton household, a mingling of cookery and paint. Something was baking in the kitchen, and

Mr Houghton was down on all fours on the chequered floor of the hallway, painting the skirting board. Mr Houghton was in the printing trade and worked by night on the production of a newspaper. In the mornings he slept but by three p.m. he was usually up and pursuing his hobby of do-it-yourself house improvements.

"It's like living on a building site sometimes," Brenda Houghton had said once in a moment of exasperation. "But then, it does keep the place nice for next to nothing."

"Do you want my hand, Mr Houghton?" Perry asked, on a sudden impulse, because pottering with a paintbrush looked much more like fun than struggling with the books in his brief-case.

"That's good of you. I'm about finished here but if you like, you can help me with a stopped-up bath. I'll have to have some new pipework in soon. Looking forward to Christmas? Nearly everyone's staying this year except for Jacques and Inge. About that bath," said Mr Houghton, not waiting for an answer, "I'd be glad of help but you'd better put on something that can get dirty."

"It's a pleasure, Mr Houghton," said Perry with sincerity.

In the kitchen, Nita was regretfully helping Brenda by preparing sprouts and putting them into salt water for boiling later on. The way the English ruined good vegetables by soaking and boiling the goodness out of them instead of cooking them tenderly with onions and butter and spices and minimal water caused her great sorrow. If ever she achieved a kitchen of her own, no boiled vegetable would appear in it as long as she lived.

The distant slam of the front door made her pause, head cocked. She recognised that slam, just as she recognised the brisk footsteps that now approached the kitchen. She turned towards the door as Kartar came through it.

"I thought you would be here. I have found a job," he said abruptly. "And I may have found a flat as well. Mrs Houghton, can I take Nita away from you? I want her to come and see it."

"But . . . " Nita stood, saucepan in hand and beamed. "This is so wonderful!"

Then she saw that Kartar was not smiling but looked, on the contrary, rather grim. "I wish," he said candidly, "that it were a lot more wonderful than it is."

*   *   *

42

"It will do as a start," Nita said with determined cheerfulness as they walked back to Gilmour Street. "I shall enjoy having my own kitchen. I have looked forward to that."

"They're reasonably big rooms, even if they are up under the roof," said Kartar. "Though I'm sorry about the paraffin heating. It'll be a bit of a change from the Houghtons' nice gas fires. But at least the landlady's willing to have us. There are so many advertisements which say English Only. I suppose she doesn't mind because she's West Indian."

"And it's not too far away from here," said Nita, as they turned into Gilmour Street. "We shall still be near Perry. Kartar, you haven't told me much about the job. I thought you would be so pleased, but you are not looking very pleased. You did not even tell me you had an interview today, although I guessed, when you went out in your best suit."

"The firm," said Kartar grimly, "is taking me on because they like my qualifications and because my temporary job was with a firm they know and approve of. The interviewing panel said my qualifications were better than those of any of the other candidates . . . "

"Then why . . . ?"

"Wait. They told me they were willing to stretch a point and give me a three month trial, although hitherto it has been their policy not to engage people who aren't . . . er . . . English. It can cause embarrassment, they said. My colour might make existing employees feel uncomfortable, they said. Then they had the nerve to add that they couldn't offer me a very exceptional salary. You know what that means? I will be getting less than if I had an English complexion."

"Oh, Kartar!" Nita stopped in the street and looked at him in horror. "Should you accept, on such terms?"

"Yes, I should." Kartar's voice was still grim. "I said I am meaning to work in Britain and I must make my word good. I can't pick and choose. We are managing to live because when I did that temporary job, I saved a bit. I hoped that that company would give me a permanency one day," he said bitterly, "but when I wrote to them, they said they'd been delighted with my work but hadn't any vacancies just now. And I saw an advert from them, in a Sits Vac column, for just the sort of job I meant, three days after I got their letter."

"In that case," said Nita, "you are doing the right thing." She quelled, with determination, a wave of depression. Kartar's new

43

employers had insulted him and that flat was . . . well, dingy and cold. But one must begin somewhere. "I expect Perry will be in by now," she said as they reached the front door of number thirty-eight. "We must tell him."

"He will be at his books," said Kartar. "At least, let us hope so. Perry worries me at times. He does not study hard enough, in my opinion."

Perry was not in his room, although he was obviously in the house, since his briefcase lay casually tossed on the bed, and the shirt and trousers in which he had gone out that morning were flung over a chair. "Now where can he be?" wondered Nita. "Having a bath? But his bath towel is still here."

Kartar stepped back on to the landing and shouted Perry's name. A voice answered from the distance.

"But he *is* in the bathroom," said Nita. "How strange."

"Come in!" Perry shouted. "I am helping with repairs only!"

Kartar pushed the bathroom door open and peered round it. His younger brother was perched on the edge of the tub in the bathroom of number forty, dressed in old trousers and a sweater with frayed elbows, handing bits of dismantled plumbing to Mr Houghton, splashed and grimy and apparently enjoying himself.

"I thought," said Kartar disapprovingly, "that you would be studying in your room. I was looking for you there."

"He can't study all the time. Stop nagging him," said Mr Houghton. "The brain goes stale if you overdo it. Nothing like a little working with the hands to relax the mind."

"I was not looking for him to talk of his studies anyway," said Kartar. "I have news. And Mr Houghton, it is to do with you, too."

Nita, listening while he explained about the job and the flat, both admired and grieved for the resolute way in which he kept the depression out of his voice. Robert Houghton, congratulating him, seemed to believe that Kartar was genuinely pleased. But later, when Perry encountered Nita in the hall on the way to the evening meal, he said quietly, "It is not what you and Kartar hoped, is it? But don't worry yourself. Kartar will make his way."

"I know he will." Her brother-in-law, Nita thought, was a very kind boy. "But I feel for him, that's all."

They broke off, as Inge hurried down the stairs towards them. "Mrs Virk! I have here a letter. I am most sorry; I picked it up from the hall table this morning with my own. But it is for you."

"Oh, thank you, Inge." Nita took the airmail letter, glanced at it, and slipped it into the pocket of the cardigan she wore over her sari. "It's from your mother," she said to Perry. "I'll read it later."

Deliberately, she kept it to read by herself at bedtime, while Kartar was in the bath. It was addressed to both of them and she would give it to him presently, but she knew beforehand what it would say and she wanted time to recover from it.

We do hope so much that soon you will have news of an addition to the family . . .

Every time Ranbir wrote, she put that in. This time it was worse; there was a marked note of reproof. *If there is difficulty, you should take advice. A marriage is not complete until there are children . . . Uncle Sunder and Auntie Billie keep asking me, when is my first grandchild coming . . .*

"What is it?" said Kartar, coming quietly in in his dressing-gown, towel over one shoulder.

She held out the letter. "It's from Bheji. She is writing again about children. Oh, Kartar . . . "

"Now, I have said before, there is no need to worry. There is plenty of time and we are not well placed for coping with a family yet. Perhaps that is why you haven't started any baby yet, you know. You have never felt secure enough. Even when we were first married, you knew I was going away soon."

"Bheji is so disappointed. I am so fond of her but I wish she would not keep on at us like this."

"You're disappointed too, I can see. Well, let us get into our flat and me into my job, and then perhaps something will happen."

"I hope so," said Nita bravely. At home, every couple had a baby, if they could, within a year of the wedding. It was part of the pattern which, once, she had regarded as in the nature of things.

In the Shepherd's Bush temple, most of the worshippers had arrived, but the service had not yet begun. Kartar, who had been talking quietly to one of the older men, now edged away and said to Perry, "Look at Nita."

Perry glanced across the room. Nita was deep in talk with two older ladies, whose grey hair was visible under the edges of their veils. "I have a feeling she is asking their advice," said Kartar in a low voice. "She is upset because there has been no sign of her getting in the family way. I keep telling her, we are still young and there's plenty of time but she upsets herself."

"I'm sorry," said Perry, slightly embarrassed.

"I have been thinking that a nice Christmas present might cheer her up, and I have just been asking where in London one can buy a sari. Believe it or not, there *is* somewhere. It's called Southall. Quite a lot of these people live there; it is a sort of little colony. You are finished with college till after Christmas. I want you to come with me tomorrow."

Shaking off Nita so that they could go shopping without her was not difficult. Nita was accustomed to the peculiar male habit of wandering off on mysterious men-only errands. Finding a suburb called Southall, on the other hand, required a street map of London, an Underground map, a consultation with Mr Houghton and two hours' travelling. Finding the shop which Kartar's acquaintance had recommended took another half hour of footslogging in a cold north wind, since the description of its whereabouts was somewhat vague.

"This must be it," Kartar said at last, slowing to a halt. "It is definitely an Indian shop. Look, those are Indian cotton fabrics, surely and . . . yes, look, *look!*" He flattened his nose against the window, peering into the badly lit interior. "I am sure those are saris on the shelves at the back. Come on, let's go in."

They went in, the bell tinging loudly as they pushed the door open. Afterwards, Perry remembered that bell, as though it had been a signal, like the clock that strikes the hour for a momentous appointment.

Kartar was right about the saris. The rainbow display at the rear of the shop could be nothing else. It was a small selection, but that was better than no selection at all. The proprietor was nowhere to be seen at first, until they observed a shadow beyond the frosted glass of an inner door. The shadow suddenly let out a staccato and clearly audible burst of Punjabi and could be seen to be gesturing indignantly. It was having an argument on the telephone.

" . . . I have customers and my wife is shopping, I must go. I will ring you back and I hope you will have something more hopeful to tell me . . . yes, yes, I will ring you back soon." The receiver went down with a bang and the door opened. The shopkeeper hurried in.

"I am sorry, very sorry. Suppliers make me angry. It is hard enough telephoning to India at all, and then they tell me they cannot meet my dates. I say to them, how I am to satisfy customers if you break your promises?" He was short and square and north Indian. "Someone else will set up a rival business with more reliable suppliers, I tell them, and then where will we all be? How can I help you . . . oh, good God, it's Perry! It's Perry and Kartar! How did you get here? Who told you I was here? Why did you not say you were coming?"

"We didn't know," said Perry. "I mean, we didn't know you were in this place. We were just recommended to your shop as a shop. What a coincidence!"

"What a beautiful coincidence!" said Perry's former friend from the bazaar behind Safed Gardens, Mohan Lal Bhatia.

Mohan Lal's wife, whose name, he had told them, was Leela, came back from shopping just as her husband was tenderly wrapping up the blue sari with the silver border which he said he was selling to Kartar with ten per cent off (although Perry, remembering the shrewd shopkeeper who was Mohan Lal's father. had secret doubts about this). "Mind the shop," Mohan Lal said to Leela, and seized her basket from her and hurried his customers through the rear door into the private quarters.

"You are not just members of the public," he said as they entered a gloomy, cluttered parlour, where boxes of backup stock were piled against one wall and one corner was entirely occupied by a sewing machine and a table bearing some half-finished garments. "My younger sister Shanti is over here, helping me with making ready-made things to sell, salwar kameeze and children's things. There are a few Indian ladies locally who want Indian styles; not many, but I try to cater for everyone who comes in. Sit down, sit down. Tea, coffee, or have you taken to the whisky yet? It's cold out, isn't it?"

"Yes, very," said Perry. "Er . . . "

"I have drunk whisky on occasion," said Kartar. "And I know you drank it in India sometimes, Perry. You used to get up to all sorts of things that you hoped I didn't know about. Whisky, Mohan Lal! This is a celebration."

"And now you are wondering how it is I have turned up here." Mohan Lal produced three glass tumblers and a bottle of Teachers from a cupboard, opened the bottle and grinned broadly. "My father sent me. He said there was a market for Indian fabrics in England and I was to come over and see what I could do. He gave me the money and he said ... "

Kartar broke in. "How did you get it out of India?" he enquired with interest. "Even the modest grant they allow to students took me and Perry all our time to organise. One hitch after another."

"My father has English friends, people who left after independence but still come back sometimes. Someone comes from England to see him and he gives them spending money and says to them: don't worry about repaying it yet. When you go home to England, put the same amount in English money in a bank account there. He has been doing it for years. When he had enough, he sent me over here to use it. He said it must not be wasted ... "

"And does it work?" said Kartar, once more interrupting with difficulty. "Is there a market in England for saris?"

"Not among the English, no. But for cottons and lengths of silk, oh yes, indeed. But, as I said, Indian ladies come in as well, and that is why I keep a few saris, for them. Oh, it is a struggle, yes, but I am building up ... we need water with this ... Shanti! *Shanti!*"

Both Kartar and Perry looked round with interest as Mohan Lal's sister came shyly in. Shanti was only about seventeen, a slight, doe-eyed creature who kept her dark blue veil half over her face and did not look at the guests as she asked her brother what he wanted.

"A big jug of water and some ice. We are having whisky. And some snacks, anything, whatever there is."

Shanti disappeared and Perry gazed concentratedly at the door she closed behind her. She was much the same as any other Hindu girl and in India he wouldn't have looked at her twice but here, she had the enchantment of nostalgia on top of the more commonplace charm of being pretty.

"Now," Mohan Lal was saying. "You must tell me all about why you are here. What you think of England, then, eh? It is a dreary place, isn't it? No bright sun, no bright clothes. I was saying to my wife just yesterday ... "

"There are bright patches," said Perry, amused, thinking of Christmas shop displays and Mr Houghton's socks. Mohan Lal, he thought, talked now just as his father, Mr Bhatia senior, always had: in staccato bursts, laying down the law, telling people what to think instead of listening to them, but always beaming with friendliness. "I am studying business management . . . "

"And Kartar was saying in the shop that he has a job." Mohan Lal gave him no chance to finish. "So you must be meaning to stay in London, Kartar, eh? And maybe Perry too? There are all sorts of opportunities these days . . . "

An hour and most of the bottle later, they had managed to insert enough words in edgeways to explain what they were doing in England, why and where. Mohan Lal seemed to feel that they required sympathy. "You are buying your wife a Christmas gift, Kartar, but I think Christmas is the loneliest time for Indians in England. Everyone all round is celebrating, but how can one properly take part in other people's festivals? We should have celebrations of our own, in our own way. What are you doing on Christmas Day?"

"Attending a party given by our landlord," said Perry. "I am quite looking forward to it."

"Well, Christmas Eve, then. I shall shut the shop at six and then you can come and we will have our own sort of party. Bring your wife, Kartarji. My brother-in-law, my other sister's husband, will be here. He is visiting from Delhi but he is out just now. It will be a gathering," said Mohan Lal, taking their acceptance for granted, "just like home."

49

Chapter Four

Causes of Dispute
1956-7

"It is a long time since we last went to a gathering of Indian people," Nita said thoughtfully, when Kartar explained that he and Perry had been to Southall and made contact with Perry's old friend Mohan Lal. "There are so few here. Yes, I think I should like to go. I rather wish that Perry's friends were Sikhs like ourselves, but after all, it is just a party."

"It will be a change for you," said Kartar, with feeling.

Nita nodded. Two days after the visit to Southall, she and Kartar had moved out of Gilmour Street into their flat and although it was splendid to have their own rooms, and eat in privacy, the place was unquestionably gloomy.

Unfortunately, it was all they could as yet afford. It consisted of a bedsitting room and a kitchen-diner, both of reasonable size, certainly, but attic rooms with sloping ceilings, and dismally decorated with milk chocolate paintwork and beige wallpaper. The small gas stove had only two rings, and the rooms were cold. After one day, Kartar bought a new paraffin heater to replace the one provided by the landlady because the latter smelt, but the new one wasn't much better. Mohan Lal's party would certainly be a distraction, Nita decided. She was touched when Kartar gave her the blue sari early, on Christmas Eve, so that she could wear it for the occasion.

Kartar had described Mohan Lal's parlour to her, and she saw when they arrived that the dark little room had been tidied up for the guests, the cardboard boxes pushed out of sight and chairs set in an hospitable semicircle. There were the familiar smells of Indian cooking and sandalwood from a scented taper burning in a wall bracket, and a murmur of Punjabi conversation. A number of other guests were present; evidently, some of Mohan Lal's local acquaintances had been invited in. A stocky

50

man who was on his feet, holding forth to the room in general, broke off and Mohan Lal said, "This is Dinesh Arora, my brother-in-law, who is visiting me. He has been here two weeks now and he is helping me with the business. Dinesh, this is Kartar Virk that I was telling you about and this is his brother Perry and his wife, Nita . . . "

A woman with a festive red mark on her forehead came forward. "I am Leela, Mohan Lal's wife. Give me your coat. What a nice warm one." Leela was a plump woman whom nature had intended to have an air of comfort and content. She looked, instead, both tired and harassed. But she drew Nita at once into a circle of ladies and small children who, as far as the limitations of the little parlour allowed, had formed a group of their own to one side, and were gossiping over a tray of tea and soft drinks.

Leela performed introductions. " . . . and this is my sister-in-law Shanti and these are my little girls. Sita is three and Krishna is two. And these other ladies are . . . "

Shanti was festive and exquisite in an orange and white printed sari, with a gold ribbon at the end of her thick black braid of hair. She immediately struck Nita as a delightful girl, sweet and shy, the sort who made Inge, for instance, look abrasive. The little girls, regarding her gravely out of liquid dark eyes, were somewhat dark of complexion, as their mother was, but were pretty of feature, and it was a long time since she had seen any Indian children. The other two women were older than herself, but nearer to her in age than the ladies at the Gurudwara. With a sense of homecoming, she took a seat among them, and settled into a comfortable female discussion on the ailments of the children and the difficulty of obtaining ingredients for Indian dishes.

There was, however, some difficulty too in maintaining the conversation, as it had to be conducted in opposition, so to speak, to the obtrusive tones of Dinesh Arora, who was now holding forth again and clearly liked the sound of his own voice.

"No, no, Kartar, I have not got my wife with me. I came over to bring some goods to Mohan Lal; it's all business, there would be nothing for my wife to do here. She has the children to look after. I have three sons," said Dinesh. "Do you smoke? No?" He waved a packet of cigarettes at Kartar, who shook his head. Dinesh lit one himself. "Time you had some sons, Mohan Lal," he said, blowing smoke. "You are not going to stop at two daughters, I hope."

"Plenty of time, plenty of time," said Mohan Lal. He sounded irritated.

Nita observed that he was pouring whisky. Men usually did when they got together; it was one of their odder aberrations. It made them noisy and red in the face but they didn't seem to mind. She hoped that Kartar and Perry wouldn't get drunk. They usually pretended to her that they didn't drink at all but she knew they did.

"Dinesh," Mohan Lal said to Kartar, "is helping me with my paperwork; these days it is all forms to be filling in . . . "

"No, no, forms are no trouble, it is all a matter of getting accustomed to them and seeing what it is they are driving at. They are too clever, these bureaucrats, they'll have the coat off your back if you let them, Mohan Lal, but I have great experience; I am looking after your interests . . . "

"And how many children have you got, Mrs Virk?" said Leela, handing her a cup of tea.

"None, yet. But we were hardly married before Kartar came to England. I have only just rejoined him."

"It does not do to wait too long. A baby completes a family," said one of the other women.

"Well, we certainly hope to start a family soon," said Nita mildly. A week ago, the other woman's remarks might have hurt, but not today. Today, she was full of hope. She should have started a period the day before yesterday, and hadn't. *Oh, God, let it be. Let me be pregnant at last.*

The doorbell rang and more guests arrived, all male. The room seemed to grow smaller still and the ladies, with a faint air of being squeezed out, broke off their conversation, gathered up the children and drifted quietly out to the kitchen, where food was on the stove and Leela was glad of assistance. Nita carried piles of plates into the parlour, declined Perry's chivalrous offer of help but was somewhat affronted when Dinesh said, "The kitchen's no place for you, old boy. My wife says to me sometimes, why you don't help? But I say to her, I am old-fashioned. Men should not do women's work. That is disastrous," and actually went to the length of shifting his cigarette to the same hand as his glass in order to free a hand with which to push Perry back into his chair.

"Dinesh," said his brother-in-law, "will you shut up?"

" . . . no, no, but seriously, it is disastrous. I tell you, Perry, women have no respect for a man who . . . "

Perry slid indignantly out from under Dinesh's impertinent hand and defiantly relieved Shanti of the plate of chapattis she was just bringing in. Nita hurried away. The atmosphere had suddenly become unpleasant, not so much because of the things Dinesh was saying, which were conventional enough although he was expressing them somewhat aggressively, as because of a palpable current of dislike between Dinesh and Mohan Lal. It would be rude to make any comment to Leela, since Dinesh was her guest, as indeed was Nita, but it was no wonder that Leela had that harassed air.

A few moments later, making her way along a short passage in search of some extra dishes which Leela said were to be found in a cupboard there, she discovered Mohan Lal and Perry unearthing new liquor supplies from the bottom of the cupboard, and heard Perry, less inhibited than herself, enquiring, "How in the world do you put up with Dinesh?"

"I often wonder." Mohan Lal backed out of the cupboard, saw Nita and addressed both of them impartially. "He has been here for two weeks but it seems like two centuries and I wish he would go home! I am sick of him, the loudmouth, always dominating the conversation and boasting. He is worse than I remember. No wonder my father wrote me this year that we must be careful who we find to marry Shanti because my other sister has such a life with Dinesh. He is just a bully. *I* am an old-fashioned man. I keep out of the kitchen. But I would never raise my hand to my wife."

"Does Dinesh?" said Perry.

"Yes, according to my father, he does and what's more, he is proud of it, the bastard. He even despises me because I am not like him. Perry, can you carry another bottle? I shall give him a lot more whisky in a minute."

"But that will only make him worse!" Nita said. She saw the plates she had come for and gathered them up.

"Only for a while. Then with luck he will be sick and I wish he turns his stomach inside out," said Mohan Lal with venom.

Mohan Lal's plan proved a success. After they had eaten, Dinesh took to singing songs from popular Hindi films, which, irritatingly, he did rather well. But presently he grew quieter and the other men took over what turned into a friendly competition in reciting and singing, while the women went back and forth, collecting the used plates and listening with amusement. A little later, Dinesh began to retch and was removed, sagging between Mohan Lal and Kartar, to the bathroom and the evening thereafter improved.

"But no one can say it was fun," said Kartar when they were going home afterwards on the Underground. "I am sorry. What a disappointment. Well, let us hope Mr Houghton's party tomorrow is better."

"It is kind of him to say that we should come," Nita agreed. "Since we are not his tenants any more."

The party at Gilmour Street on Christmas Day was indeed better. The sitting room was festooned with brightly coloured paper-chains and the Christmas tree with fairy lights; the singsong to the guitar was noisy and enthusiastic and there was a treasure hunt, which involved much rushing up and down the two staircases and numerous collisions on them, and although Aziz and Mr Bharucha were joint winners, they actually managed to be nice to each other about it.

Perry said he had enjoyed it immensely and told Nita that Christmas reminded him of Diwali festivals at home. "Everywhere is lit up and there is a sort of humming. It's all quite different from everyday. I actually thought Mohan Lal's place was miserable because he had no paper-chains."

Nita agreed, distractedly. The lights and the paper-chains were pretty and the games and songs were merry but they found no answering joyousness in her. On Christmas morning she had found that she was not pregnant after all.

After Christmas, Perry found the world very flat. The bitter cold of that January was something hitherto outside his experience and he was forced to spend money which he could ill afford from his modest grant on a thick topcoat. One of the Nigerians went home and there was a new face at the table, an English one this time.

Pat Holtsby came from Yorkshire, and was a bright, bouncy girl with butter-coloured curls which refused to be smoothed into any of the standard styles depicted in hairdressers' windows and in advertisements for home perms. Unexpectedly, her eyes were pansy brown. She was studying for a Bachelor of Arts degree at London University. She was one of the few among the Houghtons' paying guests who liked Hiawatha's attentions and grieved because he did not want to share her sleeping quarters for always.

Perry thought he would like to get to know her better but he had little opportunity. She seemed to have found friends at the university at once, and went out with them at weekends, and as the new term began, Perry's college work became demanding. Somehow, he had not completed his vacation assignments and now attempted to catch up by working late into the night. He felt tired. When he went to see Nita and Kartar, they did little to cheer him up. Kartar was grimly engaged in surviving his three months' trial period at his job. "I have to be twice as good as an Englishman would be, to make them think I'm equally as good." He too brought work home and toiled late.

Nita was always hospitable, but her normally sensible and cheerful nature seemed dimmed, and there was a worried line constantly between her brows. Once, when Perry had met them at a coffee bar and accompanied them home, he saw her pick up an airmail letter from the hall table between finger and thumb as though it repelled her, and when he realised that it was addressed in his mother's handwriting, he knew why.

In letters to him, more than once, Ranbir had repined, "I wish there is news soon of an addition to Kartar's family." No doubt she was pressing Nita for that news, which as yet was not forthcoming. She must be pressing hard, he thought, since at home, she and Nita had been on very good terms.

There was a telephone at the Houghtons', which the students could use "within reason", Mr Houghton said, and Mohan Lal rang up once or twice, asking Perry to visit him, but since Christmas Perry had had neither the time nor, he admitted to himself, the inclination. Mohan Lal had altered since their boyhood days in Delhi, having become both more earnest and more talkative, and Dinesh Arora was just plain obnoxious.

But on the third Monday of the term, when Brenda Houghton called him down to the phone, Mohan Lal's voice on the other end uttered not an invitation, but a plea. "Perry, I wish you will come and see me and bring Kartar too, maybe. I have a great worry on my mind; I am needing your advice. How soon you can come?"

"Well, I . . . "

"You must not say no to me again; I am worried, I tell you. This is urgent."

"What's wrong? What's the trouble?"

"Not on the phone, I can't talk on the phone. You must come to me and then I can explain."

Such an appeal had to be heeded. "I can go to see Kartar

tonight and ask him. Then I'll ring you back."

"I knew you wouldn't fail me. Old friends must stick together, eh? I'll be waiting by the phone. This is a real problem, believe me."

He had been planning to go through his notes that evening, but Kartar's flat had no telephone, so he would have to go there in person. If he set off at once, he might just get back for dinner. Reluctant but mindful of his duty to his friend, he fetched his coat and plunged out into the dark winter evening.

Kartar, as he expected, was irritated but accepting. "Yes, we shall have to go. There is obviously something very wrong. Tell him tomorrow evening, Perry. It is too late today. Do you want anything to eat? We are just about to have ours."

"You are always welcome," said Nita over her shoulder, stirring pans.

"No, thanks. I'd better get back. You know the Houghtons like you to say if you won't be in for dinner." Nita's words had been friendly, but her tone was depressed, and he found the flat chilly and dispiriting. He set off back to the Houghtons with an alacrity which he hoped his brother and sister-in-law hadn't noticed.

Well, he thought, as he walked quickly through the bone-eating cold, Mohan Lal's troubles, whatever they were, at least meant a break in the monotony. But what in the world could this problem be which was so frightful that Mohan Lal couldn't talk about it over the telephone?

He might, of course, have murdered Dinesh and be wondering how to dispose of the body. Cheered by this agreeable thought, Perry hurried up the steps of the Houghtons, let himself in, threw his coat on to a hook in the hall and made straight for the kitchen, ready with an apology for being late for dinner.

It was not required. No one was interested in Perry's lateness or could have heard his excuses. Mr Bharucha and Aziz, both shouting at once, and Mr Houghton's unheeded demands for them to stop it, filled the room.

Perry slid into his place and Brenda Houghton, making an eyes-rolled-up-to-heaven face, presented him with a plate of spaghetti bolognaise, which he began to eat while the uproar thundered back and forth across the table.

" . . . ridiculous saying Iran is a Moslem country like that. If most of the population are Moslem it is because you converted them at the point of a sword . . . "

"I have never converted anyone with a sword! I haven't even got a sword, you stupid man . . . "

"Will you two be quiet? At *once*!"

" . . . your ancestors, your people, what difference does it make? You are all the same. It was a forced conversion and . . . "

"Forced? Islam came to Persia in the seventh century and you are still here, I notice!"

"We are a remnant, barely tolerated! As a community with power we were destroyed in the thirteenth century . . . "

"That was because of the Mongol invasion; they destroyed everyone in sight. Just another pack of pagans!"

"Oh, do stop it!" said Brenda Houghton exasperatedly.

"We Zoroastrians gave Persia a culture, a literature, traditions of tolerance and good manners . . . "

"Good manners? We have no need of being taught manners by infidels . . . "

" . . . long before the seventh century. To talk about the historic Moslem traditions of Iran is the bunk, as Henry Ford says . . . "

"Henry Ford has nothing to do with it and you are not going to say that what I say is bunk!" Aziz shot to his feet and banged a clenched fist on the table, causing Pat Holtsby, who was beside him, to slop the glass of water she was pouring for herself. "I will not stand for it!" shouted Aziz.

"Then sit down, for God's sake!" said Brenda Houghton, reaching out a hand and yanking the back of his jacket. He took no notice.

"Do as my wife says!" bellowed Mr Houghton.

Brenda Houghton passed a spare plate to Pat and said, "Put this under the cloth where the puddle is."

"This man," said Aziz, appealing to the table at large, "says I am talking bunk! Who of you here would tolerate being told that and by someone who has insulted your country?"

"It's my country just as much as yours . . . "

Mr Houghton's large palm banged down on the table. "You be quiet too, Mr Bharucha!"

"It is a great pity we did not convert you all, with a sword or without one. It does not work when a small part of a population live their lives by a quite different set of rules from the rest . . . "

"Listen to him!" said Bharucha, also appealing to the table at large. "He complains of discrimination against him in this country. I have heard him say why do people give him funny looks when he is standing in a bus queue. Now listen to him talking about minorities at home!"

"That is not the same thing. While I am here, I keep the laws of this country . . . "

"I keep the laws in Iran!"

"But if we had Islamic law in Iran, would you keep that?"

"Aziz! Mr Bharucha!"

"I do not like your religion, Aziz. There is cruelty in it; I do not like laws that say it is all right to stone people, and . . . "

"And you are nothing but a pagan! You worship fire, like a savage . . . "

"Look, do calm down, old chap." That was the placid Akbar. "It's silly to argue about religion. It is best just to follow one's own and let others follow theirs."

The contestants ignored him. "How dare you call me a savage? I tell you . . . !"

"Stop it, you two, just stop it!" This time the protest was from Pat, whose elbow Aziz had now jogged as he leant across the table to shake his fist at Mr Bharucha. "Look what you've done; my spaghetti's all over the table!"

"I agree, this is a disgrace," said Chang. Senta Watanabe said something which from the tone was agreement with this. Yasmin looked distressed.

Aziz leapt from his place and started round the table towards Mr Bharucha, who sprang up with equal enthusiasm and advanced to meet him. "Savage, am I? At least I do not go about saying everyone else in my country should adopt my beliefs and I have some respect for my elders. You are a bully and a fanatic."

"I am a what? What is that you say about me?" Aziz burst into a flood of speech in his own language. Mr Bharucha turned purple and retorted with what sounded remarkably like a stream of rude epithets. It could not be said that either of them attacked first. They reached for each other's throats simultaneously and an instant later were rolling on the floor, trying their hardest to throttle each other. Mr Houghton, expanding under the influence of rage to the proportions of a colossus, shoved his chair back, marched up to them, seized one in each hand and hauled them bodily apart.

"You can just stop that, here and now! Stop it, I say! You may as well, I'm stronger than you are. I will not have my kitchen turned into a bear garden. You know my rules. I'm sick to death of you two and your quarrelling. You will both leave my house by the end of the week and . . . "

"You cannot do this! You cannot simply throw me into the street!" shouted Aziz. "And all over this . . . this . . . he has insulted my religion and me! He has offended me!"

"'E is always being offended," remarked Jacques. "'E enjoys being offended. If 'e can find a reason to go about with the set face and the nose in the air, 'e is 'appy." Jacques had difficulty with his aspirants and his definite articles, but his command of English was otherwise excellent.

"Yes, he takes himself too seriously. Such dramatics," said Inge, making history by agreeing with Jacques.

"For the moment," said Mr Houghton, "you can just go and be offended in your room, Aziz. And that applies to you as well, Mr Bharucha. I'm disgusted with you. You provoked him on purpose and you know it."

"But where am I to go? I cannot just *leave!*" Mr Bharucha tried vainly to wrench himself out of the landlord's grasp.

"Hard luck. You should have thought of that sooner!" snapped Mr Houghton unfeelingly and let go of him by virtually throwing him towards the door. Mr Bharucha attempted to take a stand on the threshold but Aziz lunged at him, almost breaking free, and Bharucha fled. Senta Watanabe came to Mr Houghton's aid, applying an armlock to the hysterical Aziz. He was understood to be informing Aziz that the armlock was a judo technique. He looked amused.

"I am fed up with religious ardour," Brenda Houghton announced, through Aziz's infuriated demands that Watanabe should release him. "It makes people impossible to live with. Give me a nice, restful atheist with a sense of humour, any day . . . "

"How can you say that? That is an outrageous thing to say! Take your hands off me, you filthy . . . !"

" . . . and I endorse every word my husband has said, Aziz. I wish you could be out of here *tomorrow*. And you will eat out for the rest of the time that you're here. I'm damned if I'll feed either you or Bharucha."

"Come on, my lad," said Houghton. "Thanks, Senta. Help me along with him. We'd better take him upstairs. Shut up, Aziz! We're taking you to your room and you'd better bloody well stay there!"

They went out. Aziz had stopped fighting but his angry voice, demanding that they should unhand him, calling Watanabe names which Watanabe probably – and fortunately – couldn't understand, and insisting that Bharucha was wholly in the wrong and that he himself was a deeply offended innocent, faded slowly along the passage.

"I hate this sort of thing!" said Pat passionately. She looked at the mess of spilt spaghetti and the patch of wet tablecloth draped over the plate, jumped up and ran out of the room.

"Oh, for goodness *sake!*" said Brenda Houghton, reaching across to spoon up the spaghetti. "Go after her, somebody; she must eat her dinner."

"I'll go." Perry left his place and hurried out. He started up the stairs meaning to tap on Pat's door but before he reached it, she came out with her coat on. She stopped when she saw him.

"Mrs Houghton sent me to find you. She is worried because you have not eaten your dinner."

"I can't eat it, not down there. Not with all that going on. I've never seen people behave like that," said Pat indignantly, "in all my born days! *Fighting!* And at a mealtime, too; spoiling it for everyone else. I'm sorry about Mrs Houghton's food being wasted, and I'll tell her so, but I'm not going back into there to eat. I'm going out. Excuse me."

"You are very upset," Perry said anxiously.

"Upset? I feel as though I'm living in a house full of madmen. They've never actually fought before but the way they go on the rest of the time, always squabbling – I've never come across such a thing in my *life!*" said Pat in outrage.

On impulse, Perry said, "I am not very fond of spaghetti, as it happens. There is a coffee bar and snack place in the main road, only ten minutes away if we walk briskly. They do cheese on toast, eggs and beans, things like that. Let us leave this Disunited Nations and go to Toni's Espresso."

Pat's brown eyes regarded him with a mixture of surprise and doubt. He could see that she wanted to say yes but was uncertain about him; especially, to judge from the way her gaze went to the top of his head, by the turban. She wasn't sure if she wanted to walk through the streets with anyone who looked so foreign.

"You are worrying about my turban," he said. "It is strange to you. But there is just an ordinary person under it, and I am very civilised. I *never* fight about religion at mealtimes."

Suddenly Pat laughed. "Yes, I'll come. I'd like to. We'll both

60

have to explain to Mrs Houghton."

"And I must make a phone call before we go, but it will take only just a moment, and perhaps you can see Mrs Houghton while I make it. I left my coat in the hall so I can pick it up on the way out."

He rang Mohan Lal while Pat went to the kitchen. "You are coming tomorrow, you and Kartar?" Mohan Lal's voice was very low; he sounded as though he feared to be overheard. "Listen, when you come you must say nothing about why you are here; pretend it is just a casual call and leave it to me to find a moment to explain. Promise. Tell Kartar."

"Yes, all right, if you like. Yes, of course. But all this sounds most mysterious; really, can't you say anything of what it's about? Kartar says . . . "

"I must go now," Mohan Lal almost whispered. Then, more clearly but further away he said, "It's just a wrong number; there are too many wrong numbers; it is such a nuisance." He put the phone down and Perry turned to find Pat waiting for him, her expression a little doubtful again. He realised that probably this was because she had heard him speak, with easy command, in a language which was not only not English, but wasn't even European.

"Well, that's done," he said lightly, fishing in his pocket for some coins to put into the box which stood by the telephone so that Mr Houghton's tenants could pay for any calls they made. "Let's go."

"What started all that uproar today?" he asked as they left the house. "I came in late and I missed the start of it."

"You didn't miss much," said Pat. "It was all so silly. Mr Bharucha was admiring the way there are no beggars in Britain and Aziz said that that wasn't so; that last weekend he and Akbar were walking along the Embankment in London and they met a beggar. Then Akbar said yes, that was true, they had come across this old tramp with newspaper sticking out of the holes in his shoes and he'd asked them for money and Aziz had given him some. Then Mr Bharucha said that that was a silly thing to do; one should never give money to tramps because they only spent it on drink and Aziz said that in his religion, giving alms was a duty . . . "

"Yes, it is. It is one of the good things in Islam."

"I suppose it's a good thing," said Pat doubtfully, "but Mr Bharucha didn't think so. *He* said that in a properly run country,

61

the state saw to people's welfare so that no one would need to beg and then Aziz said that it was better for people to give alms as individuals, that it improved them spiritually, and Mr Bharucha said in a sneering sort of way that it saved the state money too; how very convenient, and Aziz called him a communist and said he was ashamed to hear an Iranian say such things, that there was no place for communism in a good Moslem country like Iran, and that, more or less, was where you came in."

"All this," said Perry thoughtfully, "all of us Easterners with our passionate feelings about religions that are quite strange to you, it must all be very bewildering."

"Well, it is. It all seems so unnecessary, somehow."

"There was a time when people were passionate about religion here." They were striding rapidly now towards the lights of the main road. Pat marched briskly beside him, keeping step with ease. "I did English history at school . . . "

"In India?"

"Oh, yes; we do more English history than Indian." He laughed. "My mother disapproved of that! I know how Henry the Eighth broke with the Pope over Anne Boleyn, and we learned about Oliver Cromwell and the Civil War, too."

"That was hundreds of years ago," said Pat. "We don't go on like that now. That's why it seems so weird listening to Aziz and Mr Bharucha. My parents go to church sometimes, but they don't act like that about it."

"Well, in my family they don't, either." They turned into the main road and made their way rapidly along it. The night had become very bitter indeed.

"But your turban. That's something to do with religion, isn't it?"

"Yes. I can tell you about it if you like but we can talk about something else if you prefer."

"I'd like to know, I think," said Pat.

"Let's get into that nice warm coffee bar first."

Toni's Espresso had good lighting, efficient heating, wipe-clean tables flanked by padded benches covered in red imitation leather, competitive prices and it stayed open late. Across two foaming espresso coffees and two plates of Welsh rarebit, they took stock of each other. Perry did not know what she was making of him, although he was aware that in the last few months he had filled out and looked much less skinny and boyish than when he had sailed from Bombay. On his side, as he studied her, he thought that Pat was very pretty indeed. The butter-coloured curls which he had heard her complain had minds of their own looked to him delightfully disorderly and he liked her generous mouth and her fair skin with its faint golden undertones.

"This is a nice place," she said, slightly disconcerted by his scrutiny, and avoiding it by gazing round the room. "It's busy but it's quiet as well. Not even a jukebox."

"There is, but it's broken down."

"I think I like it that way. This is soothing, especially after that awful row. I had no idea this coffee bar was here. I haven't found my way round yet."

"You will get to know. All the essential places – the bank, the post office, the pub, the coffee bar . . . "

" . . . and the newspaper shop and the bus stop and the library." Pat smiled. "Sooner or later I'll feel at home, I suppose. I've never been away from home before. But you're much further away from yours. Do you feel homesick sometimes?"

"Yes, very much," said Perry truthfully. "But," he added, "I am lucky in a way because I have a brother and sister-in-law living not far from here. Have you any brothers or sisters?" he asked.

"I have an older brother, Ted."

"And is he studying in London too?"

"Well, he's been to agricultural college. We're a farming family and the farm will go to him eventually. But I'm setting out to find a career for myself. I want to get my degree and then I'll decide what I want to do. I'm the first person in our family ever to go to university so it will mean a lot to us all if I succeed."

"I wish you luck." He glanced at her left hand and saw that she wore no rings. "Will you marry?"

Pat looked mildly surprised. "I suppose so, in time. I shall have to wait and see. It isn't the sort of thing one can organise."

"No, I know. It's different here."

Pat, in the act of stirring sugar into her coffee, paused wonderingly. "Do people still really do that, where you come from? Actually arrange marriages, I mean?"

"Yes. Well . . . in our family, people are introduced to each other and if they have met a time or two and like each other, the families go ahead and fix the wedding. They are not ordered to marry this person or that person; it is not like that. They can say no. But mostly the girls trust their parents to decide."

Pat's expression was genuinely shocked. "How can they? I mean marry – commit themselves for life – to someone they hardly know, just on someone else's say-so? You can't decide whether you like someone enough to marry them if all you've done is talk to them a couple of times!"

"But we do and it works. Love comes after marriage, we say, like a kettle beginning to sing after you have put the fire under it."

"But that means" – Pat went slightly pink – "the honeymoon, having to have a honeymoon with someone you don't love, who's practically a stranger."

"By the end of the honeymoon, they are not strangers."

There was a silence, while Pat absorbed this. "You mentioned a brother and sister-in-law," she said at last. "Did they . . . ?"

"Yes. They had an arranged introduction, so to speak. The two families go to the same Gurudwara – I mean temple – and a mutual acquaintance brought them together. My mother was letting it be known that she wanted someone for Kartar, and Nita's mother was doing the same as regards Nita. I was going to explain the turban. Do you want to hear?"

"Oh, yes, of course you were. Yes, what does it mean?"

"It's a long story." Perry consumed a mouthful of cheese on toast, wondered where to begin, remembered Nita's exposition to the Houghtons and set about, as far as possible, repeating it.

Pat listened attentively, only interrupting once or twice with questions. At the end, she said, "Well, I never knew any of that before. What a difference it makes, when one understands *why*."

Perry smiled and then said, "I have a feeling that I have just been present at a remarkable moment."

"In what way?"

"A few minutes ago my turban was a quaint foreign eccentricity. Now you understand it and you see that it is a sign of dignity. That isn't a criticism of you. It is like a word in a strange language, I suppose. In India, everyone knows what a turban means but here you speak another language and the turban is like a strange word that is just a noise until someone tells you what it means."

Once more, Pat laughed, as she had done when she agreed to come with him to the Espresso. It was her own special bubbly laugh which he had liked when he heard it across the Houghtons' dinner table. "I heard you say the other day that you found report-writing the hardest part of your course. But why? You've got a real way with words."

"That's the trouble. They don't let you use any imagination. I get into trouble because my tutor says the language I use is too flowery."

"I like it."

The door of the café opened and another couple came in, talking together as they entered. Perry and Pat, recognising their voices, glanced round to behold the unlikely spectacle of Inge and Jacques in one another's company and apparently so engrossed in it that they did not notice their fellow tenants. They were discussing the scene at dinner, in scandalised voices. Their dislike of each other (which was reputedly founded in the events of the Second World War) had apparently dissolved in a mutual disapproval of Aziz and Mr Bharucha.

"And I like you, too," said Perry seriously, turning back to Pat. "You're very pretty, and you have such a nice voice."

"My Yorkshire voice?"

"You come from Yorkshire so I suppose it must be a Yorkshire voice. At any rate I think it is pleasing. Pat . . . "

"Yes?"

Perry put down his fork and reached across the table to take Pat's hand, detaching it gently from her coffee cup. It was a small, neat hand, a little sturdier in the wrist and wider across the palm than the hands of most Indian girls but with slim and tapered fingers and matt, pale cream skin.

"There's a good picture on, south of the Thames this week," he said. "Will you come with me to see it?"

Chapter Five

Shadows
1957

He would have liked to take Pat out the very next evening but he and Kartar were already engaged to go to Mohan Lal and there was nothing to be done about that. When a friend called for help, one had to respond. His date would have to wait until the evening after. Irritatedly, he forced himself to concentrate on the unknown problem in Southall. He presented himself at Kartar's flat at quarter to six and said, "I think from the way Mohan Lal sounded on the phone, we ought to pretend this is just a casual dropping-in. So Nita should come; it would be natural."

"Oh, Perry, you make it all sound like a cloak-and-dagger film," said Nita. She was cleaning the sink, and did not turn round as she spoke.

"No, I think Perry is right. You should come," said Kartar. "You are in low spirits this evening; I knew as soon as I got in, ten minutes ago. You put a pretty sari on, and we'll all go."

Perry tried to enliven the tube journey with an account of the fight between Mr Bharucha and Aziz, taking pleasure in it because it enabled him to speak Pat's name in a harmless context. He wasn't going to tell them about taking her to a coffee bar, but he could describe her outrage over her spilt spaghetti. Kartar was amused, but Nita was not. "It is not nice, such things happening. It is a good thing if those two are to leave. There could be real trouble, some sort of incident. Suppose the police had to be called?"

"Now who is being cloak and dagger?" said Kartar, trying to jolly her out of her solemnity. But her face remained grave. Nita, Perry decided, took life far too seriously. Sometimes she was nearly as bad as Aziz. His efforts to be entertaining were falling decidedly flat and he was glad when the journey was

66

over at last.

They rang Mohan Lal's bell and he let them in so quickly that he must have been hovering near the door. He beckoned them in as furtively as though he were welcoming them to some kind of criminal conspiracy, and then led them through to his parlour, saying, "Well, look who's dropped in on us!" in tones of loud and unconvincing surprise, for the benefit of Dinesh and three or four other guests, all men, whom Perry vaguely remembered having met on Christmas Eve.

They sat about in the gloomy parlour – the light bulb, thought Perry, was sixty watt at most and quite possibly forty – sipping tea and nibbling sweetmeats brought in from the kitchen by Leela and Shanti, who then withdrew once more, taking Nita with them.

Mohan Lal asked if Perry and Kartar had heard from their parents in India lately and hoped that all their people back home were well. He could have been holding hands with Pat in the Tooting Granada at this moment, thought Perry venomously.What on earth was all this *about*?

" . . . oh yes," Kartar was saying, "Nita is keeping very well. She is finding plenty to do in the flat. She is always busy."

"Not busy enough, though, eh?" said Dinesh. "Time you were having some sons, eh?"

"Perry," said Mohan Lal, "you were asking me something about your studies, about book-keeping. Shall I show you what I was trying to explain? It is really very simple."

Perry looked at him in amazement, realised that this must be a ploy to speak to him privately, wiped the surprise from his face and said, "Oh, yes, I should be so grateful."

Dinesh half rose from his chair. "Now, if it is book-keeping, I am your man. I have been telling Mohan Lal, he should let me take over his books for him; I can save him a fortune if he lets me."

"No, no," said Mohan Lal. "You are my co-host; you must stay with the guests while I see to this little matter. It is time they had some whisky; you see to that for me. This won't take long." He glanced at Perry who also rose, and then, urgently, at Kartar, who said lazily, "I am an accountant, Perry, you should have asked me. Let me come and look over your shoulder. If Mohan Lal here doesn't make himself clear, perhaps I can explain better."

" . . . Always," said Mohan Lal, when he had marshalled the

two of them up the stairs to what had once been a small back bedroom and was now a small, untidy office, with a portable typewriter on a paper-strewn desk, and some ledgers and ring-binders propped drunkenly against each other on a shelf above, "always there is a problem, getting out of Dinesh's hearing, but we must be out of his hearing because this is all to do with him. Thank God you are here."

"What is all this about?" Kartar hitched a hip on to the edge of the desk. "Perry is right; you are being very mysterious. Anyone would think you were plotting a revolution."

"I am not plotting a revolution," said Mohan Lal crossly. "I am not plotting anything. I need your help. It is that Dinesh. He has been insisting that he will help me in the shop and with the book-keeping, to save me money. But I am not a fool and I keep an eye on what he is doing, and I tell you he has had his sticky fingers in my till. I want to show you things, so that you can tell me I am not dreaming this about my own brother-in-law! And when you have convinced me," said Mohan Lal, "I want to ask you: what am I to do to get rid of him?"

It was Kartar, sensibly, who shut and locked the office door so that they could not be unexpectedly interrupted. "All right. Now. How's he been doing it?"

"Every which way!" said Mohan Lal and almost tore his hair. "I know my stock, I tell you. I am properly organised and there are codes for different items which show on the till roll against the amount when things are sold. And I have price tags, because I have English customers and the English don't like haggling." His voice was faintly pitying, as though the English didn't know what fun they were missing. "But I will reduce a price if a line moves slowly, and the first time I leave him in the shop, I am telling him, bring down the price of that mauve-coloured cotton fabric – I show him which – because it is not selling well. I tell Shanti and Leela about this, too, because sometimes they are serving in the shop, though mostly it is only when I am there, or Dinesh; you never know who comes in and Shanti especially is so pretty and anyway, she has such poor English. Then the very next week, Shanti is telling me that she took coffee to Dinesh while he was serving, and heard him sell a length of that cotton at the original price. But the till record shows the reduced price. I tell Shanti she has made a silly mistake and she is annoyed; she says she is not so foolish. And indeed, my sister is *not* foolish."

68

Mohan Lal paused for breath.

Perry said, "I take it she was right? What happened next? You must have found out more."

"Yes, I did. Next, Dinesh is telling me he has reduced some other item, a sandalwood figurine – I have some brass bowls and these wood figurines as well as fabrics nowadays but, hah! The customer comes back next day to buy another; he says he got the first one as a present but he likes it so much he wants one for his own home. He says he remembers the price and takes the money from his wallet and what he offers me is the full amount. I say, is that what you paid for the first one and he looks surprised and says yes, isn't that what's on the price tag? Well, it is, and I take the full price and he goes away thinking I am a funny sort of shopkeeper; I don't know what my own price tags say!"

"And?" said Kartar.

"And," said Mohan Lal grimly, "I sneak in here at two in the morning – into my own office I creep like a burglar at such an hour – so that Dinesh will not know and I am going through the books and all the records, one tiny bit at a time. And I find things. I look at supplier's invoices and I look at bank statements, and I see that if I look closely there are some invoices altered, very neatly, to look as if I paid more than I did. The bank statement shows what I really paid the supplier. The difference – well, sometimes I have let my brother-in-law bank my cash takings for me. I am thinking that all of it does not always get to the bank or if it does, it does not go into my account. What am I to do?" Mohan Lal banged a clenched fist on the table. "Look!" He switched on a desk lamp, and began to yank ledgers and binders from the shelf. "Let me show you. Look, look here."

They looked, at the footprints of opportunist pilferings, the neat alterations which had to be held under a bright light to be detected, the discrepancies.

"He's milked you of hundreds," said Kartar. "But he could not have hoped to get away with it for long."

"He despises me," said Mohan Lal. He pulled a chair out from the desk and sank into it. "He thinks I will never keep track of all these figures and Shanti and Leela he thinks are nothing at all. But they have been watching him too. What *am* I to do? I will end up bankrupt!"

"Challenge him," said Kartar.

"How can I? How can I do that?"

"What else is there to do?" said Perry reasonably.

"He is married to my sister in Delhi! You don't know him! He will take it out on her. It was a mistake ever to marry her to him. I *told* you. He is a bully."

"So you are just going to let him swindle you?" said Kartar.

"No, no! That is why I asked you to come. How do I protect myself and her and how do I get him to go home? He will not go home just for the asking, believe me. He thinks he has a right to bleed me, that is what it is. He asks for things sometimes. I bought him a new overcoat for winter. He said that the dowry he got with my sister was not all that was promised, so I should give him things when he asks."

Perry picked a sheaf of assorted documents off a spike and examined them curiously. "Try soaping the stairs," he suggested flippantly.

"They're carpeted, or I would!"

Kartar eyed them both reprovingly. "It's blackmail, Mohan Lal. Either you stand up to him or . . . "

"It is my sister who will have to do the standing up to him and she can't; she is a gentle, traditional girl . . . can't you think of something?" said Mohan Lal in despair.

"I can think of one thing," said Kartar candidly. "Who does your annual accounts?"

"I do. Well, Dinesh has been saying it is wasteful to hire outside accountants . . . "

"I bet he has! Damn Dinesh! Tell him you *are* going to employ an accountant. Say you think the business has grown beyond you or him to attend to and then sit back and let matters take their course."

"But an accountant would find . . . "

"Of course he would, if he were any use. And if Dinesh has even a little sense, he will know it. With any luck, he'll go home at once. How long has he been here?"

"Weeks," said Mohan Lal with a groan. "He could stay here years if he wanted to. There is nothing to stop him; he is an Indian, a Commonwealth citizen like me."

"The prospect of an accountant will stop him. But . . . " Kartar shook his head. "He will be getting away with it, still, in a fashion. It is not satisfactory. In your place, I repeat, I would call him up here, *now*, and say look, we have found what you are up to. Get out of this house and go back home, or else I will take professional advice. Then you murmur the words accountant, solicitor and police, in that order, and I bet you he will have his

70

suitcase packed before you have got to the end of the sentence, and he will know he has been caught out."

"But my sister . . . "

"If it were me in your place, she would have to take her chance," said Kartar, ruthlessly. "But it's your shop, your sister, your brother-in-law. It's up to you."

Perry said, "But you have other family members, back home. Surely they would not approve of what Dinesh is doing? Can you not say you will tell them if he ill-treats his wife? Can't *you* blackmail *him*?"

Mohan Lal stared at them and flung up his hands. "You are right, of course you are right. He will laugh at me in secret unless I face him with it. But if I do, you must be here. You will be witness if he makes threats." He took a deep breath, stumped to the door, unlocked it, went out, leant over the banisters and bellowed, "*Dinesh!*"

"You have to admit," Kartar said on the way home afterwards, "that Dinesh has all the nerve in the world."

"Too much bloody nerve," said Perry feelingly. "Brazen is the word I would use."

Dinesh, coming upstairs in response to Mohan Lal's repeated shouts, had strutted into the room and seen the three accusing faces, the handful of statements held fanwise in Perry's grasp and an open file of invoices on the desk. There was just one moment when he halted, stiffening. Then he smiled at them, with raised, questioning brows. There was an embarrassed silence, until Kartar broke it with, "There seem to be some oddities in the records you have been keeping for your brother-in-law, Dinesh. We have found some altered figures and some discrepancies. But perhaps there is an explanation?"

"Ah." The smile did not fade from Dinesh's face. "So you have rumbled my little devices." They looked at him speechlessly. "Who was it spotted them?" enquired Dinesh. "You, Mohan Lal? You are brighter than I thought."

"Then you are not denying it?" said Mohan Lal.

"Denying what? There is nothing wrong. It is all in one family and I have been working for you in your shop and doing your books, Mohan Lal, and you are not paying me a penny. So I pay myself." Dinesh beamed expansively round at them. Perry found himself gaping, and observed that Kartar was looking at Dinesh Arora as though Dinesh were something in a zoo.

Mohan Lal, who had now gone too far to retreat, took refuge in losing his temper. "Nothing wrong, you say there is nothing wrong? Are you crazy, man? *Nothing wrong?* You have been fiddling me left, right and centre and you think it is all right? Pay you? You almost forced your way into my business; you would not take no for an answer! I would have paid if you had asked; as it is, a fine coat you have had off me, food, lodging, money to go here and there and God knows what else as well. A watch you made me buy you at Christmas . . . !"

"Really?" said Kartar, and his glance fell on the broad gold band encircling Dinesh's wrist. "If that's it, I should make him give it back."

Dinesh at last reacted, putting his other hand quickly over the wrist and glaring at Kartar.

Kartar, ignoring this, said, "Mohan Lal," in a prompting tone of voice.

Mohan Lal, who had paused to collect his thoughts, visibly braced himself and said, as though he were reciting it, "Dinesh, I must ask you to leave my house. Go home to India. Go away as soon as you can and we will say no more about this."

"I shall say some more about it," said Dinesh. "If I am treated in such a way by my own in-laws, well, perhaps your sister, my wife, can talk you into changing your attitude . . . "

"I know what you mean by that," said Mohan Lal with dignity. "And I tell you, I shall write to my sister and say to her, let my father know, or let me know, if you and your parents are not treating her properly. If she complains, there are plenty in your family who will not like to hear of what you have been doing here. Your Uncle Chandra is a very decent man; what if I write to him and tell him all this?"

"Oh, what a card you are, Mohan Lal. How seriously you take everything and what things you read into what I say. Did I say I would not be kind to my wife? Of course I will be kind to her; when was I ever anything else? I meant only that I would ask her to write and soften your heart with her sisterly persuasions. Well, well, I can see I shall not be happy any longer in this house so I will take my leave as you ask. It is your house, after all. I will go to the travel bureau tomorrow and see what sailings there are. If that is your wish."

"Yes, it is," said Mohan Lal pugnaciously.

"I have left our guests by themselves downstairs. I had better get back to them so that you can be sure they are not stealing your spoons. You have such a distrustful nature, Mohan Lal," said Dinesh superbly, and went.

"*Well!*" said Perry.

"At least he's going," said Kartar. "Make sure he does, Mohan Lal. Let us know if he doesn't get on with it."

Perry was once more studying the papers in his hand. "If he has been doing your books for you, he hasn't only been fiddling them; he's badly behind. There are things here going back to last October."

Mohan Lal was wiping his forehead with a large red handkerchief. "My poor sister. I don't trust him . . . I shall write to her before I go to bed, and warn her what to do if he does not behave . . . It will take months to sort out everything he has done. There will be more than I have shown you, I am sure of it."

"Very likely. Look, can I help? It would be good practice for me, a useful practical exercise, if I tried to bring your records up to date. I promise not to swindle you," said Perry with a smile. "But I might save you some work."

"I would be grateful. But I would pay you something if you did that. It would be only fair."

"Oh, there's no need . . . "

"No," said Kartar. "It would be fair, Perry. It would release Mohan Lal from a sense of obligation. Accept, if you really want to take this on. But do remember, you have your studies. You must be careful of your time, even if this is good practice, as you say."

"You had better not come until Dinesh goes, anyway," said Mohan Lal. "But I hope he will go soon." He began to put away the files and ledgers. "He agreed too easily," he said. "I don't like it. I am afraid what he will do."

"If you take steps to protect your sister," said Kartar, "there is nothing he can do, you know."

"He has a long memory, that one," said Mohan Lal, sighing.

In the kitchen, Leela was saying, "I hope they will not be too long upstairs. The food is nearly ready. Thank you for doing the chapattis, Nita. Is Dinesh still up there with them, I wonder?"

"No, I can hear him in the parlour again now," said Shanti. "He is not a nice man. He behaves as if I am silly, and hard of hearing too. He says to my brother that he is selling this or that cheap, and then he sells at full price to the customer and he thinks I can't hear him or don't understand what I have heard!"

"Mohan Lal is so good-natured and patient," said Leela. "And he has such a sense of family. Let us hope that Kartar and Perry give him good advice. It was kind of them to come so quickly to help him. We are very grateful, Nita . . . Nita?"

"The chapatti!" cried Shanti.

Nita was standing by the stove, holding the handle of the pan in which the last chapatti was cooking. But she was gazing into infinity and appeared to be in a trance, although smoke was rising from the pan, accompanied by a fast-strengthening smell of burning. She came to at Shanti's cry.

"Oh, dear." She flipped the chapatti over quickly but it was too late. "I think I've burnt it. I'm so sorry."

The door opened, to admit Mohan Lal, Perry and Kartar. Leela, waving smoke away and gesturing to Nita to extinguish the scorched disaster in the sink, almost pulled them inside and shut the door after them. "What has been happening? What is to be done?"

"Dinesh will be leaving," Mohan Lal said. "My friends agree with me that he has been on the fiddle and they have spoken to him. Now, what are we to do about food? Because Dinesh is out there with the rest of our guests now and . . . "

"Food is ready. They can eat something here, quickly, while you tell us all about it," Leela said, reaching for bowls and dishes. Nita, visibly pulling herself together, lifted a saucepan from a back burner and turned the burner off.

While the Virks ate rapidly, on their feet, Mohan Lal gave the women a brief account of what had passed upstairs, assisted, between mouthfuls, by Kartar and Perry.

"I knew it!" Leela exclaimed. "I would not be surprised if it was more than just hundreds. And to try to use your sister against you! Oh, I am so sorry for Savitri. It is such a sad thing, Nita, isn't it?"

"Yes. Very sad," said Nita in the flat voice of someone who is saying the expected thing but does not actually care a straw.

Kartar looked at her sharply and frowned. "I think," he said, swallowing a final mouthful, "that we should go home now."

"All right," Kartar said, as soon as they were inside the chilly Clapham flat. They had parted from Perry after leaving the Underground station. "All *right*. Now tell me what is the matter with you? You have been like this all day. Withdrawn, not interested. I have never heard of anything so brazen as Dinesh; all the way home, Perry and I were talking of it, but you said nothing, even when I spoke to you and asked you what Leela had said about him. You just looked at me as though you had not understood. So what's wrong?"

"Kartar, don't, please. Don't be so . . . so aggressive. I can't help it. I'm sorry."

"*Why* can't you help it? Now, Nita . . . no, don't cry. Tell me what's wrong."

"In the bedroom. On my bedside table," said Nita jerkily. "There's a letter from Bheji, to me. It came after you'd gone to work this morning."

When Kartar came back with the letter, Nita was sitting miserably in her armchair. She had lit the paraffin heater and was holding her hands to it. He sat down opposite her to read what his mother had written. "I see," he said at length.

"I got fond of Bheji when we were living together. She doesn't mean to hurt me. I know that!" Nita burst out. "But she is hurting me just the same. How can she say that to me? That a woman is not a woman until she has had a child. Does she think we aren't trying? Does she think I can begin a child to order?"

"I expect she thinks we are avoiding one on purpose, for some reason," Kartar said mildly. "No one in our family – or hers – has ever had trouble having children as far as I know. She wouldn't think in that way."

"What am I to do? I can't write back and say *perhaps I cannot have babies*. I can't put that in a letter to Bheji! I know what she would say!" Nita was trembling. "She will say I am sub-standard, not complete. The woman in the flat above at Safed Gardens could not have children and that was what Bheji said about her."

"But, Nita, we have plenty of time. Just because things don't happen at once . . . "

"She wants them to happen at once. And that letter came at such a bad moment. This morning. I was in the bathroom when the postman came. I'd just found out . . . there's no news again. What am I supposed to do?" said Nita incoherently and then the tears would not be held back any longer. She put her head down on the worn arm of the chair, and let them go. "I'm sorry," she said again, speaking through them, "it's only this that does this to me. But what can I *do*, how can I *make* it happen, as Bheji thinks I should make it? We have done everything everyone says we should. Fourteen days before I'm due, every month, we try, and . . . I said we would have bad luck, I knew it, that first night when that cat came into our room and . . . "

"Nita, stop it! Oh, I don't want to be angry with you when you are so unhappy but you are not to talk in this way. Six months we were married before I left for England and there was no child then, either!"

"I'm sorry. I'm sorry."

"Oh, Nita, darling, it is all right, don't say sorry to me in that way, don't. It is not your fault, I am not so stupid as to think that. I think being left for three years with my mother was not good for you; she has influenced you too much with her traditional notions and her talk of fate and luck and all that kind of thing. A pity she cannot decide that this lack of a child is fate, and give up nagging you! I shall write to her and tell her that these letters of hers must cease. She is making you miserable and I will not have it. And as for this fourteen days business," Kartar added with energy, "it is just tiresome; like making love by appointment. That is not how it should be and this is not how you should be. Listen." He knelt down beside the chair and raised her face between his hands. "Now then. You are worrying yourself to death over this. I am not worrying because there is plenty of time and this is hardly the ideal place for a baby and God knows if I shall be able to hold on to this job I am in. It is so hard to make them see an accountant when they look at me, instead of a man with a different coloured face from theirs and a turban. But still . . . "

"Six months before you left India. You have just said that yourself. And now I have been here since the start of September and it is nearly the end of January; another five months. And still nothing." Nita looked at him piteously.

"I think," said Kartar, "that perhaps we should know where we stand. I am sure you are anxious for nothing but I can't see you like this. We had better make an appointment for you to see a specialist."

Chapter Six

Love Without Prospects
1957

The doctor at the South London Hospital for Women and Children was a young woman. She looked as though she were not much older than Nita herself. She had a friendly smile and a reassuring manner. "My name is Dr Hines, Julia Hines. I hope we can help you, Mrs Virk. One of the most important things, you know, is not to worry too much. If you'd just slip on to the couch . . . that's right. Nature can be very perverse – sometimes, the more you want her to perform, the more she decides not to. Sometimes, perfectly healthy couples fail to have children because the wife is too tense and anxious. Then she gives up hope and forgets about it and *crash*! She falls for a child. Now, let's have a look at you. When did you say the date of your last period was . . . ?"

Nita answered questions, returned the young doctor's smile, lay back, gazed at the striplighting on the ceiling, and endured, miserably, the painful invasion by metal instruments and a plastic-gloved, enquiring hand.

For Perry, over the next few weeks, college studies, Mohan Lal's problems, the regular visits to the Shepherd's Bush Gurudwara (which he kept up both to please Kartar and to make sure he didn't get suspicious), all shrank to the level of irrelevant interruptions to the central and glorious theme of Pat. As their friendship grew from seed to flower, he lived from one outing to the next and loved it.

Pat liked films and Pat liked dancing. "There weren't so many opportunities where I lived in Yorkshire; it was a small place. We had just one little cinema and an occasional hop." Together, they saw *Quo Vadis?* and *The Dam Busters*, from which Perry unexpectedly learned a good deal about the roots of Christian culture and the heroes of the Second World War, and they went to Hammersmith Palais, where Pat instructed him in basic ball-room dancing and he noted with interest the signs, among the English young, of rebellion against their elders' dull ideas about dress. The young might conform in the office, but for dancing, the girls went in for bright, swirling skirts with a view of shapely leg which fascinated him, and even the boys were fashion-conscious, sporting narrow trousers and startling, long-toed shoes.

In the cinema and on the dance floor alike, he could hold Pat's hand and put an arm about her. She took this for granted. It was magical.

They also, endlessly, talked. It did a good deal to improve Perry's English, which was now becoming better than Kartar's. What they talked about was usually themselves. They sat in coffee bars and pubs, and each in turn marvelled at the life the other, hitherto, had led, although Pat marvelled more than Perry, because he had known something about England before he arrived there, while Pat knew next to nothing about India.

Her own background was a grey stone farmhouse in open Yorkshire countryside. "Hills and dales, and the winters can be very cold." There wasn't much spare cash but Pat and her family had food and clothes and education and modest local entertainment and regarded themselves as adequately provided for.

They didn't have a car. "We've got a tractor and a sort of truck – we bought it when the army sold things off after the war; it's still got green and khaki camouflage painted on it. We can carry calves and pigs and sheep in it and so on." There were three working sheepdogs, too. Pat talked about them as if they were people.

A picture of her family gradually formed in his mind. They were hardworking and united, careful with money though hospitable to visitors and the family members did not go in for quarrels or dramas, which was why the excesses of Aziz and Mr Bharucha had shocked her so.

Even the war had not disturbed Pat's family unduly. Her father had wanted to join up but had been required instead to go on farming his land. "It was what they called a reserved occupation." An uncle of hers had been killed in Burma but Pat remembered very little about it, except that she could recall her grandmother sitting in their farmhouse kitchen and wiping her eyes, and her grandfather saying, in tones of bleak calm, "Well, lass, we're not the only ones to lose a son so we must just dry our eyes and keep going."

To Pat, Perry's customs were a continual astonishment. The tone of voice in which he spoke of Kartar and Nita not only surprised, but irritated her. "All right, so they're older than you but that doesn't make them *better*."

"We have feelings of respect for brothers and sisters who are elder to us."

"You keep saying that, but *why*?"

Nor – in spite of the behaviour of Aziz and Mr Bharucha – could she conceive of people killing each other for religion, or of a world in which yesterday's next door neighbour could turn overnight into today's murderous assailant. The communal riots which had accompanied the Partition of what had once been India, into India and Pakistan, were as exotically unreal to her as the activities of the Emperor Nero in *Quo Vadis?* Perry himself had not seen any of the rioting, because his family had been in Delhi, which was not too badly afflicted. "But we heard about it from relatives who fled to us from the troubles in what is now Pakistan. The Sikhs and Hindus north of the border mostly fled south and the Moslems south of it went the other way. None of the communities behaved well; you can't say any of them were worse or better than any others. Individuals varied. Some were decent and bewildered and tried to avoid trouble, and some went all out to make it."

"But *why*?"

"I don't know why. Sometimes people go mad. Well, look at the Nazis, gathering in crowds to listen to Hitler and give him clenched fist salutes. Madness can be catching, just as much as smallpox. It was like that in India."

She was muddled by the relationship between the Sikhs and the Hindus. They were sitting in Toni's Espresso and she began to stir her coffee rapidly as she always did when puzzled or irritated. "You mean that in some Hindu families, one boy would be brought up as a Sikh?"

"Yes. Well, not now, things have changed now. But at one time, yes."

"But you said the Sikhs believe in one god and the Hindus believe in a whole lot . . . "

"A pantheon, yes."

" . . . but parents always want to teach their children to believe what they believe themselves. So if the parents believe in many gods, how can they pick out one child and teach him something

79

different, that they don't think is true?"

"Well, I think mostly they sent the chosen boy to the Sikh temple and let the priests there do the teaching. But they did do it. It meant that one member of the family would belong to the military sect that protected the rest of the community. There probably isn't any parallel here."

"No, there isn't. You said it doesn't happen now?"

"Not much, no. The two communities have grown apart. The Sikhs have been very successful in northern India; they have done extremely well as farmers and so on and some disputes have arisen between Hindus and Sikhs about water supplies and electricity. We have shortages that don't happen here. And after Partition, many of the Sikh shrines were left behind in what is now Pakistan. I have heard a speaker, at our temple in Shepherd's Bush, say that losing our shrines has made the Sikhs feel lost, as if they must make a special point of holding together and being aware of themselves as separate. So we are becoming separate. There used to be intermarriages between Hindus and Sikhs; my father's mother was a Hindu, for instance. But nowadays it is rare. It is not forbidden or anything but it is happening less and less. People say now that it is best to marry within their own communities . . . tell me, changing the subject, back at home in Yorkshire, did you have dates?"

"Yes, now and then. Nothing serious. It's normal in England for young people to date, you know."

"But I suppose they were local boys. Would your family mind about you seeing me?"

Pat frowned. "Well, I just wouldn't ask."

"What if they visited you at the Houghtons and met me in the hall?"

"I'd say this is my friend Perry."

"Yes, another student in the house. But if they knew we were dating?"

Suddenly Pat looked uneasy. She turned the question aside. "What would *your* brother say if he knew? He wouldn't like it, would he?"

"Probably not," said Perry. "Oh, well, let's just not tell either your family or mine. Friends and family don't always mix." He had asked the question about dates almost idly, but somehow the conversation had acquired an alarmingly serious tone. This had never happened before, and it worried him. He changed the subject quickly. "Where shall we go next time we go out? Let's get a paper and see what's on south of the Thames next week."

"All right. By the way," Pat said, tacitly going along with the change in conversational direction, "did you realise that Inge and Jacques are going out together regularly now?"

"Are they? Whoever would have thought it? They owe it all to Aziz and Mr Bharucha."

"It's been a relief to see the last of those two, though."

Talking Houghton shop, he paid the bill and they went out, in search of a news-stand. But afterwards, sitting in his room with his textbooks and trying to attend to an exercise in critical path analysis, it occurred to him, for the first time, to wonder where this friendship between him and Pat was going, and how it would end.

The young doctor had sat down at her desk and was making notes on a file. Nita finished dressing, doing up the trousers of her salwar kameeze and pulling the tunic over her head. She pushed back the pins which were trying to slip out of her coil of hair and went slowly to sit in the green, felt-covered armchair on the patient's side of the desk. Dr Hines looked up and smiled. It was a charming smile, and so compassionate that Nita's entire inside turned over.

"The first thing," said Dr Hines, "is that there is no sign, as far as I can see, of any disease. You're a perfectly healthy woman."

"And?" said Nita.

"But your womb is still very immature. It is possible, in fact, that you have actually conceived several times. From what you tell me, I should say that ovulation is probably occurring normally, but your womb is not sufficiently developed to nurture an embryo. We can do some further tests to check on the ovulation . . . "

"What would be the point?" A lump of lead appeared to be solidifying within Nita. "If my womb won't work, that's that, isn't it? Can anything be done? Is there any treatment?"

Julia Hines shook her head. "Nothing that medical science can do. These problems sometimes right themselves in the course of time. Where there is immaturity, there is always the possibility of future development."

"But I'm already nearly twenty-one."

"You may surprise yourself and have a baby when you're thirty. But for the moment," said Dr Julia Hines, her hazel eyes very kind, "it would be far better if you put it out of your mind.

Is your husband here, by the way?"

"No. He is at work."

"If you wish to bring him to see me, I'll be happy to explain to him direct. Do you go to work yourself, by the way?"

"No," said Nita hopelessly.

"A job might be worth considering. It would keep you from brooding, you know."

"I'll think about it. Thank you, Dr Hines. I'm most grateful to you. It's better . . . better to know." The lump of lead wanted to dissolve now, into a flood of salt tears, but one mustn't cry in public. "I can tell my husband what you've said. He will understand."

He would, she knew that. She wasn't afraid of Kartar. But how in the world would she explain this to Ranbir? Bheji was old-fashioned; in her mind, fertility was part of the nature of a woman, very nearly a moral requirement, and lack of it was a flaw, a cause of blame. Bheji did not distinguish between faults like, for instance, dishonesty, which people could presumably control by an act of will, and barrenness which was out of anyone's control. She would write letters talking about the will of God, but the implication that Nita should somehow have managed to circumvent that will, would ooze out between every other line.

Dr Hines came with her to the door. Nita noticed that she wore a wedding ring. And as they said goodbye, she noticed too that although it was as yet barely visible, Dr Hines was pregnant.

On returning from the hospital, Nita found that her husband was home before her. He was in fact planted in the hall with his briefcase at his feet, barring the landlady's route back to her quarters on the ground floor while he explained in clear, decisive accents that there was a leak in the roof above the upstairs landing, that he had mentioned this to her three times already, that the weather was still chilly, and that the repairs could wait no longer and he was quite willing to contact a builder on her behalf provided she gave him the name and phone number. And paid the bill, of course, his manner unmistakably implied.

Nita waited silently until Kartar, by sheer force of personality, had induced their amiable but indolent landlady to fetch a builder's business card from her room and hand it over. "Thank you. We'll put it in hand at once," said Kartar, and then led the way upstairs. But as soon as they were in their flat, he closed the

82

door, tossed the card aside on to the table, turned to her and said, "Bad news?"

Nita nodded. It was difficult to speak. But presently, forcing it out and imposing a semblance of calm on her voice, she repeated to him what Dr Julia Hines had said.

"Sit down. I'll make tea," said Kartar.

"I'll do it."

"No, you won't. You need a bit of looking after. Listen, darling, there is a hopeful side to this. We might have a family yet, after some years. We don't have to give up hope entirely. Meanwhile, we can set about getting ourselves into better living quarters than this terrible place."

"It isn't so bad. One hears such stories about unpleasant landladies. Mrs Johnson is very nice to us really."

"Mrs Johnson just wants our rent but apart from that she doesn't want to be bothered with us or anything to do with us, including getting that roof repaired. I'll have to phone the builder from work in the morning, unless you can go out and do it from a phone box."

"I can do that. Oh, Kartar. What is Bheji going to say?"

"About our leaking roof?"

"No, of course not!" She managed a shaky giggle, as he had intended.

Kartar, with decision, put the kettle on and spooned tea into the pot. "I will write and tell her myself, and make it clear to her that she is not to mention it to you in any letter. She behaved very badly, nagging you as she did, until I put a stop to it. There will be no repetition. I was shocked at the effect she had on you. She made you weepy and unsure of yourself. I can't see such a thing. Your own mother has written you nothing but kindness and I can only apologise that mine was not so considerate. She will give you no more trouble, I promise."

Over the tea, Nita said, "The doctor thought I should take a job, to get my mind off it. Do you think that would be a good idea, or not?"

"She said that?" Kartar looked at her across his teacup, his eyebrows rising. "I have been wondering something of the sort, myself. It is not an exciting life for you, in this flat all day with only shopping and cooking and going to the launderette to pass the time. And if you had a job, we could save faster. I would like to put down a deposit on a small house. What could you do?"

"I did book-keeping as part of my college course. I could do

83

clerking of some sort."

"We'll get you a work permit," said Kartar, "and you shall have a try. It might help a lot. You would have company, other women to chat to, and your mind would be busy. Would you like a job, yourself?"

"Yes, I think I would. Walking back from the hospital, I was thinking . . . in the autumn I could go to evening classes and learn shorthand and typing too. They would be useful. If I go to work, I will try to take an interest in it and make some sort of career because . . . "

"Nita, my darling Nita. Don't cry. Please don't cry."

"I want children too. It isn't only Bheji. I want them too and so do you. I've let you down."

"Rubbish. Absolute rubbish. It isn't your fault and it may come right yet. Oh, my poor Nita."

"Bheji didn't mean to be unkind," Nita said sadly, later, as they sat together on the rug in front of the paraffin heater, clasped in each other's arms, with Kartar rocking her as though she herself were a child. "But she does so want to see the next generation come into being."

"Maybe we ought to get Perry married!" Kartar said.

Kartar wanted her to brace up and take the disaster in her stride and she tried. The astonishing thing was that life did in fact continue. There were things to do and one did them. The day after she had been as good as told that she would never be a mother, never see her sons and daughters growing up, never rejoice at their marriages or hold her grandchildren, Nita found herself mundanely going down the road to the telephone box with a builder's business card in her hand and arranging to get the roof repaired.

Then there was shopping to get and she automatically tested the quality of fruit and vegetables before buying them, clicked her tongue at a rise in the price of lamb and decided to try a new brand of instant coffee.

She also bought airmail letters at the post office, but she wrote only to her own mother. Kartar had said he would cope with Bheji, and he would have to, for it was quite beyond Nita.

She did not ask him what he had said but it must have been firm, because Bheji's letter in answer was grieved but accepting and even offered Nita sympathy. "There is still Perry," Bheji said.

84

This was an echo to Kartar's own remark, but when he read it, Kartar snorted. "If Perry is ever in a position to get married! I tell you, Nita, I am worried about that boy. He is not keeping to his studies, I know it. Whenever I go round to see him he is either over in Southall helping Mohan Lal straighten out his accounts, or up a ladder helping Mr Houghton redecorate another room or else simply out, God knows where. I hope he is not mixed up with some girl. But how he thinks he will ever pass his exams if he goes on like this, God knows."

"Mixed up with a girl? But that would be frightful. Oh, I hope not!"

"Well, I cannot live in his pocket. At least," said Kartar, "we have fixed up your work permit now and I hope you will soon be fixed up with a job. I think, too, that we should go out more. It is nearly April, and the weather will get nicer, bit by bit."

"Perry says Leela would like it if we visited there sometimes. I suppose it would do no harm. And since Perry seems to be always going there . . . " Nita left the social and religious differences between the two households hanging in the air, but Kartar understood.

"No harm at all. At least it is an Indian household. Next weekend won't do, but we could go the one after."

"But this is so nice," Leela said, opening the door to them. "Come inside. I am just getting food ready. Perry is here; he is upstairs with Mohan Lal."

"He is just coming down." Mohan Lal appeared behind his wife. "He is doing a very fine job. He has put all my books straight, and he is making me a card index for suppliers and another for stock items, all cross-referenced. He has made me buy all the cards and filing drawers. Come, come through into the parlour. He is costing me a fortune but I think it will save money in the end. You will have whisky, Kartar? Leela can get the ladies' drinks." Mohan Lal considered it beneath his dignity to make tea or pour orange juice.

"I trust you're paying him?" said Kartar drily.

"Yes, yes, I am paying him." Mohan Lal grinned. "He reminded me," he added.

"Well, it's only fair," Nita said reasonably. "Oh, here he is. We did not know you were here today, Perry." She knew that she sounded disapproving, but could not help it. Perry was *not* spending enough time at his books; Kartar was right.

85

"I've nearly finished the indexing," Perry said, joining them and accepting a drink. Leela appeared with fruit juices and they all settled into chairs. "I shall be quite sorry when the job is over," Perry remarked. "The money's been useful."

It had helped considerably in paying for outings with Pat. He was privately wondering if Mohan Lal would like him to go on keeping the records up once they were in order.

"Have you heard from home lately?" Nita enquired of Leela. "How are all your family? Do you know yet what happened when Dinesh got back?"

"Dinesh," said Mohan Lal, "will have other things to think of now besides his quarrel with me. In fact, I think now it is a pity that I faced him with what he was doing because this would have sent him home anyway, and it was not unexpected."

"But it was so sad," said Shanti shyly, coming into the room with a laden tray. "So very sad. Everyone hoped perhaps it would not happen."

"But what was it?" Nita asked.

"Dinesh had a brother," Mohan Lal said. "Only he was killed in an accident, a street accident in Delhi, five years ago. He was on a bicycle and he was knocked off it by a bus; you know how terrible the Delhi traffic is. He left a widow and a little boy and the widow suffered a great shock when he was killed. She got sick herself before long. There was a growth. Well, she has died. So Dinesh and my sister are looking after her son now and I think they will adopt him."

"Poor little boy," Leela said. "He is no more than seven years old."

"No, no, eight, he is eight years old at least."

"Well, seven or eight, what difference does it make? He is still a little boy only. To lose both parents so young; think of it."

Shanti was distributing the food. "Oh, lovely. Vegetable curry and rice," said Perry. "Mrs Houghton tries so hard but her Indian dishes aren't the real thing."

"Shanti cooked all this," Leela said. "She takes so much work off my hands these days."

Shanti, looking embarrassed, said, "We are all so sorry for Dinesh's nephew. But his uncle and aunt will take care of him."

Nita caught the eye of both Kartar and Perry and knew that they all had doubts about the standard of care if Dinesh Arora were to be the uncle in question, but Mohan Lal and his family clearly did not see it like that. They all recognised that Dinesh as a husband or a brother-in-law was an unmitigated catastrophe but in this new situation they apparently saw him simply as a protector for an orphan. Really, Nita thought, these friends of Perry's were very difficult to understand.

So difficult, in fact, that for several minutes, conversation ran aground because none of the Virks could think of any comment to make which was neither untruthful nor rude, and when Nita finally began to say something bright and complimentary to Leela about the food, Perry chose the same moment to burst into speech on the subject of the suppliers' card index. They clashed in mid-air and stopped, confused. At which Kartar, without stopping to think, rushed into the gap.

"Now that the days are getting warmer, I am thinking that Nita and I should go out and do some sightseeing at weekends. I was wondering if you'd like to come, Perry." He saw Nita looking at him and stopped short, too late. The delicate social nuances to which Nita had referred obliquely when she first proposed this visit consisted of the fact that although the Bhatias were friends of Perry's, whose home Nita and Kartar might occasionally visit as, so to speak, extensions of Perry, they were Hindu and the Virks were not, and although the Sikh Virks were not supposed to recognise caste, it still had faint reverberations: Kartar was a professional man whose father worked in the civil service, while Mohan Lal and his father were shopkeepers, which meant that it was best not to draw too close. Indeed, one of the reasons for making social calls at all was to keep an eye on Perry. Now, Kartar had put himself in a position where sheer good manners compelled him to ask them on an excursion.

He recovered himself. "You would be most welcome too," he said to Mohan Lal and Leela. "Though I know you are always very busy with the shop on Saturdays, and this would be a Saturday."

"Oh, yes, we are open all day then. Even on a Sunday, I am open part of the day," Mohan Lal said. "I am not supposed to be, I think, but round here, no one takes much notice."

"Where had you thought of going?" Perry asked.

"There is a place called Hampton Court. It's said to be not too far, and very interesting. It's by the river," Kartar said. "I think you would enjoy it, Nita."

"I'm sure I should," said Nita, who didn't know whether she would or not but knew that he meant the idea as a distraction for her, which was kind of him.

Mohan Lal and Leela were exchanging glances. "Shanti could go," Mohan Lal said suddenly. "She would like a day out, wouldn't you, Shanti? And she would be quite safe with you."

Shanti was nodding her head vigorously.

There was no getting out of it now.

"Shall we say next Saturday, then?" said Kartar.

"I didn't mean us to get saddled with Shanti," Kartar said that night as they were going to bed. "I didn't mean to mention the idea at all while we were there. But they were all being so pleased about Dinesh adopting his nephew and I couldn't say what I thought about that . . . I had to say something else quickly and Hampton Court is what came out. I thought it was safe enough. I didn't think any of them would come! Mohan Lal's whole life is his shop. He never goes out anywhere."

"Well, I can't say I like the idea of taking Shanti along," Nita said. "Not with Perry there. There are so few Indian girls about, that is the trouble."

"I have a strong suspicion," said Kartar, "that he does have an English girlfriend. I am almost sure I glimpsed him in the street with a fair-haired girl, the other day."

"Oh, Kartar! Well, in that case," said Nita, "perhaps Shanti will be a kind of counterweight. Oh dear, how complicated all these things are. One has to be so careful. She is a well-behaved girl, anyway." She put on the cheerful smile which she knew Kartar liked to see. "I expect we shall all enjoy the day very much," she said.

Chapter Seven

Positively Negative
1957

The day of the visit to Hampton Court was overcast and, to begin with, the atmosphere of the outing was not unlike the sky. This was not because of Shanti, who was delighted to be taken out and made a great effort to overcome her shyness and make conversation, but because of Perry, who seemed sullen.

But by the time they were tacking themselves on to a guided tour which they found progressing round the building, Perry had, to Nita's relief, become more sociable. Furthermore, he did so very correctly, paying Shanti no special attention beyond the merely courteous. This was as it should be, another cause for relief. Then she almost forgot them both. The guide they were following was exceptionally good.

He had a strong voice which carried clearly even to the hangers-on, and he not only knew his facts, but could interpret them. By the end of the tour, they had all learned more about the Tudors, especially Henry the Eighth and Elizabeth the First, and about the dissolution of the monasteries, and the history of English architecture than they had thought existed. And to Nita in particular, the new world thus opened came as a startling surprise. Not because she had not known anything about the Tudors already, for she had. They had been in her history curriculum at school. But because the subject had now been presented to her in a wholly different light.

She was still thinking about this while they walked in the grounds afterwards – it hadn't rained after all – lost themselves briefly in the maze, and finally, led by Kartar, made their way out of Hampton Court and into a pub.

She had been in pubs several times now, with Kartar, although she had never come to feel entirely comfortable in them, not merely because they sold alcohol, but also because of the curious atmosphere generated by the heads-together knots of regulars, which made her feel as if she had accidentally intruded on a meeting of a secret society. She wondered doubtfully if they ought to take Shanti into such a place, but supposed it was all right as long as the two of them kept to soft drinks. Her mind, in any case, was still abstracted. So much so, in fact, that as Kartar and Perry brought glasses of bitter lemon for herself and Shanti, and settled down at the table with their own whiskies, Kartar said, "Nita is thinking. What are you thinking about? Tell us."

Nita came out of her reverie. "Hampton Court. The things the guide told us. That's all."

"It was very pretty," said Shanti. "I liked the pinky-red stone. It made me think of Jaipur. I was taken there once, and Jaipur is all pink stone, too. But Hampton Court has grey battlements at the top, to make a contrast. I only noticed that because the guide pointed it out. It was very clever to use two kinds of stone in that way."

"Yes, it was. But I wasn't thinking about the stone," said Nita slowly. "I was thinking . . . well, about the English."

"Out with it!" said Kartar, laughing. "What about the English, then?"

"It's hard to find the words." Nita twiddled her glass of bitter lemon round by the stem as she strove with ideas far harder to express than the social situation between Virk and Bhatia, which she had once left in mid-air because it was so complicated.

"In India," she said at last, "people think about the English as they were in the time of the Raj – the rulers who had garden parties and clubs that we weren't invited to. But also . . . we think of them as people who are much more careless than we are, don't live by the same rules. I mean, look at those two girls over there." She used her chin to indicate the ones she meant. "They're drinking in this pub and they haven't even got a man with them. Well, Bheji used to say, of the English: take away their wealth and power and what have they got left? And she meant that they had nothing left, that they live in a sort of vacuum without any of the attitudes and customs and, well, rules that we have. As if Indian society were the standard and every-thing else is something less, inferior. As if the English were people who just lack our attitudes and rules and so on." She paused, sipping her bitter lemon and still, visibly, trying to marshall these new ideas which the guide at Hampton Court had loosed on her, like a crowd of noisy and alarming dogs.

Shanti regarded her with wide eyes.

"Bheji does think that," Kartar agreed. "But you've reached some other conclusion?"

"Yes. It isn't like that at all! They're . . . they're positive, not negative. They have a very strong past just as we have, and they have rules and customs which spring from their history just as ours emerged from *our* history. The histories are different, and so the customs are, too."

"I can see what you mean," said Kartar doubtfully. "At least, I think I can."

"I can hardly *say* what I mean! But the English are very sure of themselves and they scarcely pay any attention to religion, compared to us, and there are those two girls drinking in a pub as no Indian woman would ever do, but they regard those things as good things, because of reasons in their past. Because . . . oh, being an island nation is something to do with it, and so is Henry the Eighth breaking with the Church of Rome, and so is Elizabeth the First managing to be a successful ruler and a woman and a scholar right back in the sixteenth century. That's putting it too simply and all kinds of other things must be mixed up in it too, but I think that their history has channelled their traditions and made them what they are now, and what they are now is very . . . very strong."

"You mean they're English and not Indian," said Perry. "That's all!" He sounded ill-tempered again.

"No, it is not all!" Nita said sharply. "That is just what I am saying! They are not . . . just us with something missing."

She ran out of words. Kartar said with amusement, "Nita is starting a job on Monday, in the accounts department of a department store. You will be getting to know some of the English really well, Nita. You'll be able to decide whether all these ideas are right. Probably they are, or near to it."

"But that's just it," said Nita. "I don't think we can ever get to know them really well. If we try, there'll be some kind of clash because we're both so strong, so definite. I am sure when I am at work I shall want to make friends with the other girls there. It is natural to make friends, after all. But such friendships should not go too far; one must be very careful. It will be better to hold back too much than not enough. I don't think they want us to be too friendly, either. The people in this pub; most of them are looking the other way, at this moment."

"You know, there's a lot in that," said Kartar, and Shanti

91

looked exceedingly impressed.

Perry said nothing. He was thinking of Pat. He had wanted to go out with her today and had only come on this outing because he couldn't have refused without being asked what he was doing instead and he didn't like telling lies. Now, he was furious with Nita for implying that all Anglo-Indian friendships were automatically doomed. He would damned well not let this sort of talk affect him. Nita was too prim and careful and stick-in-the-mud for words. He was sure she'd been looking at him when she said that such friendships shouldn't go too far. He had had a nasty feeling, not long ago, that Kartar had seen him and Pat in the street. If so, Kartar had no doubt told his wife. Well, next weekend he'd take Pat out for a whole day, and he'd tell lies about spending the day at his books if he had to.

He'd visit Hampton Court again, he decided, and bring Pat to see it. He didn't think she ever had and he was sure she'd love it, and they'd come to this pub afterwards and that, symbolically, would wipe out Nita.

For Nita, finding a job had been much easier than it had been for Kartar. "Well, you're not proposing to challenge the old school tie network for a share of their power," Kartar said acutely, when at the end of one week's searching Nita announced that she was about to become an accounts clerk for a West End store and marvelled at the ease with which she had managed it.

"Are you challenging them, then?" said Nita, surprised.

"All professional men do. We have all got our eye on promotion. But I congratulate you. I hope that it turns out well."

A week was enough to assure Nita that it would. The post was not highly paid but it was interesting, and companionable. There were two older women in her department and two young unmarried ones, and although the older pair were admittedly steeped in what Kartar called "British Raj attitudes" and tended to be stand-offish, the young girls were friendly. Nita's sari fascinated them and on her very first day they were imploring her to "bring in an old one, one day, and show us how to put it on."

On her second day she obligingly did so, and spent most of a hilarious lunch-hour in the ladies' washroom, instructing them in the art of pleating and draping. By the end of the first week she had become quite fond of them. She had also learned a great deal about them.

She knew already that by her standards most English girls lived amazingly unrestrained lives, but she had never come into close contact with such girls before and had never thought that they could be either responsible or delightful. Her new colleagues were both. Yet their parents appeared scarcely to know where their daughters were half the time, and accepted with equanimity things which would have thrown Indian parents into fits of horror.

Janet and Irene went out with boys with whom they said they were in love. They were regular habitués of pubs. Janet went on holiday with her boyfriend even though they were not yet engaged. She expected that they soon would be, but Irene was less certain of her own future: her boyfriend was unreliable and sometimes failed to turn up for dates, which distressed her greatly. Neither was sleeping with her boyfriend; they were particular about that. But they did not seem to have been particular in choosing their swains in the first place. The boys had asked them out, and they went, taking what was offered because they didn't want to be left behind in the race to the altar. They pitied girls who had no boyfriends. One of the older women was unmarried and they regarded her fate with horror.

English girls, Nita thought, had a difficult time of it, expected to make judgments which they couldn't, by virtue of their youth and their propensity for being blinded by romance, be fitted to make. If she ever had a daughter . . .

But probably she never would have a daughter, or a son either. And at that thought, she would bend her head and concentrate on the columns of figures in front of her, and blink until they were no longer obscured by a mist.

She was not by nature pessimistic and hope persisted in its foolish way. When on the Friday it was demonstrated to her once again that this hope was misplaced, she returned home in a despondent mood, to find the flat empty and a note on the table, which said, "Have gone to see Mohan Lal; may be back late." The flat seemed empty and forlorn. She busied herself as best she could with domestic matters, and listened to the radio, and was still up when Kartar finally appeared at quarter to midnight.

"Oh, Nita, you should not have waited up. You must be tired. No, no, I have eaten; you need not worry for that. I am sorry I was so long. When I came home, our landlady had a message for me. Mohan Lal had phoned and was most insistent that I go to

93

see him."

"What did he want?"

Kartar told her.

Nita's tiresomeness apart, Perry had quite liked Hampton Court. But when he visited it with Pat, he liked it very much more.

For one thing, the weather was sunny, and it raised their spirits. They got themselves well and truly lost in the maze (somehow, the previous weekend, Perry hadn't felt that he was lost for long enough to appreciate it), and on emerging at last, laughing and dishevelled from running about and peering through hedges, they went inside and on Perry's recommendation found a guided tour to follow. This guide, however, had a flat voice which reduced Henry the Eighth's outrageous matrimonial career to the excitement level of the multiplication table, and the more irreverent members of his audience to near-hysteria. Pat and Perry were obliged several times to lag behind and out of sight in order to recover.

They bought sandwiches, ice-creams and coffees for lunch and afterwards Perry took her to the pub which Kartar had found the week before. Then, by bus and train, they made their way back to Clapham, in such charity with one another that without even thinking about it, they went together straight to Perry's room, where Perry sat on the bed while Pat sat in the basket chair and they shared a packet of peppermints which they had bought at the station and with much merriment set about reliving the day.

"I thought I'd die when that awful guide said, 'This is the corridor that is said to be haunted by the screams of Catherine Howard after her arrest,' in that bored voice as if he were saying this is the corridor she walked along to breakfast every morning . . . "

"It was even funnier when he was talking about the bed where Henry slept and someone in the crowd said, 'or didn't sleep,' and he looked so blank, as if he didn't know what they meant."

"I loved the maze. I thought we'd never get out, but it was such fun."

"It was, wasn't it? The best bit was when we got to the middle and no one else was there, so we kissed . . . Pat . . . "

He held out a hand to her and when she did not move, rose and went to her, drew her up from the basket chair and led her

94

to sit beside him on the bed. "Dearest Pat," Perry said, and began to kiss her again.

He himself was hardly prepared for the surge of his own feelings. He had had this in mind all day, but he had meant to go slowly, carefully. Now, suddenly, what had begun as a gentle salute became fierce and demanding. His body seized control. He was pushing her down on to the bed, nuzzling her and whispering endearments. She smelt wonderful, of shampoo and femaleness, and the warmth of her body was setting light to his own. He reached, instinctively, to unzip her skirt.

Pat thrust him off with an exclamation and a shove, and scrambled off the bed. Her face was horrified. "What do you think you're doing?"

"What? What are you talking about? Pat . . . darling . . . "

"I'm not like that. What made you think I was like that?"

"But . . . that's not fair!" Disappointment swept through him and made him angry. You've let me kiss you. You've come into my room. I thought . . . "

"Why didn't you think of asking first? Then I could just have said no!" Pat was as angry as he was, and also as hurt. Their lovely day lay between them in bright shards like a precious ceramic which somebody had dropped.

"But . . . I thought . . . I've been hoping . . . I even went to the chemist this morning!" said Perry, outraged. "So that you'd be quite safe." He found himself sitting on the bed with his head in his hands. "Where have we been going all this time?"

"Not to bed, for your information! We've been dating, enjoying each other's company. Not having an affair. I don't have affairs. I can wait till I'm married for . . . for going to bed with anyone."

"But I imagined . . . "

"I hate to think what you've imagined!"

His disappointment was almost beyond bearing. His body cried out for this girl who now stood glaring at him. He wanted to leap up and swoop on her regardless. Why not? She had led him on, hadn't she?

But she looked not only angry and hurt but also frightened. Suddenly, he understood that she was seeing not her friend Perry, but a demented stranger with a brown un-English face and a decidedly un-English headgear. She was edging away towards the door. His fury faded. He couldn't let her go like that.

"Pat. It's all right. Sit down. I'm sorry. Don't let the day end like this, please don't."

She paused. Cautiously, she moved to sit once more in the basket chair. "Well, I don't want that either. But . . . "

"But?"

"You didn't mind trying to do . . . that," said Pat slowly. "But you've never let me meet your brother or your sister-in-law."

"I see."

"You asked just now where we'd been going all this time. Well, I'll ask the question now." Her voice was strained. "Where *are* we going, Perry?"

"I don't know," said Perry wretchedly.

After a moment, she said, "It's a long journey by tube each day, going up to London University and I usually have to strap-hang all the way. I think . . . I ought to look for lodgings further into town."

Very carefully, Perry said, "When I finish my studies, I expect my parents will want me to . . . to consider marriage to some girl that they think suitable. They wanted me to marry before I left India, you know, but I said no. They even had a girl in mind – oh, not now. In her last letter my mother said Prem was married now . . . "

"I thought Prem was a man's name. It's your real name, isn't it?"

"Yes. But quite a lot of our names are for men and women equally."

"It's so . . . so unfamiliar. Though I liked what you told me the other day about all Sikh men having Singh as a second name and all the women having Kaur, and that Singh means Lion and Kaur means Princess. But I couldn't become a Sikh."

"I would never ask that thing. Such matters are personal. People should not try to convert each other. But it doesn't arise. Does it?"

Pat thought for a moment and then slowly, sadly, shook her head. "No." She looked at him unhappily. "I might be able to face it," she said, "face the stares and whispers and my own family, if you were willing to defy yours, but you're not, are you?"

"No." Perry discovered that he was not only miserable but terrified. How long had these hair-raising ideas of permanence, of . . . of *marriage* . . . been secretly fomenting in both their minds? For although the word hadn't been uttered, it was mar-

96

riage that they were discussing. And it was out of the question. He made a helpless gesture. His English wasn't equal to the enormous meaning he wanted to convey, the sheer size and force of his family's expectations – and Pat's would almost certainly have expectations just as definite – and the fearful difference between their backgrounds. Against his will, he had taken in some of what Nita had said in the pub at Hampton Court. For him and Pat to consider marriage would be like stepping into the path of an advancing Panzer tank division.

But Pat understood most of it without being told. "So that's that," she said, trying to sound bright. Then her face lost its firmness. She brushed a hand across her eyes, sprang up, and fled from the room. He heard her burst into sobs as she slammed the door behind her.

It opened again within seconds, to reveal Kartar on the threshold with Nita on his heels. Pat must have run virtually into their arms.

Chapter Eight

Kaleidoscope
1957

Perry's brother and his sister-in-law stepped into the room. They appeared to take in, with a single sweeping glance each, the disturbed bedspread on which Perry was sitting, and Perry's own glum and resentful countenance. Nita sat down in the basket chair, arranging the folds of a prettily patterned white and blue sari with a fastidious air, as though something in the room might contaminate them. Kartar remained standing, leaning on the mantelpiece over the small gas fire.

"We have just seen," he observed distantly, "a girl rush out of your room in tears."

"I hope you didn't accost her or upset her in any way," said Perry frostily.

"I doubt if she even noticed our existence. She dashed straight past us. She was obviously most upset. I think I have seen her before, Perry. I saw you with her in the street, once."

Perry shifted so that he was sitting right on the bed with his back against the wall, and could sit cross-legged. "That is not your business. You are not my keeper."

"It is not a question of keepers," said Nita. "It is a question of our responsibility towards you."

"It is possible to take these responsibilities too seriously."

"Is it? We have been growing concerned about you lately," Kartar said. "I am not asking what has just happened in this room, although I do not like to see a girl who has been in your company leaving it in such a state. I want to ask you something else. Perry, how are you doing with your studies?"

There was a silence. Then Perry said, "If you must know, not very well. There are subjects I find unfamiliar and . . . "

"You have not been working at them," said Nita accusingly. "Between Mohan Lal and all that wallpapering and this girl . . . "

"Pat is not *this girl*. She is my friend."

"Is or was?" enquired Kartar and without waiting for an answer, added, "That is what we are afraid of. You see, old chap, you are such a sincere fellow; you would be no good at having a friendship with a girl that is just on the surface. We have been worrying that you might be mixed up with some girl and now that we have seen her . . . "

"And what could you tell from just seeing her, I wonder?"

"I don't know her, of course," said Kartar seriously. "But she looked to me like a nice, decent girl, who was much distressed. Does she lodge here?"

"Yes."

"Then no doubt I am right and she is a decent girl. Mr Houghton is careful who he has in his house. And in that case, then a . . . a close friendship with you could be harmful to her, you know."

Nita spelt it out. "She was in your room, and she ran out of it in tears. It is the sort of thing that does a girl's reputation harm, Perry. People may say of her, oh, she is the kind of girl who is easy; she gets into awkward situations with foreign boys. Even the girls I work with, who are very casual compared to Indian girls, they do not want to be called easy. Their virtue means a great deal to them. Now, if Mr Houghton had met Pat as she was running from your room, what would he have thought?"

"Pat was upset," said Perry, carefully editing the truth, "because, for your information, we had just decided that our friendship should end. She is likely to leave this place soon, so we shall be shaking hands and parting. All your wild imaginings are quite unjustified," he added primly.

"That is a great relief," said Kartar. "You know very well what our parents would say if you were caught up in any, well, any entanglement. They would say that I have not guided you as I should."

"You sound like a bloody schoolmaster."

"Perry, I have been in this country longer than you and I know how easily a young man here on his own can be led into the wrong paths."

"Were you led into them?" enquired Perry with interest.

For a moment, Kartar was actually silenced. Then Nita said calmly, "Bheji said to me, before I left India, men are not like women and Kartar has been alone for three years in a strange country. There are things you must never ask him. Well, I never have and I never will. It is all right, Kartar."

"But if you were," said Perry to his brother, "then what do you mean by coming here and preaching to me?"

"I mean," said Kartar, recovering himself, "that you are a much softer character than I am. I never forgot for one moment that my real life is as an Indian, with my wife Nita. But you have no wife to steady you and as I was telling you, you are soft, sincere, and . . . " Kartar turned to address his wife. "Nita, we came here to place a proposition before Perry. We were intending to advise against it. Do you still feel that that is best?"

"No," said Nita. "I still cannot say I like it, and I think there are alternatives. But if Perry finds it acceptable, I would not advise against it, no, not now. Shanti is sweet and gentle and would fit in with our ways, I am sure."

"Shanti?" Perry gazed at her in bewilderment.

"Would you," said Kartar with a kindly, fraternal air, "consider getting married?"

"To Shanti?" Perry said after a moment.

Kartar nodded. "Mohan Lal has suggested it. He asked me to visit him in Southall and he put the idea before me. When he and Leela asked if Shanti could come on that outing with us, they were seizing a chance to let the two of you get to know one another. I said that Nita and I would think about it and talk to you. As Nita has just said, we meant to advise you to say no. In fact, frankly, our first impulse was not to mention it to you at all. But since you and Mohan Lal are close friends, he may well speak to you himself. So we decided to come here today. But we did not expect a damsel in distress to hurtle out of your room like a bullet from a rifle. It alters things."

"I'm a student," said Perry. "I can't afford to marry."

"No one is suggesting that you are married next week. But you could finish your first year's course and then get a job and do the second year at evening classes. There are evening courses, aren't there?"

"If you are willing to consider marriage," Nita said, "it need not necessarily be Shanti. Your parents would find someone and send her out to you if you would prefer that."

"I would *not* prefer that," said Perry angrily. "I am not going to marry a girl on the strength of some photograph or other. It is not fair on either party, that sort of thing." (Once, in the course or a discussion, or argument, about arranged marriages,

100

Pat had said furiously, "You'd take more care over hiring a secretary! And this is a partner for life!" He'd been annoyed at the time but later it had struck him that she had a point. One ought to interview a prospective partner personally at least once before making up one's mind.)

"There is no need to be aggressive," said Kartar. "How often must I say it? We are trying to do our best for you. We are worried about your future: your studies, your job, the marriage you must one day make."

"I am not having a bride I have never seen and who has never seen me, shipped out from India in order to keep me on the rails, so that you can say to our parents, look at the way I have taken care of my little brother!"

"In that case," said Kartar slowly, "once again I ask you: will you consider Shanti? I have a reason, in fact, for thinking it might be a good thing for you to marry, something that has nothing to do with you or . . . or Pat. Nita and I had some bad news a little while ago."

Nita rose to her feet. "Excuse me." She went out and in a moment they heard the click of the bathroom door. "She would not want to be here while I spoke of this," Kartar said. "The thing is, Perry, that we are wanting to start a family and Bheji has been pressing to know why there has been no baby. So we took medical advice and it seems that there is little chance of any child for us. I will not trouble you with details. Nita and Bheji are both very sad. But if you married and started a family of your own, our mother would be happier, at least."

Perry said nothing. He had a peculiar and unpleasant sensation that he had inadvertently stepped on to a conveyor belt and was being whisked away to some unknown but hideous fate such as a large machine full of rotor blades which would slice him to bits.

"I'm sorry about Nita. I'm sorry for you both. But I don't want to get married yet."

"You don't want to get married yet or you wish you could get married to this Pat?" said Kartar. "There was a tone of a certain kind in your voice when you said you would soon be shaking hands and parting. I think you are in love with this girl."

"We are still parting. What I feel about it is my business."

"I would like you to give some thought to this proposal, Perryi. It is your friend Mohan Lal who has made it, after all. He wants someone who will be kind to Shanti – because of the way

Dinesh treats his other sister – and . . . "

"They're Hindu," said Perry dampingly.

"Ours is a mixed family anyway and we are not living in India just now; these things don't seem to matter so much over here. We are all Indians; that is what matters here. You like her, don't you? She is very pretty."

"But . . . "

"You see," said Kartar mildly, "this girl Pat is going away, you say, but what then? Ten to one, before long there will be another English girl and as I have said, you are more vulnerable than I was. Do think, Perry, what grief it would cause our mother if I had to write to her and say, Perry is entangled with an English girl. That would grieve her far more than a marriage between you and a nice Hindu girl whose family we know well."

"Who is asking you to write to our parents about anything?" snapped Perry.

"If you are not prepared to consider marriage," said Kartar quietly, "either to Shanti or to someone found for you in India, then . . . I think I might have to warn our parents that you are worrying me and I should be glad of their advice. It is for your own good. There is this matter of the studies you are neglecting."

"How dare you try to blackmail me? You are behaving worse than Dinesh."

"It isn't blackmail, Perry, old fellow. If I am putting pressure on you, it is out of affection and wanting what is right for you. You will not see that, will you? You do not understand how concerned Nita and I feel."

"Nita doesn't want me to marry Shanti. She as good as said so."

"Nita will accept her if you accept her. She as good as said that, too."

It was like confronting . . . no, not rotor blades. He could see Shanti's shy, pretty face in his mind and there was nothing threatening about Shanti. No. It was like looking into a kaleidoscope. At one moment, his life had been set in a certain pattern: studies, Pat, Mohan Lal's books, Pat, the routine of the Houghton household, Pat . . .

Now all these elements had been shaken up to form a new design; Pat slipping out to the edge; Mohan Lal and his sister Shanti emerging in the centre.

All the same: "Let me get this clear. Unless I agree to a

102

marriage of some sort, you will report to headquarters that I am getting out of hand?"

"I wish you hadn't put it that way, but yes."

"My God, I could hit you."

"If you do, I shall hit you back and if Mr Houghton hears us fighting, he will throw you out. I think you should talk to Mohan Lal. I don't believe that you really hate the idea of Shanti. The day we went to Hampton Court, no one could have been more charming than she was."

There was no way he could prevent Kartar from carrying out that threat to write home "for advice" as he so euphemistically put it and Perry could imagine all too well what kind of letter he would shortly receive from his parents; the indignation and hurt which would leap from the page.

A fearful exhaustion overtook him, a sensation that he was trying to fight an inexorable destiny. Well, why not give in? Pat was lost to him already and life had to go on. Why not marry Shanti? It would be better at least than marrying a complete stranger.

Pat would never understand this, he thought wearily. She would never grasp the strength of his family's power over him. "Pat's family expect certain things of her," he said, speaking his thought. "They expect her, one day, to introduce them to a suitable fiancé. But they won't push one down her throat."

"If she is unlucky, she could end up as an old maid because her family did not help her. There is one at Nita's place of work and Nita says the other girls pity her. And there is a very sour one at mine, who amuses herself by being unpleasant to others. She is a secretary but she will not take my dictation because I am not English and she sniggers at my funny accent and my mistakes. As though," said Kartar, aggrieved enough to get momentarily off the point, "anyone could avoid mistakes in a language where O,U,G,H is pronounced four different ways and insensitive means not being sensitive yet inflammable, which ought to mean *not* likely to catch fire, means the opposite. It is a mad language."

"How does an accountant come to be worrying about words like inflammable?"

"I help to prepare the annual accounts for a firm that transports inflammable liquids. Listen, Perry. There are worse things than having suitable partners pushed down one's throat, as you put it. Now, are you willing to talk to Mohan Lal?"

103

"I will think about it," said Perry, huffily.

It was capitulation.

Usually, when Perry came to Mohan Lal's flat, no special preparations were made because he was coming to help with the
business only, but this time it was different and Mohan Lal and
Leela had signalled the difference by putting the sewing machine and the boxes of stock out of sight. Leela and Shanti had
spent all day in the kitchen and now, carefully dressed in one of
her most enchanting salwar kameeze suits, in bright pink with
silver edgings, Shanti handed cups of scented tea and snacks
which ranged from the sweet to the fiery, and wished her heart
wouldn't pound so much and that she could get rid of the
extraordinary trembly feeling in the pit of her stomach. She
dared not look at Perry's face, because of the things that Leela
was saying.

"Shanti has made all these snacks," Leela was explaining to the
three Virks. "I prepared the tea only. You must try this barfi. All
morning she was busy boiling down the milk for it."

In other words, Shanti was a gifted cook and industrious as
well. Her wares were being deftly placed in the shop window.
She stared down at the pattern of the faded blue and grey
carpet.

"The thing is," Kartar was saying, "there is this difference in
our communities. It is true what you say, Mohan Lal, that we
ourselves have a mixed family, but are you sure you are happy
about it?"

"I am quite happy," Mohan Lal was saying, "or I would not
have suggested it to begin with. Yes, yes, I know, you are Sikhs
and we are Hindus, and you are professional people and we are
business people but why should these things make divisions
between us?"

No one answered this, although Shanti, suddenly risking a
glance round the company, caught sight of Nita's face and knew
from its very lack of expression that to Nita Virk these things did
make a difference. If the marriage took place, Nita would be her
sister. Nita saw her looking and gave her a smile. It was rather a
polite smile but better than none at all. Shanti took heart.

"Is Shanti happy about it?" Perry enquired.

Shanti, in panic, wondered if she was supposed to reply to this
but her brother rescued her by waving a dismissive hand and
saying, "Why should she not be pleased? You are a fine hand-

104

some boy with prospects and from a good family that we know all about. What is there for her to object to?"

"I want," said Perry in resolute tones, "to talk to her alone."

"Shanti," said Leela. "We need fresh tea. Would you make it?" Shanti rose at once and withdrew quickly to the kitchen. Behind her, she heard Mohan Lal say, "Well, go on then, Perry. No one will interrupt."

In the kitchen, she began to fill a kettle. Her hands were shaking so that the bangles jingled on her slender wrists. She felt rather than saw Perry enter the room behind her. He sat down cautiously on the edge of the kitchen table, which was covered with slippery plastic in orange and white gingham checks. "Shanti?" he said.

She turned with the filled kettle in her hand. It was easier with no one else there, watching. For the first time, ever, she managed to contemplate him steadily without turning her head aside. "You . . . asked for us to talk?" she said. "But what . . . what is it you want me to say to you?"

The door was still partly open. Perry reached out and closed it. The moment the latch clicked they seemed to be shut in together, in a private world of their own.

"It isn't a question of what I want you to say to me," he said. "It's a matter of what *you* want to say. Shanti, what do you feel about this idea?"

What did she feel? He was so good-looking that she couldn't be in the same room with him without feeling dizzy and short of breath, but she couldn't say that to him. Even to Leela, she had only said, "I like Perry Virk very much. I think he looks good-natured."

Now, regarding him in close-up, within the confines of the small kitchen, she still thought so, but he also seemed larger and more real than before. He was waiting for her to say something. and she was tongue-tied. Somehow, she had supposed her brother and Leela would settle it all. To find the decision devolving on herself like this was unnerving. She turned nervously away to light the gas under the kettle and take the tea-caddy from its shelf while she tried to find a way of saying yes which would not sound eager or forward; would sound as though she were willing to comply without suggesting that if left to herself, she would actually have chosen him.

"When my sister was married to Dinesh," she said at length, "she saw him only once before the marriage and though her

105

opinion was asked and she was free to say no, she had nothing to base any opinion on. She said yes, but she is not happy, I think. But my brother has known you for years, and we know all about your family. So, if you are asking me, I am quite content with this idea. As long as you are content . . . since we come from different communities."

And that, Perry thought, is my way out. I can say the Sikh-Hindu difference, or the different work backgrounds, worry me. She will accept it. Then we can tell our families that we have talked it over and decided it won't do.

And then what? Kartar would start on him again. Kartar had been persistent from childhood and he hadn't changed. He had survived his three-month probation at his job, Perry knew, by sheer doggedness. He had worked with relentless steadiness, refusing to be put off by conversations which stopped when he entered a room or by groups of colleagues who at first went off to the pub at lunchtime without him. Matters had improved now, he had told Perry on the way here. His colleagues were getting used to him and for the last month or so he had been joining them in the King's Head at half past twelve each day. "The thing is," he had said, "never to give up."

Quite. And he probably wouldn't give up on this business of Perry's marriage, either.

Shanti was indeed very pretty. If he had never set eyes on Pat, he would be very interested in her indeed. And Pat, who had been avoiding him as far as possible ever since last weekend, even to the point of rushing her breakfast and being continually out in the evenings, would be leaving the Houghtons at the end of next week. She would be gone for good then.

"I am only concerned for you," he said to Shanti. "I have so little to offer as yet. We should have to live in very small accommodation and though I hope to finish full-time study soon, I may be staying on in England for quite some time. Will you mind that? Or were you hoping to go back to India?"

"Oh, no. I hadn't even thought about that. None of those things are so very important. If you are hard up, I could help. My English isn't good so I can't work in an office but I help my brother already by making ready-made clothes for the shop and I can do more of that, for other shops, perhaps."

"It seems to be settled," said Perry after a pause.

They gazed at each other rather awkwardly. The kettle shrilled. Perry turned the gas off, smiled at her, and held out a hand as if to a shy animal. Shanti went into his arms.

It was a very careful, very tender first embrace. But her body fitted itself easily to his and found the experience agreeable. She was not eager to draw away.

It was Perry who moved first. He had heard a small sound. The kitchen door which he had shut was, mysteriously, in the process of shutting once again, which implied that in the interim something or someone had opened it.

When they went back into the parlour, they encountered a row of smiles. Even Nita's smile was broad.

"We are thinking," said Mohan Lal cheerfully, "that you two have agreed together very well."

Chapter Nine

Drunk in Charge
1957

Kartar's letter home, announcing Perry's engagement, arrived in Delhi at breakfast time. Jog was opening bills, grunting with disapproval as he read their totals, and doing arithmetic on a pad beside his plate. He passed the airmail letter over to Ranbir. "It's from Kartar. I have these bills to worry over. You read it first."

It was a scorching morning, despite the electric ceiling fan which at this season was kept going whenever the electricity was available. They all dreaded the power cuts when the fan would slow down and stop and the heat gather like a sticky blanket. "How did one live before there were electric fans?" Ranbir sometimes wondered.

"We were all much lazier," Jog said. "And no wonder. In the hot season it was nearly impossible to move."

Even now, the butter was liquefying on its dish and the reading glasses which she and Jog both needed these days had a tendency to steam up because of the way their wearers perspired. Jog, who had put on weight lately, felt the heat more than Ranbir but they both liked hot tea at breakfast because, oddly enough, it cooled one down more effectively than cold drinks did. Ranbir slit the letter open and prepared to read the latest news from her absent son while sipping the tea at leisure.

The crash of her cup as it went back into the saucer made her husband jump.

"What's the matter?"

"This letter from Kartar! He has news about Perry; oh, what has Kartar done? Why did he not get in touch with us and ask us for our advice? He has acted by himself and . . . "

"What *has* he done?" Jog put his arithmetic aside and stretched out a hand for the letter.

108

"He is getting Perry married, that is what he has done. To a *Hindu* girl!"

"Getting Perry married?" Jog perused the letter. "But before Perry went, he said he didn't want to . . . well, well. Mohan Lal's sister. But Mohan Lal's family are all right, you know. They work hard and he and Perry were good friends."

"But his father was just a shopkeeper in the bazaar."

"And made a fair amount of money. I wouldn't despise that. You never liked the friendship but I did not mind. We have seen Mohan Lal's sister Shanti once or twice, if you remember. Before she went to England. She is a very attractive girl."

"But she's . . . "

"Yes, yes, I know; she's a Hindu. But I keep telling you, so was my mother and why should things be so different nowadays? Perhaps this is a new trend."

"There is no new trend. I am not at all easy about this."

"Shanti will adapt herself to our family, I expect." Jog scanned quickly through the rest of the letter. "They are to have a Sikh ceremony apparently, and a Registry Office ceremony as British law requires, two days before. Good. But it is odd that Kartar should have gone ahead and arranged the marriage in this way without consulting us, and that Perry has agreed. Ah . . . there is something here. Oh, yes, I see. Well, I don't know that rushing Perry into marriage is quite the answer I would have chosen but . . . "

"What? What is that? I didn't finish the letter."

"Oh, it is just to do with Nita," said Jog, handing the letter back. "Kartar seems to think that if Perry is married he will have children and this will make up for it that Nita cannot have them."

"What?" Ranbir forgot about her breakfast while she finished reading. "Oh, what a foolish idea. Oh, I dare say Kartar is meaning well but if he had written to us, I would have said to him, wait till Perry comes home and we can find a good Sikh girl. After all, with God's help, a miracle may still happen for Nita and I did not want a Hindu daughter-in-law. Oh, why did Kartar not contact us first!"

"Perhaps Perry was very keen to get married," said Jog slowly. "He may be lonely; he was always more sensitive than his brother."

"How can he be lonely when Kartar is there?"

"They are not living in the same place now and Kartar is much

taken up with his own affairs, perhaps. But if Perry was so eager
... there may be more behind this than Nita."

"But whatever the reasons, why this Shanti? I am not taking
this as easily as you, Jog." Ranbir's chin was up and her voice was
harsh with indignation. "People will wonder why a Hindu girl
when there are plenty of Sikh families needing husbands for
their daughters. Perhaps the dowry is very good, but who cares
about dowry?"

"Hush, hush, why so angry? What need is there to be so
angry? You become annoyed too easily and sometimes, especially when the weather is getting hot, I feel too tired to cope
with you. I can't see either Perry or Kartar being over-concerned
with dowry," said Jog. "I have always told them they should not
be and Kartar certainly did not consider dowry when he said he
liked Nita. There is a likelier explanation. I fancy," said Jog, with
a sudden grin, "that our Perry simply fell in love with pretty
Shanti. What is the betting that this is a good old love match,
Western-style?"

"But marriage is for life and it binds two families together; it is
a serious thing, it must be thought about!"

"I know. My father always said that getting married under the
influence of violent emotion was like driving a train while you
were drunk. But there is not much we can do, Ranbir. If we
write and say, do not proceed with this, it will cause such an
upset. Mohan Lal will probably refuse to speak to Perry ever
again and in any case," said Jog thoughtfully, "they are on the
other side of the world and perhaps they will take no notice and
proceed with the marriage anyway. If Perry is really drunk in
charge of a train . . . "

"It is not funny." Ranbir regarded him across the table, her
aquiline face severe. "Oh, this is what happens when young
people go so far away. Their elders cannot advise them properly, cannot force them into sensible behaviour. It is no use
asking me to write and say I am delighted. I am not. I will not
write to them. Above all, I will not write to this Hindu girl."

"I will write and wish them well but say to Perry, is he quite
sure he is doing what is the right thing. But if this is love," said
Jog gloomily, "he will not listen."

He said *if this is love* very much as though he were saying
if this is typhoid. When he sent the letter, he enquired if Perry
were in love and somehow, without saying as much, implied
that in his opinion this was a form of insanity. Perry, reading

110

it, laughed aloud.

It was not a mirthful laugh.

What am I doing? he had asked himself a hundred times. This is not what I meant to do when I came to England. When I came to England I was escaping; I was going to enjoy my freedom and make a new life and please myself about who and when I married. Why did I let myself be pushed into marrying the only girl who happens to be available, this Hindu Shanti who is pretty, yes, and of course I like her but she is barely educated and has no more than a few words of English, even? Why should I do this, just to please Kartar?

Because he had, in the first place, fallen in love with Pat. That was why. He had not told her of his marriage plans. She would not have understood and he dreaded that mixture of disappointment and bewilderment which always appeared on her face when the differences in their respective backgrounds showed up.

Instead, on the day she moved out to her new digs nearer to central London, he said goodbye to her in the hall as he was setting out for his college. They shook hands and wished each other well. Then she looked at him as though expecting him to say something more, such as to ask her to stay, Perry cleared his throat and said he must be on his way or he would be late, and that was that.

But he thought of her all that day and dreamed of her that night and woke in the darkness to find himself longing for her alike with body, heart and brain. And hating Kartar.

At that moment he very nearly hated Mohan Lal and Shanti as well. He had to remind himself that none of this was Shanti's fault, that she had done him no harm and would be dependent on him for her happiness, and that Mohan Lal had only tried to do his best for his sister. After Pat was gone, he nerved himself to break the news to the Houghtons and his fellow lodgers and made himself smile when they congratulated him. Robert Houghton said he was a dark horse, but added, "Well, I never did think you and Pat had a future," thus revealing that he had known about them all along. Perry, forcing an offhand note, said that oh well, that had just been a flirtation.

His father's letter, with its restrained congratulations and its wryly amusing theory that he had fallen for Shanti, was like a joke in poor taste.

111

Only Jog had signed the letter, although he made meticulous use of the pronoun *we*. "We would rather Kartar had communicated with us before going ahead so quickly . . . We are glad it is to be a Sikh ceremony. We hope there will be no difficulties arising from the fact that this is a marriage between different types of family . . . We are sure that this girl is delightful and that no doubt you care for her very much but we hope you are not being too precipitate."

A bloody sight too precipitate, Perry muttered to himself. But if he were making a hideous mistake, Shanti, who had come so confidingly into his arms, must not suffer for it. The letter he concocted in reply would have gladdened her heart, had she known of it. In it he assured his parents that he was convinced that Kartar had been wise in encouraging him to marry and that he was sure that Shanti was a most suitable partner. When they came to know her well, as one day they would, he was sure they would agree. In these days of increasing distance between Sikh and Hindu, might it not be a good thing for a few couples here and there to prove that the two could live harmoniously together as in former days? Shanti was very sweet and very beautiful and he was looking forward to the future with the utmost happiness.

"I was right," said Jog when he received this. "The boy's in love with her."

"Kartar's letters simply talk about the happiness we will have when Shanti gives us grandchildren," said Ranbir in exasperation. "When you write back, you should say to Perry that if he changes his mind, we will stand by him. Then if he is under pressure of any sort, perhaps that will help him to decide."

"But he has decided," said Jog's elder brother Sunder, who was paying a call on them, along with his wife Baljit, whom Jog insisted on calling Billie. "And perhaps he is right. I have never liked it that political considerations should push our two communities apart. Independence has caused some problems which were never there before, there is no doubt about it. When the British ran the place, at least we did not all go about saying isn't it dreadful, the government is mainly Hindu now, so the Sikhs must all be Sikhs twice as much as they were before, for fear they should be pushed out to the perimeter and have no proper voice in the lawmaking."

"Independence was long overdue," said Ranbir sharply.

"That is true," said Jog pacifically. "But all the same, it is a pity if all these political things should spoil Perry's marriage. I could have wished him to keep a cool head and look all round the matter before committing himself, but after all . . . "

"It is not as if he were marrying a Western girl. That would have been a terrible thing," said Billie kindly to Ranbir. "And you were much afraid of something of that sort." Billie was as conventional as Ranbir but it took her differently. She was of a gentle and reassuring temperament and anxious, always, to make the best of things. "This girl sounds very sweet."

Ranbir, back straight and chin up, snorted.

On the eve of the Registry Office ceremony which would, he knew, bind him to Shanti in the eyes of the law, he could not sleep. He thought of Pat and to his horror he found himself, like a lonely small boy, needing to cry.

He was lying there in the small hours when there was a wail outside his door and the sound of paws jiggling the door handle. The door opened and Hiawatha walked in. As if impelled by some mysterious awareness that one of the human beings in his house was in need of comfort, he jumped up onto Perry's bed and settled down, purring, close to the pillow.

Perry, too miserable to argue about it and not superstitious (Kartar had trained him not to be that), let the cat stay. Presently his hand strayed out to stroke the warm furry hump of Hiawatha's body.

Amazingly, there was indeed a kind of comfort in the presence of this living thing and its uncomprehending sympathy.

He had set out to England full of ideas about freedom and a new life and he had come to this. To being glad that a cat wanted to sleep on his bed, and to letting tears fall on its fur, because he was so unhappy and there was not one human being in the world to whom he could explain his grief.

Shanti had awaited her marriage with tremulous anticipation but when the time came, neither of her wedding ceremonies seemed entirely real. Her brother and her sister-in-law took charge, arranging times and places, choosing the clothes and jewellery she was to wear.

The civil ceremony came first. It took only a few minutes and the only people there were Kartar, Nita, Mohan Lal and Leela and Shanti's two small nieces. Afterwards, they went to Kartar's flat where Nita had prepared a festive dinner. She and Kartar had lately bought a record player and Mohan Lal had contributed some records of Indian film music. Although Perry and Shanti did not yet quite count as married, and Perry would go home alone to the Houghtons that night, there was already a subtle change in Mohan Lal's attitude. Shanti and Perry sat side by side and talked, and when Mohan Lal spoke to them, he addressed them as a pair. Perry talked to her easily and pleasantly, of quite everyday things such as the music and the films from which most of it came, the boyhood friendship between himself and Mohan Lal back in India. Shanti, recognising that the time for too much shyness was over, made conversation back. It seemed to go smoothly, but there was something faintly amiss in Perry; she had the impression that his mind was not wholly on her and his voice and his face did not express the joy she would so much have liked to find in them.

Oh, well. Men were different. Her mother back in India, and more recently, Leela, had warned her of that. "We never have their whole attention," Leela had said. "One mustn't expect too much. Be grateful if he is just kind."

Two days later, in the Gurudwara at Shepherd's Bush, she sat beside Perry in front of the Sikh priest and the Holy Book of the Sikhs on its embroidered cloth, with a gleaming canopy above it. Three of the Indian women who lived nearby and formed part of Leela's social circle had come in the morning to dress her and put on her make-up. She was draped in a red and gold sari, with a gold-fringed red veil pulled forward over her head and she and Perry could see very little of each other. He led her four times round the Holy Book, while their relatives guided their steps and, during the last circuit, threw confetti over them. There was a dinner, a more elaborate affair this time, provided by Mohan Lal at an Indian restaurant.

After that, she and Perry were put into a hired car and despatched to Clapham, where Kartar and Nita had lent their flat for two days. As she was helped into the car, Shanti burst into the traditional flood of tears, but not merely because they were expected. Now that the ceremony was done and she was married, she was genuinely terrified. What terrified her mostly was her own temerity. She had wanted this marriage. She had actually hinted to Leela that she liked Perry and was there any possibility that . . . ?

Now she would have to live the rest of her life by the light of that choice and who was she to be making such decisions? How could she judge what kind of man Perry was? And she was in his

114

hands now, and it was too late to retreat.

The Houghtons were going to accommodate the newlyweds for the time being, but Perry had boggled at spending his honeymoon in their house. He had boggled equally at Mohan Lal's kindly offer of a room in his. He badly wanted privacy. What if things did not go well? What if he hurt Shanti by mistake or, worst of all, couldn't manage at all? He would have liked to take her to a hotel but his money wouldn't stretch to it. There had been gifts to buy for his bride and her family and he had had to buy a wedding ring and a new suit in which to get married. So his brother and Nita were to stay with Mohan Lal, while the honeymooners used their flat.

Kartar's landlady at least had the merit of almost complete indifference to anything her tenants did and had merely nodded when Kartar took him to see her and said he was lending his attic flat to his brother and sister-in-law for forty-eight hours. He and Shanti climbed the stairs without encountering anyone, much to his relief. The tears she had shed in the car had dried now, but he was afraid their traces might still show and they made him feel uncomfortable, like an abductor.

He let them in with Kartar's borrowed key. "I'm afraid it's not much, but it's all ours for the time being," he said, and wished that he were safely back in his single bed at the Houghtons', or sitting in a coffee bar arguing with Pat, or anywhere but here.

He looked round the uninspiring flat (Kartar's lightbulbs were bright but the decor was quite as dismal as Mohan Lal's and why, oh why, didn't Kartar do something about all that terrible brown paintwork?) and remembered how he had struggled to afford to pay for dates with Pat.

Couldn't he have struggled a bit harder for his honeymoon and given Shanti something better to remember than this? Mohan Lal had presented her with a dowry of jewellery, saris and money. He had refused to consider using any of the dowry but perhaps he should have done.

He turned, miserably, to apologise to her, and found that she had gone into the bedroom and was opening her little case. As he came in, she said, a little breathlessly, "This is very nice. A whole flat to ourselves. I can pretend it is my own home. We have had a good dinner but if you feel hungry then I can make supper. Nita says she has left food in the refrigerator, and some orange juice. I think she does not quite approve of me, Perry,

115

but she has been very polite. This is so cosy. It was a good idea of yours, Perry, that we should begin our marriage in this way."

She smiled at him, and he saw the nervousness beneath the veneer of ordinary conversation, and the anxiety to please. She had put off her veil and she was, she really was, wonderfully nice to look at, with her dark gleaming hair and her sari of bridal red and gold.

It was the moment. It would be a mistake to delay. He was here and this was real; this was Shanti, his wife, and he needed to make them both believe it.

"Shanti," he said huskily, "Shanti, leave that case alone. There's something more important that we should be doing."

A long time later, they lay curled together in the double bed which usually held Kartar and Nita. It was deep in the night. He had put the bedside lamp on when night fell, wanting to see Shanti, wanting her to see him. The effects of their large dinner had indeed worn off, so Shanti had got up and heated the food left for them by Nita. She fetched it into the bedroom on a tray and they ate supper in bed. It was extraordinarily companionable, like a picnic.

It had all been much easier than he expected. Shanti, wanting to please, determined to please, had been co-operative and encouraging and even startling. "But how did you know . . . ?" he said at one point, in amazement.

"I asked Leela some things," Shanti said. "She advised me."

Shanti, lying drowsy and relaxed, was feeling better. He had been careful and thoughtful; she was surely safe with this man. Perhaps she could venture on a confidence. Softly, she said, "There's something I want to tell you."

"Oh? Some dark secret? What is that?"

"I think you are very handsome, and I have thought so since the first time you called on my brother at Southall, when you came with Kartar to buy that sari. And then you began to come often, to help my brother with his work and I could not get you out of my mind. So in the end I whispered it to Leela. I said to her, do you think there is a chance, any chance, that it might be arranged? And here we are. It is like magic. I am really in love with you."

"That's wonderful. What a compliment!" said Perry faintly, and felt a weight of responsibility descend upon him as though the ceiling had fallen in.

116

He had been braced to play the husband, to make love convincingly, to defend Shanti if necessary from his mother's long-distance disapproval and Nita's short-range doubts, braced to work and earn and set about the practical task of establishing a home.

He had hoped, even, that in time, a genuine love of the heart would come, for both of them. But he hadn't expected to be confronted with it instantly, like this. She would probably want him to love her back, at once!

He had only to shut his eyes and Pat's face would appear before him, and it was Pat whom he loved, not Shanti.

But at the very start of this honeymoon, he had reminded himself that when he made love to Shanti, he must not pretend that she was Pat. That was why he had switched on the bedside lamp as soon as it grew dark. In the dark, pretence would be too easy.

Any pretending he did would have to be, as it were, in the opposite direction. He smiled. He drew Shanti towards him and made love to her again and fell asleep at last, murmuring endearments into her hair. If the comfort he took from her warmth in some ways resembled the ersatz comfort he had taken from Hiawatha's, on the previous Wednesday night, he was the only one who knew it.

"I very much hope," said Nita, as she and Kartar settled for the night on adjacent divans in what had been Shanti's room over Mohan Lal's shop, "that we have done the right thing in arranging this marriage."

"I think we have, though I know you are uncertain and my mother . . . well," said Kartar, "you saw that letter from her. I haven't mentioned it to Perry. It is a pity she is so much against these mixed marriages. But, Nita, this marriage is better than what might have happened instead. Perry is just not safe, running about in a foreign country as a single man. Shanti was there, and they like each other. Let us just wish them happiness."

"And a family soon," said Nita with bitterness. "I still keep hoping, perhaps there will be a miracle."

"And so there may. Nita, I have some better news, which may cheer you up."

"Oh?"

"Yes. I have worked very hard for it, very hard indeed, but I

117

may be going soon to have a little promotion. It will mean more responsible work and quite a lot more money. Perhaps we might improve on that flat quite soon."

"That *is* good news," said Nita. "You must write and tell your parents; they will be pleased."

They settled to sleep. But before he dropped off, Kartar heard her sigh again, and knew that when and if Shanti had children, Nita would congratulate her, and say to him that Hindu or not Shanti was proving a good wife, would say in fact all the right things, and in her heart would suffer grievously, and there was nothing he could do to help her.

PART TWO

SHANTI

1966-71

Chapter Ten

The Day of Crisis
1966

"Be quiet, all of you, or you know what will happen: we shall have Mrs Cook up here again. Once she has been up here today already and she came yesterday and twice last week. Sunder, you are eight years old and you are big enough to understand these things and be more responsible. You will sit down, all three of you, and watch what is on the television *now* and you will not fight over changing the channel. It is a thriller; you will enjoy it. But if you make any more noise I shall turn it off altogether and then you will not watch anything. What will your father say if he comes home and the place is in such an uproar? Balbir, Satnam, be quiet, I say!"

And oh, thought Shanti Virk exhaustedly, as she wrenched her three quarrelling sons away from the controls of the television set and pushed them on to the settee, oh, if only Perry would come home. She badly needed to talk to him, and it was such a nasty evening, and he was so late.

She went to the window to peer out. The flat was on the second floor, overlooking a Wandsworth pavement, still busy because Christmas was near and some of the shops further along were still open. There was no sign yet of Perry and the December evening was now not only dark, but growing foggy. The fog was not one of the choking yellow pea-soupers she had experienced when she first came to London; the Clean Air Act had seen to that. But it was still unpleasant. It smelt damp and furtive as it seeped in through the windows, which were of the old-fashioned sash type and did not fit very well. Oh, Perry, do come home! Had she got it wrong, when this morning she had tried to make out what Mrs Cook was saying? Having bad English was such a drawback. But although she could speak very little, she understood quite a lot, and she was fairly sure she had

121

understood the landlady. Poor Perry; what would he say when she told him?

On the settee behind her, war had broken out again and worse still, her little daughter Rupa, who was only two and a half and had been put to bed some time ago, had now been woken up by her squabbling brothers and was crying in the next room.

As usual, her youngest son, Satnam, who was barely six years old, seemed to be the aggressor. Of all her four children, Satnam was easily the most temperamental and difficult. Abandoning the window, Shanti swooped upon him. "That is enough. Bed!" Satnam yelled, but she bore him off regardless. Behind her, Sunder and Balbir settled down to their viewing in something like amity while in the children's bedroom next door, Shanti set about convincing the younger pair that going to sleep was a good idea. This took nearly half an hour, and she soothed and coaxed with one ear cocked all the time for Perry's footsteps on the stairs which came straight up to the living room door, and praying that when she heard them they would indeed belong to Perry and not Mrs Cook.

When quiet was restored, she returned to the living room. There had been no footsteps yet. Mrs Cook was probably having her own dinner and Perry was still somewhere out in the fog, making his way back by train and tube from Mohan Lal's shop in Southall, where he had worked since their marriage. Shanti looked uneasily at the clock, considered making a prayer in front of the little shrine she kept in honour of Ganesh, the Hindu elephant god of joy, but did not feel capable just now of receiving joy even from a celestial source.

Instead, she stood looking round the living room and trying to see it as Mrs Cook must have seen it when she made her hateful visitation this morning. And at once felt more weary than ever and so hopeless that she would gladly have lain down on the worn carpet and cried like one of her own children.

She loved Perry so very, very much. Just as she had told him on their wedding night, she had fallen in love with him when he was visiting her brother and the first suggestion that they might marry had come from her, in a shy whisper to Leela.

Her love had, if anything, grown deeper with time and she knew that in the nine years of their marriage he had come to care for her almost, if not quite, as deeply. But that was as it should be. These things were never equal. It was for the woman

122

to love and give with all her heart and all her strength, while it was in the nature of man to reserve a part of himself for other things. As long as the other things did not include other women, she should be content. Leela had once admitted to her that Mohan Lal did occasionally have other women. But Perry was faithful. She was fortunate and knew it.

But oh, how hard it was to make herself believe it while they lived here under the thumb of Mrs Cook. They needed, so badly, a home of their own.

It had been all right in Clapham. They had stayed with the Houghtons for a while, and then when Kartar and Nita bought their house on the outskirts of Southall, and Kartar said, "Would you two like to take over our flat?" she and Perry had seized the opportunity. Perry, who had learned a good deal about interior decoration from Mr Houghton, had done much to improve the place, and the landlady there had been pleasant enough in a negative kind of way.

But the Clapham flat had only two rooms. Sunder was born ten months after their marriage and Balbir followed fourteen months after that. Shanti, to her sorrow, had not been able to feed her own children which might, the doctor said, have led to better spacing. After Balbir, Perry insisted that they should consult the Family Planning Service and obtain a diaphragm for Shanti, but she disliked it, frequently forgot to use it, and when Satnam made his existence known, it was clear that they would have to move to somewhere bigger.

And so Clapham and their first, amiable landlady passed into history and they had come here, to this grim Victorian house in Wandsworth, where they had more space but also had to cope with the gimlet-eyed young couple, Mr and Mrs Cook, who owned the house and unlike the easygoing Mrs Johnson, took far too much of an interest, most of it critical, in everything their tenants did.

The place itself was not basically so bad, Shanti thought. It had originally had a decor quite as ghastly as that of the Clapham flat before Perry set to work on it, but Perry had set to work here, too. "Fresh plaster, then paint, that's the answer," he said. "In here, we'll have three cream walls and one crimson and a nice mellow apricot in the bedrooms."

But over the years, their slowly increasing possessions and the arrival of Satnam and, three and a half years later, his sister Rupa (Perry had firmly taken control of the family planning but

Shanti kept saying wistfully that she would so like a daughter), the pretty new paintwork had virtually vanished behind a welter of paraphernalia. To help get the washing dry on wet days, Perry had rigged up a line in the living room and it seemed perpetually hung with damp garments; there were always toys strewn about the floor, and although he welcomed Shanti's continuing work with her sewing machine, which brought in money from a growing clientele, this too created clutter. There was invariably at least one chair out of action under a pile of material and now Shanti had acquired a dressmaker's dummy to stand beside the sewing machine.

The place looked a mess and it would still have looked a mess even if it had had gold leaf on the walls and crystal chandeliers hanging from the ceiling and Shanti didn't know how to help it, even though it was one of the things about which Mrs Cook complained.

She knew that her little shrine to Ganesh, the elephant god of joy in the Hindu pantheon, took up room and all the more so because Perry, although he had never objected to it, wished his children to be Sikhs and had felt it necessary to put up a second shrine in honour of his own religion's founder, Guru Nanak. The shrines now occupied rival cupboards and were a perfect nuisance, in view of the shortage of storage space.

But Ganesh meant something which she couldn't give up; a nostalgic link with the gods and ceremonies of her childhood in India, when she had gone with her parents to Hindu temples and once been taken on a visit to another city (though she was too young at the time to remember which) to attend a great festival in honour of Ganesh, when his image was taken through the streets. She was in the habit of fasting for a day in front of her little shrine whenever she felt she had cause to give thanks: for instance, every time she brought a baby successfully into the world. Perry, on these occasions, worried about her health but, "How can it be wrong to give thanks for joy?" Shanti protested and Perry would say, "Very well, do as you wish."

All the same, she had never pushed Perry's acceptance of Ganesh too far. In October, when Diwali, the Festival of Lights, came round, they could all enjoy the parties and sweetmeats because both Sikhs and Hindus celebrated the festival, albeit for different reasons, and she had been careful to take it as natural that at Diwali, Ganesh should have only tinsel round his cupboard while Guru Nanak had strings of coloured lights round his.

But if space were to get much tighter . . .

And it would. Shanti sat down on the settee with her sons and gazed unseeingly at the cops and robbers drama on the black and white screen in front of her. Rupa would need a room of her own one of these days. What a family of this size should have was a proper house of their own.

Perry, delayed on his journey by a faulty train and now strap-hanging on the District Line in the midst of commuters and Christmas shoppers, was actually thinking the same thing and wondering why it was, in all these years, he had never, somehow, managed to make the push that was necessary to achieve a mortgage and a house.

This line of thought had been occurring to him frequently of late; it was as though some unseen crisis were approaching. Perhaps, he thought, the number ten had some built-in signifi-cance. Ten years: a decade.

He had been in England now for a decade and England had changed.

The younger generation were in the ascendancy. "There was a baby boom after the war," Kartar had told him once, "and now they're in their teens and twenties and they're taking over." Gone were the gloomy clothes, the uniformly serious colours for cars, umbrellas and interior design, the pathological terror of non-conformity. He was at this moment wedged in the midst of jeans and duffle coats, pony-tails and beards, and exotic boots and brightly coloured coats which now and then swung aside to reveal glimpses of uninhibitedly long legs and mini-skirts. Sit-ting near him and clutching a monster carrier bag no doubt full of Christmas presents, was a sturdy, fair-haired girl with knee-length silver fashion boots. But Perry did not look at her too long.

She reminded him of Pat.

You put the past behind you. You went on with living. He didn't want to turn time back; he wouldn't be without Shanti and his family for all the world. It was true that Shanti still had only the most basic English and no one could call her an intellectual stimulant, but she was bright enough in practical matters and very affectionate and the children she had given him were healthy and nice-looking and promised to be bright.

But all the same, memories didn't just disappear.

125

Nowadays, a girl like Pat would very likely have let him make love to her. The sixties were a very different world indeed and there were times when he had an irritated feeling of having somehow missed a boat on which a prolonged and zestful party was taking place.

The fact was that he had lost Pat and then had his initiative hijacked when Kartar pushed him into marriage, and since then he had drifted, comforting himself in bed with pretty Shanti, breeding all these children because she wanted a big family, and beyond worrying about making sure that his children grew up to be Sikhs even though, out of sheer consideration for his wife, he must tolerate a shrine to Ganesh in the flat, he had scarcely thought of the future let alone attempted to make plans for it.

When he first went to work for Mohan Lal, keeping his books and assisting him in the shop, it had been "just for the time being, while I pass my business management exams. When I'm qualified, I'll find work where I can use the qualifications." He'd got the qualifications in the end but he had never summoned up the energy to move away from Mohan Lal although he knew quite well that he ought to.

It was all very fine for Leela to say, how nice, all the family working together. But Mohan Lal didn't pay well. An instinctive feeling that it might be easier, one day, to change his job if he were not living too close to the shop, had kept him from looking for a flat in Southall, but even that was in a sense passive, a matter of keeping still and *not* taking action. Meanwhile, he and Shanti had certainly tried to save. But building up enough for a deposit on a house was a long, hard business. They had to pay the rent on the flat meanwhile and it was like being bled to death. It was better, he sometimes said, not to look ahead too far.

Now, swaying on the Underground, he found himself wishing he could talk to somebody about this slack-mindedness and this strange new feeling that he must alter it soon but he could hardly talk to Shanti about anything involving Pat, no matter how remotely, and on the whole he had better not talk to Kartar either.

Robert Houghton might have understood, but Robert Houghton, although his soul still yearned for bathroom tiles and wallpaper stripper and the cosy snuggle of a screwdriver in the palm, had retired and been whisked away by Brenda to a bunga-low on the south coast, which was her own idea of the perfect

126

home. "It has plain white walls," he said at his last meeting with Perry, "and there's no point in putting any nice wallpaper up anyhow. Hiawatha died last month and Brenda's got two Siamese kittens and they strop their claws on everything."

Perry had even, now, lost touch with his fellow students at the Houghtons. Inge and Jacques, who had eventually married, had kept in touch for a while, sending Christmas cards from their married home in Paris, but when Perry and Shanti moved to Wandsworth, somehow they had mislaid the Paris address.

No. There was no one he could talk to. If he wanted to take control of his life again, he would have to do it by himself.

He emerged from the tube at Southfields station and began to plod homewards through the thickening fog. On impulse, as he passed an open-fronted greengrocer, he stepped in and bought a Christmas tree. Carrying it under his arm, he then crossed the road to a stationer's and bought some shiny coloured balls and a silver star for it. His two elder children had Christmas events, nativity plays and carol concerts and so forth at school and Sunder had been to a friend's Christmas party and been impressed by the tree. Oddly enough, Perry never felt that the Sikh upbringing of his offspring was threatened in the least by the surrounding English culture. Ganesh was far more of a challenge. The Christmas tree would be fun and it would do no harm.

Armed with his seasonal gifts, and putting a determined briskness into his stride, he went on his way home.

Perry's footsteps at last! Shanti opened the door before he put his key into the lock. "Oh, Perry, I am so very glad to see you. I wondered where you . . . "

She stopped, looking in astonishment at the green spiky branches in his grasp. Perry flourished the Christmas tree proudly at her. "Look what I've got!" Sunder and Balbir abandoned the television and, with whoops of joy, sprang to take his burden from him. "I've got things to hang on it, too," said Perry. "I'm sorry I'm late; there was a defective train in the tunnel ahead of mine. You are looking nice, Shanti."

She could at least keep herself from looking a mess. She made a point of always having earrings and a colourful salwar kameeze on when he came home. They won compliments from him. But this time, with the boys again making enough noise to drown a pneumatic drill, and a mind full of anxiety, she hardly noticed.

"Oh, do be quiet, the two of you; how many more times? And don't fight over where the tree will stand; we will decide that. Now, thank your father nicely for bringing it. Perry, come and sit down."

He looked tired and cold. Much as she longed to confide her trouble to him, she had better say nothing as yet. She put the tree aside, and when the boys had duly said thank you and sat down again in front of the television, she fetched tea and food for Perry, and asked after his day. But she did not sit down with him and her kind enquiry came out in a doom-laden voice. Perry was alert at once.

"What's wrong, Shanti?"

"I think," said Shanti, "that it is time we found somewhere else to live."

"Ah," said Perry. He doubled a chapatti over and scooped up a mouthful of the lamb curry which Shanti, herself a vegetarian, had originally learned to cook for her brother. Mohan Lal took it for granted that all his womenfolk were vegetarian but also took it for granted that men were not. Meat had always been served in his house, carefully prepared by people who never ate it. "Well, we have been saving for our own place," he said doubtfully, "and I suppose we could manage a deposit now . . . "

"Could we?"

"Just about. But we wouldn't have much left. If we could hold on here for a little longer, it might be better. Where's your food? Why aren't you eating?"

"I am not hungry," said Shanti mournfully, continuing to hover instead of sitting down. In Mohan Lal's house, everyone ate together but at home with her parents, Shanti had been used to seeing the menfolk served first. When under stress, she reverted.

"Look, Shanti, what *is* it? Tell me!"

Instead of answering, Shanti looked towards the door. Someone was coming upstairs. There was a sharp knock.

"That," said Shanti, "is *her*."

Perry looked at her face, and knew that the sense of approaching crisis had been genuine, and that it was not, after all, a matter of a ten-year landmark.

The crisis was standing outside the door of the flat and its name was Mrs Cook.

*   *   *

128

Shanti opened the door but Perry, signalling to the boys to turn off the television, rose to his feet as their landlady came in. The disapproving expression in her slate-coloured eyes was one with which they were all unpleasantly familiar. "I'll deal with her," said Perry to his wife, in their own language.

It added insult to injury that Mrs Cook, who complained so much, was herself sluttish. Shanti had once said that she was sure Mrs Cook regularly applied fresh make-up without removing the layer beneath. Powerfully built and thirty or so years old, the landlady was just now exceedingly pregnant and her maternity wear was too short and too tight. Standing aside to admit her, Shanti eyed her with intense dislike. Sunder and Balbir, deprived of their thriller, were also scowling. Mrs Cook, advancing on Perry, was however quite unaffected by the atmosphere of loathing.

"I'm sorry to interrupt your dinner, Mr Virk." She didn't sound sorry at all. "But the racket up here this evening's been a lot too much; I never heard such a din, and now there's *this*. It just won't do." She had a loud, harsh voice. She held out a toy cart of red and yellow wood. "I damn near tripped over it in the garden, going to the dustbin. I could have fallen down and got hurt. It's one of the toys those boys of yours play with. I've said before, I don't want tenants' children down in our garden. So how did it get there?"

It was maddening, thought Shanti, that she could understand most of this, but could not frame the words with which to answer back. She turned indignantly to Perry. "Children have to play; how can they stay inside here all the time? Boys must have room to run about. But the street is dangerous; all that traffic! It is not fair to say they must not ever go into the garden."

Perry repeated this.

"There is a common," retorted Mrs Cook. "Let them go out on to the common! You knew the rules when you came here; I made them clear enough . . . "

"They . . . not harm . . . not doing harm . . . to garden!" Shanti groped for speech in English.

It was a mistake. "Oho, don't they?" Mrs Cook's expression was almost gleeful. She shook the red and yellow cart at Shanti. "I told you; I almost tripped on this and there's another thing. Your toddler sucks her toys. When my baby comes, I shan't want him picking up some doll or other that yours has been licking and sucking. He might catch something; God knows what diseases he might get from your kids . . . "

"What is she saying?" Shanti demanded of Perry. "Is she saying my children have diseases? They are no more likely to have diseases than hers! Tell her, tell her!"

"Mrs Cook," said Perry with vigour, "we take the greatest care of our children's health. They have all the proper immunisations and . . . "

"Your family's still far too big for this flat and . . . my God, what's *that*?"

"What's what, Mrs Cook?"

"That thing over in the corner behind you. You've brought a Christmas tree in here! Well, you can get it right out again. They moult, those things do; drop needles all over the carpet and your hoovering's never been what I call up to standard. You can get nice artificial trees if you want one. Wouldn't have thought you would want one. You're not Christians. Your cooking smells like nothing on earth but at least with you people I thought there'd be no Christmas trees or drunken parties . . . "

"We are certainly not going to throw any dr . . . "

" . . . it was bad enough when you come here with two kids but I thought, well, two's normal for a family, I'll stretch a point, give you a chance. But I've never seen anything like the way you just go on and on having them. I've been hoping you'd see for yourselves but since you haven't, I think it's time I spelt it out. It'd be better if you found another place, for your children's sake as well as yours. And I don't want to see any of your kids in my garden again. Most people get themselves into a house before they have kids. That's all. Good night." She clumped away down the stairs. Shanti, biting her lip, closed the door.

"Bitch!" said Perry. "It's all right, Sunder. It's all right, Balbir. She's gone." They were looking from their father to the Christmas tree with wide dark eyes. Sunder's were smouldering but Balbir's small face was scared. "You'll have your tree," Perry said. "We'll keep her out somehow till Christmas is over."

"She wants us to leave, doesn't she?" said Shanti. "I can't always follow what she says but I got that right, I know I did."

Perry sank down again into his chair and looked at the dinner he no longer felt like eating. "Yes, Shanti, you got that right."

"She was up here this morning and she said it and I have been wanting you to come home and dreading you coming home too because it is so nasty for you. She has been coming up more and more these last few weeks, and there has been harassment."

"Harassment?"

Shanti nodded towards the laden washing line. "The weather was not nice today, but it was not raining exactly and I would rather put things outside. But she has told me I am not to put washing out in her garden any more, but today I saw the people from the basement hanging theirs. And last week she said we are not to keep our spare linen in the landing cupboard any more."

"Shanti, you should have *told* me it is getting like this. You should not have kept me in the dark. She is a beastly woman and that hard-faced husband of hers is no better and the sooner we are away from this place, the happier we shall be. I understand now. You are right, we can't manage here much longer so I must see what we can scrape together. If only, if only I can cope with a mortgage, then we will find a small house. We could let a room perhaps, as Kartar and Nita are doing in their house. I have let things slide too long; I see that now."

"There are some small houses near to my brother," said Shanti eagerly. Her face had brightened. "If we lived in Southall, or near it, you would not have such big fares to pay to get to work."

"I may still have fares to pay. If I am to afford the mortgage, I must get a better paid job." That decision, suddenly, was taken. The prospect of the dual search for a house and a job felt like a ton-weight burden on his shoulders but he must carry it somehow. A new thought occurred to him. "Shanti. You don't want to go back to India, do you?"

"I thought that you wished to stay here."

"I'm asking you what you want."

Shanti considered, dropping into the chair opposite to him. "I don't think it is best we go back to India. Since you ask me, I would say no."

"What are your reasons for saying that? No, come on, tell me."

"In all the time we have been married, never has your mother written to me, or put a message to me in any letter," said Shanti. "Not even when I had the boys, and not even when I wrote to her. Your father has written to me, very kindly, but never your mother. It is significant."

Glumly, Perry nodded. "Although if she knew you, I feel sure she would change her mind. But I understand your feelings."

"Perhaps I am wrong," Shanti said uncertainly. "Perhaps I should not let this stand in your way. I should be prepared to try to please her and encouraging you to take us back to India might

131

be a way to please her. Only I am nervous. Perry, do *you* wish to return to India? You have never said much about it. You said when we were married that you thought you would like to stay here for a time, but since then you have not spoken of it. Even then you never said for how long or why."

"When I left India," said Perry slowly, "I had an idea that I would make my way in England altogether. I wanted to get away from home and live in a new way. It hasn't worked out quite as I thought. I am not making my way very fast. I have not pushed enough yet. I must make more of myself before I go home or how will I face my relatives there? I have cousins there, all doing well. No, I think we agree, if not for the same reasons. We should stay here."

"If ever your mother visits England, I will do all I can. Perhaps I will start again, writing a little paragraph at the end of your letters, as I did when we were first married. Perhaps now she is more used to the idea of me. She may answer this time."

"You are a dear girl, you know, Shanti."

Shanti smiled and then tilted her head to one side, listening. "Is that the phone, downstairs? I hope it is not for us."

"We are allowed to receive phone calls within reason, up to ten p.m."

"Your brother phoned the day before yesterday," said Shanti, "and the evening before, Mohan Lal did. If this is for us, it is three times in one week and if Mrs Cook can find an excuse for saying we are not within reason, she'll seize it!"

Chapter Eleven

Letter from Home
1966

Nowadays, Nita had a local secretarial job and today, as usual, she was home before Kartar. She hurried through the side-turnings of Southall to their house in the adjoining district of Lanesden, and was glad to be out of the smell of the fog, back in her home, where she was greeted at once by the smell of the lavender-scented polish she used on her furniture, and, from upstairs, by the appetising aroma of chapattis. Mr and Mrs Satinder Singh, who occupied part of the upper floor, were admirable tenants and Mrs Singh was evidently making tea for the children. Her little boys, Surjit and Charan, were now aged seven and five. Both had been born after the Singhs moved in.

Nita, taking off her coat in the hall and stepping out of her court shoes into soft slippers which wouldn't be hard on the musty-pink and coffee and peacock of the carpet which covered the entire ground floor, could hear the youngsters scampering about upstairs. She smiled.

It had been very difficult at first. Just as she had forced herself to congratulate Shanti and Perry on their growing family, she had compelled herself to take a kindly and helpful interest in Mrs Singh's babies. Until that incredible December, five years ago.

She had not meant to tell Kartar of her suspicions until they were confirmed, in case, after all, she was wrong. But she was three weeks overdue and she kept on going to bed early and falling instantly asleep, and then came the day when they came home from the Gurudwara early because she was so tired, and she had been violently sick almost as soon as they were inside the door. Poor Kartar had been so alarmed. "I've been getting more and more worried about you, this last fortnight. I think you should see a doctor, Nita."

"So do I," said Nita, sitting on the edge of the bed and sipping the glass of water he had brought her. "But I think I am not ill. In another ten days, yes, I will go to the doctor."

"In another *ten days*? But . . . ?"

"By then," said Nita demurely, "I shall have missed twice, and I shall be feeling, well, more or less sure."

"Sure of what? *Nita* . . . but they said . . . "

"They said my womb was immature. I think perhaps," said Nita, "that it has grown up."

The chapattis that Mrs Singh was now cooking in the small kitchen which they had made for her out of the little back bedroom were not only for her two sons. Nita's four year old daughter Raminder, whom everyone called Rose because she was so pretty, was up there too and would partake as well, and little Amrit, who had been born only last summer, would be lying in her cradle under Mrs Singh's benevolent eye.

It was wonderful good fortune, having Mrs Singh there. Nita's children could be left with her safely so that Nita herself could continue to work. Kartar, meanwhile, had established himself with his employers. After his shaky start, Chesterton, Onyx and Crawley, Chartered Accountants, seemed to have begun appreciating him. Today he had been asked to attend the annual Christmas luncheon for the board of directors, principal clients and selected accountants from the staff below board level. He was adequately paid now and they had just invested in their first car.

She picked up an airmail letter from the hall table, observed that it was addressed to Kartar and must therefore await his return before being opened, and called, "I'm home!" up the stairs to Mrs Satinder Singh, whose rather squarely built form promptly appeared on the landing, grasping a wooden spatula in a practical manner and surrounded by a faint cloud of smoke from the chapattis.

"Do you want anything to eat, Mrs Virk? It is such a cold, misty evening."

"No, no, thank you. But if you can keep the children for a while, I can get something going on the stove for my husband. He went to an official luncheon today, but he will want something later, of course."

"Oh, yes, by all means. They are no trouble. Rose is sitting down with a colouring book and Amrit has been fed and she is fast asleep. It is an honour for Mr Virk to be asked to this luncheon?"

"Yes, it is. I pressed his best suit for him last night and sent him off this morning looking as smart as could be."

"He will have had a good time," said Mrs Singh. "But I expect it was just English cooking, all the same."

Nita was presiding over three bubbling saucepans when the front door opened and Kartar called to her. She turned down the gas, put the saucepan lids on and went out to the hall to meet him.

"Kartar, you look quite exhausted. What was the luncheon like?"

"The food was turkey and sprouts and things and Christmas pudding." He led the way into the living room and flopped into a chair, still wearing his overcoat. "It was awful," he said. "It was ghastly. I made such a fool of myself."

"Oh, I have not lost my job!" he explained, when Nita had taken his coat away, found his slippers, brought a pot of tea and sat down to share it with him, saying, "Now tell me all these gruesome details. I am sure you didn't do anything as bad as all that."

"I am in line for another promotion," Kartar said, "and I shall get it all right. There is nothing to worry about. But I have never been so embarrassed in my life. The English are impossible sometimes. It is a blessing, Nita, to come home and smell familiar food cooking and feel an Indian atmosphere round me. If I were *not* doing well here now, believe me, I would be thinking of taking us all back to India. In fact, the only reason I'm not thinking of it anyway is because I won't move out of the way to please people like that!"

"People like what?"

"Our new chairman," said Kartar grimly.

"What's wrong with him?"

"He's a type." Kartar gulped his tea. "That's what's wrong with him. I had to be introduced to him at the cocktail stage, before we all sat down. I knew what sort of man he was at once. And then . . . "

Kartar, placing his slim dark hand politely in Mr Julian Fairweather's thick, fleshy, Anglo-Saxon one, had recognised the type immediately. Men of this sort had locked up Kartar's grandfather for wanting to be ruled by his own people in his own country. He looked at Fairweather's high, polished

135

forehead and arctic blue eyes, at the deceptively boyish mouth and chin above the thick neck and body and the Saville Row suit, and remembered seeing men like this when he was a boy in Delhi, before that long-sought independence came.

Julian Fairweather was one of those who had been born to authority, reared to accept unquestioningly that his class, his sex and his race were superior to all others. His integrity was doubt-less beyond question. You could trust him with your investments or the guardianship of your children, and he might well be considerate towards those he considered his inferiors. As long as they took care to remember that they *were* his inferiors, were working people, or women, or natives, and heaven help them if they forgot.

"He asked me if I meant to stay in England and remarked that a lot of chaps like me were coming over here nowadays to get professional qualifications," Kartar said. "Then he said that he supposed British qualifications would stand one in good stead back in India. It wasn't *what* he said, exactly; it was the way he said it. I could hear him writing off any qualification obtained in India, hear him thinking it, I mean. Then he congratulated me on my good English and said that most of the English never learned a word of anyone else's language. He said the English go on holidays abroad and talk their own language at the tops of their voice and expect the natives to understand. Those are the terms he thinks in. *Natives.* And then . . . "

"He does not sound a very nice man. But surely, it doesn't matter. I cannot see what you mean when you say you were embarrassed. Surely . . . "

"I haven't finished," said Kartar gloomily. "I haven't got to the point yet. I don't really want to get to the point. I could have died. I wanted to just lose consciousness, topple on to the carpet and be taken away to a mortuary, at once. Or better still, vanish out of the world and out of everyone's memory."

"But what happened?"

"You know my Section Head, Mr Jamieson? At least, you have not met him but I have often spoken of him."

"Yes, of course. He sounds very nice. You have told me how helpful he has been to you."

"Yes. Well, he introduced us. He was there all the time we were talking. Fairweather said he was sure that I had learned a great deal from Mr Jamieson, because Jamieson is supposed to be known for being good at training staff and getting them

136

promoted, and I said, oh, yes, that was quite true, Mr Jamieson's guidance had been quite unspeakable. And there was this horrible silence. That ghastly woman Violet Steele – you know, the secretary who once refused to work for me – she was there, they always have some of the women on the staff at this luncheon, and she heard and she sniggered and I didn't know what I'd said!"

"But Kartar!" Nita was appalled. "Oh, no wonder you were embarrassed. It means . . . "

"I know what it means now! I said, have I used a wrong word? I meant to compliment Mr Jamieson on his excellent instruction, I found it first class, beyond words, unspeakably good, and then Jamieson explained. Apparently *unspeakably* used on its own always means unspeakably frightful, never unspeakably good. What a language! It is all traps."

"But whatever did you do?"

"I kept my head, I think. I laughed and said that until I had got acquainted with all the pitfalls, I would try to keep my mistakes as entertaining as this one and no doubt one day it would make my grandchildren laugh. Then it was time for the meal to start and we all took our seats and thank God I was well away from Fairweather and the Steele woman. Afterwards, Jamieson told me not to mind and that I'd created quite an impression, getting out of it as I did. But I tell you, Nita, I could have died."

"I am not surprised! Oh dear!" Nita's face was full of horror and sympathy.

"Dreadful, wasn't it?" He was resting his palms on the arms of his chair. He raised them and let them fall back in an oh-let-it-go gesture. "Well, that's why I told you it was a blessing to come home here to the feeling of an Indian household. I feel as though I'd spent the day in a hostile foreign country. At home, I can be myself."

"This will always be a proper Indian household where you can be yourself. I promise."

"Bless you, Nita." They paused, smiling at each other. Then Kartar asked, "Did we have any mail today? We both left before the postman, as usual."

"Oh, yes, there was one for you from your Uncle Sunderjit. It's on the table there. You read it while I get on with the dinner."

She gave him the letter and went back to the saucepans. But

within moments, it seemed, he was there in the doorway, the opened letter in his hand. She looked at the stricken expression on his face and said anxiously, "Kartar?"

"Our new chairman and my resounding clanger seem very unimportant now," Kartar said. "It's my father. He . . . "

"What is it? What has happened?" Nita moved quickly towards him. "Tell me!"

"You can read the letter." He pushed it at her. "He . . . I don't know how to say it. Nita, he's dead!"

"What?"

"He had a heart attack at home. Go on, read for yourself. He was taken to hospital, Uncle says, but he . . . expired before he got there. Uncle Sunderjit wrote because Bheji, he says, has no words to express her loss and her sorrow. I can't believe it. I . . . just . . . can't . . . "

"Come." Quickly, Nita guided him back into the living room and pressed him into his chair. "Sit down again."

"I can't take it in." Kartar sat staring dazedly in front of him while Nita rapidly scanned the letter. "We'll have to tell Perry," he said suddenly and began to pull himself to his feet once more. "I must telephone him."

"You stay there. I'll do it. Oh, he will be so upset. Bheji must be frantic. To happen so suddenly like that!"

Kartar's gaze focused on her and to her surprise she saw that he was not only deeply distressed but also slightly sardonic. "Uncle Sunderjit says that Bheji has no words for expressing her feelings," he said, "but he's exaggerating. She has found a few words. She has added a postscript to the letter after all."

Within an hour, the living room had filled up. Perry and Shanti were there, side by side, having come in a minicab. Sunder and Balbir sat close to them. All the smaller children, including Rose, had been deposited to sleep on various beds and divans. Mohan Lal and Leela had arrived too, with their two daughters and their seven-year-old son. The Singhs had come downstairs and were sitting quietly, speaking words of sympathy now and then; their status not that of family members, but at this moment not that of mere tenants either. They were friends and fellow-members of the Gurudwara, offering support and having it accepted.

Cups of coffee had been distributed. The letter had been passed from hand to hand and read by all the adults.

138

Perry's face was bloodless. "I can't believe we'll never see him again. Whenever I thought of home, I imagined him there, just as he used to be. I have only to look inside my head and I can see him. But he's already . . . already . . . "

Shanti put her hand on his arm. In the heat of India, funerals could not be delayed. Joginder had been ashes before Uncle Sunderjit even put pen to paper.

"I will arrange a memorial service at the Gurudwara," Kartar was saying.

"We will all come," Mohan Lal assured him.

"Everyone is feeling for you," Leela said. "And for your mother. Such a thing to happen, and in her presence, too!"

Perry was holding the letter. "This postscript," he said. "How are we to answer?"

"Oh, but it was a first reaction," Leela hurried to reassure them. "Most probably she will think differently after a while and you will get another letter saying something else."

"Perhaps, but I doubt it. Our mother is . . . tenacious," Kartar said, and across the room he and Perry looked steadily at each other.

Ranbir's postscript was hard to read, the writing sloping wildly, unlike Uncle Sunderjit's neat, controlled script, and it was blurred here and there as though Ranbir had wept over it. But what it said was concise enough. Ranbir was afraid of being left alone in the house with only the maidservant Dina coming in each day, and she did not want to live with any of her relatives in India. She wanted the company of her own sons and since they had gone to England, she could see nothing to do but follow them.

"There is no space here." Kartar's voice had steel in it. "We have two families already in this house and it would be unfair on our tenants to crowd the premises any more."

"Oh, no!" The Singhs were quick to disagree. "One can always fit in one more person, and after all, this would be your mother!" Mrs Singh protested.

But Kartar was shaking his head. "No. It is good of you but no; I repeat, it would be most unfair to you."

"Oh, come. We shall not be here for ever, you know. Indeed, I have been hearing from a cousin of mine of some good business opportunities in Bradford and perhaps we may be buying a house there soon and moving away," Mr Singh began. He then caught Kartar's eye and stopped.

139

Mohan Lal said doubtfully, "I suppose one household might move back to India," but saw the lack of response and also stopped. Perry and Kartar both gazed blankly into space, and their wives, glancing at them quickly and then glancing away, knew what they were thinking as clearly as though Perry had repeated, "I must make more of myself before I go home," and Kartar had again declared that he would not move out of the way of a man like the new chairman of Chesterton Onyx.

The silence persisted uneasily for some moments. "I don't think any of us wish to do that," said Nita at last.

Perry cleared his throat as if to speak, but seemed to think better of it. It was Shanti, after a moment, who said timidly, "It is true, what Nita says. We thought . . . Perry thinks . . . it is best to stay in England. But we are hoping to find a small house soon. We had thought of letting a room but perhaps if we can do without that – I could do more sewing, perhaps – then we might . . . it might be a good thing. I should like to get to know my mother-in-law. If Perry agrees . . . "

When, much later, they were alone in their room, in the English-style double bed which they both now favoured, Nita said to her husband, "Darling, about Bheji. Surely we ought to welcome her here? We could certainly arrange something; one can always take in a parent, no matter what. The Singhs understand."

"The Singhs don't understand and nor, apparently, do you. I am not anxious to have Bheji in this house, Nita. I have not forgotten how miserable she made you, with those continual nagging letters when you could not have babies. She hurt you and I think she should have known it, and I have not forgotten."

"But all that is in the past and we have two lovely daughters! She will not press us to try for a son, if that is what you are thinking. Perry has provided her with three grandsons and she knows that I had two caesareans and was warned that it would be best not to have more children. She wrote such a nice, understanding letter. And after all, Kartar, in our society, it is right for sons to take care of their mothers and . . . "

"I know. But there it is. What society says one should feel and what people actually do feel are not always the same thing and I do not wish Bheji to live with us. And since Perry and Shanti have offered, there is no need. In fact, I think Shanti is quite right; it would be an excellent thing if Bheji were to share their home and make friends with Shanti. It is time all this nonsense about not approving of her because she is Hindu should come to an end."

"There I agree. I have always thought Shanti a nice girl, even though I was not sure at first that Perry should marry her, but she is so loving and sweet that I have changed my mind about that, too. Only . . . "

"You think I am hard? When I saw you made so unhappy, Nita, I did become hard, towards the person who was responsible. But in other ways, I am not hard. It is like Perry said, every time I look inside my mind I can see my father there and yet I know I'll never see him again and I . . . I want to see him, Nita. It is so long since we last met, thirteen years, but I . . . I am missing him."

Nita slid her arms round him and he burrowed his head into her shoulder. It was not an amorous embrace, but one of kindness and comfort. She thought he cried a little, very quietly, in the darkness. But presently, they slept.

Chapter Twelve

Pressures
1969

Perry liked a restrained English-style breakfast: boiled egg (midway between hard and soft), toast, orange juice and coffee and twelve-year-old Sunder shared his father's tastes. The other children also liked orange juice, but Balbir and Rupa, aged ten and five respectively, preferred their eggs soft-boiled with bread and butter soldiers to dip into them and Satnam, not yet nine and always the awkward one, had to be coaxed to eat at all and would rather eat porridge than anything else.

An ideal breakfast for their grandmother Ranbir, however, consisted of puris straight out of the frying pan, fresh fruit and tea. Shanti, between them all, had no space for personal preferences and would sooner have gone without breakfast altogether. She ate it only because she needed it, and it usually took the minimal form of a piece of toast and a pot of tea shared with her mother-in-law.

She rose early, and not only so as to organise everything in good time. Ranbir was an early riser too and was certainly willing to help prepare breakfast just as she helped with the other meals. The trouble was, Shanti thought, emerging into a warm July daybreak, that having her mother-in-law's assistance was far worse than being left to do it all alone. She rushed in the hope of reaching the kitchen first in order to make breakfast in peace.

But this morning, she was still groping for her slippers when she heard Ranbir in the bathroom and knew that once again she had failed to win her private race. She seemed to want so much sleep these days. The fact that England was having a hot summer for once, made it worse. She would have given anything to stay in bed beside the still-snoring Perry.

She put on a housecoat and set off down the stairs, arranging her face into the sweet *good-morning, Bheji* smile which was expected of the perfect daughter-in-law she had tried so hard, for two long years, to be. Oh, if only, if only, Ranbir had gone to live with Kartar and Nita instead.

It was unfair that she hadn't. Kartar said that with his own two children and his upstairs tenants, he hadn't room, but this house, the best they could afford, was smaller than his and their family was bigger and . . .

According to Ranbir, the inadequate size of the house was Shanti's fault. She didn't contribute enough to the exchequer. Ranbir and also Perry, because Ranbir practically forced him to it, had both been on at her for some time to take lessons to improve her English and find an office job like Nita's.

Shanti protested that now that the Singhs had gone to Bradford and been replaced by a family of adults who all worked, she had taken over the task of looking after Nita's children while Nita was at her job. But Ranbir, snorting, said that she could take that over herself. Shanti, thus robbed of her first line of defence but terrified by the idea of a job in an English-speaking office, now just clung dumbly to her sewing machine. She knew that what she earned from it was best described as peanuts but although she had a practical intelligence and was a good manager with money, she wasn't good at studies like Nita, or as brave as Nita, and that was that.

The little house was bright with paint and cheerful wallpaper; Perry had redecorated most of it himself. He had lost his nerve only in the kitchen, where the narrow strips of ochre-coloured wall between the cooker, the fridge and the horrible cracked porcelain sink had intimidated him. The kitchen remained dingy and inconvenient, so narrow that two people could pass each other only if one breathed out while the other breathed in, and it always smelt faintly of gas. They had had to find the house in a great hurry. Mrs Cook had indeed taken offence at three phone calls in one week.

The kitchen did have the merit of opening on to a small garden where Shanti had succeeded in cultivating a tiny vegetable plot and some flowers. But although, on sunny mornings, Shanti would have liked to open the back door to let in the sight and scent of them, her mother-in-law said that in England it was never warm enough, and invariably shut it again.

In the kitchen now, Ranbir, stringy brown arms jutting from her white widow's salwar kameeze, was measuring out the porridge. The table in the adjoining room was set and the eggs were

143

lying in their saucepan waiting for the gas ring to be lit. Ranbir tossed a fold of white veiling over her shoulder out of the way as Shanti came in, and said accusingly, "I have done it nearly all for you."

"Oh, I am sorry, Bheji. I sleep too much."

"With four children, you are tired, I dare say." Ranbir's voice was brusque, not sympathetic. "Medical science has helped families. One does not have to have too many children. Among our sort of people, two or three are enough. It can alienate a man, piling too many burdens on his time and his purse, if there are too many children."

"But you cannot say we should not have had Rupa!" Shanti was shocked into arguing. "She is so lovely and we so much wanted a daughter. It is so nice, having a big family. I have never heard you say this thing before."

"I do not say Rupa is not a lovely child, and of course I love her. But there it is, these days, four is too many for people of our sort."

People of our sort meant *us Sikhs* as opposed to *you Hindus.* Shanti knew this perfectly well. She bit her lip and busied herself with cutting bread for toast, avoiding Ranbir's eye.

"Perry has got so distant since he had all this responsibility," Ranbir said, and then paused with head cocked. "Satnam is awake. I can hear him. Go and see to the children and dress yourself. I will finish here. Here, I have made tea for Perry. Take it to him."

A glance at the bedroom clock as she went in told Shanti that the tea was ten minutes late. When she woke him, Perry looked at once at the clock face and sat up sharply. "Oh, look at the time. Shanti, this isn't fair. Every day since I started this new job, I have had to rush for fear of being late. I must not be late. There is so much to do in this place."

"I'm sorry."

"Yes, well." He gulped a few mouthfuls and thrust the cup and saucer at her. "I've no time for any more. I must get up."

"I wish you didn't work so late. You get so tired. You have been bringing work home, too." She caught a complaining note in her own voice and hastily changed it to a more cheerful tone. "But you've only been there three weeks. Perhaps it will be better when you are settled in. At least there is more money. That other job where you were a book-keeper only, hardly paid more than my brother did. Mohan Lal was very naughty. He

144

admitted he milked you."

"The trouble with being more than a book-keeper is that the hours in the day are not more! I seem to be doing every other job that's going. I must keep an eye on the post room and see that everything is cleared last thing at night, and even check the soap in the men's washroom every day. They are always finding me new things to do." He swung his legs out of the bed and then sat for a moment with his head in his hands. "It is bloody tiring, Shanti, and worse when it is so hot and I can't sleep until dawn. I had all these ideas when I came to England, of making a career here and now the best I can find to do is be a dogsbody in this tinpot electrical goods manufacturers. Nita has done better than I have, learning to be a secretary, and getting such a good post. My pay is no more than reasonable however you pretend about it and it is only as good as it is because before me, they had two men to do this job! It is a silly, boring job, all trivialities, but such a mass of them, I am not sure I can go on doing even this!"

"Of course you can. You will make your way, just as your brother did."

"Kartar is far tougher than I am and harder in his nature. Shanti . . . "

"Yes?"

" . . . would you mind, Shanti, if we sleep separately for a while? I can't sleep well when I am so hot. I must disturb you too. There is that divan downstairs. I'll sleep there for the time being. At least till the weather is cooler. If you don't mind."

"No, of course I don't mind. Not if it will help you," said Shanti, and got out of the room as quickly as possible, before Perry could see her face.

She had wanted to marry him so much. And to begin with, they had been so happy.

In those days he had worked hard and often been tired but he had never taken it out on her or the children. He had been kind and easy-tempered, always.

She knew perfectly well what had changed him. Ranbir might hint that having too many children was responsible but Ranbir was wrong. The roses had begun to fade from the moment, two summers ago, when Ranbir herself, white-enswathed and un-smiling, first set foot across this threshold to take up residence in a house containing the Hindu daughter-in-law of whom she did not approve, and in whom she was not going to tolerate even the

145

most unimportant faults.

From that moment on, Perry, fretted by the strain between his wife and his mother, had begun to draw away from both of them and Ranbir, sensing his withdrawal and blaming Shanti for it, seemed every day to wind the deadly spiral tighter.

I do try, said the unspoken monologue which these days went on constantly inside Shanti's head, in silent counterpoint to her determinedly sweet smile and sprightly voice. I do everything that would make her think Shanti is a good wife, Shanti is a good daughter-in-law. And it is all no use. I can't please my mother-in-law no matter what I do. She is driving my husband away from me.

Between getting the children up and bathing her eyes in cold water to hide the traces of tears, she was late in bringing the family downstairs. Ranbir had already made her puris and given Perry his breakfast. Shanti murmured apologies and heard them fade into the air.

Perry, casting repeated glances at his watch, finished his meal in haste, seized the briefcase containing the office work he had brought home the night before, and departed at a near-run. Shanti, when the children, including the ever-reluctant Satnam, had also eaten, set about clearing away the breakfast things with Ranbir, and attempted a little conversation about the two Indian families, one Sikh and one Hindu, who had recently moved into the street.

"It is so nice to have Indian ladies nearby. We know so few people in this street. The young English couple at number sixty-six go out to work early and come home late, and the retired couple on the other side, they are almost invisible. I see Mr Brierley walk by with his morning paper sometimes, that is all. But now we have proper company close at hand," she said kindly, reminding herself with determined sympathy, how often, in those early days after Jog's death, she had found her mother-in-law quietly crying to herself over the sink or the stove. She would have comforted Ranbir if she could. The trouble was that Ranbir wouldn't let her; would always brush a hand across her eyes, raise her chin and say it was nothing, that she had a cold or had just peeled the onions.

Ranbir agreed that it was nice to have more Indian ladies nearby, regretted however that the Sharmas were not Sikhs, remarked that Mrs Swarup Sharma had a mischief-making tongue, and then cut the topic short with a reminder about

146

changing the bedsheets. And not wasting string. Shanti sighed.

Such a big family meant quantities of bedlinen to look after and Perry, in spite of being constantly worried over money, had long ago decreed that sheets must go to the laundry; there were too many to do at home. Shanti was glad of this but had unfortunately let Ranbir see it. Ranbir promptly took to urging the purchase of a washing machine (for which they hadn't room), or the launderette (a considerable trudge away), neither of which would solve the problem of the ironing in any case. Perry held out, for which Shanti was grateful, but Ranbir then fell back upon a policy of making a great fuss over the amount of string Shanti used when doing up the laundry parcels. "If you cut off long ends, they must always be knotted back on to the ball of string. With the mortgage your husband is carrying, you must save where you can."

She reminded Shanti about this constantly, usually as a lead-in to remarks about Shanti's bad English and its effect on her earning capacity. Shanti, in self-defence, now saved any oddment of string more than four inches long in silence, and tried to like it.

Ranbir insisted on other irritating economies as well (Shanti was using a faulty steam iron because until it broke down completely, her mother-in-law wouldn't hear of it being replaced) but the string was the most petty. Shanti had once sat down with pencil and paper and a measuring tape and worked out that it would take about fifteen years to save the price of a single ball of string. But Ranbir would be outraged if she said so. She didn't risk it.

Today, therefore, although she was miserable enough to feel even more rebellious than usual, she knotted string obediently, crushing her feelings down. She dared not quarrel with Bheji, for what would Perry say? Perhaps he would never come back to her bed and that she could not bear. The thought of tonight was like a heavy weight in her stomach as it was. And it was not her only worry, either. It was difficult, as she did up the parcel, to keep a frightened tearfulness at bay.

Nita was later than usual in bringing the children for the day and arrived, unexpectedly, in a colourful but casual salwar kameeze instead of the formal sari, printed cotton with a weighted hem and pleats as precise as a stone sculpture, which was her habitual business wear. She had her younger daughter Amrit in a push-chair, with seven-year-old Raminder Rose

147

(Kartar sometimes put both names together because the result was so musical) walking alongside.

Ranbir greeted the arrivals with joy, picking Rose up for a hug and giving Nita the kind of approving smile which Shanti would have appreciated but could not remember ever receiving from her. "But you are not dressed for work, Nita?"

"I am not at work today, or any day for a while," Nita said. "I have left my job. That job was too much, with the children growing as they are. I shall start a new job in September. It will have much more convenient working times. Guess what it is."

"No, no, you must tell us," said Ranbir.

"Well, it is in a school. Not one any of our children are likely to go to: it is in Hammersmith. But it is easy to get to from my home. I shall be the secretary there. I shall have the school holidays free and be home at teatime on most days. Their present secretary is retiring. Well, it will be a relief," said Nita, laughing, "I have so much to do, with the children. Though I should not grumble; once, I thought I should never have any family."

"They make work. But they are always welcome," said Ranbir in a doting voice.

Swallowing her hurt, Shanti said, "There is shopping to get. It is a lovely day, so shall we all go?"

"Let us visit that park on the outskirts of Southall," said Nita. "We can get the shopping on the way back."

"Oh, I will see to the shopping," said Ranbir. "I will make sure nothing is forgotten, and then I will do some cooking. Perry must have a good meal when he comes home."

"But I have plenty of time to shop and cook," said Shanti.

"When you come back, you will have sewing to do," said Ranbir. "So I will see to the food."

It could have been a kindly and helpful offer. Ranbir succeeded in turning it into a criticism. *I'll do the shopping and cooking while you enjoy yourself in the park so as to be fit to do all that sewing that hardly brings in any money.* Shanti knew every inflection in her mother-in-law's voice, every twitch in her facial expression. Well, at least she and Nita and the children could now go out without Ranbir. Good!

Harrison Street, in which her home was number sixty-four, was within walking distance both of Kartar's house and Mohan Lal's, but it was ten minutes slow and seven minutes fast walking from either shops or park. Nita and Shanti, encumbered by

148

their squad of small children plus Amrit's push-chair, did not hurry, but sauntered quietly in the sun. They talked as they went, on a superficial level.

With her sister-in-law, Shanti had never advanced beyond this. Nita had never been anything but pleasant and helpful but she suspected that Nita agreed, at heart, with Ranbir that Sikhs and Hindus should not marry. There was a link of loyalty between Nita and Ranbir and it made her nervous. She talked to Nita, always, with a care that verged on the formal.

They were nearly at the park, just crossing the foot of South Street, with the town hall on their left, and Shanti was remarking on the fact that the town hall had lately been the venue for a Sikh wedding and it was amazing how many guests there must have been – "we saw such a crowd going in" – when Nita said, "I am afraid things are difficult for you with your mother-in-law. I have been thinking so for some time. I am so sorry, Shanti."

Oh, no, Shanti thought. I mustn't stand on this pavement – with the children looking at me, too! – and burst out crying. What a state I am in. Just because Nita, who has always been so polite and reserved, speaks kindly to me, this is what happens.

"Shanti?" Nita's voice broke in on her. "What is it? You look as if I had said something dreadful."

"It is nothing. I am all right."

"But you are not all right. Shanti, what is it?"

"Let's get into the park," said Shanti in a shaky voice. "And find a seat."

Once in the park, with the older children instructed to go off and play but not get into mischief or trip anyone up, Nita established the push-chair under a shady tree, led Shanti to a bench and said again, "Now, what is it? Please tell me."

Shanti bit her lip. "I have never never said to you anything about Bheji. Now, have I?"

"No, no, never. But I think she is upsetting you."

Shanti stared ahead of her, to where their combined families were beginning a game of impromptu cricket. Sunder had brought a bat and Balbir had produced a soft ball. They were all such lovely children, she thought, all so good-looking and active; the boys already self-evident little Sikhs with their hair uncut, and each topknot tied neatly into a dark blue cloth; her own Sunder – she could hardly believe it – already becoming leggy and shooting up in the direction of manhood. The girls were like flowers in their bright-coloured salwar kameeze suits. They

149

could all be such a happy family, if only . . .

"I expect it is my fault," she said miserably. "I am not what she wanted for Perry."

"That means nothing, now. You are Perry's wife and we have all accepted you. Indeed we have, Shanti."

Shanti turned her head and looked at her sister-in-law with dawning surprise.

"Did you think Kartar and I did not think you were a good wife, or wished we had not encouraged the match?" said Nita gently. "You must not think that. Now, talk to me."

"She . . . I mean . . . I was happy with Perry," Shanti blurted. "To begin with, when we were first married, oh, so happy. And then . . . "

"Our mother-in-law came to live with you."

"I've tried to make her like me." Shanti regained a measure of control and turned to look at Nita's firm, sensible face, thinking that it was quite unlike her own, which was all doe eyes and delicate bones and illustrated her nature only too well. She was too gentle and timid to deal with Ranbir. "I made her welcome," she said and added carefully, "I hoped that once we met . . . if I tried hard to be the right sort of daughter-in-law, she would come to approve of me. But . . . "

"Bheji has her fixed ideas," said Nita. "She upset me at one time. Early on, when I was trying to have children and could not. She was for ever writing, asking why not. I was very miserable. She did not mean it but she made me feel a failure, and that was by letter only! She wasn't in the same house with me. I am good friends with her but I know what she is like. What is it she is doing? You have children, at least."

"Oh, yes," said Shanti bitterly, "and when it is me, *that's* wrong. I have had too many, according to Bheji! I think you could have twenty and she would not criticise, but . . . she tries to put me in a bad light to Perry. He . . . he is drifting away from me." She stopped there. She could not say, he does not want to sleep with me any more.

"Oh, my dear. These things can be so difficult; I know. Bheji is so very traditional in her attitudes. Well, so are we in our way." She glanced to where, across the grass, Rose and Rupa were picking up Satnam, who had fallen down. "Rose is getting to the age where sometimes she wants to go and play with school friends and of course, she is only a child yet; it hardly matters. But I am not easy about her visiting English houses and getting

150

to make a habit of it. Later on there could be difficulties; the English girls will have brothers and boyfriends too and the *fashions* that English teenagers are wearing these days! These short skirts that show all their legs. It is all such a worry. But I am getting off the point. Bheji can be so decided that it can be uncomfortable and yet she means well. You must try not to take everything she says to heart too much. I suppose that is not very helpful but I cannot think what else to say."

"I must just go on trying, I suppose. But it isn't fair, Nita. It isn't fair. Two years and I have never stopped trying. But nothing I do is right . . . " and before she could stop herself, out tumbled the rest of it: the laundry, the balls of string, the steam iron, the obstinately shut back door, the nagging about learning English. By the end of the recital, she was trembling, with anger and unhappiness long suppressed, and her small, slim fingers were clasping and unclasping in her lap.

"What happened," said Nita suddenly, "about the shrine to Ganesh?"

"What? I did not know you knew . . . "

"Oh, I saw it once when I came to visit you. You had left the door of the cupboard open and when I went to put my coat on the bed, I noticed there was some sort of shrine inside. I asked Perry about it. Well, and why should you not have your own private shrine? I approved of that," said Nita. "You come to the Gurudwara and the children are being reared as Sikhs. You are entitled to have your own privacies. One must have some firm foundations inside oneself. How else can we stay ourselves when we are living here in this Western place? But I have wondered, what did Bheji think?"

"Oh, Bheji was furious! Well, for a long time she did not know, of course, because the shrine's cupboard is in our room. But she came in one morning, bringing sheets, when I had the shrine open. But I said what you said just now. That the children were Sikhs and I would always go to the temple when Perry wanted me to, but this one thing I must keep. No, I said, I will not destroy my shrine. It is harmless and it means something to me. And it was my room and Perry's . . . " Her voice faltered, because tonight it wouldn't be, but she made herself go on. " . . . and if he did not mind, that was good enough. She tried to make him mind, of course, I heard her. But Perry would not give in and she went quiet. She has given up on that now. Perry is good and kind; he does his best but he is stuck in between us and . . . . "

151

"I am really sorry," said Nita. "Bheji does not know she is upsetting you so much; I am sure of it. I will drop a hint or two."

"Nita . . . "

"Yes?"

"Please can I tell you something?"

"Yes, of course. What is it? There is something more than what you have said, then?"

"There . . . yes, there is. Nita," said Shanti, bracing herself, "Bheji pressed and pressed so hard, that I should go to English classes and make myself fit for an outside job . . . I could not bear it. I wanted her to stop trying to make me do things. She was making Perry urge me too. But I'm not like you; I *can't*. So I . . . I . . . "

Nita waited. Shanti gulped. "After Rupa," she said at last, miserably, "Perry made me go on the pill. But for three weeks I didn't take my pill. I thought, they can't force me to do things if I have another baby, and after all, it is a natural thing, to have babies. Think how happy my brother and Leela were when their little boy was born. That was unexpected; Mohan Lal had said perhaps they could not afford more children, but when Chandra Lal came, by accident, they had a big party to celebrate, as soon as Leela was well again. But today Bheji said such things . . . I have *never* heard anyone say such things before, that we shouldn't have had Rupa, even, three is enough, and she talked as though I were some second-rate sort of person to want more and . . . Nita, I am in the family way again!"

"Oh dear," said Nita, commiseratingly but also guardedly, as though hiding an opinion not unlike Ranbir's. "Are you sure? You have been to the doctor and had it confirmed?"

Shanti nodded. "One morning when Bheji thought I was just taking the children out. I'm nearly three months. But now I know that Bheji will be so angry . . . I shan't dare tell her I did it on purpose. She will say I am irresponsible. It will be bad enough pretending I was just careless. She will make Perry be angry with me, too. Oh, Nita, I'm so frightened!" Try as she would to prevent it, the tears of fright began to flow.

"My dear!" said Nita, in distress. "Here, have this handkerchief. No, no, you mustn't upset yourself. It will be all right. They may be angry for a little while, but when it arrives, they will be pleased, you'll see. I shall do what I can. Do you want me to tell Bheji for you?"

Hiccuping, Shanti nodded.

152

"All right. Well," said Nita. "Congratulations! I'll pick my time with care, don't worry."

They sat on for a while, quiet in the sunshine. At length, Shanti said, "Well, I have sewing to do," and they began to make their way back, not talking very much but with a new companionship between them which Shanti found comforting. They turned the corner into Harrison Street, and then quickened pace at the sight of a Gas Board van, for standing on the pavement beside it was the unmistakable white-clad figure of Ranbir with two other people whom Shanti recognised as the retired and retiring Brierleys from next door. "Oh, what can have happened!" Shanti gasped, and Sunder and Balbir ran ahead to see.

"Oh, there you are," Ranbir said as Shanti and Nita caught up. "Back from the park." Her tone suggested that Shanti had been in the park for several hours instead of no more than thirty minutes and had gone there against orders in the first place. Nita caught Shanti's eye with a rueful look. One thing was definite: no wise person would choose today for breaking anything to Ranbir. "A fine time we have been having here!" Ranbir said.

"It's a gas leak!" said Sunder and Balbir in unison. Having got there first, they had heard the news already and were round-eyed with delight in the drama.

"Such a good thing that Mr and Mrs Brierley here have a telephone," said Ranbir. "It is time Perry had a telephone. I came back from shopping and walked into the kitchen and almost I fainted! The smell of gas was like a wall."

It was in fact seeping out of the open front door, imparting a breath-catching tang to the dusty London air in the street. "I sometimes thought I smelt it a little, in the kitchen," said Shanti. "I suppose there was a leak and it has grown bigger."

"If you smelt it, you should have done something about it!" said Ranbir crossly. "My sense of smell is not as good as yours; you are young. I did not know what to do. I went next door and it is lucky Mr and Mrs Brierley were in and could tell me what to do."

"We phoned the Gas Board for you," said Mr Brierley, cutting across what to him had been a flood of unintelligible Punjabi. "And I found the mains tap under the stairs and turned it off." He was a slightly stooped, unsmiling man. His plump wife, equally unsmiling, said, "We will make a cup of tea in a moment.

153

Goodness knows how long the men will be in there."

A Gas Board engineer came out of the front door and began to explain something. He had a thick Cockney accent and Shanti, who had followed little of anything the Brierleys said, could make nothing of the engineer at all. Her son Sunder interpreted his mother's wild expression and obligingly translated.

"He says we've got problems and they'll have to take the kitchen floor up. They'll do it tomorrow but we'll have the gas turned off until then."

"Gee," said Balbir, in transatlantic English culled from films. "We'll have to camp. Can't we do it properly and have a tent in the garden? I'd like to sleep in the garden."

"But all our cooking is on gas! All but the kettle! How will we make dinner for Perry when he comes home?" wailed Shanti.

"It is no good asking me! If only you had noticed this before it became so serious!" Ranbir snapped.

"Even Perry doesn't seem to have noticed it," said Nita crisply. "I suppose he walks into the kitchen on occasion?"

Ranbir looked at her in surprise.

"You had better all come to us this evening," Nita said. She turned to Mrs Brierley. "If you are making a cup of tea, it would be most welcome, but we must not impose on you. We are such a crowd, with all these children. My home is not far away. We can all go there."

Mrs Brierley had indeed been eyeing their exotic clothes and their retinue of small children and push-chair with a degree of disfavour. "Well, if you're sure . . . " she said, in a voice which said quite clearly that she hoped they were.

"Yes, yes, quite sure," said Nita. "It was so kind of you to turn off the gas and make the phone call."

"Pleased to help," said Mr Brierley abruptly, and turned away into his house, followed by his wife.

Nita sighed. "They're just like our neighbours. Ours are always polite if one has to speak, and they would help in a real crisis, but they're never friendly. They don't want to mix. Ah, well, one can overdo that anyway." She turned to the engineer, who was clearing his throat impatiently. "What time will you be here tomorrow?"

"I couldn't say, missus. Some time in the morning."

"You had all better stay the night as well as have your evening meal with us," said Nita, turning to Shanti. "We shall be

154

cramped but we shall cope."

"You mean," said Perry, dropping his briefcase at his feet in the hallway where Shanti had met him, "that we must all go to Kartar's to eat? How can I?" He pointed to the briefcase. "That is full of my paperwork; I have to make out orders for soap and electric light bulbs and God knows what else and all those orders must be sent off tomorrow. How can I work round at Kartar's; there is no room, not one corner."

"I am sorry," said Shanti. "Gas leaks are things that just happen. They are no one's fault."

"Did I say it was your fault?"

"No." She drew back from his tired, angry face. "But you are so annoyed."

"I'm not annoyed with you." Perry passed a hand across his forehead. "I am only worried, Shanti. I am paid better here than at your brother's shop, or at that other job I took, yes, but still, it is not enough. We have too many mouths to feed. And Sunder will want a new school uniform in September, the way he is growing and now we shall have a bill for these gas repairs and where the money is coming from, I don't know. The gas and electricity bills get bigger every year as it is. Sometimes I am wondering which way to turn."

Shanti said, "You must have an evening meal. I came back here to meet you and fetch you. Nita is making it now."

"All right, I will come. You are right, I am hungry. But then I must come back here and do my work. I will sleep here tonight, Shanti. That will make it less crowded at Kartar's."

"But your breakfast?" she said protestingly.

"The kettle at least is electric! I can eat bread and butter and fruit for once; there's no harm."

"I'll come back with you tonight and then I can get breakfast for you."

"For goodness sake, Shanti! I can manage. Bheji can't be left looking after the children without you."

"And yet," said Shanti, the words called out of her without her consent, "you are always saying, and so is she, that I should go out to work and do just that."

"Yes, in her own home with everything in order all round her. Shanti, what in the world is the matter with you?"

It isn't what's the matter with me; it's what's the matter with you? thought Shanti resentfully.

155

But Perry was tired, hungry and worried and if she spoke her mind they would only quarrel. She had been wrong to snap just now. "There is nothing the matter. Come round to Kartar's and have your dinner."

"I am sorry if I keep being short with you." Perry picked up his briefcase and together they left the house. "But I am anxious all the time these days, how to make ends meet. If I lose this job . . . "

"But are you in danger of losing it? And surely there are plenty of jobs about."

"Not the kind of job I want." Perry marched militantly along the pavement. The evening was stickily hot. "Building site or factory jobs, that's all. I may end up settling for that, but that is not what I want to be. That is not what my family expect of me."

"I should not mind."

"My mother and Kartar would mind. Perhaps we should think again of taking a lodger as we meant to do, except that Bheji came to live with us."

"And when Bheji came, we couldn't because we had no spare room. We still haven't." Shanti choked back the remark that this morning, he had proposed sleeping henceforth in the lounge.

"Well, we shall have to find a way. We can curtain off some of the front room downstairs to make a place for the boys to sleep. I will forget about moving down there myself." Shanti let out a small secret sigh of relief. "But about the lodger. We can offer breakfast and an evening meal. I think we should consider it."

"Yes, perhaps we should." He was going to stay in the same bed with her. He was still on her side, not on Ranbir's. The lodger would create work, endless work, but perhaps that would mean she would not be urged any more to go out and earn. Shanti told herself these things as bravely as possible, wishing that the thought of the lodger being crammed into the house with them all didn't make her feel as though she couldn't breathe and wishing too that Perry wouldn't walk so fast. She was so tired and her back had begun to ache, as though her lower spine were cracking.

"But I still think," said Perry, "that you should take those English classes. They cost next to nothing, you know."

"I am not quick at these things. I might learn too slowly."

"You can *try*, can't you? Even if you never became good enough for an outside job, at least you could cope better with the shopping and the neighbours and the children's teachers."

156

"All right," said Shanti breathlessly. Perry's brisk stride almost had her running. "All right, I'll try." She would do anything in her power to cross this chasm which had opened between them and which was still there, even though she and Perry would not now sleep apart. Only she was afraid that it might require efforts which weren't within her power. She didn't just now feel capable of any effort at all. The ache in her back had been reinforced by a dull, dragging ache in her lower abdomen and these localised pains were themselves only darker dots in a great grey misery which had overwhelmed her entire being.

She made a desperate attempt to make conversation. "Mohan Lal called at Nita's just before I came out to meet you. He is saying that perhaps Father will come to this side soon. He is lonely too, just like Bheji, since our mother died two years ago. He has been trying to come for a year, Mohan Lal says, but with this quota system that there is now, it is difficult; he has to queue up for entry. But it looks as if he may be able to come next year. He will help in the shop. It will be so nice . . . "

They turned into Kartar's street and she stumbled. Her knees were trying to give way and something hot and wet was running down the inside of one thigh. Oh, no. Oh, no, it couldn't, it mustn't be.

"What's the matter?" Perry put out an arm quickly to steady her. "What is it?"

"We must get there quickly." Shanti closed her teeth on her lip as the abdominal ache became an enormous and savage clenching. She clung to his arm. "I think . . . I'm . . . miscarrying."

Chapter Thirteen

If Only . . .

1969

"Really, Shanti, how you could have been so careless . . . why in the world did you not tell us? It is hardly a thing one can hide for long . . . and to let it happen just when Perry is so worried . . . "

"Well, nature has stepped in now, Bheji. We will look after Shanti here until she is better." Nita's sensible face gazed anxiously down from above the lake of anguish in which Shanti was drowning. "The doctor is coming, Shanti."

"Doctor, what need for a doctor? I had two miscarriages both at three months and never . . . "

"I have already telephoned him, Bheji," Nita's voice, good-humoured but resolute as rock. "She is in great pain and there is too much bleeding."

"Now who will look after all Shanti's children? Really, Shanti, in future you will have to be more responsible, more awake to what is going on around you . . . "

Shanti succeeded in surfacing from her hellish lake for long enough to say, "But you said you would take care of them while I went to work. This will be a few days only." She was relieved when silence fell after this remark. It set her free to sink back into her agony and loss.

"Ten days in bed, with plenty of fluids, and then you are to take it easy for a few weeks afterwards, that's what the doctor says." She'd heard him say it but only understood a smattering. Mostly, his voice had been an incomprehensible booming from somewhere above her. Perry's voice, translating, was tired but kind. Perhaps at the end of all this, the chasm between them would have closed. "When the ten days are up, we'll fetch you home." She nodded, wearily, only wanting to sleep.

Here in Nita's home she had peace, even though the house

158

was so congested. Rose and Amrit had been moved into their parents' downstairs bedroom so that Shanti could have the small back bedroom on the first floor, the only room upstairs which was not occupied by the tenants. But everyone seemed to be taking it lightly. Both Nita and Kartar came often to talk to her, or sent Rose in with orangeade or Ribena for Shanti auntie "because she must have plenty of things to drink." Rose, very solemn, with big shiny dark eyes and thick, shiny black plaits, seemed to consider this duty a privilege rather than a chore, and would carry the glass carefully to her in both hands, for fear of spilling it.

As the ten days drew to an end, indeed, Shanti realised that although she longed for her children and Perry, she dreaded being once more under the same roof as Ranbir. When she got there, the dread proved to be all too well justified.

Ranbir was abominable.

"What is this nonsense? What are you sitting here in front of this shrine for and not eating?"

"It is just for one day, Bheji. I am going on fast for just one day, because I am grateful I am well again. It is to show I am grateful."

"And how will you stay well if you do not eat and drink properly? Get up at once and come to the breakfast table . . . !"

" . . . well, you are looking better today but there is all this washing and ironing to do and I suppose the doctor's orders are that you don't do it yet!"

"I can do some ironing and I can prepare vegetables sitting down. I can sew, as well."

"Yes, you had better sew. No, no, you are not to push the sewing machine table about; I will do it. You are so feckless, Shanti. You never think before you do things."

"Thank you, Bheji."

"You may well thank me. It is better than answering me back as you did when you were ill. Where this household would be without me, this last ten days, I am not knowing."

"I really am grateful. The house is so spick and span and the children look fine."

"Good. Well, let us try to keep it like that. At least you seem to realise how careless you have been. You must never forget to take your pill again, Shanti. What is the use of all these medical advances if you cannot even be bothered to remember a simple thing like that. Now what are you rubbing your hand across

159

your forehead for?"

"I am tired, Bheji." From wanting to sleep all the time as she had when she was pregnant, Shanti had passed to a state of hardly sleeping at all. "I can't get rest at night. I lie awake and toss."

"Then you go to the doctor and get some tablets."

"Very well, Bheji."

" . . . you are looking better again. The tablets have worked. Good. You see how much better things are when you are sensible and do as I tell you."

"Yes, Bheji."

Ranbir was actually mollified. But it wouldn't last, Shanti thought miserably, and this pessimistic forecast was shortly proved to be right.

"It will soon be September and evening classes will begin. Perry has been saying to me that you said you would attend English classes."

He had remembered that rash promise, given as she stumbled along the pavement beside him, a month ago now.

"I shall be so bad at it. I was never clever at school."

"It is a matter of trying, of application. Sometimes I think you are just lazy, Shanti. You drift through life instead of having some will of your own . . . "

Just as well for you because if I had, I'd push you head-first into that bowl of washing-up water and drown you!

"Oh, it's not fair. Why are you so unkind?"

"You call me unkind; have I ever struck you? Here I am, doing half the work of this house for you . . . "

"Yes, I know, but . . . "

"But? But what?"

"You say such unkind things to me."

"What difference does it make what I say? What are words? Are you telling me, your Bheji, what I can and can't say?"

"No, of course not, but if only . . . "

"If only what? I can say some sentences beginning with if only, too. If only you were a better helpmate; if only you did not want enough children to populate a city and if only you could be some help to my son in trying to make his living in this difficult country! What about that, eh? How can you make him happy when you cannot help him?"

"We *were* happy!"

"Oh, you were happy, were you? When did you make him so

160

happy, tell me that!"

"Before you came!" said Shanti, goaded, and then retreated backwards across the kitchen as Ranbir rounded on her, eyes flashing, and brandished the wooden spoon she had been cleaning.

"Oh, so now you say it is my fault, do you?"

"No, no, I didn't say . . . "

"What on earth is going on in here? For heaven's sake!" Perry, arriving home from work, walked into the kitchen to find that the pleasant smell of food which had drawn him there was being offset by shouted recriminations and threatening gestures with dripping wet cooking utensils.

"I am glad you are here, son. Perhaps you can convince your wife she should be courteous to her Bheji!"

"I wasn't discourteous! You won't stop nagging and nagging." Shanti burst into tears, flung the end of her sari over her face and fled. Perry pursued her to the bedroom and found her face down on the bed, banging it with clenched fists. Her bangles clashed and glittered as her wrists rose and fell.

"Shanti . . . "

"It isn't fair! It isn't fair!"

"Look, what happened?"

"She keeps on and on. She wants me to go to evening classes and all I said was I might not be quick at learning and she started going on and on, saying I was lazy and made you unhappy and when I said I didn't, she turned on me and . . . "

"Oh, Shanti, for God's sake, whatever does it all matter?" Perry sighed with exasperation, sitting down on the bed beside her. "This is not what I want to come home to. I have had a hell of a day, a *hell* of a day. If there were twenty-four working hours in it, they would not be enough for all I must get through and then I come home and find you fighting with my mother . . . "

"It is your mother who is fighting with me!"

"Well, none of it is so very important from what you say. I will say to her, just forget it and let us have something to eat. Come, Shanti." He raised her, kindly enough, from the bed. "Wipe your face. That's right." He produced a handkerchief and did it for her. "It would be as well if you did at least attempt those evening classes, you know."

"All right." Shanti sat on the edge of the bed and tried not to droop visibly. At least she was still sharing the bed with Perry.

161

She did not want to jeopardise that. "I'll go to the classes. I'll try."

"There's a good girl. By the way," said Perry casually, "I've got us a lodger. He's moving in next week."

Sunder and Balbir were half excited by the novelty of sleeping downstairs behind a curtain and half annoyed at being ejected from their room and at one point, being acute enough to tell who had the most power in the household, complained to their grandmother about it. But here they misjudged her. Ranbir, usually indulgent to her grandchildren, startled them with a quelling eye and a still more quelling, "If the two of you want clothes that will fit and Sunder wants his own cricket bat next year, you'd better co-operate when your father tries to get the money to buy them with!"

The lodger himself was a gentle, well-mannered youth who worked in the civil service in some humble capacity and on his own admission wasn't likely to progress to an early promotion because his shoulder-length hair and his habit of wearing a sweater with no shirt under it raised his superiors' eyebrows too much and Rick Medway's mild exterior concealed a vein of what they called obstinacy and he called resolution. "You have to be resolute about being yourself, or people will mould you like putty."

Mr Medway was refreshingly unprejudiced and liked living in an Indian household, but irritated Perry and Ranbir by talking about the spiritual riches of India and how he longed to sit at the feet of a guru and experience a totally unmaterialistic society. "Unmaterialistic?" snorted Ranbir. "India? I'll say this for the English. They never talk about dowries!"

He also liked Indian vegetarian food and home-made music. Since providing breakfast and an evening meal was part of the arrangement, his taste in food was most convenient, but the music threatened to bring his tenancy to a premature end. It wasn't so bad when he practised playing the guitar and singing on his own; Shanti indeed liked his singing. She especially appreciated the rhythms of a song called 'If I Had A Hammer', and when Mr Medway kindly wrote down the words so that Perry could translate them for her, its impassioned desire for justice appealed to her. Shanti could have done with, not a physical, but a psychic hammer with which to hit her mother-in-law.

162

The trouble arose, however, when Mr Medway took to having friends round for group practices, usually in the evening. The singing and the music echoed through the house, disturbing Sunder's homework and waking the younger children up, intruding into the conversation when there were guests, and shaking the floor when, as frequently happened, the performers took to stamping in time with the beat. Ranbir and Perry told her to tell him that this must stop. Neither offered to do it themselves and she knew why. Ranbir considered it good training in "responsibility" and Perry was too overworked to face it.

When she finally succeeded in explaining what the problem was, Rick was apologetic. His resolution, or obstinacy, evidently didn't extend to upsetting his timidly stammering landlady. But explaining took some time because of the language barrier. It was November by then and Shanti had plodded through nearly three months of English at evening classes, but what with extra cooking and laundry for Rick and sewing the piece-work she had now taken on in an attempt to refute Ranbir's accusations of being a bad helpmate, she had no leisure and few resources of energy to devote to home study. She had learned little and was falling behind her class. In his sojourn with the Virks, Rick Medway had acquired more Punjabi than Shanti had learned English and at least half of that difficult conversation was conducted in her own tongue.

After Christmas, she caught flu and could not go to classes for the first two weeks of term. Then the weather was too cold and wet for going out in the evening. Stealthily, without actually mentioning the matter, she dropped the classes.

But it was too much to hope that Ranbir wouldn't notice.

"If only you had kept your studies up, perhaps I would not have to deal with your son's teachers instead of you . . . "

"If only you had persisted with your lessons more, perhaps you could telephone the laundry about that lost sheet . . . "

"Balbir's headmaster wants to talk to us again and if only . . . "

"If only . . . why you did not . . . if only . . . if only . . . "

"Oh, no, let her be," said Nita, when Ranbir let fly with the remark about the headmaster on a Saturday when all three households had gathered in Mohan Lal's sitting room for tea and chit-chat. "Shanti is speaking better English than she did, Bheji, and she can read the English alphabet too."

"That is true. I can go on the tube by myself now. I can read the place names," said Shanti defensively.

163

Ranbir, for once, subsided.

"Are you having some difficulty with your boys at school?" Nita enquired of Shanti and Perry both together.

"Oh, with Balbir it is nothing much except that he seems to be better with his hands than at academic things. He would rather weed the garden than study! There is a different problem with Sunder: he works hard but some of the English boys laugh at his topknot and the way we do it up in a cloth."

Perry was able to speak frankly because the April evening was dry and the boys were all out playing. There was just, barely, room for a limited game of cricket in Mohan Lal's backyard. "The other day he came home with his face skinned on one side, where he had been knocked over. He made light of it himself but really, sometimes I feel it would be better if the boys did not grow up orthodox, if they were allowed to look the same as their classmates."

Kartar, Nita and Ranbir burst into an indignant chorus of protest. Oh dear, thought Shanti, sipping tea: more arguments. She was so tired of them.

If the little boys were outside, the girls were not. Mohan Lal's daughters Sita and Krishna were handing trays, Krishna with a slightly sulky and impatient air, while Nita's daughter Rose, perched on a settee with her feet not touching the ground, was having a private, whispered conversation with Shanti's Rupa, about birthday parties. "I will be eight years old this year, Rupa, and Mummy says I can have school friends to my party."

Shanti, overhearing them, seized her chance and interrupted the uncomfortable wrangle with, "How fast Rose is growing up!"

Nita responded to the oblique appeal, opted out of the argument and said to Leela, "Your two are shooting up as well. Sita must be seventeen now and Krishna is only just over a year younger, am I right? You are hoping they will both take A-levels?"

Leela sighed. She was in a depressed mood. They all knew why. Of late, her hair had gone grey and she had acquired several pounds of weight and Mohan Lal was amusing himself elsewhere in a manner which verged upon the blatant. He had always, as part of his sales patter, been flirtatious with female customers and within the family was known to have gone further than that. But hitherto he had avoided alerting the excellent gossip network among the local women. But lately, the word had gone round that he had been seen several times in the

164

George and Dragon at Southall, with a succession of English girls. Leela was now the subject of an unpleasant combination of pity and malice. Her depression was understandable.

Mention of her daughters made her brighten a little. "Yes, Sita is studying for A-levels these days and Krishna will take her O-levels this summer. Krishna is very good at studies."

"And then what do they hope to do?" said Nita.

Mohan Lal, who had not been caught up in the argument and had been listening to the peacemaking initiative with amusement, said, "I am anxious they should be educated; I think it is right that they should be educated, but as for working, they will not need to do that. Why should they? We will find them good husbands when they leave school, who will look after them as they should, so that they have money and are protected. They will have dowries. There will be no difficulty."

"I want to work," said Krishna suddenly and mutinously, pausing, teapot in hand. "I would like to work in publishing or advertising. There are interesting jobs there. Kitchen work is not interesting."

"Now that is nonsense," said Leela. "A woman is for children and for the house, and where would anyone be without them? They are most important. She is always wanting to go here and there with English school-friends. But I say to her, no, you are an Indian girl, and you should stay at home and help your mother."

"But housework's dull," complained Krishna. "There's no adventure in it; no pushing back the frontiers."

"What frontiers? Are you going to be an explorer?" demanded Mohan Lal. "You should be grateful you have parents who can watch over you. There are many dangers out in the world for beautiful girls." Mohan Lal's tone became indulgent. "And you and your sister will both be that," he said.

This was true, Shanti thought. Although her nieces were neither of them as fair-skinned as ideal Indian beauties should be, both had lovely features. Krishna was the one who was going to be really striking, with those flying eyebrows which might have been put there by a calligrapher's brush, and those long, slanting eyes. Sita's face was rounder, less definite, but sweeter in its expression; she was the gentle one of the pair.

The one, thought Shanti suddenly, most at risk from life and men; the one to whom terrible things might be done because she would be the worst at defending herself, and to be vulnerable

165

was to invite attack.

"We are hoping," Kartar was saying, "that Rose will do well in her schooling. She might become a teacher, perhaps. But it is certainly a worry with girls, how to safeguard them especially in this society."

"We also hope," said Nita, "that whatever Rose does, she will always keep our traditional standards. But I think if we bring her up with care she will not let us down, even if she goes to an English college and leaves home to study."

"Yes." Ranbir nodded. "If a girl loses her reputation, how will she find a good match? Even her brothers and sisters may find difficulty in such a case, Perry, and that is why it is so important that they should be orthodox and have the example of orthodox parents . . . "

The conversation was in danger of returning to its earlier, quarrelsome subject. But this time Mohan Lal intervened. "Oh, let us not argue! I have some good news. I have been saving it. I have had the letter, Shanti, that says when our father will be arriving. Now I have a car like you, I can meet him at the airport. It is two and a half weeks only, till he comes. We must arrange a reception committee."

"It is good for you to go about a little and have a change of scene. Your father is coming just at the right moment," Nita said, as she and Shanti hurried from the Terminal 3 car park at Heathrow towards the Arrivals building.

"Except that it is a weekday," said Shanti.

The reception committee was female except for Mohan Lal who had left Leela in charge of the shop. But neither Kartar nor Perry could arrange time off from their jobs and would not let their children miss school, either. Nita could drive the car, and had given Shanti a lift. "They will need two cars, anyway," Kartar said. "If Shanti goes in Mohan Lal's, how will the one car bring back an extra person and his luggage? Mohan Lal says he wants his daughters to be there."

Like Kartar, Mohan Lal had insisted that his son go to school, but "with girls it does not matter so much". Ranbir had stayed behind to welcome Shanti's children home from school. She was not interested in meeting Shanti's father in any case. She hadn't cared for Mr Bhatia the shopkeeper when she knew him in Delhi and hadn't changed her opinion. "But it is natural that you want to greet your father," she said, albeit brusquely, when

166

Shanti said, "Oh, I *must* be there."

Traffic had been heavy and Nita was a cautious driver. As a result, she and Shanti had reached Heathrow later than intended. In the Arrivals building, they found that the flight they had come to meet was already in and the first of its passengers were trickling out from the obstacle course of Immigration Control and Baggage Reclaim and Customs.

Shanti vividly remembered her own scared landing in Britain, and the way she had nervously attached herself to another Indian couple and simply followed them, doing whatever they did, until at last, as she walked through the final door, she had seen Mohan Lal waving at her. She had been secretly sick with terror that he wouldn't be there, that he had mistaken the day or she had given him the wrong date or she had inadvertently disembarked in the wrong country.

At first they couldn't see Mohan Lal in the crowd and it was Sita who finally saw them instead and came running to greet them. "Oh, you are here! We were all worried that perhaps you were not coming or you had had an accident with the car."

"We took good care," Nita said. "That is a beautiful salwar kameeze you have on, Sita. That pale green suits you. Where is your father?"

"Over there, with Krishna. This is a new outfit. Krishna has one as well. Hers is flame-coloured. Mummy said we should have new things to greet Dadaji in. Look, there is Krishna, with Daddy."

"Good, you have made it." Mohan Lal, who was not tall, was craning to see over the shoulders of a row of people in front, as the trickle of disembarking passengers became a stream. "And there he is!" He backed away from the fence of people in front and began to make swimming motions with his arms, shoving through the crowd towards the short, old man in the not very well-fitting Western suit, who had walked slowly into view.

Shanti did not follow at once. She had wanted to go home when their mother died, so as to be with him, but couldn't leave her family, and Mohan Lal had said he couldn't leave his shop. She hadn't therefore seen for herself, and no one in India had written to say, how much her father had changed.

She remembered him as a brisk, sturdily built shop proprietor, alert to the chance of profit, zestfully bargaining with customers, getting the better of most of them and then asserting that he was as good as giving away his wares to charity and would

167

be ruined if this went on.

Her father now was grey and tremulous and the reason why his suit didn't fit properly was because he had lost pounds since he first bought it.

Shanti stood where she was, hanging back, rearranging her ideas. And swallowing, as quickly as possible, the disappointment of a hope she had harboured without knowing it. The father she remembered might have been able to help her, might have been able to say something to Ranbir or Perry, to make them understand her unhappiness. The father now walking beside a fellow-passenger, a bespectacled young Indian whose luggage trolley he seemed to be sharing, was too old, too frail, to carry her burdens. She would have to manage them herself.

Then she was hurrying after Mohan Lal. Their father had one hand protectively on top of the luggage on the trolley, but he forgot about it when he saw his family. He opened his arms and Mohan Lal went into them. He saw Shanti beyond, waved a knotted brown hand at her and beckoned her to share the embrace. His eyes were red-veined and dim, and they were wet with emotion. "My children, my children!"

"And seven grandchildren," said Mohan Lal proudly. "Though they are not all here. How is everyone at home? How is our sister?"

"Oh, she is well, very well. She sends messages, they all send messages, Dinesh and the children and ... " He disengaged himself from them and turned round. The young man with the trolley had halted and was waiting beside it, making no move to shift any of the luggage off. Mohan Lal and Shanti looked at him enquiringly.

"This is their message," said Mr Bhatia emotionally, catching the bespectacled young man's arm and pulling him towards them. "Oh, what a time we had arranging clearance to enter Britain so we could both come together. I would have been here before but for that. This is the ambassador from Dinesh and your sister, Mohan Lal. They have been so sad that there was a quarrel between you and Dinesh, and not once have you even put a message to Dinesh in a letter, or gone to Delhi to see them. Such a sad misunderstanding ... "

"Misunderstanding?" said Mohan Lal in amazement.

"Yes, oh yes, Dinesh explained it all to me, how he tried to help but was not clever enough and made such foolish mistakes, but he hopes you will forgive him now, after so long, and here is

168

his ambassador, as I was saying. He has come to make his way in England too. This is his adopted son, his nephew that was orphaned, Hari."

There seemed nothing wrong with Hari, who was polite, helpful about the luggage, apologetic about being sprung on them all and willing, he said, to stay in a boarding house until he could find a room somewhere. He had some money. A friend in Britain had opened a bank account for him and put some money in it. "The usual arrangement. Dinesh uncle advised me. I let my friend use some of mine when he visited India and he has paid me back this way."

"No, no, of course we can put you up," said Mohan Lal, although somewhat bemusedly. Sita and Krishna were already eyeing the unexpected arrival with shy interest. Hari was slightly built, but looked fit and was handsome in a somewhat expressionless fashion.

"Hari hopes to start a shop here," said Mr Bhatia. "I hope you will become good friends. Is it far to your place, son? I am feeling very tired. It was such a long flight."

"No, no, not far."

"Perhaps one day you will go to Delhi and make it up properly with Dinesh. Your sister is missing you and now she will be missing me and Hari as well. I should like to see all my family good friends before I die, son. Ever since your dear mother died, I am thinking, perhaps I have not long . . . "

His voice was monotonous but quite loud and when it cracked on the edge of tears, numerous pairs of eyes began swivelling towards them.

"I think," said Nita decisively, "that we should get home. Mr Bhatia is very weary, I can see that. The luggage can go in my car, as there is room, and if Sita and Krishna come with me now, then you can go with Mohan Lal and your father, Shanti, and Hari too."

Sita's expression became a little wistful and Hari looked faintly amused, as though he had not expected to be organised like this, and said mildly, "I'm sorry I can't travel in the same car with my pretty foster-cousins," but it wasn't a serious protest. Nita's arrangement was followed. Shanti sat in the back of Mohan Lal's Mini with Hari and they made polite conversation, while her father sat in Mohan Lal's front passenger seat and cried, with exhaustion and sentiment, all the way back to Southall.

169

Chapter Fourteen

Tears at the Wedding
1971

"You seem," said the spectacled woman behind the desk, "to have a thorough knowledge of office management and you're obviously willing to attend to details." She was just on the turn between youth and early middle age, with a trace of fading at the temples of the drawn-back mousey hair and a few lines round the eyes and mouth of her round, unmade-up face. She was the Chief Personnel Officer for the Allbright Group of Companies in whose head office, Allbright House, they were all sitting, but she did not seem quite sure of herself. She glanced at the men on either side of her and looked relieved when they nodded agreement.

Her colleagues had been introduced to Perry as the Group Security Officer and the Chief Office Manager. The latter, who was wiry and dark and chain-smoked with an air of suppressed energy, said, "Your duties would centre mainly on this building where you would be my assistant. But I sometimes make trips to deal with other Group buildings – leasing new ones, deciding on refurbishment programmes and so forth – and then you would have to deputise for me here. We have a permanent maintenance team for the air conditioning and other mechanical services; you would be responsible for summoning them if a fault occurred but otherwise, you would be carrying out routine office checks, ensuring that anything that's wanted, from the soap in the washrooms to the Xerox toner to new furniture, is supplied on time and in the right quantity." His alert brown eyes kept scanning Perry from head to foot, possibly assessing the keenness of Perry's own eyesight when it came to registering dwindling soap supplies or rickety chairs. "It's a responsible job," he said.

"This is of course purely an office building," said the personnel officer, reassuringly. "We do have factories; one of our companies manufactures the Allbright cleaning products, like polishes and oven cleaners, and another makes vacuum cleaners and the like. But you wouldn't be involved with them. Your hours would be nine to five thirty, five days a week and you would not normally be expected to come early or leave late."

"My staff open and close the building," the security man agreed. He was burly and watchful and might as well have had *Ex-CID* tattooed on his forehead.

"You might occasionally be asked to attend at a weekend or in the evening," said the personnel officer. Her name was Miss Derwent. "Courses and seminars are sometimes held then, in which case it would be your job to arrange tables and easels or slide equipment and order coffee. But these occasions are rare and you would be paid overtime."

"You might also be called out at night in case of an emergency, such as fire or flood or break-in," said the office manager, a little pugnaciously. "And that would *not* mean extra pay. It's regarded as built-in to the job."

"I understand," said Perry. "But," he added with a smile, "I don't imagine that such things occur every five minutes. I live quite close, anyway."

Miss Derwent smiled back at him and said, "You feel you are up to the task, then?"

He was going to get it, Perry thought. He could hardly wait. Allbright House was purpose-built, with huge bronzed windows, granite-faced pillars in the reception area, strip-lighting, air conditioning and a lift which had wafted him from the ground floor to the fifth with swift, purring precision.

His present employers inhabited a tall, narrow, Dickensian affair with sub-standard plumbing, electricity installed as an afterthought and a dreadful lift which stuck so often that most people preferred to climb the stairs. This building, by contrast, would be a pleasure to work in.

"I feel quite sure that I'm up to it," he said firmly. "I think I can do it not just adequately, but well. The hours and conditions are quite acceptable." They were a damn sight more acceptable than the present regime of early starts, late returns home and books on the dining room table every weekend in a desperate effort to keep up with an impossible workload. The money was much better, too.

The burly security officer was scribbling something on a pad.

171

He pushed it in front of the others. The interviewers exchanged glances. Miss Derwent frowned. A wordless message appeared to pass from mind to mind. With the air of one acting under some kind of psychic duress, Miss Derwent turned back to Perry. She gave him a winning smile. "Would you be kind enough to wait outside for a moment while we confer?"

The outer office was quiet and comfortable, with low seats covered in orange moquette, a rubber plant in one corner and reading matter – a house journal, the *Financial Times* and a copy of *Punch* – spread invitingly out on the smoked glass top of a coffee table.

There was also an L-shaped unit complete with secretary, who was busy with phone and typewriter but paused to enquire if he would like some tea or coffee. "No, thank you," said Perry. He was as taut as the strings of Rick Medway's guitar. He wanted this job. He could do it and he needed it; nothing must go wrong now. He sank into one of the orange-covered seats and waited, quivering.

After what seemed a very long time, the phone buzzed and the secretary, having answered it and listened, looked his way and said, "Please go in again, Mr Virk."

The panel were sitting behind their table as he had left them. Their faces were serious and they had a markedly shoulder-to-shoulder, safety-in-numbers air. Before Miss Derwent had opened her mouth, he knew what her first words would be. She looked so extremely reluctant to say them.

"We are so sorry, Mr Virk. We probably led you to think . . . the fact is, your experience is excellent – excellent, exactly what we are looking for. But there is another applicant with virtually the same experience, and slightly more of it, and although it is a very near thing, we feel . . . we should tell you at once, and not just send you off to wait for a letter. We feel that you are really keen about this post and we wouldn't like to think that you might let an offer go because you were hoping . . . I'm sorry."

Perry looked her in the eye and heard himself say, quite calmly and as if from a long way off, "If the fact that I am not English has anything to do with it, I would prefer it if you told me."

If he had stood up and removed his trousers, they could not have looked more embarrassed.

"Please, Mr Virk! I can assure you . . . " began Miss Derwent in a scandalised voice.

The chain-smoking office manager stopped her, ramming the stub of his latest cigarette violently into an ashtray and twisting it into extinction as though it were a personal enemy. "For God's sake, let's tell the man the truth! I get sick of flummery and doubletalk. He's entitled to know."

"There's nothing to be gained by . . . " The security officer's eyes did not meet Perry's as he started his protest. The office manager cut him short as well.

"There might be something to be gained from his point of view. Why shouldn't he know where he stands? Mr Virk, it is not a matter of you being Indian. We have other Indian employees here, and we have experienced no difficulties. But you are in a separate category, Mr Virk. You wear a turban. It makes you look different . . . "

"I'm a Sikh," said Perry. His voice still sounded toneless and remote. "It is a requirement of my religion. I regard the turban as something to be proud of, an honourable symbol."

"I realise that and so do we all, at this table. I served in India during the war and met Sikh officers. But to many people – to many in this building, I'm afraid – you would simply appear outlandish and they might find it hard to accept you."

"You see," said Miss Derwent, grabbing the initiative back, "you would have to deal personally with so many people. Office managers come into contact with everyone from the chief executive down to the post room boy. There could be difficulties with some individuals."

"After a time," said Perry, speaking up for himself largely because there seemed to be nothing to lose, "they would get used to it and then they wouldn't notice."

"That could be true," said the security officer, while his office management colleague convulsively lit another cigarette. "But if you were wrong, if things didn't go well, you would feel worse than if you never took the job on in the first place. Angrier, I fancy."

"I'd be prepared to risk it."

Why am I bothering? he asked himself. I'm desperate to find another job but I don't need to exhibit that to these people. I should shut up.

Personnel and Security were trying simultaneously to bring the interview to a close, and interrupting each other. Each stopped courteously to allow the other to speak, and gave him an opportunity to invade the resultant vacuum.

173

"Are you saying that if I were not a Sikh, I would be appointed?"

There was a silence. Then the security officer said shortly, "Yes. I think it's fair to say that."

"I see. And if I came back next week without a turban, I would get the job?"

"We couldn't possibly give an undertaking like that," said Miss Derwent in a shocked voice.

"Another suitable applicant could come along in the interim and be appointed," explained the office manager.

"But you have in fact no such applicant in view now?" said Perry. "You said you had at first but I take it that that was just an excuse?"

"Mr Virk, we would not for the world offer you inducements to abandon your convictions."

"I think," said the security officer, moving in on the conversation with massive authority, "that this interview should terminate. It is becoming embarrassing."

He raged inwardly all the way home, glaring at startled strangers on the bus and in the street. *Embarrassing*, indeed! *Difficulties*, indeed! There are worse things than either of those and one was being stuck in a job which was hell and having no alternative but unemployment. You try it and see how you like it. You won't talk fastidious nonsense about embarrassment and difficulties then. You'll have bigger things to worry about. And what the devil do you mean by saying you wouldn't for the world offer inducements? You're doing precisely that; can't you hear yourself?

He had had real hopes of that job. It was right for him and he was right for it; he was even right as the assistant to that chain-smoking bundle of suppressed energy, the Chief Office Manager. There was a directness about him which Perry liked. I could get on with him, Perry thought. The security man, who had written the note, might be another matter but perhaps he would get through even to him, in the end.

But he wouldn't have the chance. Once again, he was to be pushed back into the muddy pond of the job that he'd been trying to climb out of now for the best part of a year. This was the fourth time he had got to interview stage, only to be turned away as soon as they actually saw him.

He had taken a day of his precious annual leave in order to attend this interview. Not that he ever did much with his annual

174

leave except sleep. They couldn't afford to go away anywhere and he was usually so tired that he didn't mind. But that was precisely why he wanted a different job. He wanted to enjoy life a little, and see something more of England than just London. He'd like to take Shanti and the children on a proper holiday, to Bournemouth, perhaps, or Cornwall. One or two people at work had spoken highly of Cornwall. Would he ever manage it now?

He strode militantly up his little front path, shoved his door key roughly into the lock and marched in, slamming the door after him. And then paused, head cocked, at the tang of sandal-wood incense and the sound of female singing from the living room.

There was a Sangeet party going on in there, the traditional ladies' gathering before a marriage, at which they sang songs to encourage and congratulate the prospective bride.

He had completely forgotten that Shanti had offered to accommodate this one. He had completely forgotten that, in two days time, it would be Sita's wedding.

He stepped over the pile of abandoned footwear which lay outside the living room door, and peered in. The furniture had been pushed back against the wall and the floor spread with white sheeting and the ladies, in their most colourful silks, sat on it swaying and singing like a melodious flower-bed. Ranbir was seated cross-legged in the middle of the floor, wearing her best ivory-coloured salwar kameeze and tapping a hand-drum. Sita, the only one in dull clothes, donned on purpose so that her wedding day beauty should make a greater impact, was enthroned on a pile of cushions. She was smiling. Shanti, sitting with her back propped against the opposite wall, saw her husband's head come round the door and smiled too, but with a movement of her own head, signed to him to leave them to it.

She did not hurry out to ask him how the interview had gone for the very good reason that he hadn't told her about it. He'd left the house at the usual time and taken a bus to the British Museum for the morning instead. He had no business to feel aggrieved now.

He withdrew, feeling extremely aggrieved. He'd given permission for the Sangeet to be held here but he disapproved intensely of the marriage to which it was attached and he'd said so, loudly, although nobody had listened, and certainly not Shanti, who took the view that it was romantic, a real love-match.

175

This in Perry's opinion was balderdash but when he said that to Shanti, she had been hurt. That, he now recalled, was the moment when he consented to hosting the Sangeet. Which had robbed him of Shanti's attention just when he wanted it most.

He stood glowering in the hallway and then realised that Sangeet or no Sangeet, he needed food. He made for the kitchen and found a number of men, the escorts of the singing ladies, helping themselves to curry and an array of savoury snacks which had been left ready.

There were murmurs of greeting and Mohan Lal advanced on him beaming. "I am always telling Leela, she should learn to cook like Shanti!"

"I'm sure Leela's grateful for the advice," said Perry nastily. "So you're going ahead with this . . . this farce!"

"Of course we are going ahead with it! What a persistent fellow you are, Perry. The Registry Office ceremony is tomorrow and we have booked Southall Town Hall for Saturday and that is that. My goodness, Perry, it will be a great big wedding and the local press and TV are coming; it is to be part of some big TV programme on Indian immigrants in England. How could we disappoint them, eh? Anyone would think you had something personal against Hari, the way you talk."

"He is too close a member of your family to be marrying your daughter, for one thing . . . "

"Oh, come on now, Perry. There is no blood relationship. He is the nephew of my sister's husband."

"Who adopted him. That makes him Sita's cousin in effect, and it is not Sikh or Hindu custom to marry cousins, even adopted ones. It makes families too inward-looking," said Perry contentiously. It was perfectly obvious that the marriage was going ahead and he had indeed said all this before to no avail, but he was in a mood to squabble with somebody.

"Nevertheless, there is no law against it either; there would be no law against it even if they were cousins by blood instead of by courtesy," said Mohan Lal. "And I tell you, he has fallen for Sita. From the first day he was with us, he could not keep his eyes off her. What if custom is being broken? It was against today's customs when you married Shanti!"

"Shanti wasn't brought up by Dinesh." Perry seized a plate and supplied himself with viands, which he would have to eat standing up, since all the seats at the kitchen table were occupied. It was the end of the working day and all the menfolk

176

seemed to have arrived, except for Kartar. "I say it to you again, that he has Dinesh for a foster-parent is quite a drawback."

Mohan Lal rolled his eyes upwards and proceeded to herd Perry, plate of food and all, out into the comparative privacy of the hallway. "Now, listen. All that is over. How many more times must I tell you? When I went to India two months ago, I put everything right between me and Dinesh. He made me understand, he did not mean to make so many muddles, and he thought he was entitled to what he paid himself . . . "

"To what he grabbed, you mean."

"No, no, you are too severe. He has treated my sister better, too; I asked her and she said she had no complaints. Poor Savitri, she has not been so well this last year – she has had some woman's complaint or other. But Dinesh has been very patient, she says. I think he has made a good job of bringing up Hari. There is just nothing against the boy. Sita is not complaining," said Mohan Lal. "He is a good-looking boy with charming manners . . . "

"They're all on the surface," said Perry. "You can't tell what he's thinking. He says all the right things but it is just words."

"Now how do you know that? Upon my word, I can't make you out. You come rushing round to warn me against Hari as soon as you hear of my plans but you have no *reason*, no reason at all, except for this talk of adopted cousins and Dinesh. Hari is hardworking enough. He has arranged to take on a small shop already; he had quite a lot of money over here. He has been planning to come to this side for years and he has been preparing the ground for years too, with his father's help . . . "

"No doubt that means money that Dinesh filched from his customers, suppliers and personal friends!"

"What is *wrong* with you these days, Perry? You carp at everything. I tell you I have done my best for Sita. I am giving them the deposit on a house. There's no accommodation over Hari's shop but after all, a house is a better investment. And my father is so pleased. It means so much to him that all should be put right within the family. There is no rift now, and we are cementing the bond with this marriage. My father is not shaking his head because Hari is an adopted cousin. What of it? he says. Hari and Sita do not think of each other as cousins; they met as strangers would. Why let custom stand in their way? Times are changing. He is overjoyed, I am telling you."

Perry refrained from saying that Mr Bhatia senior had in his

177

old age turned into a sentimental nitwit and asked instead, "Where is he, your father?"

"Oh, minding the shop. He likes doing that, it keeps him busy, and it gives Leela more free time. But we shall shut the shop on Saturday. That will be a special occasion. The first wedding among our children, eh, Perry? That's an occasion to remember for ever."

The doorbell rang. "That's probably Kartar," said Perry, glad enough to change the subject. There was no sense in trying to stop a juggernaut. He'd said what he thought and he could do no more. He hardly knew himself why he was so instinctively and intensely against this marriage. It was certainly not just that it was against tradition. He had once been nearer breaking with tradition than Mohan Lal knew. Mohan Lal knew nothing at all about Pat Holtsby. He gave up. On Saturday, he would do what was expected of him as a family member and arrive at the town hall early to help put up the decorations.

Sita was certainly not unhappy. As Leela and Shanti led her into the town hall on the Saturday morning, she tried to droop and look reluctant but her eyes were sparkling beneath her veil.

But Perry, standing with the rest of the earlier arrivals to watch her enter, thought she was a touching figure all the same, so small and pliant-shouldered, and so enswathed, head to foot, in her scarlet silk wedding finery criss-crossed with thick gold embroidery, that despite those gleaming eyes, it was difficult to think of her as Sita and not as an anonymous gift-wrapped parcel.

Even her hands were netted with fine gold chains and another chain, set with rubies, ran from nostril to ear. Leela had had some of her own wedding jewellery cleaned and reset for Sita. The rest had been bought in advance over the years.

There would be a similar set for Krishna, one day. Shanti had had such wedding jewellery, too. At his own marriage, it had not occurred to Perry that his bride looked as though she were wearing highly ornamental fetters. When he glanced at Sita, it was the first thing that sprang to his mind.

Not to anyone else's mind, however. Most of the guests were already assembled in the hall and appreciative murmurs greeted the entrance of the bride. Perry, watching in the company of Ranbir and the children, marvelled at how big the Indian population now was in this south west corner of London, and also how big an acquaintance Mohan Lal had made among them.

He recognised Mohan Lal's close friends, because they came to the Bhatia flat often. There was the enormous Sharma family who lived in his own street, who always had battalions of friends and relatives staying with them (and seemed today to have brought the lot); the lean, Nehru-like Dr Chowdhuri who had lately bought the local GP's practice; the Patels who ran the coffee shop; Mr Wali from the post office.

Kartar had brought along his present tenants and some extra guests too. His first family of tenants, Mr and Mrs Satinder Singh and their two sons Surjit and Charan, had come from Bradford to visit relatives who had lately settled in Southall, had called on Kartar and been swept in. Surjit and Charan were now twelve and ten respectively and except that Charan was slightly shorter, looked nearly identical in their clean white shirts, long grey trousers and dark blue topknot caps.

But there were many other guests who were either strangers to Perry, or were faces which he had seen but to which he could not put names. The hall was full, and it was far from small.

The hall's interior had been transformed and Perry's arms were aching from the part he had played in transforming it, standing on stepladders and leaning at impossible angles to hammer in the tacks which held the paper-chains and bunches of balloons. Seats had been arranged in rows, with a gangway down the middle. A long table bearing refreshments under clingfilm wraps had been set up at one end and a portable platform had been assembled at the other. It had corner posts twined with tinsel and connected at their tops by crosspieces, to make a frame over which the embroidered canopy could be hung. In the middle of the platform, in a shallow iron receptacle on a low tripod, a small fire was burning, presided over by an elderly priest.

Sita's attendants took her across the hall, not straight to the platform, but to a couple of chairs which had been arranged to one side. They enthroned her on one of them, carefully arranging the glittering gold-encrusted pleats of her sari. There was a surge forward as guests unslung cameras and hastened to jostle the press and TV for the best positions. Perry, joining in automatically, helped the TV crew to shoo people out of the way of the camera, and when Hari arrived, escorted by Mohan Lal and Kartar and peering from behind the fringe of his gold head-dress, he helped in clearing a path so that Sita could rise and be led to meet her bridegroom.

He stepped back to watch the ceremony, and a woman reporter, notebook in hand, edged up alongside him. She studied the scene intently as Sita's veil and Hari's headdress were put back so that they could see each other's faces and then turned to Perry. "I thought I heard you speak English to someone a moment ago. Yes? I'm from the *Lanesden Advertiser*. Tell me, have they met before? Or are they complete strangers?"

"No, no. They know each other quite well; in fact, the groom has lived in the bride's household as a guest for some time. He has stayed with another friend – my brother, as it happens – for the past week, though. It's all been arranged with the approval of the families, of course, but no one has been pushed into anything."

"Is this now the way things are being done? We have always understood that the couple usually had little choice and often did not know each other at all."

"Well, it varies a good deal. But there was certainly choice and previous acquaintance with Sita and Hari. The ceremony of introducing them to each other, that you saw just now, was just a . . . a ritual."

The couple had now been enthroned side by side and the photography had started up again. The reporter moved away and Shanti appeared with Nita, both of them very elegant, respectively in deep crimson, and royal blue with gold embroidery. Shanti, however, seemed tired, perhaps because she had risen early to go to her brother's house and help the bride to dress, but also perhaps because the atmosphere in their own house had not, last night, been happy. Perry admitted regretfully to himself that because of his disappointment over Allbrights, he had let his irritation over the Sangeet show too much. Shanti was not responsible for the Allbright debacle and she was within her rights in offering to accommodate a Sangeet for a niece whose own home had no room big enough.

He had in fact behaved badly and he knew it. That his mother had taken a cue from him and positively harried Shanti over some ridiculous triviality concerned apparently with the consumption of string on a laundry parcel, did not make him feel any better.

"Well," said Shanti, "this is it for Sita."

"This was it yesterday morning, at the Registrar's," said Perry with gloom, but also with an attempt at a friendly, husbandly exchange with her. "That was when they were married according to the law of the land."

"It will be all right. Why shouldn't it?" Shanti looked with smiling approval at the principals. Hari was sitting very upright, headdress folded into a glittering crown, well-scrubbed hands flat on his knees. He had a new grey suit for the occasion and he was undeniably handsome.

"I think perhaps it will be," said Nita. She and Kartar too had shaken their heads over the cousinship and over Hari's connection with Dinesh. But now she said, "We have had Hari with us for a week, you know. He has made himself very agreeable. I know Dinesh is no good. But Hari isn't his son; he's only a nephew. He may be quite different."

"Let us hope so," said Perry.

A few feet away, Ranbir too had been buttonholed by a reporter, a TV man this time, who had apparently covered a Sikh wedding in the past and was intrigued because the Hindu ceremony was different. "Yes, you are right, Hindu weddings are differently arranged," Ranbir was saying, and if there was a trace of disapproval in her voice, at least the reporter probably couldn't detect it. Perry reckoned with a private grin that his mother was relieved to be rescued from Mrs Swarup Sharma, whose carping tongue she disliked and who had been grumbling into her ear because meat dishes were being served.

"At a Sikh wedding," Ranbir now explained, as a cameraman moved towards her, trailing flex, "everyone is seated on the floor and men would be on one side and women on the other . . . the couple would walk round our Holy Book instead of round a fire . . . yes, that is the fire, up on the platform. They're just going up now . . . "

"And what," the reporter was saying to Ranbir, "is really the difference between Hindus and Sikhs? Sikh men wear turbans, of course; I take it that there is a religious significance . . . ?"

The ceremony continued. On the platform the priest was reading a religious text, but quietly, for the benefit of the couple and their immediate sponsors: Mohan Lal and Leela. Mohan Lal's twelve year old son Chandra Lal was on the platform too, taking it all very seriously, carrying out his first duty as a man. He was very much like his sister Krishna, with the same winged eyebrows and fair complexion.

People moved into place in the rows of seats, but did so restlessly, from time to time moving out again to partake of the refreshments, from which the wraps had now been removed by the caterers' staff. The TV camera crew were trying to set up their camera anew to focus on the platform and were having trouble. "Whichever way we aim the lens, we've either got the canopy's gold fringe in the way, or else it's a tinsel-twined upright," one of the crew explained, as they gave up trying to shoot from the sides of the hall and wheeled their apparatus squarely in the middle of the gangway. "Sorry about this, folks," he added to a group of people who were attempting to use the gangway. "But we can't shoot from anywhere else. Maybe you can squeeze past." The guests squeezed by good-humouredly enough but the camera rocked alarmingly; the film was likely to show the ceremony pictured at some avant garde angles.

The following week, however, Perry was wryly impressed when he saw the wedding featured in the programme about immigrants. Most of the avant garde angles had been edited out, and Ranbir, whose interview was included, was a figure of stature and authority as she held forth on the difference between the Sikh and Hindu communities.

He watched the programme, however, with considerable cynicism. For all the while he had stood there, listening to his mother, the memory of that interview at Allbrights had been smouldering inside his brain, and behind the pleasant smile appropriate to a wedding guest, his spirit had been not smiling in the least.

The couple circumnavigated the holy fire, Sita following Hari. A poem of wellwishing was read, which someone had written for the occasion. The cold refreshments proved to have been merely a snack. "No, no, that's nothing," said Mohan Lal when Perry, making sociable conversation, complimented him on the arrangements. "There will be a proper hot sit-down meal in another room soon."

The meal was duly served, the bride and groom seated side by side at the centre of the main table. When it was over, a black Pontiac drew up outside the town hall and in a flurry of excitement, the guests poured out on to the steps and the pavement to see Sita drive away with Hari. They were going straight back to Mohan Lal's flat. "They are using the girls' room," Mohan Lal said, "and Krishna has a camp-bed in ours. Chandra Lal is relieved he does not have to have Hari squeezed in with him any more, the way he was at first."

Sita had continued to smile and sparkle quietly all through the day but when it came to getting into the car beside Hari, her eyes filled and overflowed. Leela, Krishna and then Shanti overflowed with her, and even Nita and Ranbir showed signs of becoming tearful.

"My goodness, she is not even going away!" Mohan Lal said. "Look at my womenfolk, Perry; what a sight. Those two will be living with us until they find a house and here are all the women weeping as though they were going to the ends of the earth for good. Why do women always cry at weddings? I am the one who should be crying. The bills I shall have to pay for all this! I pity any man who has six daughters instead of only two. Two are bad enough."

"Tell me," Perry said idly to Shanti later, as they prepared for the night, "why *do* women always cry at weddings?"

"Mmm?" Shanti was very tired indeed. She sat on her dressing table stool and brushed her long hair with slow sweeps as though the brush were heavy.

"I said, why do women burst into tears at weddings? And why do the brides themselves dissolve like that? Even you did, I remember."

"We get scared. It's the moment when we leave our own families and join a strange one," said Shanti, putting the brush back on the dressing table and tidying some make-up items rather concentratedly. "And sometimes girls are nervous of the wedding night or their mothers-in-law."

"Oh? Well, I can understand the brides crying," said Perry in a mild voice. "But why the other women?"

"Most of the others are already married," said Shanti. Her voice was toneless. "The brides might be frightened about the unknown but they all think, beneath all that, that once they are used to the unknown, they are going to be marvellously happy. But the other women know . . . what life is really like. We cry for the brides because they don't."

There was a silence. "Are you," said Perry carefully, at last, "trying to tell me something, Shanti?"

"Perhaps." Shanti went on rearranging bottles and jars, pushing them round the dressing table with a persistent scrape-scrape.

"Well, *what* are you trying to tell me? Stop fiddling with those things there, Shanti, and turn round and look at me. If you have anything to say, then come out with it. Don't hint."

183

"I am not hinting. I am just saying." Shanti's hands became still but she would not look round at him.

"But what are you saying? That Sita may not be happy with Hari? Well, I said I did not like this match but it is Mohan Lal and Leela's business, I suppose, and perhaps I am wrong, and I for one certainly hope so. You seemed to think it was all right. Perhaps," said Perry, coming to the point, "you are trying to tell me that you are not happy with me?"

Shanti still would not speak. Her loose hair swung forward, hiding her face.

"I've tried to be a good husband, to look after you and the children. I've never ill-treated you or been unfaithful to you. Have I?"

"No."

"Then what," said Perry, "is your complaint?"

Shanti's head came up. "You know what is the answer. You *know* what is the answer! Why do you make me say it? You are always so . . . so far away, so preoccupied; work, work, work, you never come home but you bring work with you and you swallow your food and lose yourself in this work . . . "

"If I didn't, I'd like to know where we'd be! I earn my living doing this job and I must get it done somehow."

"I know that and I try to understand and help you but it is always, always: there is no let-up and you always have such a cross face; I am tired of seeing your cross face! Why do you not get another job? This one is hell for us all; it is hell for me and for the children . . . "

"For the children? Well, if I am sometimes impatient with the children, at least I feed and clothe them. A bit of impatience will do them no harm. When have I ever been unkind to them or not interested in their doings and their education? Someone must be firm with Balbir, he does not study enough for a boy turned eleven and . . . "

"Yes, you are impatient with them and not only when they are behaving badly. It is all the time! It's not fair. It's *not fair!*" Shanti suddenly banged small clenched fists on her knees. "You and your mother too, you are not fair to me. You were not fair to me, being angry about the Sangeet. You *said* we could have it here, you *knew* it would be going on. And that is just one thing. I try so hard and I love you so much and it all goes for nothing. I work and work – you think I don't but I do; so much sewing I do, my eyes ache with it, my head aches. For months now I have had to take two Anadin tablets when first I wake up, because I wake up with headaches. And always, all I see at breakfast or when you come home at night is your cross face, and all day long it is your mother's cross face. I am using too much string, I should be learning English, I am not working hard enough, I am this, I am that, and all of it wrong. No, I am not happy, I am not happy, and it *isn't fair*!" Shanti's voice shot up to a shriek.

"Sssh. Bheji will hear."

"Let her! I don't care! You don't know what she is like when you're not here. You see glimpses only!" said Shanti on a hiccup, and buried her face in her hands.

"Shanti . . . "

He was angry, partly because much of what she said was perfectly true. But he had expected his gentle Shanti, somehow, to understand, to make allowances for his short temper, to find ways of pleasing her mother-in-law, and it seemed to him that she had failed him.

He wanted to shout back at her, to relieve his secret rage once more by attacking someone else. But he knew he must not.

As kindly as he could, he took her hand and led her from the dressing table to the bed and got into it with her, lying with her in his arms, cradling her against him, stroking her thick, dark, shampoo-scented hair and murmuring comforting endearments.

She moved against him and he knew that she wanted him to make love to her but he could not. It was as if his bitterness had gone deep within him and corroded even his manhood. For the first time in his life, he could not spring erect at will.

In Mohan Lal's flat, Sita also lay in her husband's arms. They held her firmly and Hari too was murmuring contented endearments into his wife's hair. Sita sighed, filled with gladness and relief.

She had been nervous. When it came to it, to the point of being alone with Hari and getting into bed with him, she had forgotten that during the fourteen months she had known him she had fallen in love with him, and remembered only that he was a stranger from India, that her father had once disliked and distrusted his foster-father, and that Uncle Perry had come to the house and spent hours trying to talk Mohan Lal out of arranging this marriage.

But after all, it was all right. No bridegroom could have loved more gently, more expertly, more patiently, making her laugh by taking his glasses off to come to bed and then saying that he couldn't see her clearly without his glasses so that he could only discover how beautiful she was by touch; and caressing her until she was ready for him and then slipping into her as easily as a hand into a silken glove.

There was nothing to fear. They were going to be happy. Tomorrow they would have a day out in London, a married couple, unchaperoned, free to enjoy each other's company all they liked, and tomorrow night she would come to bed with joy, unafraid, to explore anew this magical business of making love.

She might even have conceived their first child already.

With her head in the curve of Hari's shoulder, Sita fell asleep.

Chapter Fifteen

Desperation
1971

On the Monday following the wedding, Shanti as usual rose early. As the children grew older there seemed ever more and more to do. Sunder was not a problem as far as getting him off on time was concerned; he was interested in his studies, had already decided to become an engineer and usually had his homework done and his satchel packed the night before. But since he had become part of the cricket team he was demanding about having clean white shirts and trousers for cricket days and Shanti never could remember which days they were. The school timetable was based on seven days instead of five, which meant that if Day One was on a Monday one week, it would fall on a Wednesday the following week, and it was hopelessly confusing.

On the other hand, Balbir, who was now nearly twelve, was the devil incarnate when it came to getting him off to school. His satchel was never ready and Balbir himself would do his best to vanish. He would never become an engineer. "He might become a gardener!" Perry said sometimes in despair, when his second son had once again been found, just as it was time to go to school, pushing a mower or crouched among Shanti's sweet peas with a trowel. Balbir actually enjoyed weeding and watering, cutting grass and clipping the hedge. There were times when his parents appreciated this. "But not at eight-thirty on weekdays in term-time," said Shanti wearily.

Seven-year-old Rupa was not intentionally difficult but she was small enough still to need help. Her hair must be braided and her shoelaces checked and if she were left to herself, Rupa would always do her cardigan buttons up wrong.

Satnam, at ten years old, had until recently been fairly co-operative, needing only to be reminded about this and that ("Have you got your lunch money safely? What about your gym

187

shoes?"). But since starting at his present school, he had slowly become mutinous in a sullen, self-contained way, scowling over his breakfast, eating it as reluctantly as when he was small, and dragging his feet when he left the house.

Both Shanti and Perry had tried to coax him into saying what was wrong, thinking that perhaps he was upset because he was not going to the same school as his brothers. Theirs was over-full and Lanesden Middle School, newly opened and taking children from nine to thirteen, had room; that is the only reason, they explained.

But Satnam merely said abruptly that it wasn't that and then zipped his mouth shut and would say no more. Perry, once, had taken a day of his annual leave in order to make anxious enquiries of the headmaster and Satnam's form master, but without result. The boy's work was adequate, they said, not brilliant, but steady; he was polite to the teachers and appeared to get on well with his classmates.

This statement didn't agree with the fact that Satnam, although he dismissed his bruises and grazes as accidents at football or slipping in the playground, had certainly on occasion been fighting and Perry did not think this bland information reliable. "But there's nothing to get hold of," he said to Shanti. "Let's hope that Satnam is just going through a phase that will pass. Possibly, this is just Satnam being awkward and squabbling with his schoolmates out of sight of the staff."

Awkward, thought Shanti on that Monday morning, as she rounded them all up to set them on their way, was a mild term for it. Satnam was at his very worst. His father had to shout at him to make him eat up, while Balbir had vanished again and Sunder, sent to look for him, had finally found him not in their own garden, but in next door's, where he was helpfully offering to mow elderly Mr Brierley's grass for him. Sunder brought him back and Perry shouted at Balbir, too. Shanti, in an attempt at peacemaking, said that it was kind of Balbir to offer help to a neighbour. Ranbir told her sharply not to make excuses. "You would spoil your children completely, Shanti, if I were not here to check you!" Rupa, upset by the anger in the air, burst into loud roars.

Well before they finally left, Shanti's habitual early morning headache had soared above its habitual Anadin and turned into a series of rhythmic hammer blows. She longed to spend a quiet hour meditating in front of Ganesh but there was shopping to

188

get, and washing, and then she must sit down at her sewing machine and work hard. She was behind schedule, what with the Sangeet party and the wedding.

Shopping came first, and Ranbir went with her. Since they both quite enjoyed the task, it was usually one of their more amicable times, and the fresh air, Shanti thought, might make her head feel better.

But not this time. Ranbir, irritated by the scene at breakfast, spoiled the usual leisurely wander from shop to shop along Southall Broadway, and Shanti suspected that her mother-in-law knew she was spoiling it, and was doing so on purpose.

The Broadway, now, was like a small piece of Delhi transplanted. Shanti normally found pleasure in examining the windows of jewellers displaying twenty-two carat wedding jewellery. Sita's marriage had made her think of Rupa's future and today she began to wonder if she and Perry shouldn't buy a few items in advance. They had an insurance policy for the purpose, which would produce a lump sum in ten years' time but the value of money might well fall; perhaps they should make a start now.

But an attempt to discuss this with Ranbir merely resulted in a dismissive recommendation to wait till Rupa was older. They moved on to a greengrocer's where as a rule they became almost united over the business of examining fruit and vegetables for freshness and ripeness, and planning dishes on the basis of what was available. This time Ranbir quarrelled with everything Shanti wanted to choose. The stop at the general store was as bad ("You have plenty of paprika in the house and why this brand of tinned peaches? That other is better") and Shanti did not dare to propose that they stopped to have coffee although her drooping spirits and throbbing temples cried out for a stimulant. Instead, with Shanti dragging the laden trolley, they went home.

The Anadin was in the bathroom. Shanti, who had been thinking yearningly about it all the way back from Southall Broadway, pulled the trolley into the kitchen, murmured, "Excuse me a moment," and sped upstairs in search of an extra dose of relief.

When she entered the bathroom, she found it occupied already. A man in trousers and singlet was standing at the washbasin, drying his face. He turned as the door opened and Shanti found herself gazing at a complete stranger. He put the

189

towel down, smiled ingratiatingly and advanced on her with an outstretched hand and Shanti fled, screaming, out of the bathroom and down the stairs.

At the foot of them she bumped into Ranbir, who had run from the kitchen. She clutched her mother-in-law and pointed, frantically, up the stairs. The stranger appeared on the landing and began to descend towards them. The clutching became mutual, a panicky search for support. "Stop!" Ranbir shouted at the man. "Don't come a step nearer!" The phone, which Perry had mercifully had installed the previous year, was in the front room. Ranbir began to edge that way, taking Shanti with her.

"Don't be ridiculous," said the apparition, in a perfectly familiar voice, and leapt down the last few steps to stand beside them. "I'm Perry. Shanti, can't you recognise your own husband?"

They gaped at him.

"But . . . your hair!" Ranbir gasped, pointing at his short back and sides. "What have you done? Your hair is short and you've shaved off! I can't believe this that I am seeing! What would your father have said? *I can't believe this*!"

"But what are you here for at this time of day?" cried Shanti. "You should be at work!"

"I called in sick from a phone box and went to a barber instead. He did my hair and shaved me. But it feels strange." Perry rubbed a hand over his head and jaw. "Draughty, as a matter of fact. So when I came back here, I gave my face a wash. I thought it might make it feel more normal."

"Normal! Nothing will ever make you feel normal, or look normal like that!" Ranbir stopped on an indrawn breath as if lost for any more words.

"I don't understand," said Shanti, bewildered. She gestured towards the kitchen. "Let us go there. Why stand talking at the foot of the stairs?"

In the kitchen, where the light was better, she looked at her husband and found it quite impossible to imagine that she had been married to this man for fourteen years and had had four children by him. He still looked so unfamiliar that she found herself standing nervously several feet away from him. Perry peered at himself in the mirror which hung on the wall above a sentimental calendar with cooing turtledoves on it (Shanti had chosen it and Ranbir, predictably, had snorted).

"I suppose it's natural that you didn't know me. I hardly

know myself."

"But why did you do it?" said Shanti and Ranbir in unison although in differing tones of voice. Shanti's voice was puzzled but Ranbir's was furious.

Perry sat down at the kitchen table. "I've been offered a job," he said succinctly. "Better pay — much better pay and far more reasonable working conditions. Less late working and no more files on the table evening after evening and weekend after weekend, Shanti. I wanted that job and they would only offer it to someone who looked like other people. So I decided to look like other people. I made two calls from that phone box this morning. After I'd rung my own office, I rang these other people, Allbrights, their name is. I told them I had cut my hair and given up the turban and was the job still open. They said it was. I'm to see them again this afternoon. So I went to the barber to make it true, what I had told them. I think I shall have the post. But this is the price."

"So!" said Ranbir, and folded her arms grimly across her chest. "*So!*"

Perry looked at her uneasily. But Ranbir's fierce gaze was not directed at him. She had turned it on to Shanti. "This," she said, "is your doing."

There was an awful silence. Shanti took a step backwards and then another. Her eyes were fixed on Ranbir's face. When at last she spoke, her trembling voice held fear and anger in equal proportions.

"No. It isn't true. It isn't my fault!"

"Isn't it, indeed? *You*," said Ranbir, "you and this family you have had which is too big, you that can't do more to help than a little sewing but that doesn't stop you wanting this and wanting that . . . "

"Wanting *what*?" There was a sob in Shanti's voice now.

"Today who was wanting to buy gold bangles for Rupa's wedding when she is still only seven, and who is it who would like a car?"

"I have said once only that a car would be nice; I have never said that we should buy one, no, I know we cannot afford it . . . "

" . . . always nag-nagging your husband because he brings work home, trying to make up for the support you are not giving him . . . "

"Bheji, please! I came to this decision for my own private

191

reasons and it isn't Shanti's fault!"

"You would never have had those reasons but for this piece of human rubbish you saw fit to marry without consulting your father or me . . . !"

"I am not rubbish!"

"Mother, you are not to call Shanti names!"

" . . . I will call her what I like! Kartar was not old enough to advise you wisely and now look at what has happened! You have abandoned the laws of your ancestors and betrayed your whole community! That it should be my fate to have such a son! You cannot even speak politely now to your own mother and who is to tell you now from a Hindu?"

"There is nothing wrong with being a Hindu," said Shanti in a trembling voice.

"I did not say there was anything wrong with being a Hindu, but a Sikh should not look like a Hindu! Should not! Should not!" Ranbir stepped up to Shanti and shook an infuriated finger in her face. Shanti backed away from her towards Perry, turned as Perry put a would-be kind hand on her shoulder, recoiled from the sheer unfamiliarity of his shorn, uncovered head and shaven face, pulled the end of her sari over her own head and rushed out of the room.

"Now see what you have done!" said Perry angrily to his mother.

"I will go after her."

"You will not. You have done harm enough. What a to-do! I suggest, Mother, that you should turn to and think about food for the evening. Rick Medway will want his dinner if we do not. I will go and find Shanti. And I suggest that when you see her again, you are pleasant to her."

"Have you no respect for your mother?"

"I expect my mother to have some consideration for my wife, who incidentally is also a mother, of *my* children," said Perry sharply, and strode out of the kitchen.

He found Shanti in the bedroom. Ganesh's cupboard was open. On a mat on the floor in front of it sat Shanti, cross-legged, with a glass of water beside her. She did not move when he entered, not even to turn her head. "Shanti?"

She did not answer. He went round to where he could see her face and she glanced up at him. Her own face was calm, not marked by tears as he had expected. "Shanti?" he said again.

She withdrew her gaze from his and resumed her contem-

192

plation of the shrine to Ganesh. "I am going on fast," she said. "I am going on fast until all in this house is quiet again. I cannot bear all this quarrelling and nastiness. I cannot bear the things Bheji has said to me. It must all stop and she must take them back and if she does not, I shall fast until I die."

"No, Bheji, she is still fasting. She comes to bed at night and sleeps but all she will take is water."

And that was the sober truth, Perry thought. She wasn't taking her pill, either. Not that it mattered. Regardless of that, he had tried to recall her to the everyday world by making love to her, but she had refused him, turning her back.

"She is being ridiculous. She started this on Monday and it is Wednesday now. All this melodrama, it is absurd."

"Shanti did not create this melodrama, Bheji."

"She is creating it now. How she is behaving! She sits and stares at that . . . that god . . . and pays no attention to anything. She will not speak to me; she will not even speak to her children! I am doing it all; getting the children to school and seeing to them when they come home, and Nita's girls too. It is upsetting them all. You must talk to her, son, you must get her to see sense."

"You shouldn't have called her rubbish, Bheji."

"I will call her worse than that unless this nonsense stops soon. Oh, if only you had not done this mad thing! Can nothing I say make you change your mind? Put your turban on again and grow your beard, do it to please me."

"I start at Allbrights in two weeks. They kept their word and when I went to see them they confirmed my appointment. I told them I accepted that it is best when one is living in a country not one's own to blend with the background as much as possible, and the Chief Office Manager, who will be my boss, said he was sorry I had had to make such a choice, but he thought my decision was wise. I don't propose to go back on it. And nothing you say will change my mind, no."

"Perry!" said Nita, so shaken by her brother-in-law's appearance that she almost forgot the purpose of their visit, which was to try to coax Shanti out of the fast which by Wednesday evening was still in force. "Oh, Perry, this is so shocking; how could you do such a thing?"

"Quite easily, when it comes to desperation point. I had to get

193

out of that place, *had* to. This was the only way."

"Kartar, you must talk to him."

"I shouldn't, if I were you," said Perry steadily to Kartar. "It won't do any good and we might quarrel. I don't want that. But I think I should make it clear that I chose to do what I have done for what I consider to be good reasons and as I have already said to Bheji, I shan't change my mind."

"He keeps on saying that," said Ranbir. "But you are his elder brother, Kartar. He is disgracing the family. It is for you to insist that he behaves himself."

"You can't." Perry's eyes were still steadily fixed on Kartar. "You can decide to quarrel or not quarrel; you can decide to know me or not know me. But you can't decide for me whether I wear the turban and beard or not. That is my decision. I am a grown man, not a child to be commanded."

"I should try not knowing him," said Ranbir. "It need not affect the arrangements for the children, but if you refused to talk to him, Kartar, perhaps that will bring him to his senses."

"I'm not out of them," said Perry coldly. "And I was under the impression that Kartar and Nita had come to see Shanti. You'll find her . . . "

"You see? He is so obstinate and the way he disregards the wishes of his family is a disgrace. *Talk* to him, Kartar!" demanded Ranbir.

"I can't," said Kartar.

Chapter Sixteen

The Way Out
1971

"What do you mean, you can't?" Ranbir demanded. She glared at her elder son across Perry's dining room, in which they were all uneasily standing. Sunder and Balbir, who had abandoned their homework at the sound of the doorbell and were listening on the periphery, also stared at their uncle.

"He's done what he's done in order to further his career," said Kartar calmly. "In this country, it is easy to find yourself being driven to do things you don't want to do, just to have a decent standard of living and use your qualifications."

"But . . . !" If Perry and Ranbir were startled at hearing these sentiments from the orthodox Kartar, Sunder was quite obviously horrified. His thirteen-year-old face, on which the planes of adulthood and the first signs of his future beard were now appearing, was stricken. "I have been punched at school," he said, "and so have my brothers, for wearing topknots and looking funny. But we did not say anything, because Father has always said to us that we must never forget we were Sikhs and told us so many stories of valiant Sikhs who would never give in or pretend to be other than what they were. And now . . . !" He turned accusingly towards his father. "Now see what has happened!"

"You see?" cried Ranbir with energy. "Your sons are better Sikhs than you are, Perry! It is shocking that there is so much prejudice, but it must not be given in to and . . . "

"Sometimes it may be better to give in a little," said Perry. "And I here and now give you and Balbir and Satnam permission to do the same if you so wish."

"*Prem!*" Ranbir's cry was one of sheer horror.

Perry did not glance at her as he said to his sons, "The choice is yours. I would rather you remained orthodox. I would rather

195

remain orthodox myself. I have not found it possible to do so. If you can prove yourselves better than I, I shall be proud of you but I shall not criticise you if you decide to look like your schoolfellows instead of drawing their attention by seeming different." He turned to Kartar. "I'm glad you understand. I won't ask what has happened to make you understand."

"Thank you," said Kartar.

"What are you talking about?" demanded Ranbir. "What is wrong with you, Kartar, that you take this attitude?"

Kartar glanced at her. "Perry is right. Something has occurred which has made me feel that I cannot now reprove him. Bheji, you do not know what it is like for men here. The business world is hard and competitive and full of entrenched attitudes. Last week, I had to do what was a shocking thing. I tell you, I cringe to think of it."

"What shocking thing? What do you mean? How can you have done a shocking thing?"

Kartar met Perry's eyes almost apologetically. "You said you wouldn't ask, but I will tell you," he said. "Each year, we all have to write appraisal reports on our subordinates, and say if they are fitted for promotion. I have a West Indian secretary. She is a good secretary and I do not want to lose her but I would not want to stand in her way either and she is ambitious. She would like to be a secretary to a member of the board and there will soon be a vacancy for such a post. She wants that post. There would be more money for her then."

"What is all this about secretaries? What has that to do with Perry and..?"

"Let him finish," said Perry.

"We know what goes into our appraisal reports," said Kartar. "Our superiors discuss them with us. I have been recommended for promotion myself and I am ambitious too. But I would not be promoted just on my superior's recommendation: the board would have to agree. A broad hint was dropped that if I gave my girl Jennifer too good a report, it might damage my chances. The director whose secretary she might become – his present one is leaving because her husband's job is taking him to Birmingham – does not want a West Indian working for him. He is not very keen on me, either, but he has got used to me over a period of time and he does not have to see so much of me as he does of his own secretary. But, to put it crudely, if I land him with Jennifer Mackenzie, he will try to block my promotion and

196

he has great influence on the board. He would probably succeed. The chairman would back him up. Mr Fairweather doesn't like me very much either."

"Because you're Indian?" said Perry.

"And because I insist on wearing this turban."

"But at least you insist!" cried Ranbir.

"Yes. And sometimes I wonder if I am right."

"How can you say that!"

"I shall have my promotion, I think," said Kartar quietly. "I said in her report that Jennifer's telephone manner was not quite good enough for a director's secretary. I was lying. It is more than good enough. I had to discuss her appraisal with her and a more unpleasant interview I have never had. I tried to pretend that I was trying to protect her, that she did not know how high is the standard that is expected of senior secretaries. I said, perhaps next year. But she is not a fool and the secretaries always know what is going on. She knows why I did it. She is leaving the company in disgust and I am not surprised. But I am ashamed of myself. It seems to be a moot point whether preserving one's turban is more of a moral obligation than treating one's subordinates decently and honestly." He looked at his mother. "The job situation gets worse and worse. I do not say that I agree with what Perry has done, no, but I will respect his decision."

"But at the Gurudwara, people will say to you, look at how your brother is behaving!"

"There's no law against going into the temple without a turban. There are plenty now who have removed their turbans. They cover their heads with handkerchiefs. Perry will be only one more."

"But the example to the children! Oh!" cried Ranbir suddenly, "I have a good mind to go on fast myself! Perhaps when I am taken to hospital, you will all see sense!"

"Please don't, Mother," said Kartar. "It is trouble enough having Shanti on the verge of being taken to hospital, isn't it? Perry, will you take us upstairs, please? After all, to help Shanti is why we are here, since she will not listen to Mohan Lal or Leela. We will try what we can do."

They went upstairs. Shanti, dressed in an old and unbecoming cotton sari, with large mauve flowers on a fawn ground, sat cross-legged on her mat with her glass of water to hand. She was gazing at Ganesh in his shrine. When they spoke to her, she ignored them as thoroughly as though she had been deaf.

"I will take nothing back," Ranbir said to Perry when the others had gone. "Do you hear?"

"But, Bheji, she is getting so weak and so thin. She can barely totter to bed or to the bathroom."

"When she is hungry enough, she will eat."

"I'm so afraid she won't."

"Then let her just sit there, and totter occasionally to her bed or to the bathroom. I shall take no notice of her!"

"Mr Virk, you must be worried about your wife."

"That's kind of you, Rick." Perry, who had indeed been driven by sheer anxiety to seek refuge in physical toil, was helping Balbir to weed the cabbages before breakfast. He sat back on his heels as his lodger came across the small grass patch and sank down to squat at Perry's side. "I suppose you must have gathered . . . well, I don't mind admitting it, I am worried, yes."

He didn't mind the admission because Rick was part of the household now and because Rick himself was a remarkably soothing influence. He had in the last year become slightly more conventional in appearance. His hair was now only an inch or so longer than average and he was occasionally (though not frequently) seen in a shirt and tie. But he was still, essentially, a guitar-playing freethinker, and the latter made him oddly restful. Rick played traditional folk music, but he himself lived without traditions. He did not think in clichés.

"I live in the same house with you," he said now, "and I understand a little of your language. Your younger children have talked in front of me, too. I don't mean you," he said reassuringly as Balbir looked indignant. "Only the smaller ones. But anyway, I do know roughly what's happening. I don't want to interfere. But" – he reached out a helpful hand and began to twist a dandelion out of the ground – "I'm going to be home for a week or so and . . . "

"Holiday?" asked Perry politely, handing him a trowel.

"No. Look, I'd like to keep the room on and I'll pay in advance, but at the end of a week from today, I shall be away for a bit. I've left my job, Mr Virk. The musical group that I'm a part of – you know that we play for hire at parties and so forth, evenings and weekends?"

"Yes. I admire your enterprise."

"Well, we've been offered a tour as a backing group with a

198

well-known singer. We're going to chance our luck and see how it goes. We're all leaving our regular work."

"Really?" said Perry distractedly. "That's very brave of you."

"I'm not sure I've made the right decision," said Rick Medway. He tossed the uprooted dandelion on to a pile of other torn-up weeds. "The civil service was safe even if it was dull, but it never felt right for me. It was a dandelion in my life while playing the guitar and singing, well, that feels like a cabbage – or a rose or a delphinium, if you see what I mean. As if it had a right to be there. It's my proper job and the civil service isn't and if I let this chance go, it may never come again."

"If you feel like that then probably your choice is right. If something is your proper job, you ought to do it. Good luck to you."

"Thank you. But that isn't what I started out to say. I was going to say, rather diffidently, that although for the next week, I shan't be in all the time, obviously, I'll be here much more than usual and perhaps I can help a bit, as from today as a matter of fact. If this goes on, I mean."

"God forbid," said Perry. "Her brother and sister-in-law are coming again this evening, to try to talk her out of it."

"But if they can't, well, your mother is busy and has to go out at times and can't keep an eye on Mrs Virk all the time, but maybe someone ought to. If you leave her door open – Mrs Virk's door, I mean – I can look in from the landing any time I happen to pass, and at least make sure she hasn't fainted or anything like that."

"That's kind of you. Yes, I'll do that."

Mohan Lal and Leela duly came again that evening. They had already made one unsuccessful attempt to reason with Shanti. Their new effort was just as unavailing. They were reinforced, that same evening, by further worried visitors: Mr and Mrs Sodhi, who were Kartar's neighbours and were also Sikh elders – "she comes to the Gurudwara with us so perhaps she will listen to them; they have such authority," Ranbir said – and Dr Chowdhuri. Shanti remained impervious alike to relatives, old friends, Sikh elders and general practitioners. Ranbir recommended removing the shrine but Dr Chowdhuri shook his head and said Shanti's mind might be harmed if they did that.

"You think her mind is healthy now?" demanded Ranbir, but Dr Chowdhuri went on shaking his head and Perry said the shrine should not be touched. Nor should any attempt be made to remove Shanti bodily from in front of it, he added.

He could have said "nor should any further attempt be made." He and Ranbir had tried that once. Shanti had begun to shriek, short, piercing cries like a tormented animal, which horrified them so much that they instantly let go of her.

"She must come out of it of her own free will," Perry said.

Afterwards, he said once more to Ranbir, "If you would only do what she has asked, and take back what you have said . . . "

"I will not be blackmailed. Nor will I tell lies. What she is doing to you and to the children! I think what I said is more true now than ever!"

Friday dawned. Ranbir once more assumed control of the house and the children. Without Shanti, they seemed disoriented, as if they had reverted to younger ages. They forgot things, and were apt not to wash their faces properly. Only Sunder, who seemed now to have a grasp of the situation, was anything like himself. He tried to support Ranbir as a species of second-in-command. He also tried, though vainly, to reason with his mother, and to reassure his father. "I'm sure Mum will come out of it soon. Maybe the less notice we take, the better." He had apparently decided to accept his father's shorn head and shaven face and had actually stepped in between Perry and Mr Sodhi when the latter tried to take Perry to task. "Excuse me, but I think my father has enough to worry him just now."

As far as Perry's changed appearance was concerned, Balbir and Rupa followed Sunder's lead, bewildered but still affectionate, flinging themselves on their father when he came home from work as though afraid that he, like their mother, might suddenly withdraw from them.

Only Satnam kept aloof, staring at his father's hair but hardly ever speaking to him, which would have hurt Perry considerably, except that Perry, who was feeling increasingly dazed, scarcely noticed. All week, he had stumbled back and forth to work, from time to time wondering (aloud, in Shanti's hearing) how he would manage his new job if she were in hospital or dead by the time he joined it. At intervals he pleaded again with Ranbir to end the crisis by apologising even if she didn't mean it. Ranbir refused.

On that Friday, as she set breakfast before Perry and the children, Ranbir said, "It is time that all this nonsense ended. We should have been more firm. We have respected this fast too

200

much. After all, it is a thing which honourable people have often done for honourable reasons. But this is a trivial reason and I shall put a stop to it. Leave it to me, son."

"What are you going to do?" asked Perry uneasily. "I cannot agree to you touching the shrine or dragging Shanti away from it by force."

"I'm not going to do either."

"Then what?"

"I'm going to feed her, of course," said Ranbir shortly. "You go to work, and you children go to school. I will see to it all."

Shanti had long gone past the state of being hungry. Even the stomach cramps had lessened, along with the diarrhoea which had set in on the second day. Now she scarcely needed to move from her place from morning until dusk, and she felt light, of brain as well as body; it was growing more and more difficult to hold on to reality. It was easy, at times, to imagine that she might drift up from the floor and hover somewhere near the ceiling. But there was one thing in her which remained solid and rock-hard, and that was her determination not to yield. This time, Ranbir should be the one who yielded, or else she, Shanti, would keep this fast until death.

She had not herself known what hardness and strength lay hidden within her until that moment when Ranbir called her rubbish and in so doing, had taken just one step too far.

Then she heard Ranbir's purposeful tread on the stair and as though her mind, floating easily free of her increasingly insubstantial flesh, had penetrated her mother-in-law's mind, she knew what Ranbir intended, and knew, with a fury and despair which vibrated through her like a silent shriek, that what was marching solidly towards her was defeat.

Ranbir walked into the room. Shanti did not take her eyes from Ganesh, but the smell of soup reached her nostrils.

"It's thin vegetable soup," said Ranbir. "Nothing to hurt you, after your abstinence. But you'll eat it. I'm not standing for any argument."

Shanti did not move until Ranbir caught hold of her. Then she struggled and tried to scream but she had no strength and Ranbir was not only a vigorous woman but an angry one. Ranbir sat down behind her and jerked her off balance so that she fell backwards. Ignoring the weak flailing of Shanti's skeletal arms and hands, Ranbir held her daughter-in-law's nose with one hand and spooned soup ruthlessly into her mouth with the

201

other. Shanti, willy nilly, swallowed.

"I'll drink salt water!" she screamed when Ranbir at last let her go. "I won't keep it down, I won't!"

"I'll be up again in a couple of hours and I'll force-feed you again," said Ranbir coolly. "I have taken all the keys out of all the doors, by the way. You cannot lock yourself in anywhere. How lucky that the bathroom door has a key and not a bolt. Make yourself sick if you like and if you can find the salt. You have said that now, so I shall hide it. We shall see who tires of the fight first. This evening, perhaps I will try a little bread soaked in the soup. Come. You are a silly girl. Didn't the soup taste nice?"

She gathered up the empty bowl and the spoon and went. Shanti, trembling, resumed her cross-legged position in front of the shrine. But her trance was broken.

Ranbir would win, she knew it. Shanti might have discovered a new hard core within herself, but Ranbir was more obstinate, more powerful still. Shanti thought about going to the bathroom and in lieu of salt water, sticking her fingers down her throat. She felt too tired to try. The bathroom was too far away, the effort too enormous.

The warmth of the soup inside her was seductive. There hadn't been much: no more than a few spoonfuls. But it had stirred a treacherous longing. It was distracting her.

She rose shakily and then sank down on the edge of the bed, where she still slept at night with Perry. Her drifting thoughts went back to the time when Perry had first walked into Mohan Lal's dismal back room (it was no better, even now), and illuminated it for her, with his smile and his cheerful voice, his easygoing friendliness. She had been too shy to look straight at him, she remembered, but when she scurried back to the kitchen, his image, his smile, his friendly voice, had gone with her and stayed with her until he came again, and then renewed themselves. Until at last she whispered her timid dreams to Leela and her marriage was brought about. And when that happened, it was as though fate had placed a wondrous jewel in her hands, with a glowing, glittering heart into which one could gaze, and it was like gazing into another universe.

From Perry himself, she had hidden her feelings; schooling her voice when he came to ask her opinion so as to sound cool, practical, just in case nothing came of it. If that glittering and infinite wonder were not after all for her, then he should never learn that she had had the presumption to reach for it. If Perry

202

rejected her, he must not know she minded.

But Perry had not rejected her, and on her wedding night, she had even dared to admit that she loved him, for she was sure at last that that glittering other universe was truly for her. And so it had been. For a while.

Until Ranbir came and spoilt it all. She hated Ranbir quite as heartily as Ranbir hated her, but she was not effective, while Ranbir was.

Ranbir. Nagging, finding fault, blaming her for every single thing that went amiss. Perry did try to defend her sometimes, but politeness to his mother always constrained him and she knew that sometimes he saw her through Ranbir's eyes.

She had tried, fasting, to challenge Ranbir's power and she had failed.

She raised her head, looking at the door to the landing. The distance to the bathroom seemed like a thousand miles. But she must cover them. She had no choice.

From here, there was only one way she could go.

Rick Medway, coming back from an afternoon rehearsal, found the house quiet. The children were at school, Perry was at work and Ranbir, as he observed from the landing window as he went up to his room, was in the garden, hanging out clothes on the line. Shanti, he supposed, was still fasting. It was a marvel to him that anyone could sit there day after day, staring at a shrine. Quite apart from hunger and weakness, it looked so boring.

He glanced in at the open door as he passed the Virk's bedroom, and was relieved to see that she had apparently abandoned her vigil and retired to bed. She was lying under the lemon-coloured candlewick bedspread. Her dark braids trailed across it and her nose was turned into the pillow. One ivory-coloured hand drooped over the edge of the bed. Her bangles of gold and scarlet-painted ivory hung from a wrist so thin that it was painful to look at.

She was snoring faintly and lying very still. About to turn away, he hesitated, and looked again.

Then he saw, on the bedside table, the tumbler with an inch of water left in it, and the brown-tinted tablet bottle, which yesterday he had seen in the bathroom, visibly half-full, now just as visibly empty.

He strode into the room, picked up the bottle, read the label, and shook Shanti's shoulder, hard. Her head lolled back and forth on flaccid neck muscles. She moaned faintly, but she did not wake. He shook her again and shouted at her, with no better result. "Oh, bloody hell!" said Mr Medway.

A few moments later Ranbir, coming in from the garden with an empty washing bowl, heard him shouting and hurried into the hall to see their lodger descending the stairs with Shanti over his shoulder in a fireman's lift. "Whatever are you . . . ?"

"Get an ambulance!" shouted Rick Medway.

"What? What are you doing with my daughter-in-law?"

"Carrying her down the stairs, what does it look like? Get an *ambulance*! Dial 999!" Rick brandished a brown-tinted bottle in his free hand. "She's taken a good half-bottle of sleeping pills. Oh, here . . . " he pushed past Ranbir and carried his burden into the front room, followed by an expostulating Ranbir. He dumped Shanti on the couch. Her head lolled again and Ranbir, understanding at last, darted to her, exclaiming.

"Try and wake her up!" said Rick. "Shake her, shout at her! I'll do the phoning!"

Chapter Seventeen

A Place to Live
1971

She ought to be dead and out of it. Sinking into the drug-induced darkness, she had thought, this is the end of it. I shall go to sleep and not wake up and Bheji can complain and nag all she likes; I shall be beyond her reach. I wonder if Perry will mind?

But the protective shield of the dark wasn't strong enough. People broke through it, shouting, shaking, heaving her about. Voices boomed, doors slammed, engines vibrated. Her eyes, intermittently jolted open, saw strange faces above her, glimpsed hard fluorescent lights and people in white coats. There were unspeakable indignities connected with stomach pumps; needles were pushed into her; she seemed to be attached to tubes.

She heard Perry's voice somewhere, asking questions and then raised in anger. She heard Nita's voice exclaiming and Ranbir crying. She tried repeatedly to let herself slide back into comforting nothingness but never quite succeeded and each return from it brought her nearer to genuine consciousness.

Then she was awake. She was in some kind of cubicle. There were green curtains and a white ceiling. Perry was sitting on a chair at her bedside. Divested of beard and turban he still looked unfamiliar although, she now noticed, very handsome. His exposed jawline was unexpectedly strong. But on either side of his mouth, the barber had also exposed lines which she had not observed before and his eyes were bloodshot and clouded with exhaustion.

Her left arm, lying outside the covers, was bruised and various bits of her, inside and out, felt sore and aching. But when she moved, she was free of hindrances.

"The tubes are all out," said Perry. "You're all right. You can come home in a day or so. They saved your life. It was a near thing. You were so weak from starvation."

There didn't seem to be anything to say. She wanted to put out a hand and trace the line of that surprising jaw with her fingertips, but nothing in the face of this stranger with his careworn good looks gave her permission.

"I know why you did it," said Perry. "I blame myself. I should have seen how bad things were and dealt with them. They have been dealt with now: Kartar and Nita have come to the rescue. Their tenants are moving out – buying their own home, I understand – and Kartar no longer needs their rent. They have offered to have Bheji to live with them and I have told her that I wish her to do so. She is moving over there today."

"It will be better," Shanti whispered. She knew that she should say she was sorry but she did not feel sorry. Ranbir was going, and that alone made it worthwhile.

Or almost worthwhile. When she tried to smile into Perry's eyes, they remained clouded and unresponsive.

"I understand why you did it," Perry repeated. "But – Shanti – you are the centre of my home. We not only love you; we need you. It was a very unkind thing to do."

Nita took a day off to fetch her from hospital. Perry, fearful that something would go wrong with Allbrights at the last minute, was earnestly working out his notice and trying, he said, to do nothing – such as taking more time off – that might jeopardise his reference. He had already rushed away from work once, the day she was taken to hospital.

Nita drove her home and carried her small case into the house and the smell of polish met her as she crossed the threshold. Shanti had never seen her home dusted, scoured and polished to quite this extent before. "I thought I'd get it ready for you. Bheji helped," Nita told her, glancing at her sideways as she said *Bheji*.

Shanti, however, merely nodded. Ranbir was not here now; that was all that mattered.

The house was quiet. Rick Medway had left now for his tour. Sunder had been most helpful throughout the crisis, Nita said. When Ranbir was almost too frantic to see to the younger children, Sunder had done everything, including getting them off to school on time. Balbir had been taking himself off each evening, possibly to escape the situation, but he had spent the

206

time helping Mr Brierley on his allotment and now he and the formerly wary Brierleys were on positively friendly terms. Mr Brierley, aware that there was trouble in the Virk household and wishing to make a gesture of practical sympathy, had presented him with a quantity of strawberries and lettuces.

"There," said Nita, opening the dining room door to reveal a table laid for lunch, with a salad under Clingfilm and the strawberries in a bowl with cream alongside. "I've something ready to heat up in the kitchen as well; you must have plenty of hot food. But as an accompaniment, this is nice, isn't it?"

"Nita," said Shanti. "You are so kind."

"My dear," said Nita, "no one knew how it was with you. I knew a little, what you told me, but it was not enough. I have said to Perry and Kartar, you are men, you do not understand and you must not judge. Men have their world and we have ours. Only I wish you had come and asked me for more help and then all this might have been avoided. You will have to meet Bheji again soon. You know that?"

"I don't want to."

"Nevertheless . . . "

"Oh, yes," said Shanti. "Yes, I know. But if I don't want to meet her, it is not because I am ashamed but because of the thing she once called me, that she never took back."

"If I were you," said Nita, "I'd just let it go. She never will say she's sorry, you know. But she might feel it."

"I will try to think so," said Shanti.

The following Monday, Shanti stood in her kitchen, lapped in the perfect peace of solitude, listening to the steady tick of the kitchen clock, and wondered if life in her household would ever be normal again. Being alone felt so strange, yet there was no one in her family, just now, whose company was entirely pleasant.

Even the resolute normality of her son Sunder and the way Balbir kept half-timidly bringing her things, such as flowers from the garden and more lettuces from Mr Brierley's allotment, almost as though he feared he were in some inexplicable fashion to blame for the disaster: these were not blessings but subtle accusations.

Even worse was Satnam's self-contained sullenness (he scarcely spoke to his father and rejected her own attempts to get him ready for school; Sunder still had to do it and this morning he had had to slap Satnam to get him moving), while Rupa seemed afraid of her. She kept staring at her mother and then running away to take refuge with Perry.

"Well, what do you expect?" Perry had said when she showed her distress. "For days and days you were sitting up there in front of Ganesh, ignoring everybody, getting weaker and thinner every moment and radiating misery into every cranny in the house. Then, finally, the children come home from school and you're not here at all. Nobody's here but their Auntie Nita with a worried face, and when she takes them to see you, you're all pale and wan and like a stranger, lying in hospital with a drip feed plugged into you. You tore their world to pieces and especially Rupa's. Girls need their mothers."

"Oh, stop it, please stop it!"

Perry groaned. "Nita said I must not judge. And, yes, I know I am partly to blame; I should have done more to help you. If you had died, Shanti, I would have had to live with the guilt for the rest of my life. But for that very reason, trying to kill yourself was a selfish thing to do."

He saw the tears of weakness rising into her eyes and said, more gently, "I'm sorry," and they had gone to bed and he had cuddled her. But, Shanti thought, it was the way one cuddled a child or a pet, not the way a man caressed a woman. He hadn't made love to her at all since she came home. Something in him was withdrawn from her, distrustful of her, waiting, she realised with a flare of resentment, to see how she acquitted herself now.

She ought, she supposed, to be trying to regain his trust and his good opinion. On her return home, he had asked her if she needed anything to make her housework lighter and at her request, he had bought a pressure cooker and a new steam iron. There was some ironing to do today; she could start by attending to that, preparing something delicious for dinner tonight, and getting back to her sewing. But in the silence and the solitude, she could not work up a sufficient head of energy. She had come back from hospital on a Friday. Nita had stayed with her then until the children came home. This was the first time she had been alone and she did not know how to be. When the doorbell rang she answered it with alacrity, brushing a hand quickly across her eyes as she hurried through the hall.

On the doorstep, smiling cheerfully, were Nita, Mohan Lal, Sita (very bridal still in a crimson sari with a red mark on her forehead and a matching set of earrings and necklace in turquoise-studded gold) and Hari. And behind them, positioned warily in the rear, carefully dressed in her best ivory-coloured outfit, was Ranbir.

"Oh," said Shanti faintly, "how . . . how nice. Do come in."

"My dear daughter," said Ranbir. She pushed decisively forward between Hari and Sita, and folded Shanti in an affectionate embrace. "How glad I am to see you looking better."

"Hari and Sita are house-hunting," said Mohan Lal in a hearty voice. "So we are all going to help them."

"We thought," said Nita, "that you might like to come too. I have taken another day off so as to join in."

Shanti suspected that Nita had arranged the invitation as a way of bringing her into Bheji's company again, in circumstances that wouldn't be too intimate.

But she could not refuse to speak to her husband's mother, not without creating a family muddle which everyone would do their kindly best to tidy up and which would only alienate Perry further. She didn't want to talk to Bheji, let alone be embraced by her but she didn't have the strength to resist.

There seemed nothing to do but ask them in, give them coffee, change out of her old working tunic and trousers and into something more respectable, and go along.

"Yes, indeed, that looks nicer," Ranbir said busily when Shanti, who had left them with coffee and barfi sweetmeats, reappeared in a pink sari. "That gives your skin a glow. I am not against religious observances, not at all, but to fast too much is not good for the health and you are such a slight girl to start with. It is no wonder that you became so ill. You were affected in both mind and body. You must never make yourself so ill again."

This, evidently, was to be the official line. Shanti had fasted unwisely and collapsed. She had never taken an overdose of sleeping tablets and there had never been any dispute between her and her affectionate Bheji who, obviously, would never dream of calling anyone a piece of human rubbish. Ranbir was now examining Shanti's face minutely. "But you are still a little pale. You should use some make-up. Why are you using no make-up? And put on some pretty earrings."

It was nagging in a new guise but at least Ranbir would go home with Nita afterwards. Shanti put on the make-up and the earrings, and they set out together, all six of them, to find an estate agent.

Over the coffee, Mohan Lal and Hari had talked about the expedition. They had left Leela and Mr Bhatia senior in charge of their respective shops today because they considered that house-hunting should have a high priority. "Space is limited at my place," said Mohan Lal, "and besides, we always meant that Hari and Sita should buy a house, and that I should help them."

"Only the market is difficult just now," Hari said. "I gather it has not always been so but now prices are going up and so mortgages are higher and it is difficult if one gets into a chain. Somewhere along the line, up goes a house price and the buyer backs out and the chain breaks."

"But we are determined," said Sita with a smile.

"And it is surprising what one can achieve if one is determined enough," said Hari. He was wearing light-coloured trousers and a check jacket in which he appeared clean-cut and sporty, and when presently he led the way out to the two cars parked in the road, he had the brisk step of optimism.

With the prospect of dashing here and there to various houses, they would need the cars. Nita deftly steered Shanti, Sita and Hari into hers and left Ranbir to go with Mohan Lal in his Mini. Shanti wondered if this were a deliberate, tactful rationing of the contact between herself and Ranbir, and thought it was, and that her mother-in-law must be secretly conscience-stricken to have let it happen. Ranbir didn't like Mohan Lal and rarely had much to say to him.

Hari was talking about his prospective house. "We shall want to let a little space, as you are doing, so it must be quite big."

"We are losing our tenant soon," Shanti said. "Mr Medway has written to say he will be away so much, he had better not keep the room on. Perhaps now we shall be able to do without letting. Perry thinks we will."

"It is all right, as long as there is really room," Nita said. "But it is better not kept up for ever."

"I am keen on making money," said Hari. "If you don't make money when you are young, when can you make it? But I do not want Sita going out to work, except for helping in the shop. You have not seen the shop yet, Auntie Shanti. You must come. It is a corner shop, a little general grocery store. I think it will be a success. We are very healthy and hardworking. Ah. There is an estate agent. Now, where can one park?"

*   *   *

"Well, really," Nita said as they got back into the cars. "I had no idea . . . the prices! You will have a heavy responsibility, Hari, with such a mortgage. And only two houses to see that are within your range at all!"

"It is a pity," said Sita, "that there is nowhere even halfway suitable that is really near any family members. It is nice to have company near at hand. We are all living a long way from India, after all."

"There are two ways of looking at it," Nita said, watching the names of the side-roads for the left-hand turn she would need to make. The agent had arranged for them to view one of the houses at once. It didn't sound particularly promising, but Hari thought they had better look. "Kartar sometimes says that we should all spread out more, that that would make prejudice less. He is right in one way, although in another . . . "

"Yes, Nita auntie?" asked Sita.

"You will find out when you have children. I worry a good deal about my daughter Rose. She is showing quite a mathematical gift, you know, even though she is only just eleven. Her teachers are already saying if she keeps it up and it is not just a temporary phase, she could be university material. I should like her to have a degree but I feel anxious at the thought of her studying away from home. In England boys and girls are not kept apart as they are at home. We have taken care to impress on her, since she was small, how important it is for an Indian girl to keep her reputation, and tell her that one day we shall see to it that she has a husband worthy of her; she need never worry for that. But when one is young, one is giddy, and it is natural for young girls to be romantic, too. At least, if she has plenty of Indian society in her home life, that is a healthy counter-influence. But for that, one must be near plenty of Indian people. Indeed," said Nita thoughtfully, "from that point of view, I am very happy to have Bheji with us. I know she did not behave well to you, but she and I have usually been on good terms. She will be able to advise me and Rose will have the benefit of an older woman's wisdom and example."

It was a point of view which Nita had put to her husband when they realised that in sheer humanity they must take Ranbir off Perry's hands. Kartar had agreed, but only just.

"In bringing Rose up, there is a very delicate balance to be kept between the new and the old, between India and the West,

211

and Bheji is not at all wise when it comes to delicate balances. She has wrought havoc in Perry's household. I don't intend to see her wreak havoc in ours."

"I don't think that is likely, Kartar. She and I are far more compatible than was the case with her and Shanti."

"And training a daughter is mostly the women's business," Kartar admitted. "But remember, you are to tell me if she causes you any trouble. Many sons will never argue with their mothers, but if I must, I will."

"Well," said Nita pacifically, "let us hope it never comes to that. But we do have to have her; that's the truth, isn't it? Shanti nearly died."

"Yes," said Kartar sombrely. "She did."

Shanti, now, also regarded the reference to Ranbir's wisdom as unfortunate but decided to ignore it.

"I don't think Rupa will make a university student," she said. "But perhaps it is as well! She is good with her hands, as Balbir is. Her sewing is excellent. I am teaching her embroidery and she is really talented. One can't make a career out of embroidery very well, of course, and we shall want her to be able to earn her living. It has been a drawback to me that I am not well able to earn. But I think she will not go to college."

"She is a charming child. I hope she makes a good marriage," Nita said.

"Well, one is bound to hope for that, with a daughter," Shanti agreed.

No, she must not dispute with Nita about Bheji's wisdom or lack of it. Nita, after all, had saved her from her mother-in-law. She wondered if Nita could suggest any reason for Satnam's unaccountably difficult behaviour lately, or any way of curing it, and opened her mouth to ask. But Nita was signalling for the turn and Hari was saying, "From this A to Z map, it is about a mile and a half on a straight road now, and then there is a right-hand turn. You must look out for a playing field and then a church." Shanti missed her chance.

The first house had four bedrooms and a small attic conversion, was filthy, had mould on all the downstairs walls and a roof in urgent need of replacement. "We can't live there!" Sita said, holding Hari's arm as they led the retreat out of a front gate which drooped on its hinges and was therefore permanently fixed in a half-open position.

The second, which they were able to visit in the afternoon, after lunching out in Southall, had three first floor bedrooms, two attic rooms with sloping ceilings, was clean and in good order but was even further than the first from the rest of the family or Hari's shop or indeed from any shopping centre at all, and from any bus route or any form of railway travel.

"Out of the question. I have no car yet. I still have to pass my driving test," said Hari. "I think we need another estate agent."

They found another, and were offered two more addresses. The first of these had three cramped first-floor bedrooms, an attic conversion reached by a precipitous ladder and a back garden like a small-scale jungle ("Is there any risk from tigers?" Hari asked the affronted vendors blandly.)

The next, where they arrived at teatime, had four first floor bedrooms of reasonable size with recent wallpaper, two large ground floor reception rooms in which the wallpaper, far from being recent, was peeling, a somewhat basic kitchen, and electric wiring which looked sound enough but had evidently been installed after the house was built, so that it trailed like a vine along skirting boards and up walls and snaked across ceilings to reach the light fittings. It was in Hanwell, a little way distant from Southall but not too far from Hanwell Station.

"This," said Hari, as they gathered on the pavement for a council of war alongside their cars, "would do, I think."

"From what we have seen," said Sita, "we shall be lucky to find anything better that we are able to afford. We can do things to that kitchen and put some fresh wallpaper downstairs."

"I think these people are out for what they can get," Hari said. "I shall try to beat them down."

"I rather think that then they will just sell to someone else," said Nita.

"It is always worth trying," said Mohan Lal. "Well, Sita, you like this house?"

"Oh, yes, if Hari likes it, it will please me."

"Then we'll go back in," said Hari, "and make an offer."

"I am exhausted," Shanti said as Nita halted the car outside the Harrison Street house. The others had gone back to the estate agent and would then drive on to Mohan Lal's but "the children will be home from school already," Shanti had said. "Sunder and Balbir are very good. They have latchkeys now and one of them

213

will be there to meet the younger ones but still, I should be home soon now."

"I'm tired too. All that tramping round this house and that house, trying not to say rude things about them!" said Nita.

"It wasn't that. But when Hari haggled with those people at the house he wants to buy and they got so cross and nearly threw us all out; I did not like that."

"I think Hari enjoyed it. He still thinks in a very Indian way about these things; I think he did not believe they were *really* cross," said Nita. "But anyway, they did settle a figure and now Hari has gone to the agent to make the offer definite. I think Sita will be a proper housewife soon."

"I'm glad everything seems to be working out well for her. Perry was not at all happy about this marriage. But then, how is one ever to know how things will turn out?" Shanti sighed. "Nita, now that Bheji is living with you, does she ever, well, worry you about little things? Like . . . grumbling if you use too much string up on a laundry parcel?"

Nita shook her head. "No. She was always more tolerant with me. But she would not do it to you now, either. She did not understand how it was affecting you. She is a good woman at heart."

"I suppose so." Shanti began to get out of the car. "Oh, there is Sunder at the front window, looking out for me. I hope everything is all right."

Sunder opened the front door before they reached it. Balbir and Rupa were behind him. Three pairs of dark and anxious eyes looked past Nita and Shanti as if seeking, and failing to find, someone else on the path behind them.

"It's Satnam," Sunder said. "He arranged to meet Balbir on the way home from school but he did not turn up. And he still hasn't come home."

214

Chapter Eighteen

Little Hunted Hares
1971

Satnam had known since assembly that morning that it was going to be a bad day. To be precise, he had known it since the moment when, after the opening hymn and the Bible reading and the school announcements, the headmaster Mr Oliver Durrant proceeded disastrously to what he called Any Other Business.

He did not do this especially often because Oliver Durrant was on the whole an easygoing man who considered that children were best not harassed with too many rules. But once in a while, he would decide that his pupils did after all need a little restraining. Any Other Business was the method by which he usually applied the curb.

"*Some* of you," said Mr Durrant, large, untidy and informal in grey trousers and a bluish-green cardigan over a shirt in a sporty open check, "will notice when you use the washroom that the walls have been washed. I would prefer them to remain clean. They are walls, which means they are there to divide the washroom from the corridors and classrooms which adjoin it. They are not scribbling paper. I was *especially* offended by the sight of a National Front sign scrawled alongside the door in the first floor washroom. It was done with some artistic skill but I should prefer those of my pupils who have artistic ability to use it in art classes and for drawing maps and diagrams and improving their handwriting."

Here there was a faint titter, which he had intended. Mr Durrant believed that if you made friends with your pupils and taught them to enjoy listening to you and showed that you understood how their minds worked, they would respond all the better to your wishes. He was by no means wrong, either. It worked very well on the whole and there were plenty of examples of once-difficult pupils who had gone on to admirable achievements in higher education, to whom he could point as evidence.

But as Satnam could have told him, there were those with whom it failed, and others with whom it positively backfired. And Satnam, sitting cross-legged with the rest of his class on the floor of the assembly hall knew in his ten-year-old bones that it was going to backfire now.

"It isn't," said Mr Durrant embarking with the best of intentions on one of the most misconceived lectures of his whole career, "that I don't understand what is going on in the minds of the person or people who drew that sign. We all have an instinctive urge to attack in some way people who are different from ourselves. But I would have hoped that most boys and girls in this school have understood from our teaching that this instinct must be resisted. It would be a dull world if we were all alike. And let me point out, to those who I *think* may be responsible for that NF sign, that if you don't like seeing brown faces and topknots, other people don't like seeing skinhead haircuts, red braces and bovver-boots. I don't like red braces and the rest of the paraphernalia myself. The people who wear them are as good as saying that they would like to harm others. I'm sorry to say that this week, a few boys have appeared in school wearing those boots and braces. They are here now. Tomorrow morning, I expect to see every boy in this school wearing normal shoes and keeping his shorts or trousers up with a belt. Braces are for fat old men like me." Here he pulled his cardigan open and twanged the braces in question. "But you will note that they are blue, not red. From tomorrow onwards, any boy appearing in either of the banned items of dress will be sent home to change. Now, we will have the closing hymn ... "

That had done it, thought Satnam grimly. Mr Durrant, meaning well, had picked out Bill Prosser, Gary Stone and Philip Pierce and condemned them, and he had allied that condemnation to his, Satnam's, copper skin and Sikh's topknot. But conversely, and worse, he had even expressed understanding of their point of view. He hadn't approved it, but though Prosser, Stone and Pierce were older than himself, if any of them had the intelligence to distinguish between comprehension and approval, then he, Satnam, was the President of the United States. After school, he would be for it, unless he could take evasive action.

216

As he filed out with his class, through one of the hall's two doors, he caught sight of them filing towards the other door. Across the hall their eyes met his, with menace.

It was unlucky that he was the only Sikh boy in his year. The skinhead trio hated anyone with darker pigmentation than their own, but Sikhs, with their noticeable topknots, in particular drew their ire. However, they preferred to pick on one victim at a time and in most other years there were several Sikhs, who kept together and were generally let alone. They were friendly enough but his age-group did not naturally mix with theirs and they did not live in his direction. He was not going to ask them to protect him. He would rather be vulnerable than that.

The necessary evasive action might however, be possible. Lately, driven by desperation, he had been investigating alternative ways out. His secret exit was somewhat athletic and he had better leave his school-bag behind, but luckily he did not yet have much homework.

At the end of the day he made his way not out of the main gate, but across the playing field, which was not bounded by a high wall like the playground, but by a timber fence which was a mere six feet high. There was a place where one could climb a tree, scramble along an obliging branch and drop into the lane outside. He climbed, crawled, made sure that the lane was deserted, swung by his hands, using the length of his body to reduce the drop, and descended on bent knees to the ground.

On the opposite side of the lane was the blank wall of a factory. At each end, the lane ran into a T-junction with bigger streets and he could reach home by way of either. To turn left would bring him to the one where the enemy was probably waiting. The smaller T-junction to the right was his objective. He dusted tree bark off his trousers and set off.

But the enemy had been learning, too. The enemy had missed him on two or three occasions lately and had set about discovering why. The shrill whistle from behind him, from the corner of the left-hand T-junction alerted him to danger. He glanced over his shoulder, caught sight of the foe and broke into a run, just as Gary Stone sauntered round the corner ahead. He stopped, backing against the fence, mouth dry, as Pierce and Prosser came from his left at a heavy-booted jog. They and Gary reached him at the same moment.

"Well, look who's here." Gary halted in front of him, hands in pockets, teetering from toes to heels. "Been swinging from the trees, wog? Suits you, don't it? What made you come down from the trees in the first place?"

"You mean you *understood* those lessons on evolution?" said Satnam. "I'd have thought they were a bit beyond your grasp, myself."

He had, after all, nothing to lose. He was already in for the worst they could do. Which was likely to be very bad indeed. The fact that he was smaller and younger would not help him. They regarded that as an aid to more efficient terrorism.

They never went for the face. They had on occasion hit him in the face by mistake when he was trying to fight back, but their preferred technique was to go for the trunk – front or back, above or below the belt; they weren't fussy – and best of all they liked to kick. As a result, most of the damage they did wasn't apparent to the outside world.

He had developed a perverse pleasure in concealing his injuries from others. Even during swimming lessons, he had invented some effective techniques to hide his body, keeping his towel wrapped round him until the last moment and then diving in quickly. His family had noticed some of his grazes and bruises and guessed that he had been fighting, but the really horrendous marks, they had never glimpsed.

It had begun as a point of honour not to ask for help, to keep this his own private misery. But it had grown in importance since then. It was now his private payment, his apology to God for the thing his father had done, for Perry's abandonment of the turban and the long, valiant Sikh history behind it, which Satnam had been taught about in the Gurudwara and had heard reinforced by Bheji, and his Uncle Kartar, and by Perry himself in the days when Perry was still faithful.

He had made rules for himself. He could avoid or resist his attackers in any way he liked as long as he did not turn to others. This did not stop him from wishing, frequently and with all his heart, that other people, help of some kind, would spontaneously appear but God apparently drove hard bargains. Help never came. At this moment, the lane, which was little more than a wide alleyway, with very narrow pavements, was empty except for themselves and looked like remaining so.

"This one," said Bill Prosser, "thinks he's clever. Fucking wog." He moved his right hand meaningly and Satnam observed that there was a new horror. Wrapped round Bill's knuckles was a chain.

Shanti, faced with a crisis in which there were decisions to be taken and questions to be asked, was capable. "Satnam is never late except by arrangement. If he said he would meet Balbir, then that is what he meant to do. And if he had been taken ill at the school or some such thing, they would have sent word. They know to contact Leela if there is need, and no one is at home here. Oh, I hope he is not getting into mischief. He has been acting so oddly lately. Nita, you have the car. Could you drive around and just see if you can see him? Sunder, go with Auntie; you can look out of the car on the pavement side."

"I'll go right to the school," Nita said. "But surely, he isn't that much overdue? After all, boys . . . "

"I know. But we have been anxious about Satnam for some time. I said, he has been acting oddly. And it is not like him, not like him at all, to say he would join Balbir and then not come. Now he is late by one hour. He is not yet eleven years old, after all."

"All right," said Nita. "Sunder, come along."

One of the worst things lately was the fact that although they were all considerably bigger than he was, Bill in particular was actually well past his thirteenth birthday and had lately put on a spurt of growth which seemed to have embraced not only his physique but his mind as well. All three of them were streetwise and old for their years, but Bill Prosser was mentally almost an adult. An unusually obnoxious adult, at that.

He would leave at the end of the term, but that was no help at this moment. He was edging towards Satnam now, the chain-mailed fist held up as if inviting Satnam to admire the pattern of the links. In his pale, freckled face, his eyes were distended and very blue. Satnam pressed his back against the fence as though hoping to force a way through.

"'Es scared," said Gary Stone on a jeering note. Gary, so to speak, was the first mate in this appalling crew. "Poor little woggie's scared. 'Es shitting hisself."

This was very nearly true. In the English class that morning, the teacher had read them a poem called 'The Bells of Heaven', about people praying for animals: shabby tigers, dancing dogs, pit ponies and little hunted hares. It had meant little to Satnam, who had never seen a zoo or a circus and didn't know what a pit pony was; in his world, transport meant the internal combustion

219

engine. But at this moment, he felt great empathy for the hunted hares. He too was a quarry, and he was terrified.

But another of Satnam's secret rules was to show defiance at all times. His knees shook and his bowels were indeed threatening to loosen but he made himself put his nose in the air and say, "Scum like you couldn't frighten a cockroach."

"Ooh, listen to 'im! Talks big, don't 'e?" said Philip Pierce. Philip was the smallest and youngest of the gang, barely twelve, and light of build. He was on Satnam's left, which meant that if he wanted to make a bolt for it, his best chance would lie in that direction.

It wouldn't be much of a chance. He couldn't outrun either Bill Prosser or Gary Stone for long and although there would be passers-by in the main street, it was Satnam's experience that to the adult population, schoolchildren, even boys in bovver-boots, were invisible and their most lethal fights of less interest than a fight among dogs or cats. If they saw three dogs worrying a cat, they'd do something about it, but they'd probably let these three skinheads murder him before their very eyes and do nothing whatsoever.

But he must try to escape and of all the trio, Philip was the one Satnam was most likely to succeed in knocking down.

Philip was grinning at him, a gargoyle grin which bared his teeth and extended on either side towards his somewhat pointed ears. He seemed to have guessed Satnam's intention. He crouched slightly, his eyes holding Satnam's. "Yeah, come on, wog!" Uncle Kartar, who often said how important a good command of English was, would have been much saddened at the limited vocabulary of these boys, who were after all English-born. Satnam clenched his fists and sprang.

Only to stop and recoil virtually in mid-air. Today, Philip had decided to compensate for his lack of weight. Magically, in his right hand, a gleaming blade had appeared.

A heavy boot – Gary's – connected with Satnam's thigh. Bill's boot caught him just below the kneecap and the mailed fist connected almost simultaneously with his diaphragm.

He was on the ground. The pain was something almost visible, like a trio of dull grey sledgehammers. Philip was down on top of him, sitting astride him, holding that evil little blade before his face. Gary stood beside him, his shadow blocking out the sky. Bill was stooping. He caught hold of Satnam's topknot. Satnam tried to wrench his head away and the chain-wrapped fist crashed into his cheekbone. "Keep still, wog. Phil here's goin' to give you a haircut."

Satnam went mad. He heaved, shouted, fought, grabbing for Phil's knife-wrist. Gary's boot thudded repeatedly into his side. He called them all the names he could think of and even as he did so, noticed how much better his store of epithets was than theirs. He had hold of Philip's wrist. Philip wrenched it away again, leaning forward and reaching for the topknot. His face was just above Satnam's, his eyes bright with malice, his tongue just showing between his lips. Satnam shrieked a curse at him in Punjabi, and spat, straight up into the eyes.

Philip recoiled, screeching with disgust and rage. "You spat at me! You dirty little coon, you *spat!*" His right hand rose and fell. Satnam screamed and lunged, trying to draw up his knees, not able to believe what Philip was doing and knowing at the same time that it was true. The little knife blade was dripping red and the blood was his and there was a sharp, deep pain in his side, just below his belt.

Above him there was a confused shouting. Gary was yanking Philip away. Their faces stared down at him, very white, very stupid. Silly, white moon-faces, thought Satnam wildly. Then he realised, through a curious blurring of reality, that they were no longer holding him. He came up on one knee. To his surprise, his body obeyed him. He was on his feet. He was running, unevenly, because of the awful throbbing in his knee and sides, but running, and the foe was not giving chase.

The ground felt oddly insubstantial underfoot, as though it were melting, but he was covering it. He was up to the big T-junction. He was in the street, turning away from the school gates and towards home.

He wanted to be home more than anything in the world. He had forgotten that he had privately sworn never never to tell anyone about the three bullies. He needed help and knew it. His mother would be there. Balbir could play cricket without him. Home was only ten minutes away even at a walk and he was running.

But he had a stitch in his side, and something hot was running down his left leg and squelching in his shoe, and home suddenly seemed a very long way off indeed.

Mohan Lal's son Chandra Lal attended a school some way from his home and travelled to and fro by bus. Usually, he came home with a group of friends, but sometimes, as today, they went into Southall after school to roam about and, by his standards, waste their time. Chandra Lal took his studies seriously. His school-bag was heavily laden and he had a study programme for the evening which would keep him busy for a good two hours. His mother sometimes complained that he should help his father more but Mohan Lal, fortunately, was understanding.

"He will come into the business one day but he will do it all the better for being properly educated."

Chandra Lal wasn't so sure that he would ever take over his father's business. He had not said so to his father, but life as a small shopkeeper did not attract him. As far as he could see, one worked extremely long hours, mostly on one's feet, for a very modest return, and one's horizons stayed limited. Mohan Lal hardly ever felt he could leave his shop and therefore scarcely ever travelled out of Southall.

If one had a good education and passed plenty of examinations, then there would be opportunities open in other, more lucrative, more mind-broadening fields.

He hadn't chosen one yet. He was only twelve and it was too soon. But he had already decided that, scandalised as his father would no doubt be to hear it – Mohan Lal wouldn't be so understanding then – his future did not lie behind the counter of that shop in Southall.

He made the journey gazing absently out of the window, thinking of possible professions he might attempt to enter, and mulling over the studies on which he was currently engaged. His bus reached its nearest point of approach to his home and he disembarked, emerging on to a street corner. He turned to cross the road, pausing to let the bus and a little flurry of traffic pass him first. Just as a small, topknotted figure suddenly blundered past him from behind and went, blindly, head-down, straight out into the road and almost into the path of an oncoming car. Brakes screeched and a horn blared. Chandra Lal leapt, grabbed and hauled his cousin Satnam back on to the pavement out of harm's way.

"Where on earth," he said in Punjabi, "do you think you're going, young Satnam? Not safe out on your own, some of you young ones . . . here, Satnam, what is it? Hold up, are you ill? Oh, no! What's happened? You're *bleeding*!"

"We've been to the school and all round the local streets," Nita said. "He's not still at school and we didn't find him anywhere else."

"It's more than an hour and a half." Shanti in the meantime had put tea in front of Balbir and Rupa and now poured automatically for Nita. "Have this. I don't want to worry Perry at work. What can we do? Where can we enquire?"

"We could phone local hospitals," Nita suggested.

"Yes, I suppose so. But he has his name sewn inside his jacket; if he had been in a . . . a street accident . . . " Shanti's voice trembled " . . . in all this time, someone would have traced us; Virk is not a very common surname."

"It's all I can think of," Nita said worriedly.

Out in the hall, the telephone began to ring.

Chandra Lal steadied his cousin back across the pavement and sat him down against the low wall of someone's front garden. "Been stabbed. Pierce. Prosser," Satnam mumbled. "Trying to get home. Felt dizzy. Want to go to sleep."

"You've left a trail of blood all along the pavement. Don't people ever notice anything around here? Where are you hurt? Here." Chandra Lal was wadding a handkerchief into a pad. "Hold this against the wound – where is it?"

Vaguely, Satnam indicated it with a flap of his left hand. Chandra Lal undid his cousin's belt, found the place and pushed the pad down on top of it. "Hold that there. Can you? I've got to find a phone. I'll try this house."

He disappeared. Satnam rested against the wall, trying through his mental fog to remember to hold the pad to his side. The street was quiet. Though big enough to have a bus route, it was entirely residential and there were few passers-by. The other bus passengers had dispersed. No one came near. Somewhere far away he heard a doorbell ring and then voices. He felt extremely weak and, despite his cousin's kindness, he was now frightened. He also, for some reason, felt thirsty. Chandra Lal reappeared.

"Bastards. They didn't want to get involved or else they thought I was having a joke with them. I asked them to call an ambulance and they just shut the door in my face. I hate being only twelve. If I were bigger I could just carry you home, or at least to the nearest phone box. But that's three streets away. I'll try the next house along."

"Please do something quickly." He wanted to lie down. The

223

blood was seeping relentlessly through the handkerchief pad and he couldn't keep up the pressure that it needed. His hand kept going flaccid.

"Are you in need of help?"

At last, a passer-by, and one to whom schoolboys were not invisible. The face peering concernedly down at them belonged to an elderly lady. But she had an incisive voice. "The boy is bleeding all over the pavement! How did this happen?"

Chandra Lal was explaining. Satnam's eyes were dimming but he could still hear. He could also speak. He repeated, "Stabbed. Skinheads," several times over. He heard the sharp old voice above him say, "Wouldn't let you use their phone? I never heard of such a thing. That's right, press the pad firmly to the wound. You've got some sense, my boy. Leave this to me."

Chandra Lal was crouching beside him, supplying the pressure which Satnam now could not. Dimly, from far away, Satnam heard a door being subjected to a fusillade from a knocker. The voice of the septuagenarian Amazon drifted back to him. " . . . bleeding to death outside your very house . . . " Was he *dying*, then? " . . . a serious crime has been committed on your doorstep . . . what do you mean, you *thought* . . . ? You could have thought of checking! Attempted murder is a very serious matter indeed . . . Of course I know what I'm talking about; I'm a retired State Registered Nurse. I must ask you, please, to be good enough to call an ambulance immediately. And the police!"

Chapter Nineteen

Alien Life
1971

"Severe shock and loss of blood," said Perry, as calmly as he could, to Kartar, Nita, Mohan Lal and Leela as they crowded into the small hospital waiting room to join himself and Shanti in their vigil. "They're giving him a transfusion now."

"Stabbed. Chandra Lal said Satnam had been stabbed!" said Mohan Lal. "But by whom, how did this happen?"

"We don't know yet. He's unconscious. The police will want to talk to him as soon as he can speak." Perry passed a shaky hand across his hair, marvelling inwardly at the way that commonplace and homely affairs such as a wife in conflict with her mother-in-law, or a boy having problems at school, could escalate without warning into dramas with ambulances and police cars. "We think . . . someone at the school."

"Satnam is a very secretive boy, very secretive," said Shanti. "We knew he had been fighting sometimes, but now it seems he has marks on him as though he has been kicked, often. And now this! A knife!"

"What do the doctors say?" asked Nita.

"They are quite hopeful," said Perry. "But I don't know how long . . . how long it will be until we know."

"Bheji is with the children. They are all at our place now," said Nita. "Some others have come: Mr and Mrs Sodhi and Swarup Sharma and some others. Sita and Hari are there too. We can all stay and wait with you."

"Everyone is being very kind," Shanti said. "I only wish we had the name and address of the lady who helped Chandra Lal to phone for an ambulance. She was so good. I shall try to find out."

Silence fell. Perry and Shanti sat close together, as if for reassurance. They had bonded anew, Satnam's crisis obliterating

225

Shanti's. Sometimes they tried to smile reassuringly at each other. But their eyes turned quickly towards the door of the small waiting room every time they heard feet go past outside. When a nurse came in, they sprang up at once. "There is no news yet," the nurse said. "It will be a little while, I think. But please don't worry; Mr Rowlands is the best surgeon you could have. I came to say there's a refreshment place just along the corridor. You might like something to eat or drink."

Neither Perry nor Shanti was willing to leave the waiting room but the others fetched coffee and sandwiches for them all. Shanti managed to swallow a little; Perry refused the sandwiches but sipped some coffee. Time went on.

It was past ten p.m. when at last a young white-coated doctor, Indian like themselves, came in. Seeing Kartar's turban, he smiled and said in Punjabi, "I take it I have the right language?"

"Yes. Satnam – how is he?" Perry said.

"Mr Rowlands himself will come to speak to you in a moment but I thought I would let you know: the operation was successful. Your son was quite lucky; it was probably a small blade. It missed the kidney and just stopped short of the ureter. The shock and the blood loss were far and away the most serious matters and those, we hope, have been dealt with. There has been the transfusion and he has been stitched up and he is now back in his bed, sleeping off the anaesthetic. There's probably no reason why you shouldn't go home and return in the morning, when he'll be conscious, if dopey."

"He'll live? Doctor, he'll live?" Shanti's voice was sharp with fear.

"Indeed, I trust so, Mrs Virk."

"There has been something going on at his school all this time and we were too taken up with other things . . . "

"It's all right, Shanti. It's going to be all right now." Nita put an arm round her sister-in-law.

"There may very well have been something going on at the school," the doctor agreed. "The police have interviewed you already, I believe?"

"They have. But until Satnam can talk to them, what can they do?" Mohan Lal said.

"With luck," said the doctor, "he will be able to talk to them tomorrow. Ah. Here is Mr Rowlands."

"Thank God, he is awake," said Ranbir.

226

They stood round Satnam's bed in the light of morning. "Not too many people at once," the Ward Sister had said firmly. "There's a policeman in there already. There should only be two people round a bed at the same time. Well, both parents can go in, of course."

"I am his grandmother," said Ranbir. "We are a very united family."

Indian people had their own customs. They liked to do things in family groups. Since coming to work at King Edward's Hospital next door to Southall, the Ward Sister had come across this sort of thing frequently. It never actually seemed to harm Indian patients to have crowds of people round the bed, although it would have given the average English sufferer a relapse. "Very well. The parents and yourself. But no one else, not at the same time," said the Sister, and called a probationer to show Mohan Lal, Leela, Sita, Nita, Kartar, Sunder and Chandra Lal (both of whom had flatly refused to go to school that morning) to a nearby waiting room.

Satnam was pale and drowsy but he was indeed awake. His topknot cloth was missing but somebody had twisted his hair neatly up on top of his head and only a few short ends trailed on the pillow. He achieved a smile of greeting as they all leant over him. They had all come to the same side of the bed, because a young police constable was sitting with his notebook on the other side.

"Hello," said Satnam. "I'm all right. Sorry for all this." He made an effort to sit up, turned greenish, grabbed for a kidney bowl which was lying on his locker and was sick. "It's only the anaesthetic," he said, flopping down again when it was over and Shanti, clucking anxiously, had relieved him of the bowl. "That's all."

"Son, what happened to you?" Perry asked. He pulled up a stool and sat down.

"Skinheads. They jumped me in the street."

"We thought they might have come from your school," Shanti said. "You've been so funny about your school lately."

"No." Satnam looked away. The memory of his secret oath had come back to him. "I don't know who they were. They just jumped on me. On the way home."

"Thanks be to God that you are alive, anyway!" Ranbir said.

There was a quiet tap at the door and round it came the head of the police inspector who had come to the hospital the evening before. "Good morning, Mr Virk, Mrs Virk. The Sister tells me that the patient is recovering." He caught the constable's eye and raised his eyebrows questioningly.

"I'd like a word, sir," said the constable, and deftly collected Perry and Shanti with his eyes. "Outside."

They left Ranbir with Satnam and called Nita to join her. Perry then led them all back to the crowded waiting room. The inspector surveyed a gathering which now included Mohan Lal, Leela, Sita, Kartar, Sunder and Chandra Lal and said to the constable, "Is there another waiting room nearby? One that's more private?"

"We are all family members!" said Mohan Lal indignantly.

Perry shook a reproving head at him but the constable said, "Well, these two lads, sir – one's his brother and this is the boy who found him yesterday – they're concerned in what I want to say. They ought to be present, so . . . "

"Then I must certainly be present too, if my son is to be questioned," said Mohan Lal.

"It is our custom," said Perry to the inspector, "to do things together as a family."

"Oh, very well." The inspector was an impatient man and also looked disconcerted by the circle of dark, un-English eyes regarding him out of the brown un-English faces. "If there are reasons. Go ahead, Constable."

"Well, I'd just as well have all the family here, sir, in case any of them can shed some light on this. The thing is, the boy, Satnam, says he doesn't know who did it. He keeps saying they were skinheads, strangers, who jumped him in the street, when he was on his way home. But according to you, sir" – he turned to Perry – "you and your wife have noticed that something has been wrong with him, which you think is connected with his school, for some time, and that you think he's been in fights. And the doctors say he's been beaten up in the past. It looks contradictory, somehow."

"Not necessarily," said the inspector. "He could have had problems at school and still fallen foul of attackers in the street. What sort of boy is he, Mr Virk? Is he quarrelsome?"

"What is the inspector saying?" Shanti wanted to know.

"He is saying is Satnam quarrelsome?"

"Then tell him *no*, Satnam is not quarrelsome! Satnam has been stabbed and it is supposed to be his fault?"

Sunder interposed. "My brother is not yet eleven years old,

Inspector. It is a little young for serious quarrel-picking. In fact, he does not pick fights."

Perry ran a hand involuntarily over his head and jaw. Their barbered outlines still at times felt strange to him. "It's quite true that we've felt for some time that something was wrong at his school. He's been difficult about going to school, and . . . and quiet, withdrawn, not himself. We made enquiries at his school; I went to see the headmaster myself and I could not learn anything. It was all, no, he has not been in trouble with any teacher, and yes, he gets on well with his classmates, and yes, he studies hard. But something was going on, of that I am sure."

"But if he was attacked by boys from his school, why should he want to shield them?" said Mohan Lal. "Why does he not tell us who they are?"

In undertones, Leela and Sita were translating to Shanti. The inspector said, "I think we'd better go back and talk to the boy again. You and me, Mr Virk."

Shanti, in fractured but expressive English, suddenly broke out, "Skinhead boys! This National Front that is getting in all the news with its marches and its racist talk! They are just Nazis! I see those boys in the street! They are not like proper people. They are like things from some world different from our world!" Stumbling and heavily accented, it was nevertheless one of the most complex and expressive English sentences Shanti had ever uttered. Her eyes were bright with anger. "If I see them, I will kill them!"

"It's natural to feel like that, Mrs Virk. But if we can catch them, the law will do all that is necessary. Mr Virk, if we could go back to the ward . . . "

Chandra Lal said, slowly, "When I found him in the street, he said something. Well, muttered it."

"Said something?" Inspector and constable were at once alert. The inspector stopped in the act of shepherding Perry towards the door. "Something you didn't mention when we spoke to you last night?"

"I didn't think at the time that it amounted to anything." Chandra Lal's small, square face was thoughtful. "He said he'd been stabbed, and then he mumbled a couple of words and one of them was *pierce*. I thought he meant the knife – meant that it had pierced him, I mean. And then in all the upset, I just forgot about it. It's just come back to me now. *Pierce* was a funny sort of word for him to use. It's kind of poetic and Satnam doesn't talk like that. And the word after it didn't have any meaning at all; come to think of it, it could be a name, and if that's so, then so could *pierce*. There is an English surname Pierce, isn't there? The word he said after it sounded like Rosser or Prosser. I don't know if that's any help."

The constable had flipped his notebook open and was writing busily. "It could be. You never know."

"If it is," said the inspector, eyeing Perry grimly, "if this boy of yours *does* know the names of his attackers, then he has been hiding evidence and making a nuisance of himself." There was something in his face and voice which suggested that in his opinion, Satnam and his entire family were a nuisance. "The ward, Mr Virk!"

"But why, why, why didn't he say their names straight away? We cannot make it out." Perry sat with one leg tossed over the arm of his chair and addressed the company at large. Most of the family and a fair selection of friends and neighbours had gathered at Harrison Street to celebrate the news that Satnam was recovering safely and would shortly be home.

Shanti, hurrying about with refreshments, was glad that now that he had started with Allbrights he no longer brought work home and was able to join a social occasion without fretting to escape to his order forms. But she wished the conversation had taken a different turn. "It was such a crazy thing to do," Perry said, "not to give their names at once. Taking up so much police time! The inspector was very annoyed, I could tell. I shall have a word with Satnam when he comes home. At least those boys have been caught now. He will not have them at his school any more."

"I never know what is going on in his mind," Shanti said, depositing an empty tray on the table and loading it with used cups. Krishna and Nita's daughter Rose, who was now almost nine and beginning, Nita said, to be really helpful about the house, came to assist.

"Oh, it is all this terrible country!" Ranbir drained her teacup and banged it down on the tray. "We do not fit in here. British citizens we call ourselves but we are not British, are we? When will there be any brown British people? Satnam knows it; he knows he does not fit. That was why he did not want to bother talking to that inspector. He knew the inspector did not care. We should all pack up and go home!"

230

There were murmurs of mingled agreement and objection. Most, even of those who agreed, however, qualified their remarks with a *but*. Mr Sodhi, who together with his wife had come along with Kartar and his family, remarked in a distinctive bass which easily made itself heard through the rest, "So many children now are in the midst of their education and it would be a pity to disrupt them. There is much to be said for England. It is still, generally speaking, a safe country."

"*Safe!*" Ranbir snorted. "With these skinheads running about here and there and everywhere and this National Front Party holding processions and causing trouble and saying if they come to power they will throw us all o' t? We would do better at home in India. In India, that is where safety is."

"I'm not so sure." Mr Sodhi shook his head. "It has always been a place of violent feelings and communal troubles. I lost my parents in the troubles at Partition. Satnam himself is named for a friend of Perry's who was killed then, so Perry has said."

"All those troubles are over. That was years ago! Now India has her independence and things have settled down. If independence had come much sooner we should never have had all that trouble anyway," said Ranbir with vigour.

"There I am not sure I agree with you. The old violences were always there, and they still are, under the surface. There is still much bad feeling in Punjab province because it is mostly Sikhs there and yet the Sikhs do not rule it and cannot insist on quite reasonable things. The beautiful, modern town of Chandigarh where so many Sikhs live is quite naturally part of it but it took years and years before Mrs Gandhi would concede Chandigarh to the Punjab and then it was only that one Sikh leader had starved himself to death and another was going to kill himself in public, that made her relent. No, I am not sure that India is so quiet and safe a place as you think, Mrs Virk. I am quite content to stay here."

"But we are *Indian*! Look at those children's faces!" Ranbir turned to Perry and then pointed at Sunder and Balbir, who were as usual sitting side by side. "Look how puzzled their expressions are. They do not know anything about Chandigarh! They are growing up cut off from their roots. It is not right."

"The world changes, Bheji." Kartar spoke calmly. "I have no intention of returning to India except maybe in old age. I am doing very well here. I'm making a success of my career and I certainly don't intend to give it up. Nita wouldn't want me to.

231

Would you, Nita?"

Nita shook her head.

Perry said, "I would not go back to India, either. As Mr Sodhi says, it could disturb my children's education. Sunder hopes to become an engineer and he can get the best possible training here and the best career chances, too, in my view."

"I give up," said Ranbir, exasperated. "What is there in this country for us? I will never understand. Shanti, surely you would like to go home? You should persuade your husband."

"It would be nice to go for a visit. Otherwise I am content to stay here," said Shanti calmly. "Perry is right about the children's studies."

There was more to it, indeed, than that. She had raised the matter with Perry on that first night when Satnam was in hospital and despite the surgeon's reassurances, they still weren't sure if he would live or die. Holding Perry in her arms, as though he were himself a child needing comfort from its mother, soothing him when he tried to blame himself for not having found out what was amiss with Satnam, she had said, "Let's go back to India. There are no skinheads there."

And Perry had not talked of Sunder's engineering prospects then. "How can I?" he asked her. "How can I possibly go back? I came to England to make my way but how have I made it? Things are not much different from when we talked of this back in the flat at Wandsworth. Oh, it is not so bad, being part of this Allbright's office management team; it is a step up from what I was doing before, yes, but still, it is nothing much, not compared to Kartar. I cannot go back to India, where we have relatives, like Uncle Sunder who has done so well in government service, and admit that . . . well, we must face it, Shanti. I am by his standards, by my father's standards, a failure."

"But you are not a failure!"

"I am," said Perry, almost with a masochistic satisfaction in saying it, "yes, I am."

No, she would not try to persuade him to go back, although she did not intend to repeat to Ranbir any of that conversation in the dark. Any more than she would ever repeat to Perry himself what their son Sunder had told her privately, after his last visit to Satnam. Shanti had said that she never knew what was going on in Satnam's mind. This was a protective lie. She knew, in fact, an uncomfortable amount.

"Mum, I know why he didn't want to name those skinheads.

He told me. But you mustn't tell Dad," Sunder had said. "Promise."

"But why must his father not be told?"

"I think it might hurt him. I mean, I think I know what Satnam was saying even though he didn't say it . . . exactly."

"I won't tell your father anything that is likely to upset him but what did Satnam say?"

"He said he didn't want to tell because he wanted to keep it all to himself and deal with it all – deal with *them* – himself. He said he had to do it because he was a Sikh and he'd got to live up to that. He was sorry he let those names fall when he was too weak to know what he was saying. He was terribly embarrassed when he found out that it had all got into the papers. He feels like that because . . . well, it's to do with . . . well, redeeming the family honour, he said."

"I see," said Shanti. "Yes, I *do* see. Don't worry. I shall not mention it to anyone else."

She had been weak once. but she was strong now. Never again would Bheji or anyone else drive or harass Shanti into abandoning her responsibilities. When Perry, sitting tired-eyed beside her hospital bed, had said that she was not only loved but needed, she been too ill to understand. But Satnam's bloodless face on his own hospital pillow and Perry clinging to her through that dreadful night had made it plain at last. She had always thought of herself as being without importance, had thought that it would be presumptuous to imagine otherwise but she knew now that this was wrong. She knew now that she, Shanti Virk, mattered.

The topic of return to India had lapsed. The guests, sensing that to pursue it might cause discord in their host's family, had tactfully embarked once more on general conversation. Sita and Hari were talking about the house into which they hoped soon to move; Mohan Lal, since Krishna was still in the kitchen, was remarking that soon he must find her a nice Hindu boy, and in the kitchen, Leela was telling Krishna how Shanti had resourcefully advertised in order to find and thank the elderly lady whose intervention had probably saved Satnam's life.

Balbir was talking about gardening to Mrs Sodhi. Balbir's school reports continually said things like *could try harder* and *shows promise but lacks application*, but there was just about nothing Balbir didn't know about thinning tomato plants or fighting aphids. If only examination papers could ask questions like that, he'd come top every time.

Chandra Lal was saying to Mr Sodhi, "The police inspector did his job but I think he does not understand us very well. Perhaps more Indian people should join the police force."

Suddenly Shanti smiled. Even though there was a court case ahead and Satnam would have to be a witness, normal life was resuming once again.

"Here we are at last. Our very own home," said Sita.

Her voice echoed. The furniture painstakingly collected, much of it from good second-hand shops, and kindly stored meanwhile by Kartar in his garage while his car stood forlornly in the street, came nowhere near to filling the space available. They had no carpets yet, either; just a few rugs. But two of those she had hooked herself and their deep pile was real wool, in glowing colours, and she had made curtains to go with them. The previous owners of the house had left a nice gas stove behind, too.

"And here I am," she said happily, "cooking our very first dinner on our own stove. Hari, isn't it *wonderful*?"

Hari was leaning in the kitchen doorway, watching her stir the rice. He was in shirt-sleeves, his shirt open at the neck to display a brown, lightly furred V of chest. It gleamed faintly with sweat; he had been shifting the furniture about to make the best of it. His new horn-rimmed glasses gave him an intellectual look and he had dust in his hair. He was so beautiful that Sita's head swam at the sight of him.

This thing called marriage was beyond anything she had ever imagined. Her mother, carefully instructing her in the facts of life, had never talked of being intoxicated by sheer pleasure, had never told her about the freedom, the dizzy, undreamed-of freedom of drawing close to another person, letting another person right into you without having to hold timidly back for fear of overstepping some unseen boundary. No boundaries existed any more. Her mother had never told her that it was paradise on earth just to be able to say the words *I love you*.

"I want everyone in the world to be as happy as I am," Sita said ecstatically. "I want Krishna to have a husband just like you. Do you really think you know someone who might be suitable for her?"

"Yes. He's a friend that I knew in India. He came over ahead of me. In fact, I've already arranged for him to see your parents

234

and talk to Krishna. Tomorrow, it'll be. I'm very hungry. Is it nearly ready?"

"Almost. I suppose," said Sita, peering from pan to pan and carefully tasting the curry, "that we shall have to get another stove to provide a kitchen upstairs. That second-hand shop in Southall, where we got the tallboy, might have one. There's quite a few things we still have to buy. The house won't seem quite so much ours when the tenants are in, but it will be better than living with my parents."

"It will be a great deal better," Hari agreed. "With the tenants, I shall be the landlord, the one on top. I have been waiting for this day. Surely the food's done? It smells as if it is."

"Yes. Go and sit down; I'll bring it."

They had as yet only one small table and a chair each. But when she had used a wedding present of money to buy bed linen, there had been enough left over for a Nottingham lace tablecloth and a set of table mats showing views of English villages. A handsome dinner service had been given to them as another present. She thought that the table, small though it was, looked really nice. She arranged the food in the middle of it, in serving dishes: chapattis wrapped in a cloth, lamb curry for Hari, and a vegetable curry which they could share.

"We do need a three piece suite for our sitting room," she said as she sat down and filled his plate. "And buying soft furniture second-hand is so risky. One never knows what things are like inside. The springs could be weak or the stuffing going rotten. Buying new would be expensive but . . . "

"Very expensive," said Hari with his mouth full. "I have a heavy mortgage."

She wished he had said *we* instead of *I*. It was true that the mortgage was in Hari's name but she meant to contribute if she could and surely he knew that.

"I could find a job if necessary," she suggested.

"You will not find a job. I have said this before. There might be other men. Besides, I need you to do the books for the shop and perhaps help behind the counter. I need an assistant but I don't want to pay one yet; my overdraft is bad enough as it is. What are you doing?"

"What am I doing?" Sita paused with a spoonful of vegetable curry halfway to her plate. "What do you mean?"

"Yes. There." Hari pointed to the spoon. "What are you doing with that?"

"It's my vegetable curry. I'm going to eat it."

"No," said Hari. "No, you are not. Not until I've finished. Take it back to the kitchen to keep it warm and then come and serve me as a wife should. You eat afterwards."

"*What?*"

"I know that in your home everyone eats together; I have lived there and seen it. But at home with my Uncle Dinesh and my Aunt Savitri, the women wait on the men; that is the traditional way and that is how it will be in my house. Now," said Hari, "that I am in my own home, things are going to be very, very different. What are you waiting for?"

"But I'm just as hungry as you are!" Sita stared at him. It still looked like Hari sitting there opposite her and the voice was Hari's voice. But the things he was saying were the mouthings of a disagreeable stranger. "I'm going to eat my dinner. Your food is there; no one is asking you to wait. I will not hide in the kitchen while you eat . . . "

Hari, who had been doubling a chapatti over a filling of curry, set it down on the plate again, took off his glasses and polished them with a curious vigour, and stood up. "Oh, yes, you will," he said.

"No!" Sita sobbed. "No, no, no! I don't want to, I don't want sex with you, not again, not after that. How can you hit me like that and then expect me to let you . . . ?"

There had to be some limits; she still had a vestige of pride, even now. She had fought as much as she could. She had kicked him several times and broken away once; she had kept up a macabre chase round and round the meagre furniture for a long time before he finally cornered her and then she had bitten him. In the end she had been defeated, broken, forced to say yes, she would serve him at table and do everything else as he wished it, but this was a deeper thing, an attack on a private stronghold. She would not let him have sex. She would *not . . . *

But her exhaustion was too great. She had the will to fight him still but her physical strength was done for. He pushed her down and his knees shoved her thighs apart. She screamed thinly at him and tried to use her fists but her blows were as weak as a child's. He was in. He was jerking her about as though she were a mat he was shaking. He was shouting. "Respond, can't you? My God, you're no use even at this. You don't know how to serve your husband in any way at all, do you? Every woman I've ever had in my life before was better at it than this!"

Better at what? Sita wondered inside her head as the awful agonising sawing went on and on, rasping on dry tissues which didn't want him, *didn't want* him so passionately that they refused to lubricate themselves. Better at being the victims of rape?

On the first morning in her very own, her first married home, Sita gave her husband his breakfast, serving him with averted face and without speaking to him. "Not a bad meal," he said as he put on his jacket and made for the front door to go to his shop. "But do the eggs half a minute more tomorrow morning."

Sita spoke for the first time that day. "What if I go home and tell my father, show my mother, what you have done?"

"What can they do? They will not take you back; we are married and they will say it is your fault; you must have provoked me. As indeed you did. When you behave as a wife should, Sita, you will find you are happy enough. You must learn, that is all."

Then he was gone and Sita, alone in the house, climbed slowly up the stairs, lay down on the bed which was the only new item of furniture in the place, and wept.

She wept hopelessly and whimperingly, for dreams which had been shattered, and for the gentle, loving bridegroom who had after all been nothing more than a sham, a mere performance. Once she rolled on to her back and stared through blurred eyes at the walls of the bedroom. She had looked forward so much to their first night in this bedroom. Now it was no better than a prison cell.

Hari had said that today she must clean the whole house right through. He would expect to find it shining when he came home and he would go round it to see that it was. She had cried out that she would be too stiff but all he said was, "You'll work it off, and you'll be stiffer afterwards if it isn't done."

She had loved him so much. He had filled her mind with his image and her body with desire; he had kindled her deepest and most female emotions; she would have followed him to anywhere on earth, or to death as Hindu women in her ancestry had followed their husbands to the funeral pyre; had anyone attacked him she would have thrown herself into the path of bullet or knife. And she had longed to give him a son.

He wanted the son. He had said that, during last night's hideous travesty of love. "The first child had better be a boy."

237

But he wanted nothing of the rest. He simply wanted a servant, a slave, something to clean the house and cook meals and wash up the dishes and keep quiet.

He was going to find Krishna a husband, somebody just like himself. Somebody just like Hari . . .

Sita shot off the bed. The sudden movement made her cry out; all her movements this morning so far had been wary and slow. For a moment, sensing danger to her sister, she had forgotten. Suddenly seized by a spasm of nausea, she stumbled towards the bathroom. When it was over, she blew her nose, wiped her face on a cold flannel and made for the stairs. As well as a gas stove, the previous occupants had left another useful piece of apparatus behind. Their telephone was still there. Hari had said they'd need a phone and given instructions that it was not to be disconnected. It was in the hall.

"Sita! How nice! How do you like your new home?" Her mother's voice, full of innocent good cheer, was like a kick in the guts.

"Mother! Oh, thanks be to God you're there . . . "

"How are you settling in? It must be very exciting, having a whole house to get into order . . . "

"*Mother! Listen!* You must listen! This is urgent, so urgent . . . "

"But what is the matter? Sita . . . ?"

"There is a young man coming to see you all today, about Krishna. Hari has suggested him as a husband for Krishna. That's right, isn't it?"

"Why, yes, certainly. Are you coming to join us? He is arriving this afternoon. Krishna does not know yet; we are letting her think he is just a visitor, so that she will talk to him naturally . . . "

"Mother, on no account must Krishna marry this young man. Don't ask me why and above all don't ever tell Hari I have spoken to you, but *Krishna must not marry this man* . . . say you have decided she should finish her studies, that she is not yet grown up enough, say anything! Tell Father what I have said. Tell him I know what I am saying!"

"But, Sita, what is wrong with this man? And why must Hari not be told? Is something wrong between you and your husband? Sita . . . ?"

"Krishna has a mind of her own if it comes to it," said Sita. "If I must, I will speak to *her* and tell her that she must say no. It would be better if you and Father protected her but . . . "

"But why? Sita, what is the matter?"

238

"Don't ask! Just look after Krishna!" said Sita and put the receiver down, unable to endure the conversation for a moment longer. She turned to contemplate the house, wondering where to begin the giant cleaning task she had been set. It would be easier, perhaps, to do what Aunt Shanti had once tried to do, and kill herself.

Another spasm of nausea gripped her. There was no time to reach the bathroom; the kitchen sink would have to do. Not very hygienic, but it couldn't be helped.

The nausea had, she suspected, little to do with Hari's sudden metamorphosis into some form of alien life. She was three weeks overdue. She was almost certainly pregnant.

If she killed herself, she would kill her child too. It was Hari's child as well, she thought bitterly. Possibly the world would be better off without the offspring of such a man. But instinct was too strong.

She was, it seemed, condemned to life.

PART THREE

RAMINDER ROSE

1980-88

Chapter Twenty

Journeys and Meetings
1980

"What a wonderful trip this has been. How I wish we could have stayed in India," Ranbir sighed.

"Yes, I shall feel quite homesick, being in England again. It was such a pleasure, seeing all the family members and the way of life is so pleasant. Friends coming round in the evening and all of us sitting outside with cool drinks and chatting; somehow it is never like that in England," Nita agreed. "Rose, you will miss India, I think, now that you have seen it."

"Especially Uncle Sunder and Aunt Billie," said Rose. "I feel now as if I had known them always. How kind they were. It was so touching, Auntie Billie crying like that when we left."

The jumbo jet was stacked up over Heathrow and circling. Peering out of the porthole beside her, Rose could see the grey-green of England below; neat rows of houses, roads with toy cars moving along them, the steely sheen of a reservoir under a grey sky, Windsor Castle laid out below like a model fort.

She wouldn't say it, because it would annoy her grandmother, but the sight of England almost brought tears of relief to her eyes. Dear, cool, damp, orderly England, where there were no water or electricity shortages, was home. And India wasn't.

She *had* enjoyed the trip in a way. It had been the first visit any of them had managed to pay to India since the family came to Britain before she was born and everyone had been delighted to see them. Great-Uncle Sunder and Auntie Billie, along with a crowd of other friends and relatives, were at the airport in force to meet them and the hospitality had been almost embarrassingly open-handed. She and her sister Amrit had been admired, exclaimed over, given endless presents. Rose had worn her first sari in India and now had three of them, all gifts, in her luggage, together with jewellery and a marvellously embroidered silk

243

shawl. From Uncle Sunder and Auntie Billie she and Amrit had met not only with great kindness but also with approval because, "You have brought them up as proper Indian girls, Nita; they fit in with us so well and Rose especially is so well educated."

Fourteen-year-old Amrit had a cooler nature, but Rose had come to love her aunt and uncle. Yet it seemed to her that it was Amrit, not herself, who fitted best into Indian society. Rose felt as if she had been plunged into a completely alien mental world. There was much talk of politics but it was all Indian and rather alarming; mainly about Mrs Gandhi and her return to power, which seemed to worry Uncle Sunder. "This Congress Party will not care for Sikh culture; Sikhs should have their own province."

Her father had objected to that, saying that religious partitioning always caused trouble. "Look at what happened when India was partitioned in 1947 and look what is happening in Ireland now." Rose knew about the Partition riots. It was frightening to think, when she was taken on a sightseeing tour to Amritsar where the Golden Temple of the Sikhs stood, that she was in an area where some of those riots had taken place. It was for her as though the memory of that old violence still hung in the air.

A soothing female voice announced that the descent was commencing. The plane was losing height, its engine noise reduced. Across Amrit, who was dozing in the seat between them, Nita smiled at Rose. "I think you must be tired. You must rest a day or two before you begin your studies again. Auntie Billie was most impressed with the exams you are hoping to take; she thinks you should qualify for a profession. She said to us all your cousins in India are doing that and you must not lag behind. So, if your A-level results allow, you will go to university; your father and I have decided and Bheji agrees."

"I should like that," said Rose. "Very much!"

"Yes. You did not know, but there was talk of finding a marriage for you in India," Nita said. Rose, startled, sat up straight. Nita laughed and shook her head. "No, no, it is all right. We all decided that you must not waste your studies. There was a time when your father and I were not sure we wanted you to go to an English university, and Bheji had doubts, too, but now we think you should. Such a degree is valuable when it comes to looking for a good match. Besides, you have said you would like to teach and you must have a degree if you are to do that."

"There are many Indian children growing up in England," Rose said. "It will be a good thing if there are Indian teachers. I can be useful, in such a profession. Perhaps Amrit will do the same one day."

Beyond Nita, Ranbir was now complaining of earache and Kartar was leaning forward from behind to say that never mind, they were nearly down. With a rumble and an earthbound vibration, the wheels touched the runway.

"There we are," Kartar said. "Home."

"Home?" said Ranbir, and snorted.

It was a Saturday and Perry was free to meet them with the car he had now acquired. He and Shanti were waiting at the barrier, two sturdy and familiar figures. Shanti had put on a little weight with the years and the lines which both their faces had now acquired were similar. Rose thought that Uncle Perry and Aunt Shanti looked these days almost like brother and sister.

"Oh, you should have come; it was so nice, three weeks was not nearly long enough," Ranbir said as embraces of greeting were exchanged.

"We have any amount of news, and everyone has sent messages; it will have to be your turn next," Nita declared.

"We'll see," said Perry.

"Oh, you need not worry what they will say about you shaving off. Two of my cousins have done the same; people take it in their stride now."

"We have news of our own," said Perry, changing the subject. "If you are up to it tomorrow and not still sleeping the journey off, we are introducing Balbir to a prospective wife. Yes, we are thinking of getting him married. Give me that case. Sunder is bringing the car round to the front. So will you all come round for tea and supper tomorrow?"

"It's a funny way to do things," Satnam said. He used English, as he generally did when talking to his brothers and sister. He looked critically at the taper-holder he had just tacked to the wall. "Will that hold, do you think? Those sandalwood tapers don't weigh much, but every time those new people next door have another bout of hammering, the wall shakes. They seem to be reconstructing their house inside as well as outside. First of all

245

they pave the front garden to make a carport and now this. Won't you *mind*, Sunder, if Balbir gets married first?"

"Only *if*," said Balbir from an uncomfortable all-fours position under the settee. "Why is it that our mother always wants to move the furniture round when there's company? These castors are stuck on the edge of the carpet. When I have my own home, I shall have wall-to-wall carpets like Uncle Kartar. I haven't met the girl yet. Perhaps we won't like each other."

"Then they'll find you someone else," said Sunder. "And of course I don't mind. I told them I didn't want to think of marriage yet. But Balbir's willing, so good luck to him. I think he's a bit young myself, but that's his business." Sitting cross-legged on the divan which was the largest piece of furniture in the sitting room, he slit open a packet of the sandalwood tapers with which the air was to be scented during the evening which Shanti persisted in regarding as a celebration: "Just as if it were all signed and sealed and the banns posted in the Registry Office," Balbir had said with amusement.

"But now that you see arrangements actually being made to introduce him to someone?" said Satnam. At nearly twenty, he was a lean, rigid-shouldered boy whose turban looked slightly too heavy for him. He took life seriously. "Don't you . . . ?"

"No, young 'un, I do not. What a persistent brat you are. Here, put the tapers in the holders."

"I just wondered," said Satnam. "You're the only one of us who has gone English and cut his hair, though you were shocked enough when Father first cut his. I thought perhaps you were diffident in case the girls and their parents weren't keen on you because of that."

"I'm not in the least diffident," said Sunder shortly. "Everyone isn't as disapproving as you. I saw Father's point eventually, and plenty of other people think as he does."

"Then why don't you want to get married? It does not look good, the younger brother being settled first."

"I refused because I don't want to get married that way. I want to pick my own sweetheart and go out with her."

"And as I keep on telling you," said Balbir, finally releasing the settee castors, and then crawling out backwards, "I then volunteered because I thought it would make Mum and Dad happier and I quite like the idea of getting married. They were disappointed in me when I insisted that I only wanted to study horticulture at college, and they don't think much of this job I've

246

got at the garden centre, either. I thought this would please them and it has, so stop knocking it, young Satnam."

"But people are bound to whisper."

"Well, let them," said Sunder impatiently. "Pity they haven't got anything more important to whisper about! The way people in our community gossip all the time makes me tired. I'm not going to be pushed into marriage when I don't want to be, just to please the busybodies. Oh, hello, Rupa."

"Who is being a busybody?" Rupa enquired, putting a glossy dark head round the door. At sixteen, Rupa was already maturing towards exceptional good looks: Shanti's delicate bone-structure allied to the strong aquiline features of her father's family. She was well aware of it. Rupa washed her hair every day and wore gloves for housework in order to protect her hands and the transparent nail varnish which was all she was as yet allowed.

"The world in general," said Sunder. "Is the furniture to our mother's liking now, do you think?"

"Oh, yes. It's just that she always wants the settee under the window when we have visitors because she says it looks more welcoming there, even if it does mean that we can't get at the record cabinet properly. I wish we had a bigger house. It will be worse still when you bring your wife here, Balbir. You'll have to save up for a deposit on your own place as soon as possible. By the way, have you seen what is happening next door? Those people who moved in last week are having another vanload of furniture delivered. I saw from the kitchen window. Would you believe it? How much room have they got inside their house? They must be hanging chairs and tables from the ceiling!"

The new neighbours, who had bought number sixty-six Harrison Street after the death of the widowed Mrs Brierley, were of enormous interest to the young Virks, because they were English (Shanti thought this a pity but her children didn't), because the family included three youngsters in their teens or early twenties who might be willing to make friends, and because they owned not one, but two new cars. ("The latest registration!" Sunder had said, impressed.) Anything that was going on next door was worth attention.

"I think we could see best of all from my window," Rupa said helpfully.

All discord instantly forgotten, the four of them stampeded laughing out of the sitting room and up to Rupa's room. They crowded on to the deep, though not very wide sill of her little

247

dormer window and pressed their noses to the pane.

"I *say*," breathed Satnam. "Look at all that stereo equipment. I should like to have that!"

"What is their name, I wonder? I haven't found out yet," said Rupa, peering interestedly down as their neighbours darted in and out of the front door, escorting and instructing the delivery men.

"Edmonds," said Sunder. "The postman pushed one of the letters for number sixty-six into our letterbox by mistake yesterday. It was addressed to a Mr Edmonds. There's five of them, I think. Two parents, two sons and a girl, rather like us, only the girl's the oldest. That's her, look. She's pretty."

"She's got sandy hair. Ugh," said Rupa.

"Don't be rude. It's the colour of fresh ginger root. I think it's nice," said Sunder.

"Rupa thinks her hair is the best in the world," said Balbir, and pulled one of his sister's glossy blue-black plaits. Rupa jerked them away, glaring at him.

Satnam said, "Oh, well, they're English. Maybe they won't want to know us after all."

The sitting room smelt of spiced sweetmeats and of the throat-catching threads of smoke from the festive sandalwood tapers. The room was comfortably packed because Shanti had wanted it that way. "As many of us as possible and as many of the girl's family. Then both the families can see each other and get to know each other and in the midst of it all, Balbir and Narinder can slip out into another room for a chat and it will not be too noticeable. That will be less embarrassing for them. They can use the kitchen. Since you built the extension, Perry, it is quite comfortable for sitting in."

It looked as if the whole enterprise was going to be a success, Sunder thought, nursing a cup of tea and surveying the scene, from which he was keeping aloof on purpose. Balbir and Narinder ("but her school-friends shortened it to Nerin and now we all call her that," her mother said) had had their private chat and were continuing with it openly, sitting in adjacent arm-chairs, sharing the same low table for their cups and plates and picking these up without looking because their eyes were exclusively engaged with each other's faces.

Nerin was a merry little thing, with the same blackcurrant eyes and soft features that her mother had; her mother, sitting op-

248

posite and studiously not watching her daughter, was what Nerin would one day turn into. Mrs Inder Singh was admittedly overweight, with plumply dimpled arms and wrists but she wore her gold-bordered pink sari with an air and she had an attractive deep chuckle. Balbir could do worse and judging by his earnest attentiveness to Nerin, he had already reached that conclusion himself. Provided that the girl liked him in return, and she did seem to be enjoying his company, this meeting was likely to have results.

His sister Rupa and his cousin-sisters Krishna, Rose and Amrit were handing round the refreshments. Krishna was twenty-five but she was not married yet and there was no talk of it, either. There had been, some years ago, but something had gone amiss. He believed it was connected with her sister Sita's unhappy marriage, but Sunder knew no details. He knew only that Mohan Lal from time to time said things like, "It is so easy to make mistakes, being in too much of a hurry; Krishna says she will tell us when she wants something arranged," and that Sita had on several occasions turned up on her parents' doorstep in floods of tears, clutching her small son Dinesh, to be given hot drinks, comfort and advice before going miserably home – or being fetched back by Hari – in order to "try again", as her parents invariably advised. The situation had gone on for years and Sita must be fairly sick by now of being told to "try again" although she still went on dutifully doing so.

Krishna now was working as a journalist on a magazine called *Catering Chronicle*, and much of her work consisted of eating out in various restaurants and reporting on the food and service. Sunder thought it a marvel that she didn't get fat, but Krishna was svelte and sophisticated and Rupa had a crush on her.

The rest of the party were seated. His mother and his Aunt Leela were talking to Nerin's mother and another woman who, Sunder thought, was Nerin's aunt. On his other side, her father, who was a thin, somewhat self-effacing Sikh, was chatting to Mohan Lal and Uncle Kartar about the unemployment situation and beyond them, heads together, were his father, Bheji and Aunt Nita, with Satnam sitting politely by while his elders, by the sound of it, were discussing Rose.

Exquisitely pretty as a child, Rose in maturity was not as beautiful as either Rupa or Krishna. She had more austere features, a thinner mouth and a leaner jawline and she wore spectacles, although she chose the frames well: they suited her.

249

"They're talking about you," Sunder said, as she paused beside him to collect an empty cup.

"I know. It's this university business. My parents keep saying it is important I should go and then in the same breath telling me how careful I've got to be when I get there, how I should behave. And if they forget to mention it, Bheji reminds them! Just as if," said Rose rather crossly, "I don't already know! I would rather not go at all than be lectured all the time before I've had a chance to do anything wrong!"

"Come and sit here, Rose, and drink your tea," Perry called. "So if all goes well, you'll be off to college in the autumn?"

Kartar leaned across. "Well, all young people should go to college who are able, don't you think? There is plenty of choice in subjects to study. My nephew Balbir studied horticulture but he did very well. The garden centre where he works is a research establishment as well. They produce new varieties of flowers. It is all highly technical."

"Sales patter. Balbir's the merchandise," Rupa whispered to Sunder as Rose went to sit down.

"You will have a good time at university, I expect. Which one will it be? I wish Nerin could have gone, but she is a very domesticated girl and none the worse for that, but I think it is a good thing for girls to have a profession," Nerin's father said to Rose. "What do you hope to take up eventually?"

"I am hoping to teach. But I still have to take my A-levels and of course I don't yet know how well I shall do, or which university I shall be able to get into."

"I envy you," Perry said. "I went to college when I first came to this country but it was not a university and that must be quite an experience. You'll enjoy it." He laughed. "Before you go, come to me and I will show you how to dance. When I was a young man, before I was married, I used to dance at Hammersmith Palais. I know the waltz and the quickstep . . . "

"Oh, no!" Ranbir broke in quickly. "No, no, we have told Rose: she should not take part in such things!"

"Well, we would prefer it if she didn't," Nita said. "There will be no need. When you have finished your studies, Rose, and settled into your work as a teacher, we shall find you a husband; you need have no worries about that. Of course, you will mix with many people at university and make friends and perhaps we should not be too rigid but . . . "

"At Western-style dances one must dance with a partner and

then she will be urged to go out with some boy or other!" snapped Ranbir. "And that will embarrass her!"

"Yes, that's true," Kartar said. "It could be difficult to refuse. Just because we have taught you to be kind and polite, you could find yourself with problems, my Raminder Rose."

"Problems!" Out came Ranbir's familiar snort. "It will be more than that, I am telling you. Rose, if you go out with boys and that gets known, your reputation could be ruined. Before you go to university, you must promise not to go on dates or go dancing. You must promise solemnly, to your parents and to me."

"For goodness sake!" said Perry. "The poor girl! All this fuss about going to a dance. It is just harmless, I tell you!"

"No, it is not harmless!" said Ranbir dogmatically. "Perry, you are always too casual and easygoing about these things."

"It is different for men," said Nita mildly. "It is a fine line that Indian girls over here have to walk and perhaps it is better to err on the side of taking care."

"Yes, that is how one should think," said Ranbir, nodding vigorously.

In a "let's change the subject" tone of voice, Kartar said, "We have just returned from three weeks in India. Have you been at all recently? The economic situation has not improved, I'm afraid."

"No, we have not been for some years," said Nerin's father. "The fares are very costly and Nerin must have some kind of dowry. I know you are not asking for a dowry but still, as her father, it is my duty. But one does not save so very fast, running a newsagent's, although ours is a very good little business now we have a sub-post office as well . . . "

"Listen to them," said Sunder in an undertone to Rupa. Since all the seats in the immediate vicinity were full, she perched on the arm of his chair in order to eat a sweetmeat. "You're dead right. It *is* sales patter. Nerin's parents mustn't think less of Balbir because he has studied horticulture instead of engineering; he's in *research*. Our parents mustn't think that Nerin's father isn't a successful businessman; his newsagent's is a sub-post office as well and Nerin will have a dowry. God, it's all so out of date!"

"I know. I shall cringe when the time comes and all that is going on to do with me."

"It's making me cringe now! It's one reason why I didn't want them to arrange anything for me. I don't think I can listen to

251

these conversations one minute longer. I'm going out. Don't tell anyone. I shall just disappear as though I were going to the bathroom."

"Lucky thing. I wish I could do the same," said Rupa.

"You can always go and hide in the kitchen. See you later," said Sunder.

He left the hot, crowded, perfumed sitting-room quietly and with relief, closing the door after him and taking a deep breath as though he were inhaling freedom. He hadn't decided where he was going but very definitely, it was out. The hall, however, was chilly, unlike the sitting room. It must be cold outside, in which case he'd need his jacket. He went up to his room to fetch it but stopped in the act of putting it on, his attention caught by a remarkable noise from outside. A car engine was revving and fading in short, sharp bursts, accompanied by a curious grinding noise. A car door slammed and a female voice said something which sounded like an oath. The door slammed again and there was more revving. Sunder, shrugging himself the rest of the way into his jacket, went to his window.

The view it afforded of the carport of number sixty-six was more limited than that from Rupa's but it showed enough.

"I don't believe it!" said Sunder on a burst of laughter.

He was letting himself out of the front door just as his father came out of the sitting room.

"Are you going out somewhere, Sunder? You are not staying with us for the dinner?"

"Er . . . no. Well," said Sunder with a grin, "I have a mission. I've got to rescue a damsel in distress."

"What you have done," he said a few minutes later, surveying the Ford Escort in the carport of number sixty-six, "is impossible. How did you manage it?"

"I don't know. Natural genius? It is quite an achievement, isn't it?" said the sandy-haired Edmonds girl. She had climbed out of the car again when she saw him turn in at the gate. "Oh, I'm sorry. Did you want to see my father? Everyone's out, but I can take a message. If it's about all the hammering, we've nearly finished now. We realise it must be a nuisance."

"No, no, I came to see if I could help you with the car. I saw from my window that you were stuck . . . how on *earth* did you manage to hook the front bumper round the gatepost and the rear bumper round the support of that rose trellis? I don't think

252

I could do it if I tried."

"I wasn't trying," said the Edmonds girl gloomily. "I only passed my test a month ago," she added defensively. "It takes time to become really skilful. Can I get the car loose without marking it, do you think? I cashed an insurance policy to buy it. It'll break my heart if I damage it."

Her hair was neither sandy nor ginger, Sunder thought. They were flat, dull words. This girl's smooth cap of hair gleamed like old gold. She had no inhibitions about wearing pink with it: her black slacks were teamed with a shocking pink jumper. And she was right: it looked well. She had a bony freckled face and eyes which were virtually green. "If I get in again," she said, "perhaps you could guide me so that I can get the bumpers free again?"

Sunder walked round the car to inspect the problem at close quarters. "You can't. Go backwards to release the rear bumper and you'll wrench the front bumper and vice versa. Back the car about an inch, just so as to clear the trellis upright. No more than an inch! Just twitch the car backwards and then stop. Then get out again and we'll have to go round to the back and try to rock the whole car sideways. Then you can drive forward and escape from the gatepost."

She slid back behind the wheel and once more started the engine. The reverse gear went into place with a slight grinding noise. Sunder awaited the next development with some disquiet but he had misjudged her. He had said "just twitch the car backwards" and she did precisely that. She cut the engine and then looked out of the window. "Handbrake on or off?"

"I think it'll have to be on. Your carport slopes. Not much, but it would be awful if we got the car free and then it ran away from us and straight out into Harrison Street!"

"Don't!"

A few moments later, they were side by side at the boot, grasping the rear bumper. "One . . . two . . . three . . . *heave!*" said Sunder. "One . . . two . . . three . . . *again!*"

"She's moving!"

"Are cars called she as well as ships? One . . . two . . . . . . three . . . *heave!*"

" . . . that's got her!" said Sunder with satisfaction.

"Cars are called she on occasion, by their loving owners. Oh, thank goodness that's done. I can just drive off now. If I'd had to leave it there like that I'd never have heard the end of it. I've got two teenage brothers. Thank you very much indeed. What's your name, by the way? If we're going to live next door to each other, we ought to know each other's names. I'm Lynn Edmonds."

"I'm Sunder Virk."

"Yours is a Sikh family, isn't it? At least . . . " Lynn hesitated.

"It's a complicated situation. My younger brothers are orthodox, my father and I are not and my mother's Hindu."

"I am trying to learn something about these things. I have to deal with Indian families sometimes. I'm a social worker. I've a job in this area and of course, there's a big Indian community here."

They smiled at each other, each aware suddenly that the other was young and good-looking and friendly.

"I must go," said Lynn. "I'm on my way to a committee meeting."

"You're going to work?"

"Oh, no. This is a club I belong to. I'm interested in the history of London and I'm a member of a society which goes in for studying it. I'm on the committee."

On impulse, Sunder said, "You have a boyfriend?"

Lynn's face grew shadowed. "I . . . no. I had, but not now."

"Do you ever go dancing?" said Sunder.

Chapter Twenty-One

Shall We Dance?

1981

"Look, Cinderella," said Anne-Marie Devereux, sinking to her heels on the hearth-rug, the better to manage coffee cups on a table only fifteen inches high, "it's for *charity. Everyone's* going." She turned a bright, triangular face up to Rose. "Gawdstrewth, it's in aid of the anti-apartheid movement!" Anne-Marie had a French grandfather. She herself spoke pure home counties with occasional interjections of Cockney.

"I could buy a ticket or make a contribution," said Rose reasonably. "I don't actually have to go to the dance."

"It's a supper party as much as a dance. A do-it-yourself party, to keep expenses down so that as much money as possible can go to the movement," said Roger Havers. He was Anne-Marie's boyfriend, and was also one of her fellow-tenants in this house which was rented between six. Their relationship seemed to Rose extraordinarily casual. Anne-Marie was her friend but there were things about her which were bewildering. "Neither of us want to be committed yet," Anne-Marie had once said to her.

"We've hired the hall," Roger explained. "But everything else is being contributed – the food, the drink, the band, everything."

There were ten or twelve people squeezed into the dusty living room for this coffee party. Anne-Marie, Roger and their four co-tenants did the minimum of housework and appeared to support life mainly on takeaways and sandwiches. Most of their gatherings were the coffee-and-conversation kind with which she normally felt at ease. They were all hard up and bottle parties, which made her uncomfortable, occurred only rarely.

This party, however, looked like becoming uncomfortable for another reason. A murmur of approval and persuasion had arisen round her as Roger spoke. "Rose, you *must* come," said a plump girl called Joan, who was reading history and wanted to become an archaeologist although Rose found it difficult to imagine anyone with a figure like Joan's crouching with a trowel to excavate pottery from a muddy trench, or crawling, flashlight in hand, through a dusty aperture into a newly opened Egyptian tomb. "You never join in anything," said Joan.

"There are things my parents wouldn't like me to do. Our culture is different from yours. Things that you can do without thinking about it, would be wrong for me."

"Asha doesn't seem to think so," said someone, and raised a laugh. Asha was a second-year student of Indian extraction. She had won a prize for Latin-American dancing, and was currently playing off three boyfriends against each other.

"Asha's different," Rose said hastily. "She is quite Westernised and so are all her family."

"You don't need a partner; plenty of people are going just in groups or even as singles," said Anne-Marie, handing cups and sugar. "You needn't dance! You could sit and watch and enjoy some of the food."

It was embarrassing. Her parents had not understood, when they sent her to Oxford, how difficult it would be for her to live by a different set of standards from everyone around her.

Her fellow-students wanted to make friends but friendship was a two-way process; one had to join in with the things one's friends did. Besides . . .

"You know," said a boy called Nick, who was perched in an armchair, cross-legged like a lanky Buddha, if Buddha had ever gone in for azure polo-neck sweaters, "you don't mean it but with all due respect, Rose, you're being remarkably rude."

"Rude?"

"Oh, no," said Anne-Marie, quick to her defence. "Rose would never be that. No, Nick, you can't say that."

"I said, I know she doesn't mean to be. But you *are*, you know. You're taking the attitude that attending this charity supper dance would be somehow or other improper, because there's going to be a hop. You're drawing your skirts aside from us and implying that we have lower moral standards than you."

"No, no. Just different standards." Rose was mortified.

"That's not how it comes over. It comes over as an unspoken suggestion that we – in fact all Westerners – are slightly dubious people. Frankly, I resent it. There's nothing immoral in danc-ing!"

"I know, but in my community . . . "

"You're not in your community now. You're in ours. And candidly . . . "

"Oh, leave it out, Nick," said Joan. "Live and let live."

"Look," said Rose, "I could come and contribute in another way. You like my Indian cooking . . . "

"Oh, yes, we *do*," said Anne-Marie. "When you came over and cooked for our party last week, it was a revelation. I never knew how delicious Indian food could be."

"Well, I could bring some dishes – sweetmeats and a curry. I'd like to do something to help, even if I don't dance."

"Oh, Rose, *would* you?" said Anne-Marie, and Nick said, "In that case, darling, you're forgiven."

In a parked car behind a Thames-side pub, as the autumn dusk came down, Sunder Virk and Lynn Edmonds sat in silent misery.

It was a silence which had been trying to establish itself all evening, ever since they set out, with Sunder driving too fast as though attempting to outdistance the argument which had sprung up at their previous date, the evening before. They had tried, this evening, to make conversation. But stiff comments about the weather had faltered hopelessly, until Sunder turned the car into a quiet lane, parked and tried to take Lynn in his arms, only to be angrily pushed away.

"All right, let's go and have a drink," he snapped, with vague hopes that the snug atmosphere of the Schooner Inn would soothe their nerves and somehow put things right.

But even the friendly smell of beer and the crackling wood fire in the wide brick hearth of the Captain's Bar had had no effect and the intimacy of the inglenook seat only served to drive home the fact that although they were physically close together, in spirit they were a thousand miles apart. Leaving their lagers half drunk, they had come out to the car again.

And now here they sat, knowing that they could not stay like this for ever, knowing that now, tonight, irrevocable things must be said and final decisions made, and unable, either of them, to come to the point.

Sunder turned his head to look at Lynn. In the dusk he could see little except the outline of a chiselled profile and a lean jaw. Seen in silhouette like that, her face looked stern, unfeminine; one could not see its asymmetric charm.

He imagined it instead and his stomach did a somersault.

He was going to lose her. And she was part of him now.

At the edge of the car park, a lamppost suddenly lit up, catching the highlights on Lynn's prominent cheekbones. And the sparkle of tears.

He was able to break the silence at last. "Lynn. What is it you want us to do?"

She turned to him, but away from the light so that now he could hardly see her face at all although he could feel the emanation of her anger. There was a fierceness in Lynn which both excited and bewildered him.

"I don't know. I'm not asking anything. I know – I've seen – how it is with your family. They are good neighbours; they asked us to your brother's wedding; they always say hello if I see them in the street or in the garden but although they know – they *must* know – that we are seeing each other . . . "

"We are lovers."

"I imagine they guess that as well. But they're not going to admit it. They smile at me and they're always polite but they're pretending all the time that I'm just the daughter of Mr and Mrs Edmonds next door, that there's nothing else to it, and they're going to go on doing that until it becomes real. You're in a good job now. One of these days your parents will invite some friends to tea and they'll bring an attractive daughter with them and before you know it, you'll be sitting beside her in the temple, both of you festooned in garlands, getting married. It'll just happen. I could get a transfer to another part of the country and I think I ought to."

"Lynn . . . "

"Well, what else is there to do? There's no future for us. My mother keeps asking and I keep staving her off. She doesn't mind and even my father's come round. He's got used to finding you on the doorstep and he's never been what you could describe as colour-conscious, anyway. My young brothers like you, too. But your people . . . "

"Lynn, I wish you'd say clearly what you're talking about."

"Isn't this where we came in? Wasn't that phrase the one that had us parting in a rage last night? What do you mean, what are we talking about? What do you *think* were talking about?"

"I keep asking, and you keep on not telling me."

"I said to you last night that I couldn't go on like this, being secretive, making love to you in the backs of cars or in snatches

258

at home when by sheer good fortune everyone else is out. It isn't
. . . it isn't enough."

"What is it you want, then?"

"Oh, don't ask silly questions!"

"It's news to me that I'm silly," said Sunder huffily.

"If your family did produce a nice girl for you to marry, say at
a tea-party tomorrow, what would you say? What would you do?
Would you agree?"

"No, I wouldn't. I've refused before and I will again."

"Why? You'll want to get married sooner or later. Who," said
Lynn coldly, "are you saving yourself for? Why won't you consider the girls your family offers you?"

"Because I want a love-match. I want to marry a girl of my
own choice, someone I'm in love with."

"Thanks. What am I, then? A stop-gap?"

"No! But, Lynn . . . "

"Well? Are you in love with me or not? It's been a hell of a
long time we've been making love in corners, let me point out.
About eighteen months, to be precise. Haven't you made up
your mind yet?"

"I think," said Sunder slowly, gazing out through the wind-
screen and fixing his eyes on the lamppost, "that I've been
waiting for you to . . . tire of me. I thought you were bound to, in
the end. You've never seemed to want to come too close. You've
so many things in your life: your work, and this club you belong
to. I felt that soon you'd find someone else you liked better.
Then this would end of itself and . . . "

"And you'd be relieved?"

"No. No! Do you think I'm relieved now? Because we are
breaking up, aren't we? This is it, now, tonight. And I'm not glad
of it, no. God help me, I can't find words . . . !"

"Words for what?"

Sunder was silent again, struggling with his feelings.

"Words for *what*?" Lynn persisted.

"When I first asked you out," said Sunder huskily, "it was just
. . . just instinct. The male courting the female, not looking
ahead, just following nature. Later, when you had become *you*,
and making love with you wasn't just sex any more, it was me
and you talking with our bodies, I didn't think it could last like
that. It was magical but I couldn't see that there was any way
ahead. I didn't see how you could go on feeling like that . . . I
couldn't," said Sunder, "bring myself to be the one to end it and

259

I knew that when the moment came for us to say goodbye, it would be as though you'd put a knife into me. I've been bracing myself for it . . . "

"But I don't want to say goodbye!"

"Don't you? But isn't that what you were beginning to say, last night, when you said you couldn't go on like this?"

"No."

"What, then?"

"I'm leaving it up to you," said Lynn. "Can't you understand? I can't go on being secretive, having a love affair that is just that and nothing more. I'm not made that way. I've had one love affair already that didn't come to anything. Well, it was a mistake. He wasn't right for me, nor I for him. But all the same, when it dragged on and on and led nowhere, it gave me a sort of sick feeling, as if I'd . . . planted a tree and it wasn't thriving. I was watching it wither. I'd sooner chop a tree down than watch it slowly die."

"Lynn, what on earth are you talking about?"

"Oh, Sunder, you can be so *dense*. I'm telling you that either tonight is the last time we ever go out together again or else tonight is the night we get engaged! Is that plain enough for you?"

"Get . . . you mean you'd marry me?"

"Of course I would! If you ever got round to asking me, of course. If you actually want to ask me."

"You'd . . . *marry* me?"

"Not in a temple ceremony," said Lynn, wiping her eyes. "That would feel too strange, I think. In a Registry Office. Yes, I would. But since I don't think you're going to ask me, perhaps we'd better just drive home and say goodnight with a handshake."

"You'd really . . . ?"

"Face your family? Well, you know them better than I do. If you think it's impossible, that their opposition would be too strong, well just forget it," said Lynn, in a loud, firm and determinedly sensible voice. "No hard feelings. As I said, we'll shake hands and part. But if you want me to help you face them, I'll do that instead. You tell me what you want, then we'll both know where we are."

After a moment, Sunder said, "You love me . . . that much?"

"Yes, if you want to know. The question just now seems to be, how much do you love me? But I repeat, I'm not trying to push you into anything against your will. I'm just saying . . . I am just saying, I love you," said Lynn, in a voice now low and trembling. "Do what you like about it. But there it is."

"Lynn . . . "

"Yes?"

It felt like jumping off a cliff. It also felt gloriously and liberatingly right. It was the thing he had been searching for since the day he first declined his parents' offer of a bride. "Will you marry me?" said Sunder.

The supper-dance in aid of the anti-apartheid movement was being held outside college premises, in a community centre which had kitchen facilities. "Some of us want to cook things on the spot," Anne-Marie had said, "so it's ideal. And there's plenty of space for dancing and the buffet."

The atmosphere felt familiar to Rose; it reminded her of the Gurudwara in Southall, where food was cooked on the premises by volunteers and every service was followed by a meal. As she carried her mighty casserole full of chicken curry into the kitchen, she was at once plunged into the comfortable, accustomed air of bustle and turning-to. And the presence, too, of brown faces, for the people who stood round the two big stoves were of assorted ethnic origins. To judge from the spicy smells in the air, so were the contents of the saucepans bubbling on the hotplates.

A young West Indian man with smoothly moulded features and steel-framed spectacles was arranging slices of quiche on a serving plate with the precision of a professional chef and a girl in a long limp polka-dot skirt and black sweater, although unmistakably an English student, was tossing a salad as Rose's mother always did, with just the same movements. She needn't, Rose thought, have worried so much about the evening. It was all just ordinary.

"Now, you're not going to spend the evening lurking in here," said Anne-Marie, reappearing, Cheshire Cat fashion, a few minutes later to find Rose industriously setting out dishes on the long trestle tables in the buffet room next to the kitchen. "We have three dozen pairs of hands for this job and it'll be done in five minutes at suppertime. Come on out where the action is and show off that pretty sari. I'm glad you came in a sari; you look marvellous."

"I was afraid I might be overdressed," said Rose. "I didn't

261

know what to wear, really. I just guessed."

"People wear anything they like at these affairs," said Anne-Marie, who, unlike the girl in the polka dots and black sweater, had done justice to the occasion in burgundy-coloured taffeta. "Just wait till you see the Nigerian contingent we've got coming. They all *promised* to arrive in flowing robes. If you've got a gorgeous national dress, why not wear it? You never have to worry about deciding what kind of evening dress to wear, do you? You just pick out any ornamental sari and wrap it round you. Do fashions in saris change, ever?"

"Oh, yes. I put this one on, with the gold border, because I thought you might like to see it but the fashion just now is for printed patterns rather than plain colours, and some Japanese designs are very popular."

"Well, to me, that plain turquoise and gold edging look *fantastic*. Come on out and let's all get an eyeful. I mean it, Rose. You look beautiful."

"Oh, no," said Rose deprecatingly, as she followed her friend obediently out. "Now that, I am definitely not."

She had known from the age of thirteen that she was leaving her childhood prettiness behind. Her cousin Rupa was developing features which were a mixture of the elegant and the strong; Rupa's cousin Krishna was dramatically handsome, and Sita's face had a softly lovely shape, though Sita's looks were dimmed somehow, prematurely lined, and Mother said it was because she was unhappy. Rupa's new sister-in-law Nerin was plump in the face but she had generously curved lips which repaid adornment with moist, dark-red lipsticks. Rose's own little sister Amrit was going to have classically regular features and long doe eyes.

But Rose, studying her own face in the mirror, had long ago decided that she would have to make do with looking brainy. She had been told (by Mrs Sodhi, trying to be kind) that her looks were intelligent and would wear well. Which, Rose thought glumly, meant that at the age of nineteen, she already resembled a middle-aged schoolteacher.

Well, she was going to be a teacher, so perhaps it was appropriate, and perhaps small, neat features would gain more respect in the classroom than romantic ones.

It therefore gave her a surprise, when she walked into the main room of the community centre and came immediately face to face with Nick, the one who had accused her of rudeness, to see his eyes scan her swiftly from head to foot and then light up with undoubted appreciation.

"You look stunning," said Nick. He was unnervingly handsome himself, although Rose suspected that he knew it and went in for sweaters of that shade of blue because it matched his eyes. "Come and have a drink," said Nick persuasively.

"Oh, no, thank you."

"You can just have orange juice," said Anne-Marie. "Here's Roger. Let's all have something. We did lash out a bit on providing a bar otherwise the party wouldn't go with a swing. We may as well. The dancing hasn't begun yet. The band's only just arrived."

From the band on the dais there now came a series of startling twangs on an electronic guitar, and a couple of experimental crashes from cymbals and drums. "Things will soon warm up," said Roger, joining them and catching this last remark. "We sold right out of tickets."

He looked round the room, at the anti-apartheid posters pinned up on either side of the door, at the busily tuning-up band, the rapidly filling canvas chairs all round the room, and the coloured lighting which Nick was now adjusting from halfway up a stepladder. "We've called it a supper-dance," Roger remarked cheerfully. "All the old-fashioned names for things are in, this year. But it's really just a good old disco, with food, and it's going to be a humdinger."

It was clear, before an hour had passed, that the event was indeed headed for success. The room was acquiring the characteristic psychological warmth generated by large numbers of people enjoying themselves and the band had by now set to work with eardrum-cracking vigour (the boy on the kettledrums was extremely energetic and already had sweat streaming down his temples). The Nigerian students had kept their word and were now on the dance floor, gyrating with spirit and suppleness, their embroidered robes billowing like sails. There were two other Indian girls, one of them in a sari, and a Japanese couple, the female half of it in an elaborate kimono which flashed with gold thread under the slowly revolving multi-coloured lights.

"We're going to have a fine old traditional conga after the supper," said Joan, materialising out of the crowd and thumping down into an empty chair beside Rose. "I've been having a word with the band leader. Do you know what a conga is?"

"No, what is it?"

263

"A sort of musical follow-my-leader. You all get in a line, holding the waist of the person in front and do a one two three hop step all round the room and probably we'll go through the kitchen and out of the window and round the car park as well."

"How can you do one two three hop out of a window?"

"With difficulty! But it's fun trying. Oh, come and dance, Rose. Look, there are some girls just dancing together in a circle; that's harmless, surely?"

"Of course it's harmless but honestly, I would rather watch. I'm enjoying myself very much, Joan, really I am. And I want to go and heat up my curry in a moment. The supper's going to be served at nine, isn't it?"

"And it's only eight thirty now. Oh, *Rose!* Can't you loosen up just a bit?"

"Hi," said Nick, strolling up. He had shed his blue sweater to reveal a sparkling white shirt. "Rose, may I have this dance?"

"That's very kind of you, but you know that I don't dance."

"What a terribly good girl you are," said Nick in a teasing voice and eyes full of challenge.

"I couldn't, anyhow," said Rose, flustered. "I don't know the English way."

"Now's the time to learn. It's easy. You don't have to know any steps. You just stand opposite me and sway about in time to the music."

"No, really. Thank you very much."

"Leave her alone, Nick. She has her reasons," said Joan.

"Oh, please yourself," said Nick to Rose, and strolled away.

Joan watched him go, a curiously pained expression on her face. Then she jumped up and joined the circle of girls on the dance floor and Rose, as if a light had come on to illuminate the workings of Joan's mind, suddenly saw that plump would-be archaeologist Joan wanted Nick, had hoped when Rose turned him down that he would ask her to dance instead, and was bitterly disappointed to see him saunter off.

To her own horror, she experienced a surge of exhilaration. She, plain Rose with the features which looked intelligent and would wear well (ugh!), had been picked out as attractive over and above another girl. She quelled this frightful and unkind manifestation of female competitiveness at once. Poor Joan. Unfashionably bulky and decidedly managing, Joan did not attract much male attention, certainly not from highly charged males like Nick, who could pick and choose. And Joan's parents would never do anything to help her. They would never search out marriageable young men for her; what she couldn't arrange for herself would never get arranged at all. What if Nick had decided that Rose was better-looking? It wasn't saying much, after all. She was ashamed of herself and sorry for Joan.

She pushed the incident out of her mind and tried to concentrate on watching the dancing. And was taken by surprise by an overwhelming desire to join in. The music was having an effect on her which she had not anticipated. There was something about the rhythm which got inside one, made one's body want to move in time to it, made one's feet try to tap, made one feel . . . well, reckless.

Well, this wouldn't do. She'd better escape to the kitchen and help with the buffet. Sitting here, she was feeling left out and it was awful.

It was also unfair. Even at home, in Southall, things were changing. When Balbir and Nerin were married, there had been a band and dancing. Boys and girls hadn't danced together, but in separate groups, but still, they'd danced, on the same floor at the same time. Yes, she remembered that she had longed to join in then. It had been Western music, on records. She had not let herself take part but probably her parents wouldn't have minded. They wouldn't have minded because it was all happening within their own community and she would have been under their eye. But why was this so different? Why did it *matter* so much to them? Occasionally they showed signs of wanting to loosen their attitudes, but every time this happened, Bheji would jerk them back to the rulings of tradition. Her mother always listened to Bheji, possibly in order to maintain the peace of the household, but also because in so many ways, she agreed with her. Her father had been known to disagree with Bheji but not over this; he seemed to feel that bringing up a daughter was mainly the women's business.

And this was the result. She felt morally obliged to withdraw to the kitchen and busy herself with heating up the curry. But why *should* she be cut off from the fun her friends were having and feel obliged instead to go and be, well, just catering staff?

Before leaving home for Oxford, she had promised. Bheji had insisted and she had promised to maintain their own values while she was out in the dangerous world of a Western university. But just now, Rose felt mutinous.

The dancers had paused for breath as the band pounded its

way to the end of a number. She caught Joan's eye and smiled brightly. The band struck up again. Rose stood up to take herself to the kitchen out of harm's way, and then Joan ran forward, caught her hands, and dragged her willy nilly into the throng. "You *shall* dance! I'm a rotten beast, just leaving you there and not insisting. You've got to enjoy yourself properly. There's nothing wrong in it. Come on, dance with us!"

It was heavenly. It was magic. The beat seemed to pick up her feet and move them for her. The movements of the Indian dancing which was the only sort she knew, and in which she had joined on ladies-only occasions at home, such as bridal Sangeets, fitted naturally into the rhythm. She could feel herself coming alive and alight. She saw Anne-Marie in the distance, jiving with Roger, and Anne-Marie waved before vanishing beyond a swirling Nigerian robe. But there was Joan, opposite her, trying to imitate her hand movements, getting them wrong, and laughing at herself. The revolving lights turned the room from red to green to purple and the cymbals crashed. A hand came down on her shoulder and spun her round, transferred its grip to her wrist, pulled her out of the circle of girls, flung her away, snatched her back, set her spinning, caught her hand, and pulled her again towards a tall figure which changed rapidly through deep purple, crimson, amber and blue and became recognisable as Nick.

"This is called an Excuse-Me," he informed her. "When one marches on to a dance floor and snatches a partner from someone else or in this case a whole lot of someone elses. What do you mean, you can't dance? You're a natural."

There was nothing to be done; she couldn't just break away and leave the floor. That really would be rude. Besides, she didn't want to. This was a whole new kind of dancing, this following of a partner's lead, this blending of two sets of movements. This contact of warm hand with warm hand, this extraordinary awareness of the man's strength and nearness, this amazing delight in it.

Her feet, hands, body, seemed to know what to do all by themselves. She stamped, spun, swayed forward and back, was flung and retrieved. Nick used a girder-like wrist as if it were a wall and she a ball which bounced repeatedly against it, until, at will, he chose to pull her in instead of bouncing her off, pulled her against him and whirled them both in a step which Rose thought was a sort of very fast waltz, such as she had occasionally

266

seen demonstrated on television.

And then, as the number reached its climax with a roll and crash, the kettle-drummer on the dais going apparently berserk with his drumsticks, he pulled her in one last time, drew her tightly up against him, and before she could stop him, or had even understood what he intended, he had jammed his mouth down on to hers and somehow or other succeeded in thrusting his tongue between her teeth.

There was a split second during which her entire body moved towards him and pressed against his and she felt as though she might open herself to him as a bud might open to the sun. Then she gasped and choked. The tongue was hot and slimy and tasted the way beer smelt and seemed to fill her mouth completely. She bit it, hard. It was withdrawn and there was Nick, grinning down at her. "Little viper. Your first kiss, was it? Well, you're learning about the world now and I've had the privilege of giving you your introductory lesson."

"I never thought . . . " She wanted to wipe her mouth. It felt unclean. "I never thought you'd do that," said Rose in a thin voice. The magic, the delight, the glow of movement and music, had all gone as if someone had tipped a bucket of icy water over her. She turned away. Let him call her rude, in that light, sardonic voice of his. What of it? Who was he, anyway? As she walked away, she saw Joan's hurt eyes and registered the fact that despite the hurt, Joan's mouth was still smiling at her in a determinedly jolly I'm-not-going-to-be-petty-or-show-that-I-mind manner.

She couldn't bear it. She broke into a run and got herself out of the room as quickly as she could. In the kitchen, the last items were being prepared for the buffet; someone else had tipped her curry into a saucepan and was already heating it up. There was nothing for her to do.

Another dance was under way and there was a crowd round the bar. Everyone was preoccupied in one way or another. She caught a glimpse of Nick, now dancing with another girl. Not Joan. Oh, poor Joan. But no one would notice if she, Rose, were to slip away. She fetched her coat and did precisely that.

Roger and Anne-Marie had given her a lift to the community centre but it was actually within walking distance. She hurried or rather fled through Oxford on foot, passing the splendid frontage of Balliol College, almost getting run over as she crossed a road in too much haste, frantic to get back to her own college, as though she were a rabbit seeking a burrow.

When she arrived, there was a message for her. She had had a telephone call from home. Would she ring her parents as soon as possible?

She had come out without a handbag, just slipping a lipstick and comb and a purse with a small amount of money into her coat pocket. But she had enough small change to ring London from one of the public telephones in the entrance hall.

It was a good line. Her mother's voice sounded astonishingly clear and near, sending a jolt of guilt and alarm through Rose. The sound of Nita's familiar tones brought back so vividly that loving list of dos and don'ts with which her mother had sent her off to Oxford. It was impossible that her mother could know what she had been doing but . . .

"Mother? Did you ring me?"

"Yes, dear. You've been out this evening?"

"Yes. To a . . . a supper given in aid of the anti-apartheid movement." Well, it was true, and put like that it sounded not only innocent, but virtuous.

"That's good. You are getting involved in the right kind of activities," said Nita. "But, Rose, Diwali is next weekend and we would like you to come home for it. It is most important. There is some family news."

"Yes? Good or bad?" said Rose. Her mother's voice, she thought, now sounded a little odd, strained.

"Well . . . both," said Nita. "The thing is, your cousin-brother Sunder is going to get married but . . . "

"Oh," said Rose.

"Well, yes. It is this English girl, the next-door neighbour, that he has been seeing. He's going to marry *her*," said Nita. "Your aunt and uncle are being so good; they are taking it all in their stride and of course times are different and there are many such marriages nowadays but in our family . . . well, will you come for Diwali? You are not too busy with your studies and your activities?"

She'd known, as they all had, that Sunder was having this affair with an English girl but English girls were different and it was natural for young men to experiment. But this . . .

"Bheji," said her mother, "is most upset, most upset. We were quite frightened; we thought she might be really ill."

"Oh, goodness," said Rose weakly, and leaned against the wall

268

in the college phone booth, remembering that awful moment when Nick had forced his tongue into her mouth and her own even more awful first reaction, when she had almost returned the kiss, when her body had momentarily betrayed her, trying to melt into his.

She saw herself as her parents, as Bheji, would see her and shuddered, ashamed and disgusted. If Bheji were to learn of it, she might be more than ill; she was getting on in years; older people could die of such shocks. The way she had behaved tonight could *kill* someone like Bheji.

"No, no, of course I'm not too busy. I'll certainly come home for Diwali."

"Rose, are you all right?" said her mother anxiously. "Your voice has faded. You are almost whispering."

"Yes, I am all right. It is just the line, I think. I will see you all at Diwali."

Chapter Twenty-Two

Drama at Diwali
1981

If the Diwali party at Kartar's house in October was less a celebration than a melodrama, neither Rose nor Sunder were responsible. No one had the slightest idea that Rose had anything to be ashamed of, and Sunder was not ashamed at all. The excitement, as it turned out, sprang from other causes.

Though Sunder and his engagement were of course the main talking point when the plans for Diwali were first made.

"I'm his father and Shanti is his mother and we are accepting this," said Perry calmly when Ranbir, Kartar and Nita, who had been informed of the engagement by telephone, responded by arriving en masse at his door. "Times are very different from when we first came to England and such marriages were hardly to be thought of."

His eyes met first Kartar's and then Nita's steadily and with meaning and they understood.

"What is the girl like?" Kartar said.

"A social worker. Very nice, sensible, a good girl. We like her and we propose to make her welcome in the family."

Ranbir had been waiting for Kartar to do his duty as an elder brother and take Perry severely to task. Since Kartar said nothing more, it was too much to hope that Ranbir would stay quiet.

"This is a most terrible thing that Sunder is doing. Can you not talk to him, tell him that in our family, never has there been such a thing . . . ?"

"He wouldn't listen. He is in love."

"Love!" Ranbir was outraged. "What do young people know about love? Marriage is a serious business . . . "

"Sunder and Lynn are taking it seriously, believe me. So are her parents. You will like her parents."

"I will never like her parents. My father was imprisoned in the cause of India's freedom from the British. I did not think to see my own grandson marrying a British girl!"

"Why not? He's a British boy," said Perry. "He was born here. Bheji, this marriage is going forward. We are all coming to Kartar's Diwali party and with his permission, we propose to bring Lynn and her father and mother. Her father teaches at a school in Greenford and her mother is a commercial artist and does voluntary work for the Samaritans. They are most worthy people. Her brothers are nice lads, too. I trust that you will treat the Edmonds family with every courtesy."

"Oh, I shall be courteous! If neither of my sons can see their duty in this, who am I to argue? I am only your mother. I shall be courteous, and I shall break my heart in private," said Ranbir, and flounced away to the kitchen, from which quarter her voice was presently heard, repeating it all to Shanti.

"It will be all right," said Nita. "If you have accepted this, Perry, then we all must. Sunder is your son, not ours. Perhaps I agree with Bheji at heart but . . . you need not worry."

Kartar said quietly, "I suppose that you have never quite forgotten your own English girlfriend, Perry. Is that by any chance behind your – indulgence – towards Sunder?"

"You could say that."

"But you have been happy with Shanti!" protested Nita.

"Yes. And I do not know if I would have been happy with Pat. But I do know that I regret never thinking that I was free to choose. I see Sunder look at Lynn and I know what he is feeling. I will not take his freedom to choose away from him. I can bring Lynn and Mr and Mrs Edmonds to your party, then? It will introduce them to the family and the community if you are agreeable."

"Certainly," said Kartar.

Ranbir bounced out of the kitchen again. "Oh, if only you had come back to India years ago when I begged you to, Perry. But no, you must make your way in England first and how have you made your way? This place Allbrights where you are working, you say may be taken over and then perhaps you will be redundant. So what have you stayed here for?"

"I have my reasons," said Perry, in a voice so like a brick wall that for once, Ranbir was silenced.

Mohan Lal, when informed of the engagement, was inclined to

take it in his stride. "These things are happening. It is not as bad as a daughter marrying out of the community. If this girl is all you say, she will fit in, she will fit in."

Mohan Lal, anyway, had worries of his own.

"Children these days are such a problem. Things are not better with Sita. I have tried to talk to Hari but all he says is that he treats Sita perfectly well, that we have spoilt her so that she does not want to be a proper Hindu wife and that she tells lies about him. I do not think she tells lies but there is nothing that can be done; marriage is marriage. And as for Krishna and Chandra Lal . . . !"

"Is Krishna still in the same job?"

"Yes, and it is worrying us more and more, all this going about; she is doing so much more of it now. Sometimes she spends nights away from home, staying in hotels to report on them. We never know who she may be meeting and she eats meat now, too; her mother can hardly believe it. We did not think this job would grow in this way. She is not getting any younger and who will marry her if she has lived such a rackety life? She does not even stay home in the evenings although I suppose evening classes in French and Spanish are respectable enough but why she wants to study them I can't understand. We know Sita was right to warn us against marrying her to Hari's friend, since we have seen how wretched Sita is. We thought after that we must not rush things with Krishna, so we let her go to work, but now she says she does not want to marry at all! I tell her that if she is not careful, she will never get the chance!"

"What's wrong with Chandra Lal?" said Perry, largely in order to stop the flood.

"He has joined the police force, that is what is wrong with him! I said to him: here is a business all ready for you to take over one day when I retire but no, he wants to be a *policeman*!" said Mohan Lal in scandalised tones. "I said to him, when my shop was burgled two years ago, the police were so offhand, they were no help, and they were not so friendly either when Satnam had that trouble and was stabbed. The boys were caught but only because Satnam named them in the end. Why Chandra Lal is wanting to join the police, I cannot understand."

"Perhaps he feels that if there are Indians in the police force, that would improve," suggested Perry.

"Well, I do not agree. Besides, I am old-fashioned; a son should follow his father's trade." As he grew older, Perry thought, Mohan Lal was getting more and more dogmatic and it was becoming very plain that logic wasn't his strong point. A man who said marriage was marriage in that tone of voice, shouldn't upset his wife by having affairs, to start with.

But if his preoccupation with the shortcomings of his off-spring would keep him from seeing shortcomings in Perry's, that was all right with Perry. He said, "Well, well," in a pacific tone of voice, and smiled.

The Diwali party was to be held on a Sunday. On the previous Wednesday, three unidentifiable figures with stocking masks over their faces barged into Hari's shop just as he was about to close it, punched Hari, brandished an iron bar at him, robbed his till and swept quantities of his goods into a holdall.

Sita, who had been in the shop with her husband, checking on the shelves of tinned food, took in the stocking masks and the iron bar in a single instant and slid out of sight through the door to the storeroom. She shot the bolts stealthily, standing to one side so that her silhouette could not be seen through the frosted glass panel. Then she stood listening, heart thumping wildly with hope.

There was so much violence in society these days. Those former tenants of Kartar Virk, the Satinder Singhs, they had come back to Southall from Bradford, having had a very bad time there. Someone had put burning rags through their letter-box. Young criminals today were like savages.

Was there a chance (oh, please God, let it be so!) that this particular tribe of savages would actually murder Hari?

It wouldn't be like widowhood in the old days. She had a son; the house and shop would be nine-year-old Dinesh's inheritance. She would presumably go on living in the house, looking after it for him; if she couldn't manage the shop alone, she could put in a manager. She would be free, her own woman, no longer Hari's submissive, unappreciated slave.

If only, if only, those young devils in there would do one simple thing: beat Hari's brains out with that iron bar.

There was a splintering crash, followed by the sound of tins falling, and laughter. Hari's voice yelled, "My spectacles!" Footsteps clattered away; a door slammed, hard enough to shake the building. There was a fumbling noise and through the frosted pane she could see a blurred shape moving about on the floor. Hari, presumably. Injured? Dying? No, the shape seemed to be

273

groping about, as though searching for something. His glasses, most likely. Suddenly the shape stood up, advanced on the door and rattled the handle. Sick with shock and disappointment, she drew the bolts. Hari barged through. "Did you phone the police? There is an extension in here, have you called the police?"

Beyond him, she could see that the shop was wrecked. The long freestanding run of shelves down the middle had been thrown over. Packets and tins littered the floor, and the sliding glass doors of the cold cabinet had been smashed, strewing glass over the sausages and the butter. But Hari, apart from a red lump on his forehead and the fact that the frame of his spectacles, which he was once more wearing, was askew, seemed to be unhurt. He caught hold of her and thrust his face at her. "Answer me! *Did you phone the police?*"

"No, no, I was too frightened. Oh, Hari, I thought they would murder us both!"

"And so you did not even lift the phone! I thought they had broken my glasses and I am half-blind without them, and for all the use *you* are, I could just go up in smoke in the crematorium!"

Oh, how I wish you would!

"I was just too terrified to think . . . no, Hari . . . oh, Hari, it isn't my fault, don't . . . "

A moment later, she picked herself up from the floor to which his blow had sent her, and leant against the door listening while he called the police from the telephone beside the cash desk. "They're coming," he said, as he hung up. "We had better list what has been taken. If you are too stupid to phone for help, perhaps you can still count! It is fortunate that I am insured. In future, I shall keep an iron bar handy as well."

Hours later, back in their house, having collected Dinesh from the neighbour where he had spent the evening, Sita silently made food for her husband and son and then went upstairs, to be alone, to tremble, to cry, to look at the Sita who had for a moment seen an upraised iron bar in the hands of a violent youth as a half-opened door through which light and joy were streaming, and try to understand that incredible, hate-filled, new person who was herself.

She sat shaking on her bed for several moments and then, hearing Hari's tread on the stairs, jumped up and looked for something to be doing. He could not bear to see her sitting idle. ("Have you nothing to do in the house? My mother never sat

274

about with empty hands.") She pulled open the wardrobe where her saris hung and jerked out a couple at random.

"What are you doing? What are you skulking up here for? The washing-up has all been left."

"I just wanted to . . . I was going to press some of my things tonight. I was just looking to see what needs to be done."

"Looking out finery for your family's Diwali party, I suppose? We are robbed and I am nearly killed, but you come up here and choose saris for a party . . . "

"No, I'm not; I'd forgotten all about the Diwali party . . . "

"Well, we have been robbed and there is no question of going to parties. We will not be celebrating Diwali or visiting any relatives this weekend. Rest assured of that."

Except that Hari and Sita were not there – what a shocking thing that attack on their shop had been – the Diwali party seemed to be going well, Perry thought, glancing round his brother's crowded sitting room. It was a relief. Kartar and Nita hadn't let him down. They had, in fact, gone to considerable lengths for him. They had laid in among other things, malt whisky, two kinds of sherry and an enormous selection of festive sweetmeats and they had never strung fairy lights in the window at previous Diwalis. Even Bheji was keeping her promise to be courteous. She had greeted the Edmonds politely and if she had kept well away from them since, in the crowd they probably wouldn't notice.

All round the room was the hum of well-lubricated conversation and the sound of East and West explaining themselves to each other.

Nita, though keeping a wary eye on Ranbir, was being the perfect hostess to the Edmonds, offering them snacks and introducing them to people. She had begun by taking Lynn's hands and giving her a kiss, and since then had promised to show her how to put on a sari. "It is no use asking Sunder. Men only have the vaguest idea. They know when the pleats look right but how to get them like that is the ladies' secret."

The Satinder Singhs – both man and wife actually had Satinder as their first names – had after their unhappy years in Bradford now bought themselves a house in Trinity Road off the Broadway in Southall, and had arrived for the party along with their two sons. They had evidently taken to Mr and Mrs Edmonds. Mrs Satinder had been telling Mrs Edmonds about the thugs in Hari's shop, and now the two of them were deep in talk about social conditions in London and Bradford, and the work of the Samaritans.

Mr Satinder, meanwhile, was trying to explain Diwali to Mr Edmonds. Perry leaned back in his chair and listened with half-closed eyes and some amusement. Mr Edmonds was a spare, ginger-bearded individual who looked too young to have a grown-up daughter. "Teaching ten-year-olds keeps me in trim," he had said when Perry once remarked on this. He was a casual dresser with a preference for slacks, sweaters and running shoes, but he took life in general seriously. He was now leaning forward, listening to Satinder as though the latter were liable to question him later on the content of the lecture. " . . . the name means the Festival of Lights. Both the Hindus and the Sikhs celebrate Diwali but for different reasons. In Hindu mythology, the lord Rama was exiled for fourteen years before he became king, but when at last he returned, he came home after dark and people ran out to light his way. But the Sikhs keep the feast in memory of a great leader who was imprisoned by the Moghuls along with many of his men. He was finally released and told that as many of his men could go with him, as could hold on to his cloak. So he cut his cloak into streamers, and a hundred of his men were able to hold a bit of it . . . oh, yes, they were all let out; the Moghul king kept his word . . . "

Sunder, who had been sitting with his bride-to-be, had been drawn away into a political discussion with Satnam and Mr Sodhi, and had shifted his seat. Lynn, left behind, had apparently asked Rose and the younger Satinder boy, Charan, to explain the politics in question to her and they were now trying to bring her up to date with the current situation in India.

This was an intimidating task but Charan, who was doing most of the talking, wasn't making too bad an attempt. "It is very complicated but I will leave out the fine detail. For a long time there has been tension between the Sikhs, who are the majority in the Punjab – that is in northern India – and neighbouring states which are mostly Hindu . . . oh, there were all sort of reasons – water is one of them. The Sikh farmers in the Punjab felt that they needed the rivers that flow from the Himalayas, down through their province, for their crops. The Punjab is the granary of India. But the water was also needed by the other states. The government did not help much: they kept arguing about the legal entitlements of the other states, instead of pointing out that there is *enough* water if only it is properly used. So much of it flows to the sea not used at all, as things stand. But anyway there has been tension . . . "

"I have been to India not so long ago," said Rose. "It is true, these things are being very much talked about just now. And now, there is this Bhindranwale."

"I've heard the name – well, seen it; it gets into the papers. But I don't understand at all who he is," Lynn said.

"Oh, he came into prominence because of political manoeuvring," said Charan in a voice of distaste. He had actually dropped out of studying political science at college and was now working in a photographic studio. Having grasped some of the essentials in matters political, he had decided that not only did politics not appeal to him, they actively repelled him. "It was one of those moves that people in power will make to undermine an opposition. The opposition in this case was a coalition party which included the Sikhs. Bhindranwale is a fundamentalist Sikh who is very much against certain other Sikh sects . . . oh, yes, we have sects, just as Christians have the Church of England and the Methodists and the Baptists . . . "

"And the Jehovah's Witnesses?"

"Yes, and the Pentecostal Mission," said Rose. They all laughed. Rose sounded quite animated, Perry was relieved to hear. Kartar had said earlier that when she came home for Diwali, he felt worried about her because she seemed so subdued. "She says she has been overworking so perhaps that is it but I hope she is herself again soon." Earlier in the evening, she had sat very quietly, not helping her mother and Shanti to hand food and not joining in the lively conversation which Krishna was having with her mother and Rupa, about make-up techniques. But by the sound of it, she was feeling better now.

"Yes," Charan was saying, "very like that. So he was encouraged and brought forward to cause dissension among the Sikhs. But now he is too powerful, a threat to the government itself, even. He wants a separate Sikh state to be declared and there is so much trouble. A journalist who wrote something criticising this idea has been murdered. Bhindranwale has been arrested now but his supporters are angry; Sikh extremists on motorbikes have been shooting his opponents; they have shot both Hindus and other Sikhs and there have been many other things too. I think it is all very dreadful and I do not approve of this Bhindranwale."

277

"Bhindranwale," said Satnam, sauntering up and dropping to his haunches beside Charan, "is a saint."

Sunder had come with him. "No, now, Satnam, don't . . . "

"But," said Lynn protestingly, "are this man's supporters really killing people openly like that?"

"They are loyal to their leader and his ideas. He is a saint, a great leader like Guru Hargobind whom we remember at Diwali. It is the government's fault. They should give the Sikhs their own state and then there would be no . . . "

"I can't agree with you there, Satnam," said Lynn mildly. "I can't possibly agree that murder is excusable. If he has been encouraging killings, or even if he has just not tried to stop them, then he is certainly no saint."

"He has the integrity of the Sikhs at heart. It is too easy for us to forget who we are in this world which tempts us to abandon our traditions and become like anyone else but . . . "

"Satnam," said Sunder angrily, "for goodness sake . . . !"

"I take it," said Lynn, "that you don't approve of my engagement to your brother?"

She said it in tones of polite enquiry, without either indignation or visible distress. Satnam stared at her and then at Sunder and appeared to withdraw into himself. "I did not say that. I respect my elder brother and I shall respect you too as my sister."

"Well, that's a relief," said Lynn, and gave Sunder a laughing glance. Perry, who had been about to rise and intervene, settled back once more.

Too soon. "But," said Satnam, "in a Sikh state, under Sikh law, there would be no temptation to wander from the true path or forget our identity. The Moslems have a state of their own in Pakistan, why should the Sikh state of Khalistan not be established? If it is . . . "

Over Satnam's head, Sunder caught his father's eye and Perry rose to his feet. "Excuse me, but there is something I want Satnam to do. You'll find, Lynn, that we use our young people as spare pairs of hands whenever there are big occasions and jobs to be done. Come with me, Satnam." He shepherded Satnam out into the hall and shut the door after them. "I brought you out here, my lad, to tell you to shut up. Just that, do you hear? *Shut up*. This is a Diwali party and an engagement celebration. We need your fire-eating the way we need a hole in the head, is that clear? How dare you try to embarrass your brother's future

278

wife? That is what you were doing, don't deny it! I think she's one too many for you, but she's still entitled to my protection. My God, I'm furious with you. I know that our religion means a great deal to you and that it began to mean even more after you were attacked with a knife because of it, but it is time you tried to put that behind you. You seem to regard the whole world as an enemy: Westerners first and now apparently you have started on the Hindus! No one would think you were the son of a Hindu mother!"

Satnam looked mutinous for a moment and then upset. "I never think of Mother as not being one of us."

Perry sighed. "You're young. I suppose you'll grow out of it. But for the time being, you will be kind enough to behave. I don't want to hear another word about Bhindranwale or Khalistan today. This affair is going very smoothly and it is to continue in that way . . . now who is that at the door? Some late arrival, I suppose. Come, let us let them in and look hospitable."

They opened the front door. Standing in the porch was Sita. She was holding her son Dinesh by the hand. It was raining and they were both soaking wet, their topcoats dark with it. Dinesh, who looked pale and bewildered, wore a drenched school cap, and Sita's hair trailed in damp tendrils from under a saturated headscarf. But the streaks of water on her face were not merely rain and the discolouration round her left eye was not the result of wet mascara. She was breathless. She stumbled in, dropped a bulging holdall on the floor and turned to shut the door herself, quickly, as though she feared pursuit.

"We've come on foot all the way from our house. I've run away. He went out to a pub and left us. He did not think I would do this, but I have. I have left Hari. And I am not going back, I am not going back, *I will not go back.*"

"Satnam," said Perry, "go and fetch Auntie Nita. She'll take you upstairs where you can rest, Sita, and bring you something hot to drink. Dinesh, would you like to go upstairs with Mummy or would you like to go into the kitchen for cakes and Coke? You'd better both get out of those wet things . . . "

"No!" said Sita. She was not referring to the wet things, which she and Dinesh were already shedding. "I will not be pushed off upstairs out of the way where I will not be an embarrassment!" Coats, cap and drenched headscarf were tossed on to the hall-stand. "I am tired to death of not being an embarrassment, of hiding my unhappy situation in some corner!" Her voice was high and rapid as though it might slip out of control at any moment, but there was steel beneath the hysteria. "I will see Nita Auntie, yes, in the room where the party is and I will tell them all what I have just told you. It is all right, Dinesh. Go along with Satnam to the kitchen now and have something nice to eat and drink. It is all right here, Mummy is quite safe here. I will see you in a minute." She achieved a calm voice while she spoke to her son but Satnam gave her a sharp look and without comment led Dinesh away. The child had said nothing at all, but he looked back anxiously over his shoulder, towards his mother, as he went.

Sita turned to Perry once more. *"I say again: I will not go back!"* All the shrill tension was there once again. Without waiting for him to answer, she led the way into the sitting room.

"Sita!" cried several voices as she marched in. "So you have come after all!"

"Oh, and look at her; those robbers must have hit her, look at her poor face! No wonder they have not let anyone go to see them after it has happened!" In a swirl of ivory-toned polyester, Ranbir started towards her. Ranbir, these days, was gentler towards the Hindu members of her family and she liked Sita, whose natural sweetness appealed to her. "How brave of you to come after all. Where is Hari ?"

Sita stopped her with an upraised palm. "Hari is not here. It was he who did this to me, not the robbers and I have run away. My son is with me; he saw what his father did. He tried to stop him but Hari shut him in a cupboard. He cried and cried in there, while Hari was hitting me. I have come to tell everyone. Oh, Mother, Mother!" said Sita as Leela, followed by Shanti, Krishna and Rupa, all came running from the kitchen, exclaiming that little Dinesh had suddenly appeared there and surely they had heard Sita's voice. Sita threw herself into her mother's arms. "I am too frightened to go back. Say I can stay with you, say I can stay!"

Leela caught hold of her and steadied her to a settee. "But why did he do this? What happened?"

"Yes, indeed, what made him do such a thing?" Mohan Lal hastened to sit beside his daughter. Other guests, who included the Sodhis and several of the Sharma clan, were watching doubtfully. Mrs Swarup Sharma, who had been seated between two other ladies, began whispering explanations behind her hand. Rose and the Satinder Singhs were also trying to explain to

280

Lynn and her parents.

"I said, couldn't we come to the Diwali party after all," wailed Sita. "Nothing more!"

"Just that? That is all you said?" demanded Kartar.

"Yes! There was no reason why not. It was not so bad, what happened to us. They took the money from our till and some tins and frozen food but we had enough stock left, still, and when we had put the shelves up again next day, we could open. Our bank balance was all right; we could order more things. Why we should not just come to the party for a little while? Hari had a bruise on his face; he was not hurt otherwise . . . "

"Pity," remarked Krishna candidly.

" . . . so today, I just said, couldn't we drop in at this party and now see what he has done to me!" cried Sita.

"This is very sad, very sad." Mr Sodhi shook his head gravely. "But you cannot stay away from your husband and home for ever; that would not do."

"Why won't it do?" enquired Nita. "Sita, here's a cup of hot tea and a luddhu sweetmeat. You should have something sweet after a shock. If someone twice your size kept giving you black eyes, Mr Sodhi, you would want to be where they were not! This is not the first time this has happened!"

"Well said," approved Perry.

Shanti said, "I will go and see to Dinesh. He is with Satnam in the kitchen," and hurried off.

"I will speak to Hari again," declared Mohan Lal. "I shall tell him he is not to behave like this . . . "

"It won't be any use!" Sita ignored the tea and the luddhu. "He makes promises and then he breaks them!"

"Yes, that is true. Sita must be protected," Ranbir said, shocked for once out of her automatic support for traditional standards.

"Which means, she cannot stay with Hari," Leela agreed.

"But it is her *home* and there is the child!" argued Mohan Lal. "His father will want him back."

"No, no, your husband is right, Mrs Bhatia. Husbands and wives should stay together. The honour of the family is bound up with it," Mr Sodhi persisted. "No doubt Hari knows where his wife has gone and he will come in search of her; we cannot withhold her from him."

"I am not a parcel to be handed this way and that. What if I say I will not be handed?" shrieked Sita.

"But you have brought his son away!"

"He's my son too!"

"If Hari shows his face in this house, I shall break the bastard's neck," announced Kartar.

Outside in the hall, the phone began to ring. Kartar strode out to answer it and a moment later his voice drifted back to them. "No, of course Sita is not here, why should she be? You told us neither of you would come, on account of the upset over your shop being robbed. Is there any news about that; have they been caught? . . . No, I do *not* know where Sita and Dinesh are. They have not come, Sita has not phoned. The way you behave to her, she has probably thrown herself and Dinesh in some river. Goodnight, Hari!"

The receiver went down with a crash. Sita let out her breath in a great sigh. As Kartar came back into the room, she said, "Thank you. I am grateful."

"But how," said Lynn to Rose, "can anyone want her to go back to him? Is that really what that older man in the white turban was saying?"

"Well, he is old-fashioned. He feels that wives should accommodate themselves and that if they do, their husbands will love them. He thinks that if Sita's husband has hit her, it is probably Sita's fault."

"That's absolutely outrageous!"

"I think most of us agree with you," said Charan. "Wouldn't you say so, Rose?"

"Yes, oh, yes. Sita is so sweet; I'm sure she has not provoked Hari. She has always tried to make the marriage work, because of her sister Krishna. Krishna is not yet married and some families look askance at a girl from a family where there has been a divorce or anything like that."

"So Sita is to be just a sacrifice? She has no rights of her own?" said Lynn, appalled.

"Well, some of the older people would think that way," Rose agreed.

"Was it an arranged match?" Lynn asked.

"This is going to be girl talk. I'm going to get a drink," said Charan, although he grinned at Rose as he said it, in a way which removed all trace of disparagement from the words.

Rose smiled back. As he moved away, she returned her attention to Lynn. "How best can I explain the strange concept of the arranged marriage to you? This one was half and half. It was

282

supposed to be a love match, but Sita's grandfather – he died some years ago – very much wanted it, so you could say, half and half."

Rupa came over and joined in. "My father never liked the match." She nodded towards Perry, where he stood in the group round Sita. "When it is time for me to get married, I shall trust his judgement. He will not make such a mistake as to land me with a Hari. Arrangements are not so bad, Lynn. Mostly, it is a matter of arranged introductions. Our parents will not just say to us you are to marry this one or that one. But they see that we meet suitable young men, who are interested in marriage, and sooner or later, quite naturally, a couple are attracted to each other, and then they are married."

"Yes, and it saves so much heartburning," Rose said. "The English girls are sorry for us because we have no freedom, but we do not lie awake crying because we have no dates or because our boyfriends haven't telephoned us. Most of us think that we are the lucky ones! There is a girl I know at university . . . "

Carefully, avoiding any reference to Nick's advances to herself, she began to tell them about Joan and Nick and the supper-disco. She must, she thought, learn to think of that horrible evening in a calmer way. It could not be undone, so she must accept it as an instructive experience. After all, nothing drastic had happened. In future she would be more careful and she would be very grateful, *very* grateful, in due course, to have a safe, approved partner found for her.

Falling in love, said Rose to herself, very firmly, was a frightful mistake.

A few seats away, Mrs Satinder and Mrs Edmonds were talking together and glancing towards Sita. Suddenly, Mrs Satinder rose to her feet, dusting orange luddhu crumbs off her violet silk salwar kameeze, and went over to the settee.

"I think," she said in her commonsense voice, and in English out of deference to the English guests, "that we should offer to help. Mrs Edmonds, who assists the Samaritans, wishes for Asian volunteers and I have just offered myself. Perhaps I can make a practical beginning. It may well be difficult for Sita's family to withhold her or her son from her husband but they could stay with me. Satinder, you would not object? Mr Sodhi, there *are* such things as desperate and frightened women. Men are not all angels! Sometimes women must defend themselves. And it cannot be good for her child to be in such an atmosphere. He too will be better for spending time in a calm household. Meanwhile, Sita can consider quietly what to do."

An interested babble broke out, approval and disapproval mingled. Mr Satinder Singh cut it short. "If Sita is agreeable, then I am certainly willing. By all means she can come to us until something can be sorted out. It will be best, because Hari is sure to come to see if she is with her parents . . . "

Nita and Leela were encouraging Sita to let them take her upstairs to lie down until such time as she and Dinesh could go home with the Satinder Singhs. The party slowly relapsed into its chairs and normal conversation resumed. Satnam reappeared from the kitchen and joined the rest of his generation. Charan said something which made Rose laugh.

Perry, relaxing once more, was very relieved that the crisis was over. He had things on his mind. Though his worries, he thought, were in a fair way to being resolved. He had almost come to a decision about what he would do if the threatened redundancy from Allbrights became a fact, as it was all too likely to do, although he had settled well in his time with the company, and even got along with the security manager who had shown signs, initially, of being awkward.

He had spoken on the telephone to Robert Houghton in his Sussex bungalow and Houghton had said, *Come and see me. I'll advise you if I can.*

Perry was in his mid-forties but he was fit and he had certain skills. He'd learned a great deal at Allbrights as well as from Robert Houghton long ago. And however much his mother sighed, he intended to stay in England. He certainly wasn't going to go crawling back to India, disrupting his family and admitting defeat. He wasn't defeated. If it came to it, he'd go self-employed, as an interior decorator.

When Nita came back into the room, after seeing Sita upstairs, Lynn went to her. "Can I do anything to help in any way? She did look ill. I'm so very sorry."

Nita looked at her in slight surprise and hesitated.

"I hope to become a member of this family," said Lynn. "I realise that I've come as a shock to . . . to many of you, but I hope to make Sunder happy and be happy myself. The sooner I start to be part of the family, and useful to it, the better."

Suddenly, Nita smiled. "I am making fresh tea. Perhaps you could take a cup up to her. She's in the front bedroom."

"Thank you. I'd like to do that."

Nita's smile broadened. They studied each other. Lynn had been wary of her hostess when she first arrived, sensing the unspoken reservations behind Nita's outwardly friendly welcome, instinctively aware that this dignified woman, Sunder's aunt, was highly respected in the community, and that her opinion would carry more weight than that of Sunder's own mother.

On her side, Nita had not known what to make of this English girl with the angular, asymmetrical face and the remarkable green eyes, this girl whose customs were so different from her own and who had almost certainly been to bed with Sunder. She might, after marriage, separate him from the rest of his family and his community. She might think herself superior to them.

Now each began to revise her ideas about the other.

Bheji would probably not like it if Nita made friends with this girl but over this, Nita found herself prepared to be firm.

"You know," she said, "I think you'll do."

Chapter Twenty-Three

Dreams and Reality
1984

"So you're going to have a ladies' video party here this evening?" Kartar said across the breakfast table to his wife and elder daughter. "Well, you can have the front room to yourselves. I shall not interrupt. I will watch the portable in the other room."

"No one will keep you out," Nita said, laughing.

"I shall keep myself out. I hate Indian romantic films," Kartar assured her.

"But it is all right? You don't mind?" Rose asked. "I thought of it only last night, and telephoned round. After all, I don't know how long I shall be still in England and it is nice to see one's friends while one can."

"No, I don't mind," Kartar said. "Not that there's much chance of you going to India for at least a year. Northern India is not a happy place since Bhindranwale embattled himself in the Golden Temple and the army attacked it to get him out. I think that attack was very wrong; it is no wonder that Sikhs everywhere are so angry and resentful. I feel angry myself. But I think that the atmosphere in India is such that it is best you stay here for the time being." He picked up the *Guardian* and began to scan the financial pages, but added from behind them, "I don't really know why you want to go. When we visited it, I thought you were quite glad to come back here. This is a nice new house we've moved into. Stay and enjoy it with us for a while!"

"This house is lovely," Rose agreed. The move, to the outer edge of Southall, had been the result of her father's latest promotion and accompanying rise. They were still within walking distance of other family members but this house was semi-detached, possessed of garage and drive, and they were now eating breakfast in the sunny breakfast room attached to the big fitted kitchen. "I *was* happy to come home from India, too," Rose said, "though I did like Uncle Sunder and Auntie Billie very much. But that was then. Since I've been away to university, I've changed. I don't mind the thought of going away so much now and I think if someone of my generation went back to live in India, it would please Bheji so much. She has had to absorb so many shocks."

Her parents nodded. They knew exactly what she meant. And though they would not criticise Bheji in front of her, she knew that they wished Ranbir's absorptive powers were somewhat better, and were thinking of her formal politeness towards Sunder's wife Lynn, and her horror when Perry, having duly become redundant from Allbrights, first went to Sussex to spend a week with his ex-landlord, the do-it-yourself fanatic Robert Houghton, and then turned into a self-employed interior decorator.

Although, said Perry, Mr Houghton now looked very old and was too shaky to stand safely on a ladder or even hold a paintbrush very well, he was only too glad to advise on how to set up a decorating business, and Perry trusted that he would make a success of it. He intended to enjoy trying, anyway.

Bheji, appalled at the spectacle of Perry in paint-stained boiler suits, and more appalled still when he bought a second-hand van which he drove around the locality with ladders fastened to its roof, lamented bitterly that this was not the way in which she expected her sons to earn their living. Perry appeared to be enjoying himself and he and Shanti now seemed to feel financially confident enough for Shanti to give up her sewing, which meant that their house was much less cluttered and much more homely, but even these things could not comfort Ranbir.

"She is always saying how Western ways have got hold of my generation – the way she says it sounds as if she imagines Western ways are a lot of bandits hiding round corners and pouncing out at people," Rose said. "Sometimes, I want to laugh. Then at other times I feel cross. I feel annoyed when she backs Satnam up in some of the things he says. Really, I think Satnam ought to go and live in India himself! But in a way, I understand what she means. I am quite happy to go, once things are calmer."

Her parents were smiling. She had once overheard her mother saying, "Bheji is really comical over Satnam. Because he is so orthodox, she will forgive him anything. She does not

287

approve of Perry's new business because she says he is wasting his studies, but Satnam refused to go to college at all and is working as a motor mechanic and all she says is, how useful."

"It is funny," Kartar had said, "but in a way, Satnam is just like his father. They both like to work with their hands. But Perry is a tranquil fellow while Satnam is all passion."

Rose privately considered that the trouble with Satnam was that he had no sense of humour. It was an attribute she valued. She knew that she took life rather seriously herself and she liked people who could make her laugh.

"It is a great pity that you couldn't have married the Satinder Singhs' younger boy, as we once hoped," Nita was saying. "Charan was so nice. But, well, it would not have done. He had no steady job and now, of course, he has gone right away. When you go to India, your Uncle Sunderjit has promised he will look round and find you someone really worthwhile: a doctor or the son of some well-to-do businessman. Someone you will like; you will say yes or no, of course."

"I am really looking forward now to going," Rose said earnestly. "Auntie Billie says I can find a teaching job there easily if I want one, now that I have some experience in England. I wish all this uproar would stop. It seems a pity that people cannot follow their religion peacefully and not have all this fighting."

Her father folded down his paper and smiled at her over the top of it. "You're a good girl, Rose. We are very proud of you and Amrit. To think, our second daughter has just gone to university! I'm in no hurry to send you away, I must say. I think myself that it is a pity Charan Singh is out of the running. Your cousin Rupa and Charan's brother Surjit are obviously so happy together. Before you run off to India, I think we might look about for another local family similar to the Satinder Singhs."

"If you think it best. I am really quite willing to do what you advise," said Rose, trying not to sound bleak.

She had made up her mind, at that appalling supper-dance, that never, never would she allow any man to approach her again without her parents' knowledge and sanction, and never, never would she make Joan's mistake and fall in love before she was safely married.

And then what had happened? She came home for that Diwali, and sat talking to Lynn and Charan Singh had joined in, explaining to Lynn who Bhindranwale was. They had all begun to laugh over some silly joke to do with Christian sects . . . and she had looked at Charan's strong young face, and the way his genial smile showed his beautiful teeth, and she had listened to the refreshing, commonsense remarks he made in that downright voice of his, and before she knew it, she was imagining what it would be like to dance with Charan instead of Nick, thinking how different that kiss would have been if Charan had been the man instead of Nick . . . and there she was, just as she had sworn never to be, lost overboard, like a cruise passenger in a freak storm.

She could remember how, through all the rest of that evening, and the subsequent days, she had fought herself, pretending that nothing had happened. She went back to university and studied frenziedly and came home at Christmas half-longing, half-terrified, at the thought of seeing Charan Singh again. She went on feeling like that, every single time she came home, all through the rest of her university course.

It didn't help that Charan seemed to single her out, that when they met, as they often did, at social gatherings, he would smile at her the moment he saw her, would come and talk to her and make her laugh. Above all else, he could make her laugh.

And then after she had finished at university and had begun her teaching course, her mother told her one day, quite casually, that the Satinder Singhs had approached them about a marriage between her and Charan, and they had turned it down, because Charan was not in a sufficiently good job and Kartar, making a few quiet enquiries, had discovered that the one he did have was not secure.

But why didn't Charan speak to *me*? she had whispered in passionate fury, in her room with the door locked, lying face down on her bed and thumping it with her fists. Shoulder to shoulder, they might have prevailed. But he had left it to their elders to arrange their lives for them and not even made sure that she was consulted. She'd been obedient and modest, all the things her parents expected of her, and this was her reward. This was what you got for being good: you got ignored and passed over even in matters which concerned you and your whole life.

She wanted to ask Charan why he hadn't talked to her but he disappeared from most social functions and when she did catch sight of him, at someone else's wedding, he looked away.

She couldn't telephone; she guessed that his parents had approached hers at his request but wasn't sure and it would be very embarrassing if it turned out not to be so. There was no knowing who would answer the phone, either. If one of his parents did, what would they think if she asked to speak to him? They'd know her voice even if she didn't give her name.

For similar reasons, she could not write to him. She was too shy and what if someone else read the letter?

There was, however, Rupa.

Rupa, in the past, had heard from Rose all about the complicated love lives of Rose's fellow-students at university. Rupa wasn't university material herself, but like Satnam she was good with her hands. She also had a knack with make-up. On leaving school she had gone to train as a beautician and hairdresser. Ranbir disapproved of this ("Oh, she will mix with girls who think of nothing but being attractive; the next thing, she will want to go out with boys. As if Sunder were not bad enough!") but Perry said that Rupa should choose her own work.

Her training was enlivened by the on-off engagement of another, slightly older, trainee called Gillian, whose lukewarm fiancé kept delaying their marriage plans – once because he wanted to buy another car and once with no excuse whatsoever – and finally announced that he was going to work abroad for an unspecified time, and went. As a result of this, for a long time, Gillian's eyes kept filling with tears at unexpected moments and as a result of *that*, a client who had wanted a very discreet reddish tint emerged from the salon looking like a bush fire and refusing to pay even the reduced bill available to clients who let trainees practise on them.

Rupa went home and said candidly to her parents that English girls seemed to go through hell on the way to the altar, and that she would get married whenever they thought fit and would be only too happy to have potential partners found for her.

"You see?" Perry said to Ranbir. "You are always worrying about Western influences on the children, but Rupa has chosen all by herself to go about things the Indian way."

The upshot, amid much family satisfaction, was that at the beginning of the year, Rupa had married Surjit, the elder Satinder Singh boy, who unlike Charan was in a very good job as a business equipment salesman.

To Rupa, Rose told the story of the refused proposal and her distress that Charan had never spoken to her directly. She did not ask Rupa to mention this either to Surjit or to Charan but Rupa understood. A week later, as she made her way home from the school, Satnam's old school, where she had begun teaching, she found Charan waiting for her in the road.

"Rose! I wanted to see you. Rupa said you were upset. She told Surjit and he told me. I'm sorry, I didn't know. I mean, I didn't know you had been told anything at all about it. About my parents approaching yours, that is."

Now that he was there, she didn't know what to do or how to speak to him. She stood looking down at the gutter and moving the toe of one foot uneasily about.

"I'm sorry your parents wouldn't agree," said Charan. "But I was afraid they wouldn't. And perhaps they were right. I'm only here now, at half past four in the afternoon, because I've no work to go to at present. My company folded last week and I don't have a job. I was afraid it was going to happen. I didn't talk to you directly because I didn't . . . I didn't want to make you care and then perhaps you would be disappointed. If you cared anyway . . . I'm glad with half of me and very very sorry with the other half. I wish things could have been different."

She looked up once, into his dear face, and then down again before the hunger and unhappiness in her own could show too clearly. "Thank you for coming and saying this to me. I understand now. I'm so sorry about your firm. I hope you find something soon."

"I'm going to Canada. I have cousins there. I hope to make a better success of life there than here, with all this unemployment. I'm leaving in a month. I'm sorry. Good luck, Rose."

Then he smiled and walked away and left her thinking miserably how kind and good he was and how desperately much she would prefer to chance all and go to Canada with him, and knowing that she would be allowed to do no such thing.

Halfway home, she suddenly remembered that horrible supper-dance again and thought, if Charan knew, he wouldn't look at me. Thanks be to God, no one knows but me.

By the following day, she had faced it. Between Charan and herself it was over and that was final. It hardly seemed to matter what she did with the rest of her life.

The day after that, she said to her mother, "I think I would rather like to go back to India to get married. I wouldn't mind that at all. Would it be possible?".

Now, across the breakfast table, her mother's voice broke in on her thoughts. "Where is Bheji?"

"I think I can hear her moving," said Kartar. He had gone

291

back behind his newspaper. "She is not as lively in the mornings as she used to be. We all get older, gradually. It'll happen to you too, one day, Rose."

"The children at the school keep me young," said Rose. "I have to keep remembering to think as they think. They told us that during our training, but now I see what it means."

"Wait till you have children of your own," said her father. "They'll have the opposite effect. They'll *age* you." He glanced round the side of the paper and saw Rose looking bewildered and slightly hurt. He chuckled. "Oh, no, you are too sensitive. I didn't mean it. I hope you enjoy your video party."

Rose said, "Lynn is coming."

Lynn was not a film fan, and the advent of the video, which enabled people to go the pictures at will, without leaving their houses, had not struck her as the best technological advance of the century. "At least you could go round to someone's house then and not have to watch a film."

"Indian people like films very much," said Sunder mildly. "We are all getting videos."

"So I notice! And the films they watch are nearly always Hindi films."

"Well, that's natural."

"But they're so unrealistic."

"Indian audiences don't want kitchen sink dramas. They like glamour, and some songs and dances."

"But there's never anything to make one *think*."

"In Indian society," said Sunder, "films that make people think don't make money."

"But you don't care for Hindi films either!"

"No, I don't," Sunder agreed. "But it's kind of you to say you'll go to Rose's video party. She'll appreciate it."

"I know," said Lynn resignedly. "That's why I'm going."

The participants in the party were to include most of the women in the family, except for Krishna, who was working away from home, and Sita, who rarely joined in anything. Sita's final decision, after a long series of family conferences and some solemn undertakings from Hari, to return to him with Dinesh, had horrified many members of the family, quite apart from Lynn. "He will never keep his word," said Sunder.

But Sita had gone, saying that she had been hysterical on the day when she burst into the Diwali party and that Dinesh would one day inherit his father's business and should be brought up in it. She had not run away again but on the rare occasions when any of them saw her, she was always quiet and pale.

They all worried about her and discussed her often, but there had been no more dramatic developments.

Sunder commuted by train and Lynn used their car for work. On the day of the video party, she went straight from work to pick up some of the other guests. Balbir and Nerin now had two small boys and Nerin did not go out to work, but had that afternoon been entertaining her own mother and her mother-in-law Ranbir. Wearing jeans and a sweater, she greeted Lynn with pleasure and took her into the kitchen where saucepans were being briskly stirred.

Ranbir glanced round at Lynn without speaking, but Nerin's mother said cheerfully, "You shall eat something before you set off. I am not coming; we are taking care of the little boys this evening instead. They are out in the garden with my husband. He came here from work and went straight out. They love the garden already. Karnail is only two, but still he knows to pull up dandelions."

Lynn laughed. "I remember, Nerin, when you and Balbir bought this place, the big garden was the thing you liked about it most. You didn't mind what state it was in, but you had to have a big garden."

"They are mad," Perry had said, flinging up his hands in despair after being taken to see the house. "Oh, the wiring is all right and the roof will do for a few years yet but it all wants redecorating and when I said so, all Balbir said was, Oh, does it? They hadn't even noticed. All they care for is the garden and *that's* just a wilderness of grass and weeds! The place has been empty for months and the last occupiers were no gardeners. But Nerin simply laughs and says they will see to it and they are getting it cheap because of the weeds. But Balbir works such long hours; how will he have time to do so much at home? I will have to help with the wallpapering, but I'm no gardener, either."

"No," Nerin said later when this comment reached her. "But *my* father is."

Nerin's father had been born on a Punjab farm and both father and daughter possessed that talent known as green fingers.

With both of them working on it, aided by Balbir whenever he could, the garden had been transformed. Lynn looked out of the kitchen window on to a smooth lawn between neatly clipped hedges and flower-beds, the latter no longer colourful now that it was autumn, but being dug over by Nerin's father, with his two small grandsons helping him. Through a gap in an evergreen hedge beyond, a kitchen garden and greenhouse could be seen.

"I was out there myself till just an hour ago. That's why I am in these rough clothes," Nerin said. "We are planning to have a bigger greenhouse and grow more tomatoes next year. And I shall have a bed of rhubarb; I have got a taste for very tender young rhubarb. We are trying to think how to grow more potatoes without stealing ground from anything else. Oh, one has never enough space!"

"Nerin would buy a great big farm if she could," said her mother.

"My father has bought some land in India," Nerin said. "It is being managed for him now." She looked at her mother. "I think you will go back home one day. I wish you could buy land and work it here in England instead."

"Oh, not in England, one cannot do that in England," said Ranbir, lifting a saucepan off the stove. "Buying land in a country, that is really giving yourself to the place, sinking your money in it."

"No, we would never feel enough at home in England," Nerin's mother agreed. "We would never fit in with an English farming community. I cannot see my husband joining the Farmers' Union and being part of the scenery."

"I tell him," said Nerin, "that it is a matter of people getting used to you. Now, Balbir has won prizes for the potatoes and cucumbers he has grown here in this garden. He has joined a Middlesex club and he exhibits at their shows. He says many of the people at the club are very conventional and at first some of them were doubtful about him, but he just took no notice and talked to anyone he felt like talking to and joined in with everything and now they take him for granted, turban and all. He says that people would get to take a man with two heads for granted, if they saw him every day."

"I am not so sure," said her mother. "When the riots broke out at the time of Partition, people turned on their near neighbours. Shopkeepers were attacked by customers they had seen every day for years. Suddenly, people could not any longer see the individual they were used to: all they could see was a Hindu or a

Moslem, and they killed them and all past friendships went for nothing."

"Not all," said Nerin. "You yourself have told me that there were some decent people on both sides who protected neighbours, respectable Moslems who hid Hindu friends in their houses and Hindus and Sikhs who did the same for frightened Moslem neighbours."

"But not enough," said Ranbir. "They are never in the majority, those people."

"Ah well. Nerin, call your father and the boys in from the garden," said her mother. "Then we will eat something, and then you can go on your way."

"So nice for you," said Ranbir, ladling food into serving dishes, "having your grandsons to yourselves for an evening; it is such a joy to have grandchildren. There is nothing as wonderful for a woman as having babies and seeing them grow up and have children of their own. Sita has sacrificed herself I think, for Dinesh's sake; you see the power of her feelings for him."

"He's twelve now," said Nerin. "He's growing up. Divorces are becoming quite common now, even in the Indian community. No one would blame Sita if she went in for one. I am sure Hari still ill-treats her. She always looks so ill and miserable."

"But at least she has her son," said Ranbir.

Lynn, taking her place at the table, was silent. She had heard Ranbir talking about children in that unmistakable, persistent tone of voice before. Ranbir might be apparently discussing Sita, but her remarks were actually aimed at Lynn. A moment later, Ranbir, provoked by the silence, made another and more direct attempt, as Lynn had feared she would.

"Sita is a good girl," said Ranbir. "She is doing her best to make things work. One must admire that. As people grow older, sometimes they mellow; things may settle down. It is a pity there were no more children. It is such happy news that Rupa is in the family way. When will Sunder and Lynn be giving us an addition to the family, I wonder?"

I knew it, thought Lynn gloomily.

Nerin said, "We all thought, when you came back from your holiday in Spain this summer, Lynn, that perhaps soon you would have something to tell us. One hears such things about Spain; all the romance and warm nights."

"We're going again next year," said Lynn. "We're not in that much of a hurry to start a family."

295

"Oh, but you should not leave it too late." Ranbir insisted. "These holidays are all very well but there is nothing like an ordinary family life. You should have a baby soon. You have been married nearly three years now."

Lynn smiled politely and said no more. Ranbir, having realised that Lynn was there in the family, for better or worse, and would have to be endured, had very soon started a stealthy campaign to press her firmly into an Indian mould. Lynn usually dealt with it as she was doing now, by determinedly failing to react.

But it was always uncomfortable. She and Sunder meant to please themselves about when or even if they started their family, but withstanding this kind of barrage could be positively exhausting. She was relieved when the meal was over, and she and Nerin and Ranbir were in the car and bound for Rose's home, with Ranbir in the back seat and the conversation resolutely turning on the films they were to see.

From the day of the Diwali-cum-engagement party, Lynn and Rose had been friends, and Lynn had formed friendships too with most of the other women in the family. Leela had for a time regarded her rather as though she were a bomb that might go off at any moment, but this too had settled down. Lynn might not be looking forward particularly to the Hindi films, but the atmosphere would be friendly, and Ranbir, having had her say once, would probably not resume the attack until another time. It would be a pleasant enough occasion, she thought.

There were more things to eat when all the guests had arrived. This time the refreshments took the form of snacks which they put on low tables in front of the chairs and couches which Rose had put in a semicircle round the TV in the big front room. Nita, who occasionally drank a sherry these days, smilingly handed one to Lynn and poured one for herself but Shanti vetoed Rupa's request for one. "Not in your condition."

Rose said how lovely it was to see them all together and what a shame Sita and Krishna could not be there.

As Rose set the video going, Nerin said to Lynn, "Can you follow Hindi films? It must be difficult, with the language gap."

"I manage," Lynn said. "One can usually follow the plot, more or less." She added, politely, "The Indian settings are interesting; I haven't been out there yet. And I like the music and the dancing."

296

"The first film won't have music or dancing," Rose said. "But I hope you'll enjoy it. It is said to be very sad and romantic. Let us all settle down and have a good cry."

As the screen came to life, Lynn settled herself in the depths of a large armchair and prepared to concentrate. She might not like Hindi films very much as entertainment, but there was no doubt that if you wanted to learn about India and Indian culture, they could be very instructive. They also gave her a chance to hear Hindi, which, if not quite the same as her husband's Punjabi, was a related tongue and the official language of India, spoken continuously for a couple of hours at a time. She was trying to learn it and had mastered the alphabet and a few phrases, but one of the most important things in learning a new language was to accustom oneself to the sound. She proposed to treat the film as though she were a student.

But halfway through, it was borne in upon Lynn that this particular cinematic drama was different.

As the final credits rolled, Rose switched off the video and said, "I think that was the saddest story I ever heard of. And it was so well acted! It made you feel it was almost real. Shall we have another film, or would that spoil it?"

"I think another film would be an anti-climax," said Rupa. "Did you like it, Lynn? It was easy to follow, wasn't it? And I thought the acting was very fine. I was crying, I don't mind admitting it."

"Crying?" said Lynn. Both Rose and Rupa looked at her, somewhat startled by her tone, and she knew that her greenish eyes were probably hard and that her ginger hair was all but bristling with wrath. But sometimes, white lies could not be told in the name of politeness. Sometimes, it was asking just too much. "Crying?" she said again. "Well, maybe with rage! Of all the dangerous, sentimental, saccharine . . . !"

"Rage?" said Nerin, puzzled. "Why rage?"

"*Why?* That girl, the heroine, why did she go and throw herself into the river?"

"The villain had raped her," said Nita reasonably, from the other end of the couch. "She felt she had been defiled."

"I know, and that's why I'm in a rage! She wasn't defiled; she'd been the victim of a criminal assault! Why should she have to die? The only person who was defiled was the villain! *He* was the criminal. Nobody else!"

297

"Well, it is a different society," said Ranbir. "In that society, and among the people the film was made for, the girl would be thought to be dishonoured and her fiancé could not have married her."

"Why not? *Why not?* How can anyone just accept it like that? The girl was the *victim*. It's unfair, unjust, *monstrous* that the girl should have to pay. She'd done nothing wrong. She wasn't unfit for society or marriage. What sort of damn stupid man can't *see* that?" Lynn had been simmering for too long to make even a pretence of being polite to Ranbir now. "And that ghastly syrupy ending, when the hero killed the villain and then collapsed dying, clutching the heroine's photograph, and everyone stood round weeping. If she hadn't gone and drowned herself, I suppose they'd have refused to speak to her! All right to sentimentalise over her as long as she's conveniently dead!"

"Well, perhaps it is unfair," Nita said doubtfully, "but . . . "

"Yes, it is." Rose, who had been thinking it over, suddenly joined in. "Lynn is right. It was not *just*."

"In India there are many old prejudices," Nita agreed, "and it is a pity, but these attitudes are almost born in people. In time, things may change and perhaps they should but . . . "

"I do not agree!" Ranbir turned her shoulder to Lynn and addressed Nita and Rose. "These old ideas, they have served very well for thousands of years. They *protect* girls; you should realise that. Girls in our society value their honour, and so they take extra care to look after it, and their parents take care to guard them, because they know that if anything happens, yes, the girl will be called dishonoured, and there will be whispers, people will say perhaps it was her fault."

"But if the facts are known and everyone knows it was not her fault?" protested Rose.

"Then there may be suffering, but for every girl who suffers in that way, ten thousand more are saved, because they take care they would not take otherwise," said Ranbir.

"The horror of the thing itself would make most girls want to avoid it! You can't excuse an outrageous injustice on those grounds!" Lynn shot back. "In fact, you can't excuse outrageous injustice on *any* ground!"

"You are too passionate," said Ranbir coldly. "It does not do to be so passionate."

"About that kind of injustice I will always be passionate!" Lynn would not be placated.

"But it is only a film . . . " began Nerin.

"*Only* a film? Millions of people see these films, from what you've told me. Films have power, just because of that. Instead of reinforcing that wicked, cruel, unjust ethic, they should be using their power to question it. That film was a *disgrace*; in effect, it was just saying to women, if you're unfortunate enough to be the victim of an attack like that, you've no right to live. How about the sanctity of human life?"

"A girl's honour is sacred also," said Ranbir angrily.

"What honour? If someone breaks into your house and steals your spoons you don't talk about being dishonoured! You send for the police and say you've been robbed! You don't apologise for the bad taste of having been burgled, sorry I've embarrassed everyone, where's the nearest river? How about being sensitive over injustice? How about being sensitive about *human rights*?"

"Lynn, please!" said Nita rather sharply.

"But it is not so different here," said Nerin. "I have read in papers about how lawyers will try to blame the women when there is a rape case; they will say she should not have been in such a lonely place by herself or that she encouraged the man in some way . . . "

"I know, I'm a social worker. I go into families where all kinds of things have happened and I've come across a woman who was afraid to take a rapist to court because her husband had rejected her on account of the rape, and she couldn't take any more. She had *not* invited trouble. She was attacked by a housebreaker. Not that it would have made any difference if she'd been walking in a wood. Woods are beautiful and we've as much right to walk in them as anyone else. I am not supposed to lose my temper," said Lynn grimly, "but I told the husband what I thought of him. And I wrote a letter to the *Guardian*, and it was printed. Yes, women do get blamed here, too, but here it makes women angry. And it's not just women; plenty of men can see how wrong and unfair it is. There are newspaper articles and TV programmes condemning attitudes like that and groups have formed to fight against them. The prejudice still exists here but society doesn't back it up. The society that film was about *does* back it up and it's shameful, shameful! Why aren't you all angry? I can't understand it! Oh, I'm sorry, Rose. I didn't mean to upset you after you'd organised this party so beautifully. But I can't help it, that ethic shocks me."

"But it is the way people in India think and a film which

questioned it would probably not be a box office success. So it would not wield much power after all," said Nita mildly.

"I wonder," snapped Ranbir, "what Sunder would say if such a thing happened to you?"

"I hope," said Lynn with emphasis, "that I would get sympathy and support. Not condemnation!"

"I expect he would try," said Nita, "But it would be very difficult for him. It is best, perhaps, that girls should just be very careful. I understand what Bheji is saying. Some things go against a man's instincts."

"Then I'd quarrel with those instincts! At least I could do that! At least I could stand up and shout at him that I *was* a victim, that I *refused* to be blamed! At least I could kick up hell about it. I wouldn't just accept it!"

"There are things one has to accept," said Ranbir flatly. "If you marry amongst us, there are things you must realise will not change; you must learn to think in a different way."

"Let us all pray that nothing so dreadful ever happens," said Shanti. Her English was still limited but she could now understand and contribute to conversations which were not too complex. In the brisk let's-restore-normality way for which, of late years, she had become noted, she added, "Nita, shall I help you make some tea?" Shanti nowadays was resolute and efficient in times of crisis.

"I'll help," said Lynn. "I've said my bit!"

"You have a good heart," said Nita kindly, as they moved towards the kitchen. "But Bheji will not change her attitudes, I fear."

"I've probably offended her, but I can't help it." Lynn glanced over her shoulder to where Ranbir was sitting, face closed. "Sometimes one must speak up."

"Yes, and one must respect that. In time she will get over it," said Nita.

Rose, now busy removing the cassette from the video, was feeling depressed.

It was always the same. Her parents were inclined enough as it was to cling too firmly to the attitudes of their own youth. Her mother took an especially earnest view of life but she did not think she had ever heard either of them utter that restful phrase, "Oh, well, it doesn't matter," about anything at all.

But on the rare occasions when they did show signs of softening, of wanting to take a short excursion down an easygoing

Western side road, what happened? Bheji was there, planted in the way like a No Entry sign, to make sure that they stayed on the traditional highway.

Dimly, listening to Lynn's outburst, she had perceived one of the differences between her society and Lynn's, glimpsed a world in which people defined themselves and did not feel forced to accept what others thought of them as the truth. In that world . . . she and Charan could have said they wanted to marry, and got engaged and paid no heed to anyone else's opinion.

But for her, in this household, in this society, that world was out of reach, and she did not want to quarrel with those around her. But she felt obscurely that life would be easier. that she would not, for instance, still feel a haunting guilt about that awful dance with Nick, if only her parents would relax just a little.

If only Bheji would let them!

It took Rose a long time to get to sleep that night. The film, Lynn, her doubts of her own chosen course, whirled round and round in her head and would not let her go. When at last she did fall asleep, she had a nightmare. Charan was angry with her. She ran away from him and fell into a swift river and was swept away. A black cavern yawned ahead. She fought to reach the shore but the waters tossed her from side to side and her efforts were useless. Then she woke suddenly and found that her father was shaking her arm.

"Raminder Rose, wake up. Wake up! Something terrible has happened."

"Something terrible?" She sat up, staring at him in alarm. "What? Is it Mother? Bheji..?"

"No, no, it is nothing to do with this house. It is in India. But it is so terrible. Mrs Gandhi has been assassinated in Delhi. Her own Sikh bodyguard have shot her. I am afraid there will be such trouble."

Chapter Twenty-Four

The Vigil
1984

"I knew it!" said Kartar grimly, turning the television off as the newsreader went on to a domestic item which did not interest them. Rose wished she hadn't had to see the one on events in Delhi.

She had been to Delhi. She might, quite easily, have sat in a bus beside some quite ordinary, harmless looking man who was now running amok with knives and petrol cans, murdering total strangers, just because they happened to be Sikhs and Mrs Gandhi's assassins had been Sikhs too.

It was the insane logic of Alice in Wonderland. You were not responsible for someone else's behaviour merely because you belonged to the same religion or race. She was herself a British citizen. So were a good many of the inhabitants of Pentonville and Wormwood Scrubs. Being British didn't make her responsible for their murders and bank robberies. A child ought to know that.

A large proportion of the inhabitants of Delhi didn't appear to know anything of the sort.

And the horrors she had just seen on the television screen were no invented drama; not even historical footage from the days of Partition. They were happening in the real world, now.

Her father was looking at her. "Rose, you should sleep. It will be a long night. My God, it's been a long day."

Rose nodded. Trying not to worry, she had gone to work that morning. She taught at Lanesden Middle School, which Satnam had once attended. She had instructed a class of ten-year-olds on the difference between adverbs and adjectives, and the distinction between a tributary and a distributary, supervised break, attended a staff meeting. And come home to find that her parents hadn't gone to work at all. They had spent the day switching on every TV or radio news bulletin available, ringing friends to find out if they had any further information, or alternatively, being rung up by them.

Kartar had gone out briefly only twice, to buy the newspapers which were now strewn round the room. There was tea in the pot and sandwiches to eat but, "I can't settle to cooking proper meals," said Nita. "I am too distracted. The news is so terrible, so terrible. I just keep making tea."

Ranbir, huddled wretchedly in a corner of the settee, was lamenting. "For once I am glad I have left India. It is the only time I am glad Jog is dead and gone and never lived to see this! They are dragging people off trains and out of their houses and butchering them; no one is safe, not even tiny children. They are making fires and throwing little children into them . . . !"

"Uncle Sunderjit and Aunt Billie are in Delhi," Kartar said. "I hope to God they are safe. It is not clear just where these atrocities are occurring. Delhi is a big place."

The phone rang and Rose, who was nearest the door, went out to the hall to answer it. "Rose?" said her sister Amrit's voice. "I have seen the news. I'm coming home. I'll be with you by tomorrow midday. Is there any news of Uncle Sunder and Aunt Billie?"

"No, Father was just saying he hoped to God they were safe. Oh, Amrit, it is so awful!"

"I know, I keep crying. I would come home tonight but I am so upset I feel ill; I can't set out yet . . . "

"Who is it?" said Kartar, at Rose's elbow. "Amrit?"

"Yes." Rose relinquished the receiver.

"Amrit . . . ? No, no, of course you can't start out now; you will be arriving at some unearthly hour and we do not like you being out late, alone, no matter what the circumstances. Have a good night's sleep and come tomorrow. We will be here. Yes, it is dreadful, unbelievable . . . "

The phone rang again the instant he put down the receiver and he caught it up. "Virk here. Perry!"

"Mohan Lal and his family are with me." Perry's voice came clearly to Rose. "They came for Shanti's sake and to tell us that there are some Hindus who have not gone crazy. They are in as bad a state as we are. Kartar, we want to try and ring Uncle Sunderjit tonight. He has a telephone, hasn't he? But I haven't got his number. Have you?"

"Yes. Hold on and I'll get it for you."

"No, look, why don't you come over and join us? We shall feel better if we are all together. We shall try to ring at about one a.m.; it will be very early morning in India then but perhaps not so many people will be jamming the lines this end. It would be no good ringing now; every Sikh household in England is probably trying to raise Delhi by phone."

"All right," said Kartar.

In times of trouble, people found comfort in being together. Perry's house had somehow or other become the centre of such a gathering. Nearly all the extended family had arrived there. Mr Satinder Singh opened the door to them and immediately behind him were Rupa and Surjit. "This is so awful!" Rupa said. "In this day and age, too. Rose, you can never go to India now!"

"No, I know. I would be too frightened. Even when all is quiet again, I would still be frightened."

"Come inside and have some tea," called Shanti's voice.

In Perry's house too, people had been making tea rather as if the continual swallowing of that restoring and ordinary beverage were a form of magic spell, through which normality might somehow be restored worldwide. In the sitting room, crowded with anxious faces, used cups were everywhere and Shanti was dispensing fresh supplies from a huge, steaming pot. But at the sight of Nita and Ranbir, she put the pot down and dropped her hands into her lap. Ranbir looked at her briefly and then went with Rupa to sit on a couch beside Nerin. Shanti, the brisk common sense of her recent years suddenly vanishing, began to shake. Her face crumpled.

Nita went straight to her and put her arms round her. "Shanti, Shanti, it is not your fault."

"I am so ashamed. How people can behave in such a way . . . "

"Hush. Hush. We are all one family and we are all in this together."

"My people are murdering yours. I can't bear it."

"We will set them a good example. Pour me some tea, Shanti. I'm parched. We've had nothing for hours," said Nita untruthfully, on the principle that upset people were the better for being kept occupied. "Here is Rose. Amrit is coming tomorrow. Will Sita come?"

"No, we telephoned and she said she would but she didn't, so Leela rang again and Sita said she couldn't come; Hari didn't think it necessary. Krishna's not here; she is away on some job

304

again and Chandra Lal is at work; all police leave has been stopped round here, in case trouble breaks out among the Indian communities here as well, I suppose. Lynn and Sunder will come soon. I will be glad to see Sunder. Satnam has been shooting his mouth off; he came in late from his work and then we heard nothing but the sound of his voice until Mohan Lal came and then Perry would not stand it any more, but he had to shout at Satnam to stop him saying, oh, such dreadful things. He never thinks how he is hurting me . . . "

It was noticeable that Satnam was indeed sitting in a corner on his own, scowling and being ignored by the rest of his family. Nerin and Balbir had brought their two small boys and these, aged three and two respectively, were sitting on cushions on the floor and regarding him with large round eyes, half fascinated by him and half afraid of him.

"Never mind him," said Nita firmly. "He is not yet old enough to know what he is talking about. He is only in his twenties and he is young for his age in some ways. He does not yet understand that other people have feelings. To Satnam, other people are not yet real."

"There are too many people about who don't know that other people are real and some of them are a good deal older than Satnam is. Delhi is full of them. That is what has caused all this; people not knowing that others are real. And it is nearly time for the nine o'clock news," said Shanti wretchedly. "Yes, Perry is turning on the television. I don't want to see. I don't want to hear. I am going to the kitchen!"

She fled, as the sound of BBC Channel 1 came on. Rose soon wished that she had fled as well. But . . . no, she thought, sitting as rigidly as though she had been paralysed, while a new catalogue of horrors was displayed upon the screen. No, it was better to know the facts; it was even a duty. If they had been living in India, they would have been in the midst of this. People they knew and loved were in the midst of it still and from half a world away, one could not help them. Here we sit, she thought, perfectly safe but what right have we to be safe when other people, like nice Uncle Sunder and kind Auntie Billie are in such danger?

She was undeservedly fortunate to be threatened by nothing worse than a news bulletin and the least she could do was refrain from running away from it.

The unspeakable report from Delhi seemed to go on for ever.

There was an interview with a frantic woman whose husband and son had been murdered in front of her; another interview with a shocked man, an entirely respectable Hindu who had seen a Sikh dragged from the train in which they were both passengers. "We all told him he was in danger; we tried to get him to take off his turban and cut his hair before the train got into the station but he wouldn't . . . "

The doorbell rang and they heard Shanti's footsteps going to answer it. A moment later, Lynn and Sunder slipped quietly into the room. Those already present acknowledged them with silent nods; even Ranbir. Yesterday's argument with Lynn had clearly been wiped out of her mind. Lynn and Sunder also signalled greetings without speech, concerned not to interrupt the viewing. On the screen, the bulletin had now shifted to an interview with Sikh representatives in various English towns.

" . . . a march took place in the early evening in Southall . . . "

"I saw it," said Satinder Singh. "Mr Sodhi was in it. I preferred not to be. It was a shocking thing to send soldiers into the Golden Temple but I can't agree with assassination . . . "

He stopped short. The camera had swooped in close and the interviewer had buttonholed some of the marchers at random to let them have their say. An angry young face, the neck muscles corded with rage below the bearded jaw, appeared, enlarged, staring straight into the camera lens. "We are pleased that this assassination has been carried out. This is our day of rejoicing!"

Perry pounced across the room, yanked Satnam out of his seat and shook him hard. "You bloody young fool! So you were *not* at work today! And what possessed you to talk like that to an interviewer? Look what is happening because of this thing you are so proud of!"

"We hadn't heard the news about the riots when that was filmed!" Satnam protested, tearing himself free.

"What were you doing in that march at all? You should have been at your work!"

"This was more important than to go to work."

"Making an exhibition of us all on British TV? You haven't the sense you were born with! We were all grieved that the temple should be the centre of such terrible events, but it is a private thing, private to us. The English don't give a damn about Sikhs and Hindus and most of them have never even heard of the Golden Temple. Do you think all this shouting and demonstrating about things that mean nothing to them will impress

306

them? They will just say, oh, hysterical foreigners, and switch their sets off and then there will be more prejudice against us in this country. And meanwhile, you will make trouble between the communities here. What do you want, bloodshed in the streets here in Southall?"

Satnam's neck muscles were knotted into cords once more. "Our great shrine was desecrated! We were entitled to our revenge!"

"Revenge is a questionable thing," said Mr Satinder Singh slowly. "It so often leads to blood feuds and to innocent people being killed just for belonging to the wrong community."

Satnam's scowl deepened.

Kartar said, "I knew the moment I heard of the assassination that there would be a backlash. You were foolish not to realise that too, Satnam."

"Yes, I agree." Lynn joined in. "Oh, Satnam, your face on TV just now was . . . was dreadful. It was all distorted with hate. How could you?"

"If Canterbury Cathedral were attacked by armed men, sent in by the Prime Minister, perhaps your face would be distorted, too!"

"I doubt it. I don't subscribe to any religion. I'm a humanist. And there isn't one single solitary building on earth, no matter how beautiful or holy, that I'd put above a human life. And if Canterbury Cathedral were suddenly taken over by a lot of born-again Christians, armed to the teeth, I don't think the Archbishop would like it a bit. He'd *want* them removed!"

"It is not the same thing, not the same thing at all."

"Oh, do stop it!" Rose cried out. "Stop it, stop it! We are all worried out of our minds about Uncle Sunder and Auntie Billie, yes, and there are others, too, who will be in danger, and all you do, Satnam, is pull haughty faces and shout about temples and revenge! I would see every temple in the world blown up, just to know Uncle and Auntie are safe, yes I would! When we went to India we stayed with them and they were so kind to me! And when I think what may be happening to them . . . oh, shut up, Satnam, just shut up!" Rose dissolved into tears.

Her mother went to her. "Now, let us be a little calm. We must not have all this trouble among ourselves!" said Nita. "I do not know why you are like this these days, Satnam."

"It is a matter of our identity. Everywhere the Sikhs go, their identity is threatened. I was stabbed by skinheads because of my topknot, here in London; now in India, Sikhs are being murdered. We have to stand up and show we cannot be intimidated. We must be like the Israelis, like . . . !"

"Satnam!" shouted Sunder. "Will you for God's sake get down off that soapbox you carry about everywhere with you! We are all sick of your opinionated talk."

Sunder's voice was so very loud and furious that Satnam was actually silenced for a moment.

"Oh, it ought not to be like this!" cried Ranbir. "What is happening? Satnam is a good Sikh boy; I have been so proud of him being such a good boy, but it is all going wrong; he ought to care more for his uncle and aunt!" Ranbir's face was genuinely bewildered.

"Satnam," said Perry. "You are upsetting us all. You have upset your mother so that she will not come back into this room. That's enough. You will now go to your own room and I shall fetch your mother back to join us. Please do not cause her any more distress."

Satnam muttered something like an oath and rushed out.

Perry said, "If you've got that phone number, Kartar, I'll try to get through now. There isn't much chance of a free line but let's try. It'll be the middle of night in India, but I doubt if Uncle Sunder is asleep."

Two a.m.

Lynn's parents from next door had been in to express their horror and their sympathy, had drunk tea, and then, as if fearing that their presence might be somehow intrusive, quietly returned home. Their house was now in darkness. But in other houses nearby, in Harrison Street and in the road that backed on to it, windows were still lit. There too, people must be awake, keeping vigil; there too would be the murmur of voices and the never-ending clink of teacups.

In Perry's house exhaustion had overtaken a few. Rupa, being pregnant, had been sent upstairs by Surjit. Nerin and Balbir, who were now sharing an armchair, had fallen asleep slumped together. Their two children were asleep on their cushions, curled up like puppies; Ranbir too was dozing uneasily, sagging against the arm of a settee, her face old and tired. Even Perry's repeated endeavours at the telephone could not disturb them.

His efforts so far had been all in vain. "There's no way to get through," he said, putting the receiver down for the seventh

308

time. "The operators in Delhi are not answering. Probably they are not at their posts. Who can blame them?"

Kartar nodded. The last news bulletin, picked up on the radio, had been a nightmare to hear, the newsreader's British voice grey and heavy with the horror he could not express in any other way.

The phone had rung once, with an incoming call, but it was from Robert Houghton, calling to express his distress and give his anxious good wishes for the safety of Perry's family in India. His voice had sounded old and shocked.

"If only," said Nita, "there were direct dialling to Delhi. If only they had STD."

"There must be codes." Kartar sat with his hands hanging between his knees. "The operators use them; if we knew what they were, we could get through direct. But they have not been published."

"It's the sort of thing Mr Sodhi might know," Nita said. "He knows so many things, so many people."

"Let's ring him up and ask him," said Sunder.

"He'll be in bed," Nita protested.

"On a night like this?" Kartar had jerked upright. "If he is in bed, he has no business to be! Let's wake him up! Perry, do you have *his* number, by any chance?"

Two forty-five a.m.

The tea had long since been augmented by whisky and then by black coffee. A litter of used glasses now reinforced the cups.

"It's no use. I think the number Mr Sodhi gave us is right, for the phone is ringing. But no one is picking up the call." Perry sat down. His hair fell into his eyes and he pushed it exhaustedly back. Rose, half-drowsing in a chair, heard his voice as if through a haze. "They are not home or else I'm ringing the wrong number."

"No one is home, it seems." Satinder Singh had a brother in Delhi and had been trying to telephone him as well, with a similar lack of success.

"They may have got out of Delhi," said Nita hopefully. "It seems it is worst there."

"My sister Savitri and her husband have a telephone." Mohan Lal sounded slightly apologetic. "They will not be in danger, since they are not Sikhs. But perhaps they can find something out tomorrow. Perry, if I may use the phone . . . ?"

309

Three-thirty a.m.

There had been movement outside in the darkness; the swish of a passing car, footsteps, somewhere a door slamming. Other households were not only wakeful like theirs, but clustering together like theirs as well. Once, Rose, going to the bathroom which was at the rear of the house, heard wailing from a house in the adjacent street. She stood trembling at the washbasin, feeling her skin prickle.

Downstairs, Mohan Lal was on the telephone again. As she came back into the room, he was speaking over his shoulder. "I've got Savitri at last." His attempts at direct dialling had been balked at first by a lack of free telephone lines and then by a blizzard of interference. He concentrated once more on the receiver and spoke rapidly.

"Oh, Mohan Lal will be so glad if Savitri can help," Leela whispered to Nita. "He is so sad about all of this."

Savitri was evidently agreeing to something. "Yes . . . Perry's uncle and aunt and Satinder's brother . . . yes, I have the names and addresses here . . . can you hear me? . . . yes, first is . . . "

Presently he put the phone down. "She will find out what she can. She is distressed; it is all so terrible, she says. I did not speak to Dinesh; he is ill in bed. His health is not so good these days and I am not sorry. He is still a surly fellow; Hari learned his bad ways from him, I think. Savitri will do her best. Thank God she has her own health again now. Maybe tomorrow we will get news."

"I think we shall have to leave it to her for the time being," said Perry exhaustedly. "I am too tired to think. I can't think how to go to sleep but I need sleep; we all do."

"Yes. There is no more we can do here tonight," Kartar agreed. "Rose? Are you awake?"

"Yes." She forced her leaden eyelids to rise. "Yes."

"I think," Kartar said, "that we should go home."

"We should, too," said Satinder Singh. "Charan may be trying to get through to us from Canada."

Even in the midst of nightmare, private, personal thoughts sometimes intruded. Rose longed to say, "Remember me to him if he does." But knew that she must not.

Amrit reached home at noon, pale and frightened, with dark-circled eyes. They were still compulsively turning on news bulletins "though the news only gets worse, which one wouldn't have thought possible, yesterday," Rose said.

Perry rang at six that evening and Rose took the call.

"Tell your father, that I would like you all to come round here, as soon as possible," he said, and rang off.

Twenty minutes later, they were once more in Perry's sitting-room. "Shanti is upstairs," he said. "She won't come down. Mohan Lal got through to Savitri an hour ago. She'd been trying to reach him but she couldn't. She told him . . . he wouldn't come himself. He gave us her news by phone. He can't face us. He . . . the Satinder Singhs are coming; it's as bad for them. The news is . . . "

"Get on with it!" said Kartar.

But they already knew what Perry was going to say. His face was enough.

"They're dead," he said. "Satinder Singh's brother. Uncle Sunderjit. Auntie Billie. They're *all dead*."

Chapter Twenty-Five

The Nightmare
1984

The gathering of the previous night was forming anew. As each family arrived, Perry drew them in and broke the news. People turned to each other and clung together, weeping and exclaiming. Ranbir became faint and Rose helped her to a seat and sat with her, holding her hand. Lynn came, with Sunder, and sat down beside him, white-faced and shivering. When Surjit, arriving with Rupa, said, "How did they die?" Rose wanted to shout out to him not to ask but the answer was given before she could protest.

Satnam, who had been once more sitting in a corner, was the one who gave it. "Mr Satinder Singh's brother was beaten to death in the street. Uncle Sunderjit and Auntie Billie were attacked in their house. They were set on fire, with petrol. That is what happened. It is too monstrous to think of. Can you imagine it? People broke in and . . . "

"Don't go on!" pleaded Rose. The images of horror which the media had been thrusting at them now for so long had risen up in her mind's eye with Uncle Sunder and Auntie Billie caught up in them. The kindness they had shown her when she visited them, the terror and agony of their deaths, were displayed on a nightmare screen inside her head and neither closing her eyes nor turning away could shut it out.

"But we must think of these things! Now perhaps you will understand why I say that there must be Khalistan. No Sikh is safe in Hindu India. It is too horrible to imagine. They threw petrol . . . "

"It *is* too horrible to imagine!" Rose cut him short. She got up, walked out of the room with a fair imitation of steadiness and then pounded up the stairs at a run. She stumbled into the bathroom, grabbed at the sink with both hands, and was violently sick into it.

Presently, having wiped her face with a cold flannel and drunk some water, she made her way down again. As she came back into the sitting room, she heard her Uncle Perry say, "It is as if the whole world were disintegrating."

Satnam had blessedly fallen silent. Lynn's parents and brothers had arrived, having seen Lynn go into Perry's house and decided to enquire once more after her husband's family.

"We don't want to intrude but we know you must be worrying about your people in India," her father said. "We only want to say again how sorry we are and is there any news?"

"There's news," said Perry. "The worst. But come in, come in. You are part of the family now."

The English in-laws, thought Rose distractedly, came among them more easily than Satnam's own mother. Shanti had hidden herself upstairs. Rupa went once to try to coax her mother down but failed. "She is just lying on the bed and will not get up." Nita went into Shanti's kitchen and began, as if automatically, the inevitable business of making tea.

But an hour later, the situation changed. Perry and Kartar, seeing the Edmonds out, saw two figures approaching hurriedly along the street and held the door open for them. Mohan Lal and his son Chandra Lal greeted the Edmonds briefly as they passed them and hastened inside.

"We had to come. We are so sorry for what has happened; more sorry than we can say," said Chandra Lal. "But there is more news, and things are happening; it is important that we visit you. I have dragged my father here, more or less. You do not mind?"

They had seen little of Chandra Lal in the last few years. He had left home during his initial training for the police, and although he had returned to work locally, he had been aloof from all but the most important family gatherings. This was partly because of his hours of duty but also, Rose had heard her parents say, partly from choice although no one knew quite why. "I think he feels that many people do not approve of what he has done," Kartar had said on one occasion. But Chandra Lal's sister Krishna, who chanced to be present, shook her head. "It isn't that. There are only a few who think that. We need Indian policemen; it is a help to have them and most people know that.

313

No, it is that he thinks he must learn to see his own people from a distance, that in his work he must be impartial to all sections of the community."

"Don't English policemen take part in their own families' affairs, then?" said Nita in surprise.

"Yes, but the English do not have such close family ties," said Krishna. "And they do not think of themselves as being in a community so much."

"They are a cold people," said Nita. "I have heard that after a funeral, they will practically throw a party!" The conversation then went on to other things.

Now, as Chandra Lal came in and sat down, Rose wondered which explanation of his aloofness was the true one and decided that it couldn't possibly be fear of criticism. He looked far too self-possessed for that. He was not burly in the way that many of his English colleagues were, but he had nevertheless filled out in the last few years and his quiet, controlled movements spoke of an underlying physical strength. He was a contrast to his father, who seemed to have shrunk inside his clothes and was hardly able to meet anyone's eyes. As they sank into armchairs and thanked Nita for the tea she at once handed to them, it was Chandra Lal who was dominant.

"What is this news you have?" said Satnam in a slightly hectoring tone.

Chandra Lal looked at his father. "I have been in touch with my sister Savitri again," said Mohan Lal eagerly. "There is better news of some other family members. She has found out a lot and it was brave of her, for the streets are not safe for anyone. But she knows the wife of the local chief of police . . . "

Ranbir leaned forward anxiously. "My cousins? You have heard about my cousins? And my friends . . . ?" She recited a list of names, most of which Rose remembered as the names of people to whom she had been introduced in India.

Mohan Lal nodded vigorously. "Yes, they are all safe, so far. They are all all right. There is great disruption, still anything may happen, but at the moment they are all right. Camps are being set up outside Delhi for Sikhs escaping from the violence; some of them are there." He began to give more details, still in the same anxious, eager voice, as though his news were a passport back into acceptance.

"Thank God," Perry said. "Thank God *someone* has got through safely."

314

Ranbir was in tears again. "It is grief and relief both mixed up."

Satnam said in a stiff voice, "We must thank you both for bringing this news to us. You have taken a great deal of trouble to obtain it."

Chandra Lal set down his teacup on top of a bookcase and turned to him. "Satnam, I'm still the same boy who picked you up bleeding from that pavement, you know. And my father is still your father's old friend. We're all the same people that we were before. Which brings me to the other reason why we're here. I said, things are happening, and they are. Mr Sodhi was with the police last night and so were some of the other community leaders . . . "

"With the *police*?" Ranbir wiped her eyes and sat up. "But why were they with the police? What have they done?"

"Been involved in inflammatory marches and said inflammatory things on the media, for a start," said Chandra Lal drily. "But this wasn't to do with that as it happens. The police wanted to talk to the leaders of the Hindu and Sikh communities to get them to co-operate in keeping the peace here. Our chief superintendent's quite determined that none of the violence in India is going to spread to the streets of Britain and he's taking steps. Much the same thing's happening in places like Leeds and Bradford. Chief constables are sending directives but the local levels hardly needed telling . . . "

"Is all this," enquired Satnam, "leading up to you forbidding me to take part in any more demonstrations? Because if so . . . "

"I'd be glad not to see a repetition of yesterday's performance," said Chandra Lal calmly. "I saw you on television. You were a depressing spectacle. But as to forbidding you to take part in demonstrations, no, not exactly. There is a demonstration being planned, with police permission, which Mr Sodhi will certainly tell you about soon. Sikhs and Hindus are to march together, holding hands, to show that here in England we are friends and that we reject what is happening in Delhi. It is a demonstration of solidarity. It was Mr Sodhi's idea. When the trouble in Delhi broke out, he was very shocked. It made him think afresh and he thought of this. Personally, I'd prefer to see no demonstrations at all, but I came to tell you that this one is legal, provided that everyone understands that it must be peaceful. I am fairly sure that some of you will want to take part; so I am just telling you that."

"A *solidarity* demonstration?" Satnam snorted. "You need not worry. I shall never take part in such a thing!"

"No, I hardly thought you would. But I trust you won't try to disrupt it, either," said Chandra Lal.

"I might join it," Surjit said slowly. "But when is it to take place?"

"Tomorrow," said Chandra Lal, watching them with serious eyes. "Krishna is home and she and Mother have gone to see Sita and Hari, to try and persuade them to come along."

"If only you would all come. It would make me so happy. I have felt so terrible," said Mohan Lal. "We will be peaceful, son, you need not worry. We won't let you down."

"I cannot march with Hindus," said Satnam. "I say nothing about you, Chandra Lal, or other members of our family; you are in a different category. But with others, no. I cannot take Hindu hands and walk down the street with them. Their touch would make me sick!"

"How can you, Satnam?" cried Rupa. "What would Mother say? Oh, why does Mother not come down?"

"Probably because she doesn't want to listen to Satnam," said Sunder exasperatedly.

"Yes, where is she?" Mohan Lal looked round as though noticing for the first time that Shanti was not there.

"Upstairs, hiding," said Perry. "I can't get her to come down; even Rupa can't. But we must try again. Come with me, Mohan Lal . . . oh, who is that at the door?"

"I will go," said Kartar.

He came back in a moment, pushing Leela and Krishna in front of him. "Of course you are welcome, and yes, Mohan Lal is here. We have heard all about the solidarity march and yes, we will help. I think I will march myself. Chandra Lal has told us that we must be careful but of course we will be that. Sit down. How did you get on with Sita?"

"We failed," said Leela, sitting down miserably. "It is no use trying there; that Hari would not listen to us. He . . . oh, he is impossible!"

"Said he wouldn't march with Sikhs, I suppose," said Satnam. "Well, for once I am at one with Hari. I say it again, I will not march with Hindus!"

"No, you will only march in crowds shouting big words about rejoicing and revenge, and now see what has come of it!"

The whole gathering swung round, to find Shanti in the

doorway. Her face was hollowed with sleeplessness and sorrow but she held herself straight and she was glaring at Satnam. "Bred in this household, you should know better than to put people into lumps called Sikh and Hindu and say one is all good and one is all bad. You should know that people are themselves. But you do not know and I am ashamed I have such a foolish son!" said Shanti furiously.

"Thank you," said Satnam, equally furiously, and charged out of the room. They heard the hallstand rock as he grabbed a coat, and then the front door slammed.

"Oh, my God," said Perry, and sank into a chair, hiding his face in his hands. Shanti went to him, perching on the arm of his chair and putting her arms round him. Her self-possession had returned, regenerated by anger. "It is a pity he could not learn from us. But in time perhaps he will. All this will pass, you will see."

Sunder looked at Chandra Lal. "We will march tomorrow. Lynn and I will march."

"Does Lynn want to?" asked Kartar. "I mean, since she is English . . . "

"I'm one of you now," said Lynn. "I will be there."

"There can be no question of opening the shop today," Hari had said that morning. "Very likely some Sikh boys would charge in and I should be knocked on the head again. We will stay home and stay quiet. It is just as well it is a Saturday. If it were a weekday, I would keep Dinesh home from school."

"Why?" said Dinesh. He was a well-grown twelve-year-old and developing a mind of his own. "All these things are happening in India, not here."

"It would be better. Things can reach out from long distances," said Hari. "Yes, indeed they can."

The events in Delhi had certainly reached out to her husband, Sita thought miserably. He had watched all the TV bulletins with close attention, hunched forward, his eyes fixed on the screen, and his face full of a queer, frightening excitement and last night, he had wanted sex.

In the course of her marriage with Hari, there were times, which could be quite prolonged, when as long as she kept his rules, lived within the bounds which he dictated, life was bearable in an arid fashion, much as existence in a desert might be. He seemed to regard sex as a weapon, a way of demonstrating

317

his power, and he was liable to want variations which Sita found objectionable, but he was not sufficiently interested in her or indeed, she suspected, in sex in general, to inflict himself on her very often.

He sometimes complained because there had been no more children, but he seemed to have grown used to this now. Again, Sita suspected that he was fundamentally indifferent to the appeal of family life. He complained because it was another way of attacking her rather than because he really cared. He had his son Dinesh and that was enough.

The reason why there had been no more children was because Sita had made sure of it. Much as Hari would have liked to control her every movement, this was impossible. He had given up having tenants after Sita had twice made friends with the wives but she had to go to the shops to buy goods not available through the suppliers of Hari's own shop, and sometimes she was obliged to visit the doctor with Dinesh, for vaccinations or to deal with childish illnesses. Sita had obtained the pill. Hari would be furious if he knew. (He had once said, "I hope you're not doing anything to stop yourself getting pregnant because I shan't like that.") But her supplies were carefully hidden in the hem of a little-used sari in her wardrobe. She felt irrationally guilty about this, but she kept on with it. She was not going to give Hari any more hostages. Two were enough.

One was their son Dinesh himself. It was true that although Hari had several times threatened, when displeased with her, to ill-use or disinherit Dinesh, he always did so out of the boy's hearing and it was quite possible that he thought enough of his son to render the threats empty, but Sita could not be sure of that. She had returned to Hari mainly to save Dinesh's inheritance and hoped she would succeed in this but doubt and fear were always there.

The other hostage was her Aunt Savitri. He sometimes threatened to write to his stepfather. "He will take it out on your aunt. All the family elders there have died; she will have no one to turn to now."

Another child would be just one more victim for Hari to bully, especially if it should be that despised thing, a daughter. Therefore, there must be no other child.

On the night after the news of the riots had aroused him, she was glad all over again that she had the pill's protection. A child born of such a night would surely have been somehow warped at conception. She had never known Hari so crude, and so per-verse. He clutched and bit with the intention of doing damage and his mouth and loins felt red-hot. Spent at midnight, his frenzy awoke in full again before dawn, and in between, although he slept, he woke when once she tried to leave the bed, to get away from his contaminating presence and to wash herself and rinse her mouth. "Want to wash me off, do you? Think Ill stand for an insult like that?"

Now, at breakfast in the light of morning, announcing that Dinesh was to stay indoors, he was still dangerous and Sita was keenly aware of it, although Dinesh at first was not.

"But I *did* want to go to the school today," Dinesh protested. "There's a football practice. Nothing's going to happen to me there. I'm the only Indian in the team."

"You'll stay home," said Hari. "Don't argue."

"Oh, Dad . . . !"

"I said, don't argue!"

"Dinesh. Do as your father says," said Sita in a warning tone. Her son looked at her, with eyes which she knew were more understanding than the eyes of a twelve-year old ought to be, and was silent. It occurred to her, for the first time, that perhaps when she was out of earshot, Hari might be controlling Dinesh by making threats against *her*; that she too was a hostage.

At any rate, Dinesh said no more then. When, much later in the day, peering disconsolately from a window, he announced that Auntie Krishna and Grandmother were approaching, he spoke it in an aggrieved tone of voice but he only added, "*They're* not afraid to go out," in a whisper to his mother while Hari was answering the door.

The visitors did not stay long. "That's settled them," said Hari with satisfaction after Leela and Krishna had taken their leave. "Solidarity march indeed! Who wants to show solidarity with trash like these murderous Sikhs? What is your family doing, mixed up with that sort of person?"

"I did not know that you disapproved so much of my Sikh relatives," said Sita. She would rather not have said anything at all but he had used the tone which she knew demanded an answer, and staying silent would cause as much trouble as answering.

Sure enough, he pounced. "You did not know? Well, how would I expect you to know? You do not know half the things about me that you should know because you do not take the

319

interest in me that you should take."

Oh, thought Sita, if *only* those people who broke into the shop had had a gun and shot him dead. He was in a terrible mood today. He might do anything. She tried to read his face but couldn't. He had needed stronger glasses lately and he had gone in for tinted lenses. They made his face both sinister and inscrutable.

"Well, what have you to say?" Hari demanded.

Since he would quarrel with anything she said, she might as well say what she thought. "All those Sikh people in the family were very kind to you when you first came to England."

Hari ignored this. "You saw your cousin Satnam on TV yesterday; boasting of this murder they have committed. I tell you, Sita, it is no wonder all this uproar has broken out in Delhi, it is no wonder at all. They have asked for it."

"Oh, come on, Dad." Dinesh, who had sat down to study a sports magazine featuring football teams and boxing heroes, put it aside. "In Delhi completely innocent people are being murdered, just because they happen to be Sikhs. They haven't asked for it."

One blessing about Dinesh, Sita thought gratefully, was that although he resembled his father a little in feature, he had openness and warmth of heart. He had not inherited Hari's unloving temperament, or his horrible ability to dissemble. Another reason for having no more children was that the next one might not be so fortunate. She didn't want to be responsible for presenting the world with another Hari.

"I am not talking to you," Hari said. "You are just a child and you don't know what is what. I do not like those people and I hope they are all wiped out, every one!"

"You can't say that!" Sheer horror struck the protest out of Sita. She stared at him, sickened, recognising in his face the same unhealthy excitement which had filled it during the TV bulletins. "You can't, you can't! You were attacked once, you remember what it was like! You can't wish that . . . and so much worse than that . . . on thousands of people you have never met, who have done you no harm . . . "

"Oh, yes, I can and I do! You are a silly woman with a silly soft heart."

It was never any use trying to appeal to Hari but she tried anyway. "Hari, why are you so hard? Why are you so aggressive with me?"

"Aggressive with you? Who is shouting at me and arguing with me, I should like to know?"

"But I cannot bear it, that you say such terrible things. What harm has any Sikh ever done to you?"

"What harm? When my stepfather that Dinesh is named for was over here, wasn't it your Aunt Shanti's husband and his brother that said things against him so that your father threw him out of the house? And aren't they Sikhs? And that Mrs Satinder Singh is a Sikh, isn't she? Didn't she harbour you when you ran off from your own husband? Mm? Mm?"

Suddenly, he came towards her and thrust his face into hers. Sita backed away. He followed. "You say, what harm has a Sikh ever done to me, when once they tempted my own wife away from me! What harm? What harm? You can ask what harm?"

"I ran away from you!" Sita cried out. "Why I should not run away from you, the way you have treated me?"

"Treated you? You do not know how badly I could treat you if I wanted to. I have been forbearing; you have no idea!"

"Father . . . !" Dinesh tried to push his way in between them but Hari thrust him aside, hard enough to send him staggering against the wall.

"But why should you have to be forbearing? What is so terrible about me?" Sita cried.

"Dinesh," said Hari, "get out. Go up to your room."

"Why?"

"Do as you're told!" shouted Hari and Sita, looking at his face, added, "Yes, Dinesh, go," in the desperate hope that she could somehow, by compliance, stave off or at least reduce whatever ugly thing Hari was preparing for her.

Dinesh went. Sita allowed herself to be pulled over to the sofa. Oh, no, she thought, not again, not so soon, not more of what happened in the night. He was stronger than she was and resistance only made things worse in the end. Besides, he had long ago overcome most of her will to resist. His very presence paralysed her.

He shoved her on to the sofa, but then paused, looking at her. His expression frightened her. He smiled, which frightened her still more.

"I think I will tell you," he said. "I have never been sure whether to tell you or not. I have saved it up, thinking, perhaps one day, or perhaps not. Perhaps it is better if she does not know, if she stays for ever, trying to get round me, being

321

bewildered; pleading with me sometimes. I enjoy that. It is fun. But perhaps now I shall tell you, because that will be fun, too, a new kind of fun and it is good to have a change sometimes."

"Tell me what? What are you talking about?"

Hari's smile widened. His eyes were very bright. The shocking exaltation engendered in him by the reports of violence was gathering power again.

"Why, tell you why I came to England," he said. "Tell you why I married you. My stepfather sent me, Sita darling. Because when *he* came to England and stayed with his brother-in-law, that bastard Mohan Lal, he was thrown out. Mohan Lal and his Sikh friends – that man who married Shanti, and his brother – they accused him of all manner of things, and they even threatened him with the police. So he told me, you go over there, Hari, and get my own back for me. Marry one of the daughters and give her hell. Then I shall be happy because I shall have got even. That's what he said. I told Dinesh just now, things can reach out from long distances. And so they can. Old wrongs can. Your father wronged my stepfather, and my stepfather has reached out across time and space and got hold of you, my dear, and I am the arm he has reached with."

Sita said nothing.

"Did you hear me?" said Hari.

"Yes. Yes, I heard you."

"Do you understand me?"

"Yes."

She both understood and believed him. Everything made sense now: his courtship of her in the face of custom, the way he had changed towards her the moment they were out of Mohan Lal's house, the monstrous nature of that change.

"So," Hari said. "You understand. And what have you to say?"

"What can I say?" She spoke quite calmly, to her own surprise. But Hari's revelation had cast a quite new light on Hari. Before, he had been Her Husband, the figure of authority she had been taught from childhood she must one day respect, the source of a power to which a woman was by nature subject, from which she had no right to flee. But now he had shown himself to be something else.

He was an enemy both to her and to her family. And with that, the accustomed feeling that when Hari was in the room, he filled it up, grew less. She could look at him now as if from a distance. "I loved you once," she said. "I wanted to make you

322

happy. But you have never let me."

"Oh, but I have been very happy, I assure you," he said.

And that, she thought bitterly, was most probably true. And he would go on being happy for she could never get away. Her family had encouraged her to go back to him, because they did not know the truth, and now that she knew the truth, she could not tell them. Her father's heart would break and she herself would be shamed beyond bearing. The very offences which might range her family on her side, were by their very nature the offences she must hide from them most carefully.

He was smiling at her, that disturbing light still in his eyes. He moved towards the door, giving her a moment of relief, and then she saw that he only meant to turn the key in the lock.

He turned back to her. "We don't want Dinesh bursting in while we're making love, do we?"

It was bad; worse even than the night before. But she was free now of the guilt which had haunted her in the past, because she wished him dead and because she feared that in some way she had merited mistreatment.

She was free at last to hate him. He had been shaped from childhood for an evil purpose by a man whose petty dishonesty had at last tipped over the brink into wickedness, and he had had, beyond question, flaws in his nature which made him apt for the shaping.

She shut from her mind the things he was doing to her, and gave her imagination up to fantasies of murdering him. This new, shameless hatred would be henceforth her secret source of strength.

Chapter Twenty-Six

Demonstration

1984

It was good weather for a march, Chandra Lal thought, without enthusiasm. The early November sky was a cool blue, and the brisk breeze spun yellowed leaves down from the little trees in the side roads of Southall.

He had had a faint hope that the notoriously capricious English climate would oblige with a good soaking downpour, preferably linked to an autumn gale, and force the march to be called off, but it wasn't going to happen. No such luck.

"No, I do not want you to go into the police. I have a nice business here for you to take over one day and it is our custom that sons follow in their fathers' callings," Mohan Lal had said to him, when Chandra Lal first announced his intentions. "I cannot understand why you do not accept this."

"Father, if sons always followed their fathers, then the world would never advance. No new professions would ever get started. Somebody had to be the first full-time motor mechanic or computer programmer and he can't have been following his father."

It had been Kartar who had almost deflected him, by saying, "You know, Chandra Lal, you won't have too easy a time in the police force. I know we need to be represented there but it's going to be damned hard on the individuals. The police have some very entrenched attitudes, you'll find. There'll be bullying."

What had pushed him on, in the end, had been the memory of Satnam lying on that pavement with the blood oozing from his stab wounds. Law and order mattered. If he met with prejudice in the police force, then he must deal with it as best he could. Those prejudices were in fact the whole point. Satnam's assailants had had them too. Anything he could do to reduce them was worth doing.

So he had joined the force and encountered the prejudice and dealt with it. He had managed it mainly with the help of two natural attributes. One was imperturbability and the other was physical fitness.

Armed with these, he had succeeded in coping alike with edged remarks and with the regrettable tendency which his first colleague on the beat had shown to stand back and see how he coped if obliged to deal virtually alone with some loitering and cheeky youth or drunken motorist.

He had had to deal with only one serious incident, which took place in a washroom during his training. A fellow-trainee, who had already taken offence because Chandra Lal performed role-playing exercises better than he did, had been further irritated on that morning's assault course to notice that Chandra Lal was also defter than he was at swinging across a stream on a rope. "I don't want to use the same soap as a monkey," he said with distaste, reaching for a bar of soap from another basin.

It had raised a laugh and it was quite impossible simply to pretend that he hadn't heard. Chandra Lal considered the provocation for a private count of three, decided to lose his temper, devoted a further count of two to making up his mind whether to do so in the manner of a volcano or an iceberg, opted for the iceberg, and said frigidly, "If I am a monkey, then you are a sheep. You make offensive remarks to get a laugh, because silly racist remarks are fashionable among your mates and you want to go with the crowd. You must go where the flock goes. Baa! Baa!" His tone remained completely level throughout and he took his tormenter wholly by surprise when with a panache which would have gladdened the heart of the unarmed combat instructor, he seized the offender's wrist and with a sharp twist sent his victim slithering to a sitting position under the wash-basin. In the startled pause which followed, he brushed his palms together, surveyed the semicircle of watching eyes, smiled at them, said, "And you," went calmly to the nearest basin, soaped his hands and rubbed them over his face.

It was a gamble, because with his eyes closed against the soap, he was vulnerable. His seeming indifference to this would either provoke an attack or else put him in command. Self-confidence could carry the day if one could carry it off.

He carried it off.

When he was posted back to Southall, he was a constable with great self-confidence, which of itself was a bulwark against prejudice. As time went on, and it was found that when called out to deal with members of the public who were liable under stress to relapse into Asian languages, Chandra Lal could frequently understand them, he began to be valued. When it was also realised that he was impervious to the occasional attempts by members of the Indian community, when stopped, to trade on the fact that Chandra Lal was Indian too, he began definitely to make himself a niche.

He only hoped that nothing would happen today to damage that niche. He had already, over coffee the previous day, had a colleague saying frankly, "It may be difficult for you, policing this march. One thing we've all learned this year is that all Indians belong to one community or another – Hindu, Sikh or Moslem. You're Hindu. So how do you stop being partisan? This is supposed to be a solidarity march, but if trouble breaks out and Hindus cause it, how will you feel?"

The man asking the question was a constable called Jeremy Hogan. He had a precise, almost schoolmasterish manner, and because of this no one had ever shortened his name. In a world full of Rods and Alfs and Bernies and Jims, a world in which Chandra Lal himself was usually called just Lal, he remained indestructibly Jeremy.

Chandra Lal stirred his coffee consideringly. Once or twice of late, usually at three in the morning, he had asked himself the same question. But he could not afford to be in doubt of the answer. "My family is mixed, as it happens," he said calmly. "It contains both Hindu and Sikh. I am not very partisan. And I am not, in any case, concerned with the rights and wrongs of the two sides. I am a policeman. Whatever the disputes may be among my own people, if I see them breaking the law in the course of their disputing, I will take the appropriate action for a policeman. It is that simple."

Jeremy's expression warmed a little and he nodded approvingly.

But the other man at the same table, PC Rod Jones, said, "You're a cold fish, aren't you, Lal?"

"I have to be," said Chandra Lal.

"This what I call good-tempered weather," said PC Jeremy Hogan, now surveying the growing assembly in front of Southall town hall with a professional eye. The traffic diversion was already in force and someone with a loudspeaker was telling onlookers to move back. The marchers were getting into line. "There are two kinds of weather I hate, for this kind of thing," said Jeremy. "Hot and sweltering, or cold and raw. They both turn people vicious. But this is all right."

"It would be better still if there were no march at all," said Chandra Lal with a sigh.

"Never mind. With luck we'll all just go for a nice quiet walk, or ride, in the case of the mounted division," said Rod. "No riot gear in sight, no shields, no weapons. Just a friendly stroll in the sun. What could be nicer?"

The riot gear was available, Chandra Lal knew. It was out of sight inside strategically placed police vans. Behind the scenes, there had been Scotland Yard briefings for senior officers, and massive reinforcements had been brought in from other districts. He just hoped that none of the disasters for which these preparations had been made would materialise.

The march moved off, with its cordon of police keeping pace on either side. Not far ahead, Chandra Lal could see members of his own family. Ranbir, he knew, had refused to come, but Perry and Shanti were there, together with Sunder and Lynn behind a row of men, alternately Sikh and Hindu, who were leading the way, arms linked, striding towards the wheeled TV cameras which were backing along the street in front of them. His father Mohan Lal was in that line, with Kartar on one side of him and Balbir on the other and they were chanting although he was too far back to catch the words. Balbir was carrying a banner with the words *Peace and Amity* painted on it.

Chandra Lal himself was keeping pace beside a group of women, several rows of them, who held hands as they walked along. Every now and then they swung their joined hands high and shouted slogans about sisterhood and solidarity, sometimes in English and sometimes in Punjabi. He glimpsed Rose, marching between Leela and Krishna. The women too had a standard-bearer, whom he recognised as Swarup Sharma. *All women are sisters,* declared her banner, red on white, rippling out in the brisk wind. Chandra Lal grinned faintly. Stout, busy Swarup was probably responsible for the good turnout of Hindu women. She knew an immense number of people. She also knew most of their private business and never minded gossiping about it; Swarup Sharma enjoyed reporting erring children to their

327

parents and erring spouses to each other. Few people liked her but most were rather afraid of her. It gave her considerable powers of leverage.

There was a scatter of onlookers along the Broadway as the march proceeded, but this was also a shopping centre and a good many people were simply trying to go about their everyday business, slightly hampered by the traffic diversion. The Moslem section of the local population was not involved and only mildly interested, and although most of the indigenous English knew about the assassination of Mrs Gandhi and the rioting in Delhi, few of them understood the issues and the English faces watching the parade mostly looked bewildered.

The march was well and truly swinging by now. The men's chant was growing louder. The numbers had swelled; people had come from their homes and shops to join it, some carrying baskets of shopping. They slipped through the police lines to join hands with the other marchers; others simply walked along outside the police cordon, joining in the chants, forming lines of their own, spilling on to the pavement.

As the march entered the Lanesden district, there was one bad moment. A small crowd of young Sikhs were waiting round a corner. They shouted insults at the marchers and they too had a banner. Chandra Lal looked at it and had to crush down a surge of rage.

No, partisanship was not easy to abandon. The ugly caricature on that banner, shown clutching a firebrand, referred to Hindus, and that meant Chandra Lal as much as anyone else. He was relieved that policemen ahead of him were the ones who stepped aside and chivvied the counter-demonstrators away.

By the time they had negotiated most of their route and were in South Road, with the green railings of the town hall steps again visible straight ahead, the crowd was dense and somewhat noisy. Some West Indians had joined in, apparently for fun, and had started an impromptu calypso about brotherhood. A new party of Sikh and Hindu youths had tacked on to the back of the procession and were waving a banner proclaiming, in gold on red, the words *We're Just Good Friends*. The march was nearly over.

He was thankful. It had gone very well but with so many tensions under the surface, one could never be sure that the good nature would hold. But in a few minutes they would be at the town hall. The community leaders would give brief speeches

– they had promised to keep them brief, and also calm – and then the gathering would disperse, encouraged to do so by careful shepherding on the part of the police. There had only been that one unpleasant incident. They had got away lightly. The head of the procession was almost at the town hall already.

The interruption burst out of a cul-de-sac on the left, and its constituents did not have brown faces. It consisted of a crowd of English youths in motor cycle helmets, jeans and black bomber jackets festooned with chains and adorned with swastika arm-bands.

It had been a carefully laid ambush. The cul-de-sac had a sharp right-angle in it; they must have been waiting beyond it, out of sight.

They were armed. Half a brick knocked off Chandra Lal's helmet, and a shower of stones went over his head into the marchers on his right. A wave of noise went up, made of shouts and screams and a wild scrambling as youths and marchers collided and scuffled. Banners swayed and lurched; out of the corner of his eye Chandra Lal saw one being used as a weapon. Two women coming out of a shop gasped in terror and fled back inside. There was a crash of broken glass and the proprietor of another shop rushed out shouting. Leaving his helmet to its fate, Chandra Lal went for the attackers. Rod and Jeremy were beside him. Half a dozen other constables were with them and over the heads of the crowd he could see mounted police approaching. "Drive them back up the cul-de-sac!" Jeremy snapped. "We'll corner them there!"

The youths, however, did not intend to be cornered. They had chosen their moment with skill. They hurled their missiles, ran and scuffled and dodged straight across the road through the midst of the marchers. On the far side, they took to a side turning. Chandra Lal, pelting in pursuit, caught hold of a slippery jacket sleeve. It ran through his fingers as though it had been oiled. He saw his intended captive grin and two fingers were outrageously raised in his face. Then he saw the parked motor bikes. There were six flying leaps, six coughing roars as the engines started and the riders gunned them, and then they were gone in a cloud of exhaust fumes.

"Didn't get any of the numbers! Wrong angle," snarled Rod, catching up. "Did you get any numbers?"

"No. What's *that*?" Chandra Lal swung round, alerted by an uproar from the direction of the march.

Jeremy, behind him, was speaking rapidly into a walkie-talkie, reporting the actions and the direction taken by six fleeing motor cyclists with swastika armbands. He thrust it back into his jacket, cocked his head and said, "More trouble!" and in a moment, they were pounding back the way they had come.

They had all recognised, subconsciously, the way the angry shouts and alarmed shrieks of the disturbed marchers had faded as the youths fled and now they recognised, with equal certainty, the tumult of renewed violence.

But not, this time, by youths with swastika badges. The break they had made in the police cordon had been deftly exploited by another band of assailants, who must also have been waiting close by, possibly lurking inside a shop. These were Sikhs, mostly young, an infuriated knot of them, wrestling with the marchers, shouting slogans about Khalistan, flourishing yet another banner, on which the Hindus were defamed collectively and the establishment of the Sikh state was demanded forthwith; and attempting apparently to snatch away the peace banners.

Chandra Lal hurled himself forward, shoulder to shoulder with his colleagues, caught hold of the nearest attacker, dragged him back and threw him to a policeman behind, rather in the manner of someone passing a fire-bucket along a human chain.

He plunged further and grabbed the arm of the man with the Khalistan standard. He was savagely kicked. "Pig!" yelled the owner of the arm. "Brothers, get this pig!" Furious, bearded faces bore down on Chandra Lal. They then abruptly disappeared as a police horse thrust its way in between. Chandra Lal wrested the banner away and jerked the bearer's arm up behind his back. The latter let out a stream of invective.

"I might have known it," said Chandra Lal, hauling him away. "What a damned young hotheaded fool you are, Satnam."

"Let go of me! Let *go* . . . look here," said Satnam furiously, as Chandra Lal marched him briskly towards a police van which had appeared from somewhere and pulled up with its rear doors invitingly open, "you can't arrest me!"

"How wrong can you be?" said Chandra Lal.

"We were making a protest! Our people have been murdered!"

Satnam resisted fiercely as his cousin ran him up to the van. "Those marchers are traitors . . . you can't arrest me, where's your sense of family . . . ?"

"Where's yours?" said Chandra Lal shortly and tumbled his

cousin unceremoniously into the van. Jeremy, coming up beside him, lent a helping hand.

Satnam glared out at them. His face was taut with rage and the hard blaze in his young eyes was a shock; the feeling there seemed much too strong for his safety or anyone else's.

"I won't forget this! You haven't heard the last of me! Hindu!"

"Policeman," corrected Chandra Lal coldly.

Long ago, on a pavement beside a bus stop, they had been cousin-brothers, fellow-Indians, united against a hostile European world. Chandra Lal saw now that in Satnam's eyes was not only fury but astonishment that his cousin had this time not stood between him and disaster, but picked him up and flung him bodily into it.

There was still an uproar behind him. A siren was wailing and one of his superior officers was shouting to his men; there was more work to be done. He turned and sped back to the scene. The riot gear was out. The scrimmage was shortlived, but seemed to him long. It seemed a hundred years before it was all over and he was back in the police station, seeing to the formalities. Which among other things included charging Satnam Singh Virk with incitement to violence, assault and resisting arrest.

It was not until afterwards that it occurred to him that when he recognised his captive as Satnam, he had felt no desire to let him go or to shelter him from arrest, no distress at the thought of tumbling him into that van, no emotion at all except exasperation with Satnam for getting into such a plight; and that even now he felt no regret and no anxiety about what family and friends might say when they heard what he had done.

All he felt was relief, because when it came to the point, he had withstood the test. When it came to the point, he had seen Satnam as neither a cousin nor an enemy but simply as a lawbreaker.

He knew now that from the beginning of his career in the police he had harboured a secret fear that his tangled communal and familial loyalties might one day come between him and his duty. He had denied it to his colleagues, but the doubt had been there.

Now he knew that it was groundless, and with that certainty came a sense of strength and freedom. As though, until this moment, he had been living in a half-light and now, at last, the light was full and he could see clearly.

Chapter Twenty-Seven

Polarisation
1984

Winter set in, with the frosts and mists and the dripping wet days which were so much part of England, so different from Delhi, where Rose had discovered blazing sunshine and red dust so pervasive that she had to wash her hair every day.

Well, she would not marry in India now. Her life was set in England after all. But it had become a double life.

At Christmas, the English shops were full of Yuletide displays and at the school where she taught she had to help organise a nativity play and marshal her class to and from a church to give a carol concert.

Rose's fellow-teachers were not indifferent to the world outside. They had been concerned about the riots, asking her to explain the issues to them, and been kind and shocked about the deaths in her family. The school had improved since Satnam had nearly been murdered by three of his fellow pupils. It had moved into more spacious premises and somehow, at the same time, acquired an air of greater dignity. The headmaster, mindful of his many Indian pupils, gave an impressive address one morning on the immorality of vengeance as a concept.

But as events in Delhi faded from the headlines and Christmas took over, Rose, sensitive to atmosphere, stopped talking about Indian politics in the staffroom. There were new talking points. Two teachers who had been engaged became disengaged and caused discomfort in the staffroom because they would not speak to each other, and the school caretaker caught some youths one evening smoking pot in the shrubbery between the drive and the netball courts, which were all features of the new premises, and made an official complaint that the grounds were too easy to get into and that he needed an assistant.

Shortly after that, a squabble arose over the nativity play

because according to Mrs Hoxley who was producing it, Mr Sanderton, who taught singing and was in charge of the angel choir, seemed to think that the choir should dominate the entire play. She did not, she said, mind them singing behind the scenes while Mary and Joseph were on their way to Bethlehem, but if they were encouraged to sing so loudly that the audience couldn't hear what Mary and Joseph were saying to each other, there wasn't much point in having any dialogue, was there? The argument escalated, Mrs Hoxley resigned as producer, and Rose found herself taking the task on instead, considerably to her embarrassment because she was shy of Mr Sanderton who, notwithstanding the fact that he was thirty-eight and divorced, had once tried to persuade her to go out with him.

Rose, after spending a day devoted to arithmetic and geography and coaxing Mr Sanderton to tone his angel choir down (by the unobtrusive backhanded method of urging Joseph and Mary to "come more to the front of the stage, dears, and try to speak a little louder"), would change from English to Indian clothes, collect her coat and scarf from their peg and go home to a different world, where no one wanted to hear about angel choirs or angry caretakers, but where the issues of revenge or peace, Khalistan or a united India were still obsessively alive, and the conversation centred on the latest news from Delhi and the fact that Satnam, in the cause of fundamentalism, had gone vegetarian. At times, it made her dizzy.

Some of the argumentativeness within her community was not directly concerned with the political issues but seemed to be a weird spin-off from it.

"I simply do not know what is the matter with Sunder," said Lynn crossly, when Rose called on her one Sunday afternoon, largely in the hope that Lynn's home would be some kind of haven from matters political. The small house that Lynn and Sunder were buying on the outskirts of Southall was busy and colourful, with Sunder's engineering and Lynn's social services spilling cheerfully into every room: a table littered with drawings, rulers and set squares in a corner of the dining room, briefcases tossed casually down on the settee in the sitting room, shelves of reference books and case histories everywhere.

This time, however, Lynn was in the kitchen, beating eggs as though she wished to murder them. "I just don't know what's wrong with him. It's been since this business in Delhi. It's hard to explain, Rose, and maybe if I try to explain, I'll offend you but if

I don't talk to someone I'll burst. I know he's Indian but he's never been *that* Indian ... I mean, he's got a lot of attitudes which are just the same as the English ones, or were, but now ... "

"What's he done? You can tell me, I won't be upset," said Rose.

"Done! He wants me to give up going to my club, you know, the London History Group. I only go once a month but all of a sudden he's started saying that he doesn't like me going out in the evenings without him; I'm neglecting my home! You'd think to listen to him that my home were a sort of prison instead of the place where I happen to live!"

"What did you say?"

"That I'm not going to give up my club, and I'm not, and that's that. That was yesterday. Today, we're not speaking."

"Oh, Lynn!"

"We shall get over it," said Lynn grimly. "But I'm not giving in. My God! I said to him, what has he got against my club and he said I might meet other men there! Well, of course I do! But I've belonged to the club for years and never slept with any of the men in it yet and I don't propose to start now! I was *furious* with him, *furious*!"

"Oh, dear," said Rose helplessly.

She returned home, saddened and jaded, and Krishna arrived almost at once, exuding, if anything, even more indignation than Lynn.

"I don't know what the matter is with my father! All these years I have got on with my job and on occasion he has said he does not like it, that I am sometimes away overnight, and I am staying in hotels and he doesn't know who I mix with but it has been just talk. He would never push me into marriage because of what happened with Sita. But now! I'm getting too English! I'm mixing with too many people outside the community, I'm forgetting who I am and where I come from, it's time I gave up all this roaming around and settled down to be a good Indian wife. Because of Sita, he has waited for me to choose the moment and he has hoped that in our community I will meet someone whom I like, but now he's tired of waiting and how will I ever find anyone suitable if I go on like this; it will hurt my reputation. I don't *want* to get married, but he won't *listen* and my mother won't help, all she says is, 'Your father is right, dear.'

She always accepts everything he does, the way she used to accept it when he had affairs with his female customers . . . he's stopped that now and gone all virtuous; I suppose that's one good thing! But he does not like my English dresses and hairstyle! He says I should dress Indian fashion and hide my legs and he does not like to see my hair permed and waving round my shoulders like some movie star! I have looked like this for years and years and I am still a virgin and he has always trusted me but now . . . !"

Krishna ran out of breath and stopped, tossing back the black wavy hair to which Mohan Lal was objecting. She leant back in her chair and defiantly crossed the knees which her fashionable orange dress did not conceal.

Over the last few years, Krishna and Rose had formed a solid friendship, based, like Rose's friendship with Lynn, on the fact that they were so different. To Rose, Krishna and her adventurous job were glamorous and exhilarating, and so were Lynn's English attitudes and looks, while Krishna and Lynn both found Rose restful.

"They haven't suggested anyone for you yet, have they?" Rose asked, worried by Krishna's frantic expression.

"As a matter of fact," said Krishna furiously, "yes! They come from Leeds. The whole damn family came to look me over as though I were a prospective purchase! My father said afterwards that they told him that I seemed very modern, but that he told them I would soon adapt to them once I was away from the influence of my job – as though it were some form of drug addiction! He is giving me a good dowry, and believe me, that's what they're interested in!"

"What's the boy like?"

Krishna laughed shortly. "Harmless and hopeless. He helps his father and brothers run a hardware shop. He counts for nothing in that house. He'll be someone I'm supposed to have sex with, that's all. His mother rules the house and she's a bully."

"Can't your brother help? What does he think about all this?"

"Chandra Lal? We hardly see him since he moved out to live in a flat. I've seen him once, but all he said was that it was up to me to decide. He's so remote these days; he's hardly human any more."

"You've been lucky in some ways," Rose said. "I was always surprised that your parents let you stay in that job. My parents would not like me to do such a job. In fact, I don't think I'd like it myself. I admire your enterprise. You just seem to go here and there, when and how you please, in that little Toyota of yours and you are not questioned. My parents worry if I am ten minutes late home."

"My father's started asking questions now," said Krishna angrily. "Sometimes he tries to pretend it's just kindness talking. Some girl was followed in the street near our house the other day – it was in the paper – and he was on to that at once! We get anxious about you, something could have happened to you, how would we know, what a terrible thing it would be if some man attacked you, on and on but all the time, behind it, he just wants to put me in protective custody, and then marry me off to this awful family. I've said *no*, but I think he's just going to go ahead with the arrangements . . . I'm terrified I'll just be dragged along . . . it is wearing me out, having to *resist* all the time. I can't stand it! Oh, what is happening to everyone?" Krishna's strong, beautiful face, with its vigorous cheekbones and slanting eyebrows, was alive and angry. "There was a time when we were living in England and trying to get along with people here. Now, you wouldn't think England existed any more. Do you know, the Sharmas are not even taking English papers any more? Everyone is too busy remembering they are Hindu or Sikh to notice any longer that they're Indians living in England!"

"And that is quite right." Ranbir and Nita came into the room. Krishna had been speaking English, but Ranbir's interruption was in Punjabi. "We were forgetting who we were and although what has happened is a terrible thing, at least it has done that; it has reminded us. It has reminded other people too; it has shown everyone that we are not just English people with brown faces, we are a different people, and not all the same people, either." Her sharp dark eyes raked Krishna from head to foot. Rose wondered whether the disapproval in them was for Krishna as a Hindu or Krishna as a Westernised young lady with waved hair and a revealing orange dress.

"Bheji," said Nita soothingly, "let us all be calm. You are up early from your rest. You were so tired this morning."

"I am getting on in years; you will be tired when you are my age. I will sit in here for a while and then I will change my clothes ready to go to Perry's as usual on Sundays. They are so relieved that Satnam is home. Krishna, I hear your father has not been to see them since Satnam was freed. Perhaps he is wise. Satnam can be very outspoken."

336

"He hasn't forgiven my brother for arresting him," said Krishna. "I know that. But I am proud of Chandra Lal. He did the right thing."

"You do not know enough about it," said Ranbir. "Satnam says too much at times and he is too much a hothead, but he is a good Sikh boy; his heart is in the right place and when he is older, he will know better what are the right things to say and do. But you will never know, how can you? You know nothing except England. You are so Westernised, you are west of sunset. I cannot get down the stairs very quickly now and when I was making my way down them, I heard you saying your father thinks it is time you left that job and got married. There I agree with him; he is quite right. It is time Rose here was married, too."

Nita's eyes sought her daughter and Rose, recognising an appeal to help stop this argument, said, "We have some snacks in the kitchen. Krishna, come and help me bring them."

"Sorry," said Krishna when they were in the kitchen.

"It's no good talking to Bheji, she'll never change and I don't think she's very well, just now. Where did you buy that dress, Krishna? I want some new dresses, for work."

"I got this at Selfridges. Your parents don't mind you wearing European clothes for work, then?"

"They never actually see them," said Rose. "I travel to and fro in salwar kameeze tunic and trousers and change in and out of English dress at the school. I keep English clothes there. I've never discussed it with my parents; they can be so funny about that sort of thing. Uncle Perry wouldn't be, he never minded what Rupa wore, even before she was married. But my family . . . " Rose sighed. "They want to get on in England without compromising with the English. That's how it was with them even before all the trouble broke out. It can be most exhausting to live with. I am always having to remember when to stop going along with what the others do, because it isn't right for me to do this or that, my family wouldn't like it. Even if, sometimes, I feel I could talk my parents round, Bheji would soon talk them back again. They agree with her at heart, about most things. She just . . . shores them up."

"You ought to get married, that's true enough. To someone with modern ideas," said Krishna.

"You could be right, at that." Rose shook her head sadly. "Even Uncle Perry," she said, "isn't as easygoing as he was."

She had always liked visiting Uncle Perry but since Satnam came home, having been given a few stern words from the Bench and been bound over, the atmosphere of the Harrison Street house had changed.

Perry said he had got off lightly. But although Perry did not approve in the least of his son's behaviour, Satnam's presence made a difference. There was a tautness in the air. Violent political argument was liable to break out at any moment, and Perry had startled everyone by suddenly growing a beard and resuming his turban. He said he had resumed Sikh dress out of respect for Uncle Sunderjit and Auntie Billie and no doubt, thought Rose, he meant what he said. Yet she did not miss the careful way he treated Satnam, as though his son were a force he was simply weary of resisting.

Sunday tea at Perry's was a habit the Sikh members of the family had fallen into as a preliminary to going to the Gurudwara. Mourning had not interrupted the custom, since all the family were grieving together. Rose, greeting her relatives, saw that although nearly everyone was present, Satnam didn't appear to be there, and was relieved. Then she noticed that as yet, Sunder and Lynn hadn't appeared. She wondered if they would come or not. She had not thought to ask Lynn earlier. She was glad when the doorbell rang, and the two of them came into the room smiling pleasantly, though she was sorry to see them take seats a considerable distance apart instead of next to each other as they usually did. Lynn handed over a cake she had brought, which probably contained the eggs she had been so vigorously assaulting earlier in the day. She was wearing a sari, but the pleats didn't seem to be quite right, as though she had been fumble-fingered with them or else not taken much trouble, and Rose, observing her closely, saw that her green eyes were still too fiercely bright. Ranbir also noticed, and remarked to Nita, in a sharp aside, "I see that Lynn is still getting into passions. She should put some energy into having children." The memory of the disastrous video show had evidently revived. Ranbir spoke audibly and in English and judging from Lynn's suddenly tightened mouth, she had overheard.

Then, evidently drawn by the sound of rattling crockery, Satnam appeared from upstairs, and instantly, as though her nervous system possessed a set of antennae which had picked up secret signals from both Satnam and Lynn, Rose knew that this

338

was going to be a much more calamitous gathering than the video show.

It was, however, Uncle Kartar, with the most amiable intentions, who started it, by saying jovially to Satnam, "And what have you been doing with yourself?"

Whereupon, Satnam took the floor.

"I've joined a pro-Khalistan group and we're starting a magazine. It will carry articles on the importance of establishing the state of Khalistan and news reports on anything relevant, attacks on Sikhs in India and the actions of the British and Indian governments where they bear on the matter. I am writing the first leader."

Mr Satinder Singh, who along with his wife and Rupa and Surjit, was a regular at these Sunday teas, said, "Now that is a pity. Things would be better left to settle down."

"Some things cannot be left to settle down," Satnam snapped. "Some things must be dealt with!"

"Oh, Satnam. Not now," said Perry, but not as though he expected to be heeded.

"But what," said Surjit, "is the purpose of such a paper? What do you hope it will achieve, Satnam?"

"It will inform people and win converts to the idea of Khalistan, people who are willing to fight for it!"

"Look, there's been enough fighting." This was Sunder.

"In any case," said Surjit, "is Khalistan really the best answer? In the modern world . . . "

Perry protested again but was overborne. The battle was joined.

Half an hour later it was still raging. The conflict had gone in hideous circles: violence versus peaceful campaigning, Khalistan versus united India, collective vengeance versus the pursuit of guilty individuals: round and round, thought Rose, whose head had begun to ache, and for what? Nothing would bring back the dead; must there be more dead, and then more, for ever? Who would take the responsibility for saying *stop*?

Certainly not Satnam. Nostrils flaring, eyes burning with evangelistic fervour, Satnam was out of reach of reason. "Why not violence? There may have to be violence before Khalistan is a reality. There will be sacrifices, martyrs!"

As often happened, the room had become divided between men and women, but Lynn, although not sitting next to Sunder, was among the men; in fact only two seats away from Satnam.

339

Lynn never observed the informal male-female divisions on these occasions, and indeed never seemed aware of them. She was in the heart of the battlefield. Lynn, like a landmine, now exploded. "Martyrs! Sacrifices! *More* killing! And some of the dead would be just ordinary harmless people, on both sides, who only want to be allowed to get on with their lives in peace! Have you asked the permission of your prospective sacrificial victims? You're living in a . . . a . . . cultural and religious hothouse, Satnam, and . . . "

"You do not understand. No English person can understand . . . "

"No, Lynn is perfectly right." Sunder, who had kept out of the argument hitherto, now joined in with spirit. "Nothing can undo the mess that is the past, but it might be kinder to the children who are now being born not to saddle them with a blood feud that is none of their making. We do have to consider the future."

"Yes, what *about* the future?" demanded Lynn. "The world's shrinking, Satnam. Things like data transmission and Concorde are making it smaller and smaller and countries and cultures are getting more and more interdependent. People need to come out of their tight little cultural groups, not withdraw into them and put glass walls round themselves . . . and I hate all this talk of fighting and vengeance, it's frightening and it's useless . . . Oh!" Lynn suddenly struck clenched fists against her forehead in a gesture of despair. "I've heard nothing but talk of killing and religion, religion and killing, for weeks and weeks and *weeks*. I wish to God that I were on the Spanish Costa Brava, dancing the night away to romantic Spanish guitars and stoned out of my mind on sangria!"

"Yes, Lynn, I dare say you do. That is the sort of thing one might expect from a European who has no religion and no morals. You are lax in the West; there are people living together who are not married and illegitimate children being born, and all these things come from this dancing and drinking that you admire. You are just a hedonistic pagan and . . . "

"Lynn is a social worker and does much good in society, and takes her work most seriously!" cried Nita indignantly.

"Yes, I do take my work seriously. And then I go on holiday and enjoy myself," said Lynn. "And why not? Don't be so bloody pompous, Satnam! Stop trying to pretend you're a repository of all the virtues! There's one thing to be said for us immoral, pagan hedonists! We don't start wars!"

340

"I agree with Lynn. I wish I were on the Costa Brava, too!" announced Sunder.

Satnam rounded on him but Kartar crashed a fist on to a table. "Stop this! Be quiet, all of you!"

Satnam looked at him. "I am giving an address at the Gurudwara this evening. I shall say it all again, there."

Shanti had been in and out of the room, dispensing refreshments, taking no part in the wrangle and apparently ignoring her son. But now she stopped, with a tray of empty cups and plates in her hands. She stepped in front of Satnam. "I have had enough of this," she said.

Silence fell. Perry cleared his throat but did not actually speak. It was Shanti, after the pause had gone on for what seemed like a very long time, who broke it.

"It is not just I who say this. You make such a fuss about Sikh and Hindu that anyone would think to hear you that they were different creatures like cats and dogs. Do you think your father and I do not talk to each other? We have done much talking to each other. And I have been saying to him it may come to this and now I think it has. And it is fitting that the moment should arrive while these others are here. Satnam, you have insulted my people before others, after all. Perry?"

Perry's face was drawn. He looked as though he were desperately tired, or in pain. "I want some peace under this roof," he said. "Yes, tell him."

Shanti turned once more to her son. "It is for me to say it, me, your own mother, because your father is so kind, so gentle, he cannot bring himself to say such harsh things. We want you to leave this house. You have friends, any amount of friends, some at the Gurudwara, who think as you do. One of them will give you a bed, until you can find a room or some such thing. Go and pack, Satnam. Take your things with you to the temple where you are going to make all these firebreathing speeches. From tonight, you live elsewhere, not in this house. We do not want a son here who calls his mother's people his enemy."

"I have never said *you* were my enemy, Mother."

"But you have shouted about the Hindus this and the Hindus that. I am a Hindu! I keep a shrine to Ganesh upstairs. When you shout and scream about the Hindus; well, I am one of them!"

"Mother, you're different." Satnam had quietened. He sounded hunted.

"But I am not different. I refuse to be different. And now," said Shanti relentlessly, "*go!*"

Satnam stood up. He had gone pale. His face seemed to have grown older, all in a few moments. "Very well," he said. "Yes. Perhaps I too will be happier, among people who think as I do, who understand what I am saying."

He walked calmly out of the room. Presently, they heard his footsteps overhead, moving back and forth, and the sound of drawers opening and closing. The movements sounded methodical, unhurried. Perry put his face in his hands.

"I am sorry," Shanti said to him. She was still standing there with the tray in her hands. "But it is best."

"I know," said Perry in a muffled voice. "And he is old enough to leave home; he is a man, not a child. I should have told him after the business on that march that he should make his own life in future. I was too soft." He looked up. "I find I wish after all that it hadn't happened in front of everyone like this. But you have put up with too much, Shanti; as you say, it may be . . . fitting."

"I would not go on that march because I knew it would be trouble," said Ranbir. "But that the trouble should reach right into our homes and divide mother from son . . . !"

Into the renewed silence which now fell, Rose heard herself say with truth, "I have a splitting headache. I am not going to the Gurudwara. I think I'd like to go home."

Rose's parents said they would go to the temple as usual. "Oh, we shall not worry about Satnam and his speech, if he still comes and makes one," her father said, catching her in the hall as she came downstairs with her wrap. "All this is natural, under the circumstances, you know. We are all raw and hurt. But it will pass, as the troubles at Partition passed. Satnam will make it up with his parents one day. As you grow older, you see these things."

"I still want to go home."

"All right. We'll see you later, then. Off you go. It's getting dark, so take care. I think we ought to buy you a car soon; then you won't have to walk anywhere on your own."

"But I always take care!" said Rose, somewhat indignantly.

"Well, be sure you do," said her father. "And have some food when you get home. We'll eat dinner at the Gurudwara."

She set out into the winter dusk. The street lamps were just coming on. The cold air and the solitude soothed her throbbing temples. She had turned the corner of the road when the car drew up beside her.

Someone, recently, had followed a girl in the street near here. Krishna had said so. She swung round, setting her back against a house fence. There were lights on in the house; if necessary, she would run up the path and ring the bell.

"What are you looking so scared for?" shouted Sunder's voice from inside the car. He was in the front passenger seat and Lynn was driving. "We're not a pair of wicked muggers! Want a lift? We'll run you home! We're not going to the temple either. We're willing to bet Satnam will turn up as he intended and still make that speech, and we don't want to listen to him. Maybe a few nights on other people's sofas will make him more sensible but probably they won't. Come on, jump in the back!"

"Poor Rose," Lynn said as they drove away again after dropping her at her home. "She hates quarrels and loud voices. She is so gentle and good. I'm sorry about that squabble with Satnam," she added after a pause. "But he makes me angry and frightened all at the same time. I have to react."

"And you were spoiling for a fight with someone, anyway," said Sunder. He laughed. "I daresay you enjoyed pitching into Satnam! But I agreed with you, anyway."

"Oh, Sunder. I don't want to quarrel any more. I'm tired of angry voices, too. Only you mustn't press upon me. I shall never be the same thing as an Indian wife. I'm an English wife who happens to have an Indian husband. You must let me be myself. I love you, you know. No one's going to supplant you."

"Yes, I do know that, Lynn. It's all right. Keep your club and your friends. I won't be jealous."

"Could we afford for me to give up work for a bit, Sunder? For a few years?"

"Give up work?"

"I was thinking; perhaps Bheji is right when she keeps urging us to have a baby. With all this talk of death and revenge all round me, I feel I'd like to do something creative, to show I'm on the side of life and the future! Only I don't want to work while the baby's small. I don't like the idea of baby-minders or asking relatives to look after it and besides, I'd want to look after it properly and be there when he or she says the first word, that kind of thing. Once the child is of school age, I could do part-time work, perhaps."

"You'd have to give up your club then."

"Oh, not necessarily," said Lynn demurely. "That's only once a month, not five days a week. I wouldn't mind asking Rupa, say, to babysit for me if you weren't there for any reason."

Sunder burst out laughing. Lynn began to laugh too, failed to notice that the traffic light at which she had halted had now turned green, was hooted at from behind, and let in the clutch in a hurry.

"Well, well! Yes, all right, let's see what we can do," said Sunder. "We could start tonight!"

In her bedroom above Mohan Lal's shop, Krishna sat on the edge of her bed, staring at a piece of paper. It was a Xerox copy which she had made from an announcement posted on her office noticeboard.

It would be one hell of a gamble, she thought. She wasn't sure if she dared.

But Chandra Lal, her brother, had once turned his back on a washroom full of potential foes and deliberately covered his face with soap, gambling on his own self-confidence to defend him. In Krishna too was the same ability, which was almost an urge, to hazard all, if only the prize were great enough.

And it was. Oh, yes, she thought. It was.

Chapter Twenty-Eight

Mutual Acquaintance
1985-87

"Well?" said Kartar, as Rose brought the little white Mini to a stop in a layby. "How do you like this car?"

"Very much indeed! And it is really mine?"

"I said at the end of last year that I wanted you to have a car, and I have paid for your driving lessons. You did well to pass first time like that. So here is your car. It is only two years old. I would have got you a brand new one, but . . . "

"But?" said Rose, looking out across the valley to their left. They had driven out of London and were on top of a hill overlooking a wide tract of Surrey. Below, visible through a faint grey haze, were fields patched brown and green or pale with stubble after the harvest, and clumps of trees in which the first bronzing of autumn could be seen. Soon it would be a year since that hideous night vigil while murder roared through the streets of Delhi. Here in this quiet late afternoon on a Surrey hillside, it was difficult to imagine.

"I wanted you to drive us out here as much for a quiet talk as to test-drive your car," Kartar said. "So much has happened in this past year, and most of it has been depressing. Would you not agree?"

"Yes, indeed. The Delhi troubles, and Satnam leaving home. I never thought Shanti auntie could be so hard. She has never let him come back. And then Bheji falling ill. We all thought she was just slowing down because of age, but . . . "

It was odd, she thought. At the school, in the staffroom, she had not hesitated to explain that she was worried because her grandmother had been hurried off to hospital on account of a suspected growth in her womb. But to her father, she could not bring herself to say, "When she told Mother she was bleeding."

"She seems to be recovering very well," Kartar said, "and very

345

probably, it was caught in time. But it was certainly upsetting. And then there was Krishna. Although I think myself that Mohan Lal handled that business badly. But God knows what has become of Krishna now. You haven't heard from her, have you? You and she were quite good friends. I am not saying you should betray her confidence, but if you've heard anything at all, it would be a kindness to Mohan Lal and Leela just to tell them that you know she is all right."

"I'd do that, if I'd heard. But I haven't. She is still keeping her own counsel," Rose said. "Just as she did beforehand. She never let on what she was planning, you know. But I did know she was very unhappy about this marriage that her father wanted. She kept on saying no, but he went ahead and set the wedding date and even booked the Registry Office ceremony, and paid no attention to her. I can't say I was surprised when she vanished. But I expect she's all right. Her magazine knows where she is, after all."

Krishna, one Monday morning in the previous February, had suddenly announced that she had decided to give in and make the marriage her father wished. She had tendered her notice at her job, she said. She had, however, also undertaken to do one last feature on hotels in north Wales. She was setting off forthwith but would be back home on Friday and would do no more jobs away from home while working out her notice.

She then tossed her suitcase into the back of her Toyota and drove away, and Mohan Lal was so relieved at her capitulation that instead of his usual warnings about the dire consequences which all this roving about might bring, he wished her a safe journey quite amiably.

On the following morning, she rang him up from Paris.

She had, she said, applied for and won the post of European Correspondent on her magazine. She would for the foreseeable future be travelling round western Europe, writing articles on hotel facilities in various resorts. Her editor understood the situation and would forward letters to her if they were sent care of the London office, but he would not tell anyone where she was. She had left her Toyota at Heathrow and posted the keys home, with a note of where exactly the car was parked. She recommended her father to collect the car quickly, before the parking fees became too astronomical. She would be using a company car henceforth. "I should sell the Toyota and give the money to Sita," she added to Mohan Lal, cutting across his gobbling protests. "I'm sure she needs help. I'd have needed help too, if I'd gone through with this. Give my love to her and to Mother and to Chandra Lal. Goodbye."

And that was the last anyone had heard from Krishna. Her editor had indeed refused to tell Mohan Lal where to find her, on the grounds that Krishna was over thirty and entitled to conceal her whereabouts if she so wished. When Mohan Lal, who had rushed to the magazine office in person, began to shout, the editor picked up his phone, pressed a button and said, "Security, please," in an ominous voice. Mohan Lal took the point and left.

"And so now," Mohan Lal said afterwards, "I have washed my hands of my younger daughter. I was a fool. I let her go her own way too long; the years go by and one does not notice and suddenly it is too late. Well, let her ruin her life. She will never enter this house again."

Kartar and Nita had not approved of Krishna's behaviour and when Perry, on hearing the news, let out a shout of laughter and said, "Good for Krishna! She's making a fine use of all those European languages she studied!" there was a slight coolness for a while. But it had to be admitted, Kartar said later, smoothing it over, that Mohan Lal had been foolish. Krishna was not a child but a successful career woman. It was a pity she had said no in such a dramatic manner but, well, Mohan Lal had to some extent asked for what he'd got.

"She will probably be all right in a fashion," Kartar said now. "But one day she may want to return to her family and perhaps it will be difficult. She has left her community and it may be cold and lonely out there, as she grows older."

"But there have been happy things this last year," Rose said. "Rupa's little boy is so lovely, and Lynn will have her baby any minute, and Bheji is pleased. She and Lynn quarrelled, you know, over some of the ideas in the film we were watching the day before Mrs Gandhi was killed. Perhaps Mummy told you. Bheji forgot it while all the troubles were happening, but afterwards it came back to her and she was chilly with Lynn. Now all that is all right. Those are good things."

"Yes, they are. And I think, Rose, that it is time that good things like that came along for you. Don't be afraid. I shan't behave like Mohan Lal. But you are twenty-three now. All this year, I've waited because we were all mourning; somehow it was not the right time. But if we were to look around now and find

347

you someone, you would be agreeable?"

"Yes," said Rose. "Oh, yes, of course."

When she had been planning to go to India, after all, it was with marriage in mind. She had accepted long since that Charan was lost to her and she must, after all, marry someone.

"There's no hurry," Kartar said. "You shall meet a number of prospects and take your time. I shall ask around at the Gurudwara, and we might advertise. We want you to be happy."

"Yes, I know."

It would be a relief, in a way. She would feel settled; the future would have a pattern. And once she was engaged, Mr Sanderton at the school, who had been renewing his efforts to persuade her to go out with him, would stop.

"You'll have a dowry," Kartar said. "We shall look for a family that isn't interested in dowry, but still, I want you to have something; some help towards a deposit on your home, perhaps. And that's why I saved a little, buying you a two-year old car. I am not badly off but life is so expensive these days and I will have Amrit to cater for, too. The difference between this and a new car will go to you when you marry. Every little helps." He smiled at his daughter. "I don't think it will be difficult to find you a good match."

"I'm not the pretty one. Amrit is that."

"You're nice-looking enough. I'm glad we've settled this," said Kartar. "It is time, I think, to turn back towards life."

Eighteen months later, Rose sat in front of her dressing table making up her face, and thought wryly that it wasn't proving as easy as all that. She was almost getting used to interviewing unsuitable applicants. The whole business of meeting prospective partners and their families, which had once been agonisingly embarrassing, was now turning into a standard procedure. One got past feeling either shy or expectant. The process even had a funny side.

"How many is this?" said Amrit, who was sitting on Rose's bed and watching her. "I've lost count."

"So have I."

"I think maybe you're too particular."

Amrit, who had completed an undistinguished university course and was now working as a dentist's receptionist, was far less scholarly than Rose, but had turned out exceptionally beautiful. It was a static beauty, though. Her shapely features were immobile, and Amrit cultivated this further on purpose because she was afraid of getting lines. "You already have a crease between your eyes," she had told Rose worriedly, months ago. "I have some cream which may help; let me give you some. You should try to get rid of that line. It will not help you find a match."

"You are just anxious to get me married so that it can be your turn," Rose had said.

Now she said, "Just you *wait* till it's your turn. You won't want to marry just anybody."

"The last one wasn't just anybody. He was very nice and an accountant, like Father. You would have had a good standard of living."

"I didn't like him, or his family. I like to read books, not just at school but for pleasure. His mother told me she thought reading was a waste of time, and I should have had to live in her house."

"I wonder what today's ones will be like?" mused Amrit.

"Well, it is the fourth time we have advertised for someone," Rose said drily. "We shall soon be getting applications from the first enquirers' sons, at this rate! Poor Lynn, how scandalised she was at the idea of me being advertised in that way. How do I look?"

"That salwar kameeze is a very good colour for you," Amrit said critically. "You look nice in that dark red. But you need some more eyeliner on your lower lids."

"There's a car drawing up." Rose raised her head. "I haven't time."

"Yes, you have. There is no need to rush downstairs at once. Let them come in and settle down and then make a grand, impressive entrance. Even if you decide you don't like them, there's no reason why you shouldn't make *them* like *you*."

Amrit was not coming down. She never appeared on these occasions, which was tact on her part and yet irritated Rose because the reason was that beautiful Amrit might distract attention from her less exotic elder sister. It was just rubbing it in, Rose had thought secretly, when inspecting her own face in the mirror. But this time, when she was at length fetched by her mother and led downstairs into the sitting room, she was glad. The young man who rose to his feet and smiled at her as she entered was . . .

Not Charan, of course. There would never be another Charan

in Rose's life. But this young man was something like him. A little graver, two or three years older, but the same general type, with the same frank and friendly smile.

"This is my daughter, Raminder," Nita was saying. "Only everyone calls her Rose. Rose, this is Mr and Mrs Singh from Clapham – such a coincidence, your father and I used to know Clapham well, of course – and this is Jasbir Singh, their son, and his sister Amarjit, only everyone knows her as Pet."

Rose smiled. "It is nice to meet you." She was acutely conscious of Jasbir smiling back, of his eyes taking her in. She did the expected thing and went to fetch refreshments. When she returned to the sitting room, an animated conversation was in progress among the elders, while Pet, who was small and rather chubby, sat quietly beside her brother and listened, and Jasbir put a word in occasionally.

"It is a small world," said Nita, drawing Rose into the gathering as the plates were handed round. "Would you believe it, Mr and Mrs Singh know the Sodhis quite well – yes, our Mr and Mrs Sodhi. They came to know them at a function in the big Gurudwara at Shepherd's Bush."

"A very good man, Mr Sodhi," said Mr Singh. "Very steady and wise. We have been to a gathering at his house once – no doubt it was only by chance that we did not meet you there! – and it was so easy and friendly, with guests from all parts of the community. There were at least four people from a Hindu family called Sharma . . . "

"If they're the Sharmas we know," said Nita with amusement, "they live in the same street as my brother-in-law. It *is* a small world."

"There was a Mrs Sharma who was very stout and talkative and knew nearly everyone in the room," said Mrs Singh.

"Oh, that was Swarup Sharma. It must have been. They are the same ones, for sure," Nita said.

"It is amazing," said Mr Singh. "But as I was saying, we admire Mr Sodhi. He is old-fashioned in many ways but he has a good heart and a level head. It was a shocking thing we heard, that there have been threats against him from extremists, just because he preached in the Gurudwara that Sikhs and Hindus should try to find harmony together and that in India, they should all try to be Indians first and put communal loyalties second."

"Worse than threats," said Kartar. "Someone actually shot at

350

him from a car one day, as he was walking in his street. Oh, yes, it is quite true. The bullet was dug out of a tree. But it was all so quick. He saw the gun poking out of the car but no one got the car number."

"But that is terrible. When was this? No, we hadn't heard."

"It was quite recently. Fortunately no one was harmed as things turned out. Tell me, changing the subject to something more pleasant, do you have a garden at your home? I am becoming quite a keen gardener. I have a nephew who has a wonderful garden and he gives me first-class seeds and seedlings, and gets catalogues for me."

"That is a nice hobby," said Mr Singh. "Yes, we have a garden. We cultivate roses."

"Ah, now in the other room, I have some very fine rose catalogues. Come and see them. Nita, could you bring some tea to us there . . . ?"

"I think perhaps," said Rose, after she had been left alone with Jasbir and the silence threatened to persist, "that my father did that on purpose!"

Jasbir smiled briefly. Then, becoming serious again, he said, "These can be very awkward moments. Do you think so too? I think this is very nerve-racking. Look, we both know why we're here. Let me tell you about myself. I am a chemist – I mean the sort with a shop, a pharmacy. It is quite a good living. It is in Clapham but I would move somewhere else if you . . . well, if my wife didn't like it there. I have my own flat over the shop and so I don't live with my parents. I believe you're a teacher?"

"Yes."

"What do you teach, and what age group?"

"Oh, ten-year-olds or thereabouts and mostly I teach English and some history, not very advanced, obviously, and I am interested in drama, as well. I enjoy teaching," Rose said.

"Drama? What kind of plays do you do at your school?"

In the dining room, Mrs Singh was saying to Nita, "I can hear their voices. I think they are getting on very well. I would like to talk to your daughter alone if I may, but really, she seems a very sweet girl. And it is so nice, that we all have acquaintances in common."

"Perhaps we could all visit your house sometime?"

"It is hardly the time of year," said Mr Singh, "but you could look at my rose plants."

They all laughed. There was a feeling of warmth in the house.

"Well, that completes the invitation list," Nita said, head on one side. "Now, Rose, you are quite happy about all this? You think this boy, and this family, are right for you? We are very anxious that you should be contented in your marriage. It is not a bad thing that they don't want to hold the ceremony until June, so that Mr Singh's brother can come from India to attend. It gives us time to make all the arrangements properly and you time to make up your mind finally."

"I have made it up," said Rose, from the other side of the dining table, on which they had been making the invitation list and preparing memoranda of things to be done. "It is quite all right, Mother. I have seen Jasbir several times now and I am quite sure. I think June is a good idea, too. Lynn will have had her new baby by then, so she can come as well. What a surprise that was! She didn't say a word to anyone until we began to notice. Apparently she had some difficulties early on and they didn't want to speak of it until they were fairly sure things would turn out all right."

"Difficulties are not so rare," said Nita, remembering her own barren years. "But very often they are resolved. I hope it will be all easy for you, but if it takes time to begin your family, bear that in mind."

It's April now, Rose thought. I shall be married in June. And, yes, I'll be glad.

Jasbir wasn't Charan, no. Indeed, the more she came to know him, the more she realised the differences. Charan had made her laugh but with Jasbir, if she wanted laughter, she had to create it herself, which did not come easily to her. But he was very gentle, perhaps more so than Charan, whose good nature had always had something tough in it. He would make a good husband, she thought, and he certainly seemed to want her as a wife. After his first meeting with Amrit, he had said to Rose, "You are an active sort of girl and I like that. Your sister is very pretty but I think she likes best to sit still and be admired." Rose had appreciated that.

Once installed in Jasbir's family, she thought, with chubby Pet as her sister, and parents-in-law whom she liked and who had made friends very pleasantly with her own parents, and, she hoped and prayed, with her own children coming along soon, she would be safe in a sheltered place, and love, surely, would grow in such propitious surroundings.

A year from now, if she were one of the fortunate ones who did not have difficulties, she might be about to have Jasbir's baby. Might already have done so.

A year from now, she would have forgotten Charan.

A rattle at the letterbox made her mother look up. "That must be the post. Oh, your father is going to get it, I can hear him. Now, about your changes of clothes on the day . . . "

Kartar had been reading his Saturday morning newspaper in the next room. He now came in with an ornate red and gold card. "Weddings are in the air, it seems. This is from one of the Sharmas – it's Swarup Sharma's niece, if I remember rightly. They're such a complicated family. It's for a fortnight today. Shall we go, or not? What do you think, Nita?"

"Oh, dear." Nita took the invitation from him and examined it. "Before 1984, we wouldn't even have asked the question; we'd just have gone. Bheji will probably say she'd rather not go. But . . . "

"She doesn't always feel like going out, these days, anyway," Kartar said. "Though she does seem to be getting better. But you think we should accept this?"

"Yes. Yes, I do. People should hold together, not let themselves be pushed apart. Let's go."

"My goodness," said Kartar, in mock horror. "More expense! As well as marrying off Rose here, now I shall have to buy a gift for this Sharma girl. Is there no end to it? No, you're right of course. We'll go."

"You next," said Rose's cousin Rupa, giggling, as they filled their plates from the buffet at the end of the large community hall. The formal part of the two hour marriage ceremony for Swarup Sharma's niece had now concluded and hungry guests were enthusiastically forming queues for the meal. Some of the men had drifted away to a corner of the hall where beer and whisky were available, but there were cans of soft drinks lined up on the table alongside the food.

"Don't tease," said Rose. "I shall feel so shy, when it's my turn. Everybody will be looking at me."

"Don't they all look at you when you're teaching a class? Teaching would terrify me," said Rupa. "So many expectant faces, and half of them wondering how much naughtiness they can get away with . . . "

"Oh, it's not as bad as that. Anyway, they're children. This will be quite different. You ought to know! You've been through it."

"I rather enjoyed my wedding," said Rupa reflectively. "Although I knew Surjit better, perhaps, than you know Jasbir. Perhaps that was it."

"Do you ... ?" Rose stopped. She really had no business whatever to be asking after Charan. But Rupa was looking at her enquiringly. She altered the question a little. "Does Surjit ever hear from Charan? He must do, I suppose. They're brothers, after all."

Her cousin looked at her searchingly. In looks, Rupa was not unlike Amrit, but her features were more animated. Her eyes had a shrewd sparkle which Amrit's did not. "There was some idea once of you and Charan, wasn't there? Did you mind when it came to nothing?"

"I did at the time, but it's all so long ago," said Rose. The truth was, she couldn't speak Charan's name without feeling her blood begin to race, but it was possible to conceal these effects from other people, and she did so, resolutely.

"We do hear now and then. He seems to be settled in Canada," Rupa said. "He's not a particularly good correspondent so we don't hear very often, but I think he's doing better there than he did in London."

"That's good," said Rose with determined offhandedness, disregarding Rupa's uncomfortably penetrating scrutiny. "Oh, dear, poor Mummy," she added. "Swarup Sharma's backed her into a corner. Look." Rupa did so, and chuckled anew. Nita, looking extremely flustered, was indeed quite helpless in a corner of the room, obliged to eat standing up although there were unoccupied chairs close by, because Swarup Sharma was in the way, talking and gesticulating so energetically that the loose end of her red and green printed sari kept whisking in the air and once nearly knocked Nita's plate out of her grasp.

"I think perhaps we should rescue her," said Rupa. "I expect Swarup is on about Krishna again. That was the juiciest scandal to come her way in years, and she will *not* let the subject drop. You'd think two years was long enough, but no. Well, I want to tell Auntie Nita my news, anyway."

"Your news?"

"Yes! One child keeps me busy enough, goodness knows," said Rupa. "I have parked little Davi with Nerin, since she and Balbir were not coming today, and I only hope she is behaving; she can be so lively. But just the same, I am having another one, in

354

October. Then Lynn and I will have two each." Her eyes sparkled wickedly at Rose. "You next!" she said again.

"Rupa," said her cousin as like a well-dressed relief force, they moved towards the beleaguered Nita, "you are a wretch!"

On the M4 motorway to the west of London, as the afternoon drew towards evening, Balbir and Nerin sat companionably in the car, enjoying the peace which had descended since their two small sons and Rupa's two year old daughter had all fallen asleep in the back seat. "We have an appointment on that day," Nerin had said when Rupa asked if they were going to the Sharma wedding and if not, whether they could look after Davi. "She can come with us and be welcome, but you don't mind if we take her out in the car? We're taking the boys, so we shall drive very carefully."

"Oh, yes, that is all right. But where are you going?"

"Ah," said Nerin mysteriously.

Now they were on their way home, and there was a decision to take.

"What do you reckon, Nerin? Shall we risk it? It means sinking every penny we've got and the mortgage won't be an easy prospect."

"But you're longing to, aren't you? So am I. There's just the right amount of land and the house is in good repair."

"It'll be quite a venture. There won't be any other Indian people for miles. Will you miss having family members nearby?"

"We can get to Southall in an hour or so, any time. Wiltshire isn't the Antarctic," said Nerin, amused.

"It's a strange thing," Balbir said thoughtfully. "But hardly any of my family, or yours, know much about England outside the cities. My father and my Uncle Kartar go in for family holidays sometimes, but they go to resorts like Bournemouth and Penzance, which are essentially towns. What goes on in the countryside hardly exists for most of us. Some of us drive through it occasionally and that's it! If we start market gardening in Wiltshire, we'll be real pioneers."

"But it feels right, somehow. We'll be doing what were best at – growing things, I mean. You can't do that without having land to grow them on. You don't want to go back to India to grow things, do you?"

"No, I do not," said Balbir with feeling. "It would seem like a foreign land. I don't want to lose my links with my own people;

355

I'd like the children to grow up orthodox if possible. But as you said, Southall's not so far; we can still get to the Gurudwara sometimes and see the family reasonably often. Just at the moment, I don't feel inclined to pine over not seeing Satnam too frequently, I must say!"

"We might get a bank loan," said Nerin thoughtfully.

"I think we'll have to consider the finances very carefully, yes. There'll be equipment and seed to buy, and we'll need a tide-over fund until we've raised our first crop. We'd better work out some detailed proposals for the bank. We ought to diversify to some extent."

"Could we try some organic crops? The market for that is getting bigger; people are so health-conscious these days. Organic tomatoes might do well. But we'll need more greenhouse space . . . "

Discussing the future, they drove steadily on into London.

"All off?" Rose, perched on the edge of an armchair in the sitting room, with the sunshine of a spring morning streaming through the windows, stared at her parents in disbelief. "My wedding off? But . . . but why?"

"Oh, my dear," Nita said. "We are so *sorry*. But you haven't met Jasbir so very often. I hope the disappointment won't be too great. It can be an advantage if a couple are not too closely attached before the marriage, sometimes."

"But *why*?" said Rose again.

She had known from the moment when she and Rupa interrupted Swarup Sharma yesterday that something was wrong. Her mother had looked at her wildly, veered away, and vanished in the crowd. She hadn't joined up with her parents again until it was time to leave, and in the car going home they had been almost completely silent.

When she tried to talk to them about the day's events, they had either not answered, or replied in such short, forced sentences that she desisted. They did not seem to be angry with her; it wasn't that. But there was undoubtedly something and this morning at breakfast it had been just as bad. Both her parents looked exhausted, as if they hadn't slept, and they had hardly eaten anything, and her father hadn't touched his Sunday papers. Usually he disappeared behind them for the whole of Sunday morning.

And then, her mother said, "Leave the washing up and come

356

into the other room, Rose. There's something we have to tell you."

And it was this. She couldn't believe it. It made no sense. She said, "Why?" for the third time.

"The truth is," said Kartar, unhappily, "that Jasbir's family have not been sincere with us. We want the best for you, Raminder Rose, and only the best, and this family is not what we thought. We have been awake all night discussing what to do; believe me, we are not deciding this lightly." He raised a hand before Rose could ask why yet again. "Some information came our way yesterday," he said.

"Yes. I saw that you were both upset."

"Your intended in-laws were not at that wedding," said Nita. "They know the Sharmas only slightly. But I think they would not have been asked however well they knew them. It seems that Swarup Sharma has a cousin-sister who is an auxiliary nurse in a clinic in Clapham. I was telling Swarup about your engagement, you see . . . "

Swarup wasn't gossiping about Krishna this time, after all, thought Rose. Her mother came to her and took her hand. "Dear Rose, we *are* sorry. But when I spoke of the family to Swarup, she remembered having met them and then, well, she told me what she knew about them. When the two families met at Mr Sodhi's that time, Swarup's cousin-sister was with her, and she recognised Pet, Jasbir's sister. Pet was a patient in the clinic last year. Rose, she was in there to have an abortion."

"We don't want you to be involved in a family where there is any scandal," said Kartar. "That would not be good enough for you. We don't want you to marry where there is a single breath of scandal. Bheji says the same. She is horrified by this news. She cried when she heard of it."

"But . . . there's nothing against Jasbir himself," said Rose. "He hasn't done anything wrong that we know of."

"And you feel it isn't fair?" said Kartar. "No, perhaps it isn't. For all we know, Pet herself may have been taken advantage of in some way; she may not be as bad as this makes her seem. But with a thing like that, one can never be sure. For you, Rose, it just isn't good enough. But you need not feel any embarrassment. We will deal with it all and see that everyone who knows of your engagement knows that it has been ended and not through any fault of yours. No one will mention it to you. I think we'll let the subject drop for a few months, while you get over this. Don't

357

worry, Rose. Something better will come along; you'll see."

June was a curiously empty month. She tried to concentrate on her teaching, but found little satisfaction in it. It wasn't that she was grieving for Jasbir, exactly. She hadn't known him well enough. But there was a sense of loss all the same; a vacuum where a busy family life should have been developing; a grey fog where there ought to have been a visible future.

She avoided any occasion at which she might encounter Swarup Sharma. She hated the woman and her jabbering tongue. Sometimes she felt she hated the whole Indian community of Southall. It was too claustrophobic; people whispered and chattered and minded each other's business far too much. If Swarup and her cousin-sister had only minded their own business, she thought as she set off to work one Monday morning, she would have been two days' married by this time. The Mini, which was occasionally temperamental ("Maybe I should have gone for a brand new car for you after all," Kartar had said once or twice), was reluctant to start. Rose wondered if it was possible for cars to pick up moods from their owners.

July came and towards the end of it, the schools broke up. Rose went to Bournemouth with her parents for a fortnight's holiday. August passed and September came, and the new term.

Rupa's telephone call came in the October.

Chapter Twenty-Nine

Dreams Become Reality

1987

"I said, Charan is coming back," said Rupa, repeating herself patiently down the telephone line. "He wrote to both his father and to Surjit. He's still employed by his company in Canada, in fact, that's why he's coming. They make and supply some sort of electronic equipment – desktop computers, I think – and they have a factory and distributors over here. He's been working for them as a salesman and he's coming to London to manage their showroom in Putney."

"When?" said Rose faintly.

"He'll arrive next month. He's going to stay with us while he finds a flat or a house. He can afford it now; he's been doing very well, Rose, very well indeed."

"Why . . . why are you saying this to me?" Rose said. "When Amrit answered the phone, she said you asked for me."

"Of course. Charan mentioned you in the letter. He wanted to know if you were married yet, and if not, whether the question of you marrying him could be revived. Well, Rose? Do you want him? Because if you do, just say so, here and now."

"He . . . you're . . . ?"

"If you still want to marry Charan, and you know, I've got the oddest idea that you've never forgotten him, then tell me. Because he wants to marry you. And we're all for it, I assure you. My father-in-law is delighted. He's here now. He wanted to come straight round to see your father but I said no, let me ring Rose first. Just say what you want, Rose. If you're keen, we'll all do everything we can to help."

"I can hardly believe it!"

"Means well, could try harder."

"What?"

"You're a teacher; don't you have to write reports? And aren't those the kind of thing one puts in a school report? Now I'm saying them about you. You're such a dear, Rose, but do for goodness sake, for once, make a push to get what *you* want. If it's Charan, say so! But if you'd rather not, then it's your business and we won't say anything to your parents. But this time, you be the one who says."

"I . . . please . . . yes, please."

"You would like my father-in-law and Surjit to come and see your parents?"

"Yes."

"At last! I thought I'd need thumbscrews to get it out of you. Oh, Rose, wouldn't it be marvellous? You'll be my sister-in-law as well as my cousin. I'm so thrilled. I wish I wasn't just like an elephant just now, or I'd come rushing round there to hug you. Rose? Rose? Are you still there?"

"I'm still here. I just feel . . . staggered," said Rose.

"And so after all," said Nita to the engagement party gathering, "we can bless Swarup Sharma's gossiping habits. Because this is far better, far nearer to what we always wanted for Rose and to what Rose wants for herself. It's a happy day."

"I always understood," said Mr Satinder Singh, "why you would not let the engagement proceed when it was first suggested, some years ago. I never held it against you, I assure you. But I am overjoyed now that things have come right. I can't find words to say how glad I am."

"Maybe," said Perry lazily, stretching his feet to the warmth of Kartar's handsome new imitation coal fire, "we should have asked the Sharmas to this party. What do you say, Rose? As your mother has remarked, but for Swarup, this wouldn't be happening."

"No, indeed. Well, we can ask them to the wedding," said Ranbir, also pulling her chair nearer to the warmth. The November day was cold. She nodded towards Charan and Rose, who were seated in adjacent chairs. Rose's diamond engagement ring twinkled in the gleam of a standard lamp. Jasbir had given her a bigger one, with a ruby, but she liked the simple solitaire with its pure, blue-white fire, far better. "I think it was fate," Ranbir announced. "It was the will of God, Rose, that none of the other arrangements proved suitable, and that Swarup found out what she did. This is what is right for you."

Shanti, Mohan Lal and Leela all broke into happy exclamations of agreement. Kartar remarked, "It's not the hottest day I have ever known in England but on the other hand, it is dry. Charan, if you and Rose want to put on your topcoats and go for a walk for a while, no one is stopping you."

The kindly murmurs as the two of them slipped out of the room were in the nature of a benediction.

And so here she was, walking along the pavement, side by side with Charan. It felt so natural, so familiar, that she might have done it a thousand times already. "Perhaps there is something in the theory of reincarnation," she said suddenly. "Perhaps we have been married before, in other lives."

"This one will do," Charan said. "April seems a long way off; I wish we could fix a date sooner. But it is such a performance, buying a house, and I want us to go straight into our own new home."

"There is a great deal of organising to be done for the ceremony," said Rose. "That takes time, as well."

"Yes, you've been through some of it before, haven't you? My God," Charan said, "when Rupa told me how nearly you had been married off to someone else, I went cold inside, all the way through. I knew all along that it might have happened, in fact that it was more than likely, but it made no difference. All the time I was away, Rose, I don't believe there was one moment when you were out of my mind. I kept on thinking, if only I can make it fast enough, if only I can build something up in time, I can go back for Rose."

"I nearly went to India, except that the Golden Temple business happened first."

"Well, that's an example of something good coming out of a disaster!" Charan said, and before she turned to look into his face, she knew that he was smiling his tough, merry, good-humoured smile. When she did meet his eyes, the friendship in them made her laugh aloud, for sheer joy.

There was no one else in the long quiet residential street and they were at the far end of it now, well away from Kartar's windows. She went into his arms as though she were coming home. They stood embracing for a long time, warming each other, oblivious to the cold misty air around them. Then they moved apart again but only so that he could draw her arm through his as they walked on.

Rose looked up at the dark sky, and at the haze round the

361

orange streetlamps and sniffed the winter air, and thought that for the rest of her life, cold misty nights like this would seem magical because they would remind her of today, when Charan put his diamond on her finger, and she stood in his arms on a chilly street corner and it was more utterly right than anything she had done or known before.

But they must not spoil it by doing anything amiss, even by being out too long. "Shall we walk round the block? That will be far enough, I should think, because the meal will be ready by that time."

"Yes, fine. In fact, I am hungry. I wouldn't like it if nothing was left by the time we got back, and with such a crowd there, I should say there's quite a risk."

"Yes, nearly all the family have come. It's so nice."

"Family means a lot to you, doesn't it, Rose?"

"Yes, it does. It gives me a sort of . . . of belonging feeling."

"We'll found a family of our own. Those are beautiful children that Sunder and Lynn have produced, although it seems strange to have youngsters with English names in the family. Tina and Jonathan!"

"Well, Lynn is English and Sunder's hardly orthodox. He says it will be easier for them to get along in English society if they have English names."

"Rupa's new infant is very fetching, too. Well, well, we'll see what we can do."

"I was only sorry," said Rose, becoming a little shy at this point, "about the ones who couldn't be there. Krishna does write occasionally now but she never gives an address and I don't think she'll ever come back. And Sita no one ever sees these days. While Chandra Lal seems to be permanently on duty."

PC Chandra Lal Bhatia was very much on duty at that moment. He was in fact just stepping out of a police car in Southall Broadway to investigate the small and scruffy truck which he and his more junior companion, a young constable called Bill Wragg, had just pulled over on Chandra Lal's recommendation.

Chandra Lal had concluded some time ago that although imperturbability and physical fitness were clearly valuable to a police officer, real career success would require much more. If he wanted to be promoted to sergeant, and he very much did, there were things in himself which he must improve.

His memory and powers of observation, he decided, required

honing and he set to work to hone them. His efforts had just paid off. He had recognised the number of that truck, which was on a circular which he had read only the day before. A week ago, in London at three a.m., in a vicinity where there had been a number of burglaries, the police had tried to stop that same truck. One of them was now in hospital with a broken leg because the truck instantly accelerated and knocked him down with a glancing blow.

The victim's colleagues had got the number but the vehicle must have gone to ground somewhere close by as none of the instantly alerted patrols had picked it up. They had traced the name of its legal owner but couldn't ask him to account for its movements because he was abroad. Chandra Lal advanced on the driver's cabin, alert with interest.

There was no chance that it would accelerate away this time. The police car was backed up against it and there was a traffic jam only yards ahead. Chandra Lal rapped on the driver's window, the driver opened it and Chandra Lal reached in and seized the ignition keys. Because it was after dark, they were already in his hands before he recognised the driver's face.

"You again," said the young Sikh in the driving seat. "PC Chandra Lal Bhatia, the most dedicated cop in London."

"We just want a look at whatever's under that tarpaulin in the back," said Chandra Lal to his cousin Satnam.

A second man, in the passenger seat, spoke across him. "What is all this?" He was another Sikh, Chandra Lal noted, and one who, like Satnam, wore the high, noticeable style of turban which was a sign of religious fervour.

"I think they think we've been robbing a bank," said Satnam in a disgusted voice. Admittedly, thought Chandra Lal, it was unlikely that Satnam had been committing robbery. If he had been driving that night in London, he hadn't knocked a policeman down because he had stolen goods in the back, not Satnam.

But in that case, what had there been in the truck that the police force mustn't see? And in both Satnam and his companion now there was a taut bodily stillness which sent prickles of warning down Chandra Lal's spine.

A truck which had put a policeman in hospital and was driven by a known agitator amounted in any case to a situation which Chandra Lal considered to warrant reinforcements. He kept both men inside, occupied by producing Satnam's driving licence and the vehicle documents, and invoices for the motor spares which Satnam said were in the back, while Wragg sent out a message, and another police car arrived.

Then he ordered Satnam and his companion out, and they all went to the back.

Under the tarpaulin were car exhaust assemblies, bundled together with rope, some tyres and some crates. The first of these, once the lid had been chiselled off, proved to contain car batteries.

"I told you. Spares," said Satnam.

The sergeant who had arrived with the reinforcements was studying the other crates. "All right. So now we'll have the lid off . . . that one there," he said, jabbing a finger between two boxes and indicating another crate which was lurking modestly beneath.

The chosen container was uncovered and opened. "Small parts, see?" snapped Satnam's companion as a quantity of small clear plastic bags were revealed. "Screws, plugs, valves . . . "

Chandra Lal and the sergeant tipped the crate, tumbling the packets on to the floor of the truck. At the bottom was something different, a square metal box with a catch. The sergeant opened it.

"What on earth?" said PC Wragg, leaning from the other side and prodding the contents with an interested forefinger. "It's like plasticine. Or marzipan."

"It's putty," said Satnam. He was giving off tension in pulses like a radio beacon.

"It isn't plasticine or marzipan or putty," said Chandra Lal. He knew what it was; he'd been shown it when on a course. "I saved your life once," he said in an undertone to Satnam, "but not for this." Aloud, he said, "It's Semtex."

"Very nice," said Inspector Welling. "Very nice indeed. We ought to be able to make a charge of conspiracy to murder stick. The first target was almost certainly Mr Sodhi: he's been an outspoken opponent of the Khalistan movement ever since 1984 and Satnam Virk's house is where those death threats came from. We even found a dud copy of an anonymous letter to him, screwed up and chucked in a wastepaper basket. Very nice indeed. And if it turns out that that bullet that missed Mr Sodhi last year was fired from the rifle we found in Virk's attic . . . how are we doing with Satnam Virk himself and his chum?"

"We aren't," said Detective Sergeant James. "They're still sitting with their arms folded, calling us pigs. Virk says he'll never tell us anything no matter how much we beat him up. Anyone would think he wanted us to."

"He probably does. In a perverse sort of way, he'd enjoy it even more than you did. Restrain yourself. Steady questioning and regular cups of tea, that's the answer. With any luck, he'll lose his temper and then you'll get somewhere. Have you noticed," said the inspector thoughtfully, "that there are no worry lines on his face at all? He believes absolutely in his creed and his cause and he's never lain awake at three in the morning wondering if committing squalid little murders in the name of religion really is the most reverent attitude to the deity. Even that human iceberg PC Bhatia has a few lines on his face. *He's* done some small hours worrying, I fancy."

"PC Bhatia?" said the sergeant, surprised. "He's a candidate for promotion, I'd have said. A very sound officer. Why should he worry? Because he's Indian and he's had to arrest other Indians? But . . . I'm not very up on these distinctions, but isn't there a difference between the sect with the turbans and the ones without? Bhatia doesn't wear a turban."

"Oh, I suppose you wouldn't know. You haven't been here that long. There's such a turnover in personnel these days; there's hardly anyone left who was here in 1984. That was the first time Bhatia had to arrest Satnam Virk. The Sikhs and the Hindus are separate communities but there are a few mixed families. Satnam Virk is Bhatia's first cousin."

"*What?*"

"Quite. That's why I'm not surprised that Bhatia's done some worrying. Not that it matters; you're quite right, he's a thoroughly sound officer and promotion's likely to come his way quite soon. He's very valuable in this district. But I'm glad, in a way, to see those traces of anxiety in him. I called him a human iceberg just now and so he is. And do you know, I respect him for it and yet it bothers me. He's loyal and efficient but I want to work with loyal and efficient men and women, not dedicated robots. I know how I'd feel if I had to arrest a relative. God willing, it's never happened and never will," said the inspector. "If it did, I'm not sure I'd carry it off as calmly as Bhatia. And I'm damned relieved to get the feeling that he does mind, a little."

365

Chapter Thirty

A Matter of Honour
1987

"But this is a terrible thing! It is a slur on the whole family!" Amrit cried. "My cousin will go to prison and there will be headlines and the name of Virk in the papers. Who will want to marry me after that?"

"Is that all you can think about?" said Rose indignantly. "Well, I shouldn't worry. There are plenty of people who would think a cousin in jail for this reason is a positive enhancement to you!"

"Oh, well, *you're* all right," said Amrit sulkily. "Your future father-in-law has just rung up to reassure you. No wonder you're so calm."

"I'm not calm. I'm most distressed, but I'm distressed about Satnam, not about me!"

Amrit declined to answer. She merely scowled. She then turned back to her dressing table, examined her face in the mirror and stopped scowling, for fear, Rose thought, that it would disturb the mask-like perfection of her make-up. Rupa had once been a professional beautician, and was going to do Rose's face for her on her wedding day, but Rupa had never been so obsessed with her appearance as Amrit.

Downstairs, the front doorbell rang. Someone opened the door and there was a murmur of voices. Rose, hearing Charan's voice among them, ran out of the room and went down at once, leaving Amrit to her mirror. Charan was at the foot of the stairs. He held out his hands to her. "You had my father's phone call? We've just come to make really sure you knew that this terrible thing will make no difference to you and me."

Charan's father, Satinder Singh, was in the sitting room with Rose's parents and Ranbir. "Here they are," he said as she came in with Charan. "Poor Rose, she looks quite pale, Kartar. But we are all one family already, Rose. Surjit is married to Satnam's *sister*, never mind about cousins."

"Thank you for telephoning so quickly," Rose said. "I was afraid at first . . . it is a dreadful thing, to have someone in such trouble with the police."

"Well, now you know what I think, not that it would have mattered even if I had thought quite differently. Charan would not let anything come between you."

"No, I wouldn't," said Charan. "Come and sit down, Rose. Rupa is most upset. We are so very very sorry."

"Perry has spoken to us on the phone," Nita said sadly. "Satnam is making no pretences, it seems. He has confessed. More than that! He told his father that the police made him angry and in the end he almost threw it at them. Yes, he meant to kill Mr Sodhi, and others, and he is proud of it and they can do what they like. The charge will be conspiracy to murder and I suppose that yes, all the details will end up in the papers. Perry said to us that he will not go to the temple tomorrow, and not to go over there for Sunday tea."

"Poor young devil," said Kartar heavily. "I'm sorry for Satnam, sorry that he's taken this way in life, sorry for what's going to happen to him. He told his father he was proud to be a martyr for the cause of Khalistan, but he doesn't understand what that martyrdom is going to mean."

Charan had drawn Rose to sit beside him on the couch. His warm, strong fingers closed over hers. "Try not to think about it too much," he said to her softly.

"I prefer," said Shanti, cold and calm as Perry had never known her, "not to think about it at all. To me, Satnam no longer exists. He has disgraced us all. He wished to commit murder, and for what motive? To destroy a decent man who thinks people should try to live in peace instead of shutting themselves up in separate communities and only coming out to fight each other."

Shanti still sewed a great deal, although nowadays as a hobby. She was at her sewing machine now, working it rhythmically as she talked. "No, Perry. I am sorry, but I will not go to the prison to visit him. Ever."

"He hasn't even been found guilty yet." Perry was slumped in an armchair. His eyes were strained and heavy with the sleeplessness of many nights.

"He has confessed. He intends to plead guilty," Shanti said.

"I could never have believed you could be so harsh, so . . .

What if he asks for you?" Perry cried. "He is your son!"

"Yours too. You can visit him, Perry, all you like; I will never question it. But if he wants me, let him want. He should have remembered that his mother is Hindu."

"Now who is shutting herself into a separate community?"

"Don't say that to me, Perry. It is Satnam who has shut himself away from me. It is not like that with you and me, or with your family and me."

Perry was silent. Suddenly the whirring of the sewing machine stopped. "No!" said Shanti loudly. "No, no, I will not let us be divided! Perry, say to me that we are not divided!"

"You are my wife," said Perry heavily. "So how can we be? We have had four children between us . . . "

"Three."

"Oh, God. Shanti, will you keep this up for years? If . . . when . . . he is convicted, then it will mean years in prison for him. You know that, don't you?"

"I won't be divided from you, I won't!" Shanti would not answer the question. "But I cannot see Satnam; I *cannot*!"

Perry pulled himself out of the chair and left the room. But in the night, as he once again lay open-eyed, he heard her quietly sobbing and turned to her. He must not maintain a feud with Shanti or this whole house would fall apart. Besides, Perry too needed comfort.

That Shanti, once he had taken her in his arms, then wept uncontrollably for a long time, actually provided some of that comfort. She was not weeping only for the estrangement between herself and Perry. She would not admit it but he knew that she too was grieving for Satnam, and the steel at the core of her was hurting her as much as it hurt himself or Satnam.

"I will not ask you again to visit him," he said in the darkness. "But I will see him and I shall speak of him. And when I do, you must listen. I must have an outlet. You may be able not to think about this thing which has happened to him but I am made in a different way. I will think, and I must talk. You understand?"

Muffled against his chest, Shanti whispered, "Yes."

Rose was made in Perry's mould. How, she asked herself as she prepared for work on the following Monday, could one possibly avoid thinking about it? Alongside her horror at the thing Satnam had intended to do, was a huge and aching grief for him. He would lose his youth. He would spend the years of his young manhood shut away behind rattling locks and clanging doors. How would that fierce, passionate spirit of his endure it? He would burn away within.

He could have been free and happy under the sky. He should have been making something of his life, working with the cars he liked so much, marrying, making love, having children, doing the ordinary, wholesome things which made living rich.

He had never understood about the importance of those ordinary things. With his head stuffed full of slogans and causes and dreams of martyrdom, he had dismissed everyday matters as trivial, or at least expendable. But they were neither. They were the most precious things, the greatest cause of all.

She was angry with him and she wanted to weep for him. It would be hard to wrench her thoughts away from him and concentrate on work today. She would have stayed at home, but both her father and Charan had said, "No, don't. There's nothing you can do and you'll feel better when you're with the children."

But all the same, it was hard to get herself going that morning, and she set off at length ten minutes late, and feeling harassed, and not in the least inclined to put her mind to the rehearsal of the Christmas play, of which she had become the regular producer. It wasn't a nativity play this time, but a rather ambitious attempt at a pantomime, partly written by the children themselves, with recorded pop songs as part of the musical backing. She had been enjoying it. Now, it seemed as remote and thin as the air on a far-off mountain top.

When, presently, she was halted by a traffic jam caused by roadworks, she concluded miserably that the whole day was going wrong. She'd be half an hour late, not ten minutes, by the time she actually got there. She was. The shrubbery-lined drive past the netball courts seemed a mile long and the only parking spaces left in the school car park were on the far side of it from the school. She was obliged to run in order to be at her desk before the bell rang for assembly.

The rehearsal was in the second half of the morning and before that she had to deal with the new class of which she had this term become the form mistress. "You'll feel better when you're with the children," Charan had said kindly, but Charan had never met this particular lot of children. They were a tough set, mature for their age and apt to be unruly. Mrs Hoxley, who had had them last year, said that it was a curious thing, the way each year's intake seemed to have a composite character of its own. At the start of the term, Mrs Hoxley had warned her that they would stage a trial of strength against their new form mistress. "Just stand no nonsense, right from your first day with them," advised Mrs Hoxley.

Rose had taken the advice, on the whole successfully, but the class had a fiendish ability to sense it if their teacher happened to be tired or distracted. Then they would challenge her. They had a variety of methods, ranging from whispering and passing notes to lengthy and time-wasting questions and attempts to get her off whatever was the subject in hand, to outright impertinence and noisiness. As well as checking them in and out, she had on this particular day to take them for three lessons as well, and several of them were also in the play. At lunchtime, furthermore, she caught three of them just as they were about to slip through a hole in the fence beyond the netball courts and make an illicit visit to the world outside.

The caretaker did nowadays have an assistant, but the school was in urgent need, Rose thought as she led her charges back to the building, of some maintenance work. The trouble, of course, was shortage of money. They needed all sorts of things as well as repairs to the fence. All the same, there was a staff meeting later on; she'd mention the fence. Meanwhile, she must make it plain to the would-be truants that they wouldn't get away with this. "You'll sit in the classroom for the rest of the lunch-hour and I'd remind you that you're all three extras in the play. Let me catch you misbehaving again, and I'll have you replaced."

After devoting what felt like the whole day to standing no nonsense, Rose felt as though she had been in a psychic boxing ring. She longed for nothing more than to go home, eat, bathe and sleep. But before the day could finish, there was still the staff meeting.

This was late starting because Mr Sanderton had squeezed in a short choir practice at the end of the day and they had to wait for him. Once launched, it turned out to be the kind of meeting which trailed on and on. She did succeed in mentioning the fence, but the topic somehow got lost in a welter of grumbles about dog-eared textbooks that needed replacement and the damp patch on the art room wall, and the pernicious nature of the financial cuts in education in general. She was obliged to leave the meeting once, to telephone home and say she would be late.

When, finally, she said goodnight to her fellow committee members, it was fully dark. Well, getting home wouldn't take long. It was a blessing to have a car. She hurried round the corner of the school building and across the car park, nearly empty now except for two or three committee members' cars.

The Mini refused to start. Kartar had said months ago that, really, she should have a better car; no amount of overhauling ever seemed to cure the Mini's problems permanently. But then she had got engaged and Jasbir had a car; it wasn't worth replacing the Mini. Now she was engaged again and Charan also had a car so it still wasn't worth it.

But this was maddening. She wrestled with the starter for some time, producing nothing but a series of dismal groans and coughs suggestive of a bronchitic cow, and then jumped as someone's knuckles rapped on the window. Recognising Mr Sanderton, however, she wound the window down.

"Playing up again, is it? Shall I have a look under the bonnet for you? I've got a torch."

Rose climbed out and gratefully, though shivering somewhat in the winter evening, held the torch while Mr Sanderton peered into the engine and fiddled about. "Now try her," he said at last.

She slid back behind the wheel and once more attempted to start the car. This time there was only a weak and fading groan and her second attempt was greeted by complete silence.

"Are you an AA member?" enquired Sanderton, coming round to her window again.

"No."

"You should be. Make a note of it. It looks," he said, "as though you'll have to leave it here for tonight. That garage down the road'll be shut by now. You can see them about it in the morning. Meanwhile, can I give you a lift home?"

"Oh, no . . . no, thank you." It would have been all right if he hadn't in the past asked her out, but he had, and even though he hadn't mentioned the matter for some time now, she felt awkward about being alone in a car with him. Besides, suppose someone saw them and gossiped? What if Charan heard she had been seen in a car with a man? "I can get a bus just outside the gate. It's not really late. I shall be quite all right."

Mr Sanderton's face, always somewhat tense in expression, at once showed irritation and for an uncomfortable moment, Rose thought he was going to say something, to tell her not to be silly. If he did, she wouldn't know how to answer.

371

But he thought better of it and withdrew his head from her window. "Just as you like. I've got a note of the garage's phone number somewhere. I'll look it out and leave it on your desk in the morning. You're sure . . . ?"

"Yes, thank you. It's very kind of you but the bus goes so near my home."

"All right. Goodnight," said Mr Sanderton, a little huffily, and went. She heard him slam the door as he got into his own car, and then saw his headlights veer across the asphalt as he swung towards the drive. She then regretted having refused him. The bus journey home suddenly looked very long and tiring.

She got out of the hateful Mini, which she would very much have liked to kick, and realised that the evening was now very cold indeed and likely to get colder. She preferred to use the heater and drive uncluttered, and had taken, in winter, to coming to school in slacks and sweater. She wore those at home sometimes, and so did not have the bother of changing in and out of salwar kameeze. But she kept a coat in the back of the car. She retrieved it, picked up her handbag and then, out of habit, locked her useless transport. She looked round.

There was still a light in the staffroom but none of the others lived in her direction and she did not want to be a nuisance by asking for a lift which would take someone out of their way, even if the someone were Mrs Hoxley. She shrugged into her coat and set off on foot towards the drive.

She was halfway up it, head bent into what was now a sharp wind, when from the shadowy bushes beside her, a deeper shadow emerged and solidified and there was a hand round her wrist and a voice whispered, "Hello, sweetheart." She drew back with a sharp cry, trying to wrench herself free, heart pounding and veins shot through with fear. "Come on, now. I won't hurt you if you're good," and she saw that in the man's spare hand, there was a knife.

The caretaker might have an assistant now, but they were both elderly and no doubt it was a long time since either of them had thought to push their way into the middle of the shrubbery. There was, she found a moment later as she was pulled into the heart of the bushes and shoved down on to the earth and the leafmould, a positive nest there. The pot-smoking youths of three years ago were gone but it had remained far too easy to get in through the fence. For how many weeks, she wondered, had this creature lurked here of an evening watching children and teachers go along the drive and waiting for his chance?

Blessedly alone at last, she crouched on her knees in the bushes throwing up, casting out not only the coffee and biscuits she had consumed at the meeting but the smell and touch of the man who had attacked her: his dirty, flapping greatcoat and his groping hands, his hot, slobbering mouth and the hard, throbbing part of him which he had driven into her.

When the retching stopped at last, she went on crouching, unable to make herself move because she did not know where to move to. A car went by, one of the last committee members going home, presumably. She let it pass.

She ought to get up, run back to the school or to the caretaker's house, tell someone, use the phone, call the police. But she couldn't do any of these things. The only people entitled to do indignant, authoritative things like that were people who were entitled to be alive to do them and she had no business whatsoever to be alive. She had been raped, and she hadn't fought back.

She had not fought because of the knife. She had been afraid of being killed. And so she had done nothing but try feebly and vainly to push him away, and whimper to him to stop, to let her go. She had put her life before her virtue.

She could not kneel in the shrubbery for ever. Somehow she made herself stand up. There were bruises on her arms and inside her thighs and a burning ache in her vagina but these things seemed local, even superficial. She stepped out on to the drive, took her coat off and shook it free of twigs and leafmould. Her slacks were torn but she found her handbag where she had dropped it when she was accosted, and in it were some safety pins. She secured the slacks and put on the coat again. It hid the damage. She found a handkerchief and wiped her face. Her chignon had come down but her bag held spare hairpins too. Her hands shook violently, but she managed to tidy her hair.

She could not go to the caretaker and demand a telephone. She could not possibly tell anyone what had happened. She thought about it again but was seized at once by a renewed retching.

Somehow she got over it and somehow, too, she stilled her trembling. There seemed to be nothing to do but go home.

She was on the bus before it occurred to her that she would probably have been perfectly safe with Mr Sanderton. It was black humour, in a way; a vicious jest on the part of fate.

She sat, clasping her hands tightly in her lap, fighting a surge of tears and crazy laughter, holding down hysteria.

Chapter Thirty-One

Secret
1987

Before getting off the bus, she examined her appearance in her handbag mirror, removed a few small leaves from her hair and put some make-up on her face. When she arrived home, her parents were in a fuss because she was late but the excuse that the Mini had broken down and that she had had a long, cold wait for a bus was sufficient.

No one must know what had happened. No one must ever, ever, know. She had set this up in her mind like a wall, and shock and hysteria, the desire to throw herself into her mother's arms and sob it all out, the desire to seek comfort or redress, must all be confined behind that wall.

She went to the bathroom and washed, removing the traces of blood. She changed all her clothes and put on a salwar kameeze suit, clean and fresh. She would never again wear the clothes in which she had been attacked. Tomorrow she would smuggle her stained, torn underwear out of the house and throw them in a trash bin somewhere.

She went downstairs and said that she felt off-colour; she had been fretting about Satnam all day, and she had been thoroughly chilled, waiting for that bus. After the meal, she said that she would like an early night. She went upstairs again, and back into the bathroom, where she ran a hot, deep tub. She washed herself again, this time from head to foot, including her hair. When she had got it dry, she went straight to bed, turned the light out and lay in the dark, trying once more to confront the thing which had been done to her.

She had been raped. No amount of hot baths, disinfectant or scrubbing could cleanse her of that. It was for all time.

She had only one lifeline. Except for her assailant, who was a stranger, no one knew but herself.

And once more, that single sentence recited itself over in her brain. *No one must ever know.*

As long as nobody knew, as long as she never had to speak of it, never had to relive it in words or look into the eyes of anyone who knew about it, she might one day forget it.

She ought to report it. She knew that perfectly well. Because of her silence, some other girl might meet the same fate, might even be killed. She realised this fully but there was nothing to be done. She could not go to her parents and present them with this; still less could she go into a police station. She imagined her parents' stricken faces, their recoil. She imagined the assessing eyes of a detective, the demands for detail. She had read newspaper reports of how women who complain of rape were questioned.

Can you describe the man, Miss Virk? Was it someone you knew?

No, of course not! He was a stranger in a smelly coat and . . .

Did you scream? Fight? Mark him? Are you marked yourself?

No . . .

Why not?

Because he had a knife and I was frightened. I let him do it because he was holding the knife against my throat.

Are you sure he was a stranger? Not someone you were meeting in the drive? Someone you had an argument with?

No, no, no!

What precisely did he do, Miss Virk? said a detective in a smelly overcoat, leaning over her and breathing heavily into her face. You must tell us everything, in *precise detail.* She woke up in the darkness, sobbing and nauseated.

Probably it wouldn't be like that at all. She was a girl of good character and there had been intruders in the school grounds before. Probably, the police would be perfectly considerate.

But she would have to describe what had happened and once it became official, she couldn't see how to keep it from her parents and . . .

If Charan were to find out . . .

Rose stumbled out of bed, back to the bathroom and was extremely sick for the second time.

She was rinsing her mouth out afterwards when a monstrous thought struck her. What if she were pregnant?

She knew the facts of life. She had been taught about them at school and Nita too had instructed her, simply, sensibly and in a fair amount of depth. The likeliest time for a pregnancy to start was a fortnight before a period was due. She was very regular and her next one was due in four days, in fact on Friday. Very likely, she would be all right. But the four days must be lived through first.

Afterwards, she never could remember how she succeeded in living through them. She had not the slightest idea what she would do if the worst had happened. She got up on the Tuesday morning, went to school by bus, timing the journey so that she could walk down the drive together with other people. Mr Sanderton brought the promised phone number and she arranged for the garage to remove her Mini and repair it. In the evening, to her relief, she was able to collect it and drive home.

Wednesday came, and Thursday. She marked registers, took classes, and inadvertently impressed her aggressive form so much with her cold and distant air that by the end of Thursday they were extremely well in hand. She made a good deal of fuss about the three pupils who had been caught trying to creep out through the hole in the fence and actually succeeded in getting it repaired. No one now would be able to enter the grounds except through the gates. For an intruder to reach the shrubbery unobserved would henceforth be very difficult.

On Thursday evening, she went with her parents and Charan to visit the house which he was buying and discuss carpets and kitchen fittings. She planned normal-sounding things to say, rehearsed them inside her head, and spoke them like an actress playing a part. Once, despite her efforts, Charan did notice that she seemed distracted and asked her if anything were wrong. She said hurriedly, "Oh, Satnam comes to mind sometimes," and felt ashamed, because she hadn't thought of him for days and yet was using him as an excuse.

Friday came. And disappointed her.

Throughout the day, she went to the toilet frequently, and in vain. Fear settled within her and began to grow.

She slept little that night, falling into a doze only at dawn, and woke to further disappointment. There were things to do in the house and in the afternoon she went shopping with her mother. She struggled on with her pretence of normality while her churning mind sought a way out of the trap. She would have to go to a doctor. Not Dr Chowdhuri; it would have to be someone she didn't know. Weren't there associations where girls in her probable condition could go? If she were quick enough, it might, just, be possible to have the pregnancy terminated without her family knowing. She might meanwhile try what some more hot baths could do. Perhaps she could engineer a fall downstairs. A heavy shopping bag might help. "Let me carry that one," she said to her mother. "It's too much for you, I'm sure it is."

"I really must get a trolley," said Nita, exchanging bags gratefully. "Thank you, dear. We must come shopping for your wedding clothes, soon. You're to have a sari for the first ceremony, when you and Charan meet face to face at our house, and then a salwar kameeze with a gold-embroidered veil for the Gurudwara ceremony. And about jewellery . . . "

Nita talked wedding all the way home and Rose, thankful that she need only listen, walked beside her in silence. When they arrived home, Perry and Shanti, for the first time since Satnam's arrest, were there.

Perry had seen him lately. "It is heartbreaking," he said. "He is so sullen and distant. When will he ever come home again? What future will he have? Rupa has gone to see him today. He seems to talk to her more easily than to me."

"If I were you," Kartar said, "I should wash my hands of him. He'll never bring you anything but heartbreak. Let Shanti drive home, Perry, and have a whisky. You need it."

"I can't just wash my hands of him," said Perry. "He's my son. Nothing will ever change that." He did not look towards Shanti as he spoke. He took the glass which Kartar held out to him. "He was named after a school friend of mine," said Perry wretchedly, "another Satnam, who was killed in the Partition riots. And all my Satnam wants to do is to kill. Oh, God."

"But there is other news, better news!" Shanti said in a brisk voice. "Satnam is not our only child. What a pair Balbir and Nerin are! You will never guess what they have been planning – oh, for months – and have never said a word about until now."

"Yes, I told them they should take up poker," said Perry, and they could see the effort he made to brighten. He had grey in his beard, Rose noticed. It seemed to have appeared all in a few weeks. For the first time, she realised that her father's beard was greying, too, that he was no longer a young man. If he ever learned what had befallen her, what would it do to him? Her eyes stung at the thought of it. Only one thing would hurt her more, and that would be if Charan learned of it. She shivered at the thought, and her stomach clenched.

"So, what's their secret?" Kartar was asking.

"Balbir – well, and Nerin too – are going into business. They are buying a place in Wiltshire and starting up as market gardeners. Tomatoes, potatoes, green vegetables and so forth. They've been negotiating and raising a loan and they didn't want to tell anyone until it was definite. Now," said Perry, "they've sprung it on us that they're moving in January. We shall all be asked to a party there in the summer, when they've got it straight. The house," he added, "is in a terrible state, from what they say. It's the land they care about!"

"Well, that is very good news," said Kartar in a hearty voice and frowned as Ranbir, who was sitting beside him, said dissentingly, "But they are moving away from our community. I think that is a pity."

"No, no," said Shanti protestingly. "It is so enterprising."

"And Balbir is very orthodox; I am sure that will never change," said Nita.

Rose, murmuring an excuse, slipped out of the room.

Upstairs in the toilet, she confirmed it. That dull aching clench in the abdomen had suddenly felt familiar. It had not lied. A few moments of distraction, looking at her father and at Perry, had been enough to let nature work. She was not pregnant. That anxiety at least was lifted.

In the bare, institutional room at the prison, Rupa sat and looked across the table at her brother. She had been talking of ordinary things: her children, and the gossip of the Gurudwara, and Satnam had been listening, but she knew that there was something he wanted to say. Only, he was finding it difficult. An account of how little Jaspal, only a few months old, was already beginning to look just like his father, ground to a halt. "Satnam?"

"Father came last week," said Satnam. "But not Mother. She's never come. Is she going to?"

The words came out aggressively, like a challenge. But his eyes were saying something different. Rupa read the message.

I want her to come. I need her.

She took a deep breath. Perry had warned her that this might happen. "With me he keeps up this sullen front," her father had said. "And with his brothers. But you are a girl and you say he talks to you and seems glad to see you. If he asks about your mother, the one he will ask will most likely be you. You must

379

think how to answer. But it may be no good to lie."

"Satnam. She has been so hurt. She . . . "

Rupa broke off. *She refuses to come* were words too harsh, too cruel; she could not say them to him.

But Satnam had understood. "She isn't coming, is she? She's turned her back on me. I'll be here for years; you realise that, don't you? And she'll let me rot."

"We shan't let you rot, Satnam. We'll always come: Surjit and me, and your brothers and their wives, and your father. If . . . if it is years," said Rupa valiantly, "well, Mother will come round in the end, I'm sure of it."

Satnam raised his chin. "She needn't. If she can do without me, I can do without her. You can tell her so."

"I shall tell her no such thing."

"You may as well. When she feels like coming, maybe I won't want to see her."

"Let's leave the subject," said Rupa. "Let's just leave it."

Years. Years of places like this. It was hard to imagine what it felt like to be Satnam now but when she tried, it was like peering into hell.

Two days later, Kartar went down with flu. Three days after that, Rose woke up to find herself markedly out of sorts, with a sore throat which seemed to reach right into her ears. She went to work in spite of it but during the day felt feverish and came home. Her lips hurt as well as her throat and examining herself in the mirror, she observed that she had a couple of unsightly cold sores.

Something that she had at some time read or heard drifted into her mind. A new dread, cold and ugly, took possession of her.

She had been raped by a dirty, smelly stranger. One could catch other things from that besides pregnancy. One could catch VD. One could catch Aids.

Neither her mother nor her school had given her any details of such things beyond the fact that they existed. She hadn't enough knowledge. She worried all through the long week while she was having influenza – though the flu did seem genuine – and then bethought herself of the *Encyclopedia Britannica*. There would be one in the public library. On the way home from her first day back at work, she visited the library and pored over the relevant entry.

The list of possible diseases was formidable and most of them, alarmingly, seemed to be slow developers. If she had contracted syphilis, then skin and mouth lesions might well be the first indication of which she was aware, and they could begin between ten days and ten weeks after being first infected. She touched her mouth gingerly. It was in fact much better now and her father had had cold sores too, along with his flu. Hers had appeared rather earlier than the encyclopedia said and probably meant nothing.

But she could still have syphilis. She might in due course have more sores, more fevers or headaches or bad throats, which this time would not be due to flu. And even if she didn't, it wouldn't prove that she was not infected. The disease could still be present.

If she had gonorrhoea, she should have had a slight discharge with a burning sensation, which might pass off by itself. Possibly there would be fever and pains in the lower abdomen.

She didn't know. She had stomach cramps every month anyway and she'd had a temperature with the flu. She had been sore after the attack. She hadn't noticed anything else, not after she'd cleaned up the bleeding which it had caused. But how could one tell for sure?

There was a pamphlet in the library too, about Aids. She read that as well. If she'd caught Aids, she might not know for a long, long time. But if she had, it wasn't curable.

There were ways to find out. You could go to a doctor or one of the clinics one saw advertised in public loos, and have a blood test. For Aids, you'd need another in three months' time.

Rose tried to imagine going to a clinic. There would be other victims there. They would be very different from herself. There would be people among them who came from a moral underworld which had nothing to do with her; which she could not bear the thought of entering. She could perhaps go to a doctor she didn't know, as she had thought of doing if she were pregnant.

She ought to go. If she needed treatment, she should obtain it. Fail to do so and she might pass disease on to Charan.

She went back to the encyclopedia and sat staring at it. Even her feelings about Charan had altered now. When they were married, he would make love to her. The thing first experienced in horror and fear among the bushes of the school shrubbery

381

would be legalised, honourable, part of him and her. But could she face it, now? Would her mind, her body, hopelessly confuse him with the smelly horror in the flapping greatcoat and make her shudder away even from Charan?

But I can get over that, she thought. I can, I can! Dear Charan. I won't, won't, won't, let myself mix him up with that creature in the shrubbery. They're both men but they're not the same. I won't make Charan suffer for what that creature did. I won't let love be smeared by a crude, beastly crime. I will command myself. What Charan and I will do is *making love*. I may be weak and timid and ignorant but I'm not completely useless. I will make love with Charan and learn to enjoy it. I will not hurt him.

Then she must have the blood tests. Because to marry him without making sure that she could not infect him would be to risk hurting him in about as nasty a way as could be imagined.

Getting away anywhere by herself was always difficult but she managed it the next day by leaving the school early on the plea of feeling ill. She did not go home, however, but drove to an Underground station and caught a train into London. According to the telephone directory, there was a women's hospital in Soho. She would go there. They might at least be able to advise her where best to seek help and the staff might be female, too. It would be easier to explain to a woman.

She found the hospital, walked up and down outside it for some time and went away.

Even for Charan, she couldn't do it. Even for Charan, she couldn't open her mouth and say the words *I have been raped. I'm afraid I may have VD*. To say it, she thought illogically, would make it true.

Halfway home, she realised how extremely silly she had been and took a fresh resolution. Mrs Hoxley, she knew, went to a woman doctor.

"We might move into your area after we're married," she said casually to Mrs Hoxley. After the debacle with her engagement to Jasbir, she had been shy of discussing her new engagement much. Mrs Hoxley did not know that the house was already bought, or that it was close to Rose's present home. "Do you think your area is convenient, generally speaking? What's the shopping centre like? And how far are you from your doctor? We'll need to get on to a local panel and I like the idea of a woman doctor."

Mrs Hoxley was willing to chat. Rose emerged from the conversation with not only with the name and address of Mrs Hoxley's doctor but also with innumerable details of the whereabouts of banks, building societies, supermarkets and Marks & Spencer.

She checked the doctor's phone number in the directory and used a callbox. "I'm a stranger in this district," she explained. "But I need to consult a doctor. Could I make an appointment?"

"What's your name?" said the receptionist on the other end. "Where are you staying? The address, please."

"Oh, . . . er . . . my name's Raminder Singh. Miss. I'm staying at . . . at . . . " she peered out of the telephone box and saw the name of the residential road in which it stood. "Forty two, Throgmorton Street. Could I have an appointment this evening?"

"No, not this evening. Dr Armstrong is fully booked all today. Tomorrow's Saturday and there's a slot in the morning, at five past ten. Would that suit you?"

"Oh, yes, thank you."

She would get away somehow to keep the appointment. She would say she wanted to go to the school and do something or other connected with the Christmas play. It would be held next week; the excuse was quite reasonable. This time she wouldn't lose her nerve.

When she reached home, Amrit was waiting to talk to her. "I thought we could go to the West End together for shopping tomorrow morning, Rose. I want to buy you a wedding present. Would you like a sari or some satin suit material or some earrings?"

"It isn't till April!" said Rose.

"That's no time at all. Are you going to cry on your wedding day? I shall on mine," said Amrit. "I want to do every single thing according to custom. Rose, who are you going to ask to your Sangeet? Have you thought about it yet . . . ?"

"Excuse me," mumbled Rose, and blundered out of the room. Flat on her face on her bed, she gave herself up to despair. She was never going to get to a doctor. She couldn't go tomorrow; there was no way at all she could get out of shopping with Amrit. Amrit would say, but why can't you come, it's such fun with all the Christmas crowds, what are you going to do at the school that's so important, tell me. And she'd have to invent and her brain didn't seem equal to it.

Also, a ghastly new ramification had now presented itself. What if she did have a disease? What if the wedding had to be postponed or even called off and the reason got out and caused a scandal? What of Amrit then? Her marriage prospects might not be damaged by Satnam but they would certainly be damaged by this.

Amrit would break her heart and she would very likely hold Rose to blame. Her sister, Rose thought, was very self-centred in some ways. But it was not wrong to want to be married, and not fair to have one's chances spoilt by something that had happened to somebody else.

Jasbir had had his chances spoilt by that, after all.

She didn't know what to do. She couldn't now get to the doctor tomorrow, but if she got to one later and one of the tests proved positive . . .

Even if it were curable, it might still mean delay and she would have to tell her parents and how could it be explained to Charan? In her imagination she saw the hurt in Charan's eyes, saw her mother's face as she heard how her daughter had been flung down on the leafmould under the bushes, to absorb the semen and perhaps the disease of a criminal stranger in a dirty overcoat.

Her mother came into the room. "I was looking for you, Rose . . . Rose? Whatever's the matter? Are you ill?"

She longed for her mother's comfort but dared not seek it. And although that really wasn't the worst thing her assailant had, or might have, done to her; weirdly enough, it felt as though it was.

"I just feel funny," Rose sobbed. "I don't know what's the matter with me. I just feel nervous and upset."

"Wedding nerves? Is everything all right with you and Charan? You haven't seen very much of him lately; you keep saying you're so busy with school things. Have you quarrelled?"

"No, no, it's nothing like that!"

"I think you're run down," said Nita briskly. "You're doing too much and you had that terrible cold and there is the wedding to plan as well. I think I should take you to Dr Chowdhuri."

Chapter Thirty-Two

The Bruised Apple
1987-88

Dr Chowdhuri made a few waggish and avuncular remarks about young ladies at crucial moments in their lives, assured her that before she had been married a week she would be laughing at herself, but recommended a short course of Valium meanwhile.

The Valium produced results that were nearly magical.

Calmly, she reassured Kartar when, earnestly and formally, he asked her if she were really happy about marrying Charan and told her that if she had doubts, he would take the responsibility of ending the engagement. "You can go away for a holiday."

"No, truly, I am very happy to be marrying Charan. I've been overworking, and I went back too soon after the flu."

She said the same thing to Nita when Nita came to her room one evening and said, "Rose, dear, is it the physical side you are worrying about? Have some silly women been trying to frighten you? Believe me, there is nothing at all to fear. It is the happiest thing in the world. Look round you at all the happy married women there are – they wouldn't be like that if there were anything dreadful about it."

"I know," said Rose, and repeated her little story about overwork and illness.

Charan came over to see them and she made herself talk to him cheerfully, and discuss furniture. And she nerved herself at last to find a doctor; not Mrs Hoxley's but another one, discovered by driving round until she found a brass plate proclaiming a woman doctor. She made determined excuses about staying late at the school, and took the necessary blood tests. The results were negative.

"I should say you're perfectly clear," said Dr Margaret Devine.

"When did this happen, you say? At the end of November? At the beginning of March we'll take one more test to make sure that you're not HIV-positive – that's the Aids test – but the chances are that you're not. Your wedding isn't until April, so you'll be able to be sure before that. But don't worry yourself. You're almost certainly all right. Look, you say you were attacked . . . "

"I was, but no one must know. You don't understand. In my culture, it's such a terrible thing if a girl loses her honour."

"You do realise that this man is still at large and a possible danger to others?"

"Yes, I know. But . . . " Rose looked desperate.

"All right. It's for you to say."

"Would it be possible for you to report to the police that . . . that this has happened to someone without giving details?"

"Yes, I could do that. I know some of the local police, as it happens. Doctors usually do."

"But you won't mention who I am?" said Rose in a panic.

"I certainly shan't break your confidence. Besides," said Dr Devine candidly, "I suspect I don't know who you are. I'm fairly sure you don't live where you say. But we'll let that go. Only, please come back in March."

She didn't like being dependent on Valium and stopped using it after the results of the first blood test, but returned to it in order to get herself back to the doctor for the March test. This too was negative. "You are all right," said Dr Devine. "You are *all right*. Forget what happened. Go and live your life and be happy. There is no reason at all why you shouldn't. Good luck to you and a happy wedding day."

And only five minutes later, it seemed, it was the week of her wedding and the day of her Sangeet party.

They would use the dining room for the Sangeet, Nita decided, because then they could push the dining table against one wall and set out refreshments there. They'd need plenty; there would be a big crowd of ladies. Records of Indian music would be played and there would be room too for the ladies to get up and dance. The men might come in at the end and video the dancing.

The morning was a daze of preparation. Furniture must be moved and the customary white sheet spread on the floor. Sandalwood tapers were put in place ready to be lit. There were sweetmeats to make and others to collect from the confectioner.

"You, me, Bheji, Amrit, and Rupa's coming and Lynn," Nita said, working out the numbers on her fingers. "Shanti auntie – how brave she is being. It is a terrible business with Satnam. Ten years inside; it is like a lifetime. How Shanti bears up, I do not know. We shall have Charan's mother, and Mrs Sodhi and her married daughter who is visiting from Canada, and all our friends from the Gurudwara. And Swarup Sharma and her sister and her cousin-sister and three of their daughters-in-law – I have never sorted out quite which of them is which, I must say, but how nice that in spite of all the troubles we are all still friends. Lynn's mother is coming, and Mrs Chowdhuri . . . "

"And Sita," said Rose, and they both laughed.

"It was most obliging of Hari to choose this month to visit India," Nita said. "Of course, it's right that Dinesh should see his relatives there. But best of all, it's left Sita free. She'll come with her mother. Now then, which records would you like to have?"

Since the bride didn't dress up for the Sangeet. Rose put on an old salwar kameeze in a muted pink and brown pattern, pleasing but not outstanding, and did not make up her face. Amrit, by contrast, devoted half an hour to painting her lovely, static features and emerged from her bedroom looking like a work of art, dressed in a turquoise silk tunic and trousers, her pearly fair complexion framed by long gold earrings and her gleaming black plaits threaded with gold tinsel.

"Pooh!" said Kartar, making believe to hold his nose. "What did you put your perfume on with, Amrit? A watering can?"

"Anyone would think you were the bride!" said Rose with amusement.

There was an atmosphere about a Sangeet. It was at once a time of rejoicing and dedication, of frivolity and risqué merriment, and the most reverent laying of foundations for a new family, a new partnership, from which would come a future generation.

It was early April but it was a cold day with a grey sky. The room, however, was centrally heated and beautifully lit. It possessed two gold-shaded wall lamps already and Nita, after some experiment, had augmented these with a powerful standard lamp and two small lamps borrowed from bedside tables. They all had shades in gold or pink. The overhead light was turned off and the lamps between them cast a warm, intimate glow

387

which flattered complexions and sparkled softly on bangles and silks and smiling dark eyes.

The air smelt of sandalwood from the smoking tapers, and the ladies' perfumes and, a little, of the sweetmeats which had been cooked in the kitchen next door. But at first, the recorded music was not put on. To begin with, they would make their own music. Nita and Ranbir, who were acting as the hostesses, were seated cross-legged in the middle of the carpet, each with a small hand-drum, on which they were tapping out the rhythms for the songs.

It's like a dream, Rose thought. She was, she realised, very tired and she was glad that her mother and grandmother were in charge of the occasion, that she herself had only to sit on her pile of cushions and smile and be sung to.

But it was a lovely, kind and soothing dream. No! Rose said to herself, with an unexpected lightening of the heart. It wasn't a dream; it was reality. It was the beginning of her marriage to Charan, which was her proper destiny. The horror in the shrubbery had been the dream, or nightmare.

The singing began with just her mother and grandmother and Amrit, but gradually everyone joined in. The room was crowded and few faces were missing. Nerin, busy in Wiltshire, had not been able to come, but it was wonderful to see Sita at a family occasion for once. She was subdued, as always, but at least she was here, sitting beside Leela and singing with the rest.

It was delightful too, to watch Bheji. She had made an astounding recovery from her operation, although she still, to Rose's eyes, looked a little shrunken, a little smaller than before. But her thin brown hands tapped the drum with authority, never losing the beat for an instant.

Her grandmother had mellowed, Rose thought. She was on good terms now with Lynn. The last barrier between them had gone down the moment that Lynn produced her daughter Tina, and had warmed into near-enthusiasm when Jonathan came along. Jon was now asleep in a carrycot in a corner, with his sister beside him on a cushion. Lynn was sitting between Rupa and Swarup Sharma. Lynn couldn't join in the singing very much because most of the songs were in Punjabi but her companions were whispering the gist of them to her every now and then.

It would be a good idea, Rose thought, to translate some of the traditional songs and write them down for Lynn.

"We are all getting dry!" Nita exclaimed, as they all paused for breath after a particularly lively song. "I will bring tea, and there's plenty of fruit juice in the jugs on the table there."

Ranbir started to struggle up from the floor, apparently in order to go to the refreshment table, but Swarup Sharma, rising busily to her feet, waved her back. "No, no, I have told Nita I would see to the jugs. I would like to help. I will pour you a fruit juice or would you like tea instead?"

"Oh, I will have orange juice. It is hot in here now."

"I will bring it to you, Bheji," Rose said.

She went to the table, behind which Swarup was already installed. "Your mother," said Swarup, "always does everything so well. Such a fine selection of juices. And what a happy occasion this is. Ranbir is well again, and it is so nice to see dear Sita here with us, and her mother. But it is a pity Krishna is not with us. It was a terrible thing about Krishna."

"It may have been best in the end," said Rose mildly. People were crowding round the table and she found her sister beside her. "Amrit, take this glass to Bheji. Krishna's job has taken her to Italy now," she said to Swarup. "She is earning very well."

"We all know that times are changing," Swarup said, tossing a length of violet sari out of the way over a plump, smooth shoulder as she used two hands to fill a row of cardboard beakers from a heavy jug. "But there was so much talk about that. To run off on the eve of her wedding in that fashion! She would do well to stay abroad, because people would certainly look askance at her now. It is a good thing she has no younger sisters wanting to get married; this sort of thing casts a reflection on a family. People say, now why did that girl run away, what was she afraid of? Had she some secret to hide?"

"Yes, well, it was all some time ago." Leela emerged from the throng. "I think we made a mistake when we urged her into that marriage; it was not a suitable match. At the time it seemed the best thing, but . . . "

"And why it should not be the best thing?" said Swarup with energy. "What did she have against it? Well, one is forced to wonder . . . "

"Excuse me," said Nita, arriving with a colossal teapot. It was kept for large gatherings and it was first cousin to a commercial urn. Shanti was beside her with a tray of teacups. "I need a space to put this down . . . you've spread all over the space I left, Swarup," said Nita protestingly.

"Oh, I am sorry. Here . . . " Swarup pushed beakers and jugs out of the way. "We were just saying, about Krishna, what a thing it was. Did you ever know why she did such a thing, Leela? Could there have been some man in her life and perhaps she thought her bridegroom would find out?"

"I doubt it," Leela said with a shrug. Swarup Sharma could be quite maddening, Rose thought. She never minded opening old wounds. But Leela, after all this time, had become indifferent. "We think," she said, "that it was just that she wished for her freedom and her job. Girls are different these days."

"Some things will never be different." Swarup shook her head. "If a girl does something she should not, if she is spoiled goods, well, that is a difficult thing to hide."

"Yes, that is so," Nita said. "A man always knows. These days, with tampons and so much sport at school, perhaps it is not so obvious, but there is still something different in a girl's eyes. Bheji told me that once and I think it is true. I think no man can ever quite forgive it, if after the marriage ceremony, he realises that he is not the first. We have taken such care to bring Rose up wisely, and she has not disappointed us."

Rose, desperately, buried her face in a teacup.

Mohan Lal had been with the men in the other room and helped with the camera when they came in at the end to video the ladies dancing. He and Leela gave Sita a lift home. "No, we won't come in," Leela said. "I am feeling rather tired. We will talk about it all on the phone tomorrow. What a good time we have had!" Sita stood under the lamppost by the gate to wave them goodbye as the car retreated, and went to unlock her front door. And noticed, as she stood close to its frosted glass panel, that there was a faint glow from within, as though a light were in on the rear of the house.

But Hari and Dinesh were away. Burglars? Did burglars put lights on? Didn't they use torches only? Maybe they didn't have any rules about it. She stood fearfully on the step and then heard, faintly, from within, the sound of Dinesh's favourite tape playing. She unlocked the door and went inside. Their suitcases were in the hall.

Hari came out of the dining room. "So you are home. And where have you been, may I ask?"

"To Rose's Sangeet. Shanti's niece. You know about it; she is getting married this week. She had her Sangeet party at

390

her home today."

"Come." She followed Hari dutifully back into the dining room. "I do not like it that you go gadding here and there the moment my back is turned. I am not keen on you mixing with those people; they are Sikhs and it is better we don't mix with Sikhs. How many times must I tell you?"

India had been bad for him, Sita thought unhappily. Since the day when he told her that he married her for revenge, she had despised as well as feared him and it seemed that he had sensed this and that it had somehow dulled his edge. The stretches of bearable aridity had grown longer; the patches of violence and sexual distortion briefer and less intense. During these times, she kept his rules and he made occasional threats against her or Dinesh or Aunt Savitri, but nothing actually happened. But now, she saw that he had slipped back.

"It was only a Sangeet," she said placatingly. "There was nothing political. No one said anything about . . . "

"I'm tired and hungry," said Hari. He took off his spectacles and began to polish them ominously. "I've just had a fourteen-hour flight. I come home wanting a welcome, a hot meal and someone to unpack for me and what do I find? A cold, dark, empty house, no sign of my wife . . . "

"But you didn't let me know you were coming. I'm so sorry. Of course I'd have been here if I'd known. I'll get you some food." Moving towards the kitchen, she added, trying to change the subject, "Did Dinesh like India? How is Aunt Savriti?"

"You don't get out of it that way." Hari moved quickly, interposing himself between her and the door. "I don't have to tell you my movements. I expect you to be here when you're wanted, not imagining you can go out having a good time when I'm out of sight. Your place is here in this house. You should be in it unless I've given you permission to go out."

"But," said Sita, feeling her shoulders sag, "you never do give your permission. I need friends sometimes, Hari. I need company, to talk to other ladies . . . "

"Talk to them about what? About me? You want to go and gossip to them about me, eh? Is that it?" Hari shoved his glasses back into place, caught her shoulders and began to shake her. "Will you never learn? I will make you regret this. I will write to my stepfather and say, see how your wife's niece behaves and then Savitri will regret it too!" Her head was jerking back and forth with such violence that she was afraid her neck would snap. "Stop . . . Hari . . . no, don't, please stop..!"

"Excuse me," said Dinesh politely, walking into the room. He stepped up to them, reached out with a long, well-proportioned hand, already more like a man's hand than a boy's, removed the spectacles from his father's nose, threw them on the floor and stamped on them.

There was a staggered, unbelieving pause. It was as though the foundations of the house had shifted under their feet, or the axis of the earth had tilted the other way. Then Hari recovered his powers of speech and movement.

"What the hell are you doing?" He let go of Sita and lunged for his son but Dinesh merely sidestepped and his father blundered into the sideboard. Hari swung round and lunged again, groping, inadvertently knocking a bowl of fruit off the sideboard and overturning a side table. Dinesh pushed him off balance, so that he toppled into an armchair. Sita, staring at her son in amazement, saw that although Dinesh was only just sixteen, he was extremely well-grown for his age. Even during his brief absence in India he seemed to have added height and muscle, and his face had acquired the shaping of maturity. He was extraordinarily sure in his movements, as though his body were controlled by a mind much older than its housing.

"Now then," said Dinesh, standing over his purblind parent. "You just sit there and *listen!*"

"How dare you talk to me like that? I'm your father. Sita, bring me my spare glasses."

"Don't do it, Mother." Dinesh loomed over Hari, one hand on each chair-arm. "As long as he hasn't got his glasses, he's harmless. Let's keep him that way for a while."

"You young . . . !" Hari heaved convulsively, swore and threw a punch which Dinesh parried almost casually.

"I said, *listen.*" Dinesh raised his voice. "I'm sick of your attitude to my mother. I thought it had improved lately, but evidently I was wrong. She's not dirt under your feet, you know . . . "

"I'll break your neck, you . . . "

"You will not. Mother, his spare glasses are on the mantelpiece. Put them on the table, where I can reach them and he can't. You'll listen to me, Father, or so help me God, I'll reach out and smash those as well and then where will you be? You'll need a white stick and a guide dog to get to the optician. You needn't think we'll help you. Why should we?"

392

"I've worked all my life to make an inheritance for you, that's why! "

"Oh, the shop? Forget it, Father. I don't want your rotten shop. I've decided to study engineering like Uncle Sunder . . . "

"He is not your uncle. He is your mother's cousin-brother only. What do you mean, you will study engineering? I have built this shop up . . . "

"You're welcome to it. I've more to say. I'm not only sick of your attitude to Mother, I'm also aware that at times you've blackmailed her through me and Aunt Savitri. Mother, if he ever again threatens to disinherit or otherwise misuse me, in order to make you do what he wants, ignore him. I can look after myself. As for Aunt Savitri, we left them only yesterday and you know as well as I do, Father, that Uncle Dinesh is a sick man and leans on Aunt Savitri now for everything . . . "

"What?" said Sita faintly. She was uneasily feeling her neck muscles, where they had been strained.

"Oh, yes." Dinesh did not take his eyes from his father but he spoke to her nevertheless. "There's no risk to Aunt Savitri any more, Mother. She is in control in that house and you need not fear for her ever again."

"Indeed!" said Sita. An extraordinary sensation was burgeoning in her, of lightness and liberation. For the first time in her horrible married life, she was able to think: I am not alone.

"And you, Father," said Dinesh grimly, "had better begin thinking of your future too. What with your worsening eyesight and the weight you're gaining, you'll be middle-aged before you know it and then you'll be old. What's going to happen then? I'll be adult and married in a few years; I'll offer my mother a home if necessary. I'll make it possible for her to abandon you. Then where will you be? If you want anyone to care for you when you're old, you'd better start earning the right to it now."

"Right to it? Right to it? I am a man of substance and I am only thirty-nine . . . "

"You look forty-nine. You're probably the type that ages early," said Dinesh inexorably.

Suddenly, Sita laughed.

Hari, infuriated, uttered a sound like a snarl. "Give me my glasses! Give them to me now!" He let out a volley of oaths and attempted to burst out of the chair. But Dinesh had been waiting for this. He stooped and heaved and the armchair went over backwards with Hari in it. He struggled out from under its upturned bulk, cursing and clutching at his left knee, and then made a rush towards them, hands outstretched. They evaded him easily and he blundered into the table. Dinesh neatly whisked the spare pair of glasses off it and pocketed them.

Hari veered, breath sobbing, eyes peering out of focus, identified the shadowy forms of his family and lurched forward again. The wreck of his original pair of spectacles crunched under his feet. Again his wife and son dodged, and he stopped, panting and staring; angry, frightening and also pathetic. *"Give me back my spectacles!"*

"No," said Sita. "Not yet. I want some promises from you first, Hari. And if you don't keep them, I shall pack my bags and go to stay with my mother or with friends while I divorce you. Don't think I won't. This time they will not persuade me back to try again. Times have altered. Divorce is not so unthinkable now and Dinesh has freed me from thinking I must stay here for his sake or Aunt Savitri's. But if you are nice to me, I will not expose your behaviour before a divorce court. Promise me there will be no more bullying, and that I can do reasonable, ordinary things like going to Sangeet parties when I wish, that is all. Give me your word and I will hand you your spectacles and fetch your food "

"Refuse to promise, and I'll smash the specs here and now," added Dinesh.

"Sita, I can't do without my glasses, I can't *see!*"

"I know."

"Then give them back!"

"Why?"

"Sita, give them back, you must give them back! You will in the end. You won't break them, or let Dinesh break them, you won't dare. And I warn you both, the longer you withhold them, the worse it will be for you."

"You've got that the wrong way round," observed Dinesh. "The longer you go on blustering and making threats, the worse it will be for *you.*"

"It's all right, Dinesh. Do you mean you want a divorce, Hari? You can't even cook. A fine mess you'll be in if I leave you on your own."

There was a silence.

"I'll go and get your dinner," said Sita coldly. "I'm sure it's true that you're tired and hungry."

"I can't see to eat!"

"Oh, you'll manage. Then we'll have a little talk. All I want," said Sita, "is that simple promise. And I rather think, Hari, that I'm going to get it."

"You are a bitch. All your family are worthless; now it seems I even have a worthless son!" Dinesh was right, Sita thought; her husband was putting on weight. He was standing there like a wounded bull. He was waiting his chance to charge.

"Do you remember," said Sita, "the day we were robbed in our shop? I hoped so much, that day, that those youths would actually kill you. It would have been such a relief to me. I really hate you, Hari. The things I have been tempted to do at times, you would hardly believe. I have looked at you when you were asleep and thought, shall I fetch a hammer and break your skull with it? I have made meals for you and thought how I should like to grind up a glass bangle and put that into the dish as well . . . "

They saw him break. They saw the shock strike all expression from his face, saw his jaw drop and heard him gasp.

"You . . . you . . . " It was not clear whether he was stammering over the choice of an epithet or merely trying to frame a disbelieving question. The eyes that could not see them clearly looked as though they were staring instead into a pit, whose existence they had only just discovered.

"I am sorry you had to hear that, Dinesh," Sita said. "It was most unfitting, but it had to be said. Hari, I shall bring your dinner now. There is curry ready and chapatti batter standing. It will be a good, wholesome meal; don't be afraid. And then, Hari dear, you will give me your promise and then you may have your spectacles back. And life from now on will be very very different."

At twelve forty-five a.m. Rose sat in her room, writing a letter.

It was a sad letter but she was not crying. Some things were too big, too awe-inspiring to be expressed by such commonplace things as tears.

In a couple of sentences, Swarup Sharma and her own mother had made her position plain. A few casual words, flung like fishing nets, had trawled her mind and brought from its depths the terrible thing which had lain there all along, unadmitted, all through her fear of pregnancy and the terror of disease.

She had been dishonoured. She had lost her virginity. And Charan would know.

He would know. If from nothing else, he would know from her eyes, her attitude, her thought waves. And he would turn from her in horror, for she was spoiled goods. It was not her fault but that did not matter. It was not the fault of an apple if it was pushed off a fruit-stall and bruised on the ground, but the bruise was there and a fastidious person would not want to eat that apple.

She had got through the rest of the Sangeet as a smiling automaton, while behind her bright facade she had looked at the alternatives, and reached a conclusion which now seemed so inevitable that she could hardly believe that she had woken up this morning expecting a future as Charan's wife.

There was only one way to regain her honour, only one thing to be done which would not leave her sharing the same sky with a Charan out of reach, or risk spoiling her sister Amrit's marriage chances as the harmless Jasbir's chances had been spoiled by his sister Pet.

She had thought of going without explanation, but on consideration she knew that this would not be right. Her parents and Charan were entitled to know why she had left them. Above all, Charan had to know. He could not be left thinking that she had not loved him after all.

She was very glad that Dr Chowdhuri had prescribed Valium for her and that she had got by without taking more than a small amount of it. She hoped that what was left would be enough, but she thought it would be, combined with the bottle of whisky which she had tiptoed downstairs to purloin from her father's sideboard.

She was sorry for the grief that awaited them all in the morning. When she thought about that, the tears did begin to prick her eyelids.

She experienced one moment of rebellion, of bitter resentment that she, who had done no wrong, nevertheless had no life to look forward to, must die at twenty-five with her only knowledge of love that monstrous travesty in the shrubbery.

But the rebellion passed. There was no way out but this. In time, they would all see that she had done what was best and she hoped they would remember her kindly.

Chapter Thirty-Three

Requiem
1988

The day of Rose's funeral was bright but there had been a late frost the night before. A sharp wind greeted the mourners as they parked their cars and walked up the path to where Kartar stood at the open front door to receive them.

"What do we do about the children? I can't find anyone to look after them at such short notice. And what do I wear?" Lynn said to Sunder rather nervously beforehand. "Indian mourning is pale, isn't it, not black? I want to do the right thing and so do my parents. This is so awful. Oh, poor, poor Rose. Why didn't she tell someone? To think of her brooding all alone like that. It's unbearable!"

"I know. Charan is almost beside himself. No one knows what to say to him. He was like a madman when Uncle Kartar told him, so my uncle says. We can take the children with us. They can stay back at the house while we go to the crematorium; there'll be a neighbour to keep an eye on them. Indian funerals aren't quite the same as English ones. Oh, what to wear . . . something dark will do if you feel more natural in it. I'm wearing a dark suit myself. I haven't got anything pale-coloured that looks quite right."

Kartar himself had adhered to tradition and was in a dun corduroy jacket and pale trousers. He clasped the hands of each arrival in turn. "Welcome . . . this is a sad day . . . thank you for coming . . . I'm glad you could come . . . thank you . . . " Voices were muted, tears not far below the surface. Kartar's brown eyes were bloodshot with grief. Charan was waiting in the hall behind, to give his own welcome to the mourners. He too was in an off-white suit, a lightweight probably bought to wear in the Canadian summer and pulled out of a suitcase for this horrible ceremony. He whispered the same greetings as Kartar and took their hands in the same way. His face had the blank, stricken look of someone shocked beyond the power of expressing it. Lynn and Sunder could hardly bear to meet his eyes.

Ahead of them, the door to the kitchen stood open and beyond it, the kitchen was quiet and polished and empty; the table in the middle divested even of a cloth. The whole house was hushed but not quite silent, for somewhere, the voice of a priest could be heard reading from the Sikh scriptures. Lynn, peering through the door to the dining room, glimpsed rich fabric and saw that the priest was a Sikh elder with a flowing white beard and a snow-white turban, and that he was installed in the room with his portable altar. The male mourners were gathering round him. Perry was by the door. He too murmured greetings, and then ushered Sunder forward. "Gentlemen this way, into the back room. Ladies and children in the front room. Your mother is already here, Lynn. She and your father were so early. They are very kind. People have been such a support." His voice faltered. "If only someone could have been a support to Rose."

The front room was packed. No one was missing. Nita and Ranbir, both in white, sat side by side, quiet and still as statues. Lynn went to them and embraced them. They returned the embrace, but silently, and she saw that they could not trust themselves to speak. She was glad that her own mother was there, and sat down near her, setting Jon's carrycot on the floor and taking Tina on her knee, and thought how hateful was the contrast with the Sangeet. No sandalwood tapers or music now, no gold and pink lamps picking up jewellery and silks; only cold sunlight and dull garments and faces full of sorrow.

A few ladies managed a little desultory talking. Nerin was telling someone that she and Balbir had driven up from Wiltshire that morning and how cold it had been. Swarup Sharma, speaking English as people often did when English guests were present, was telling Shanti what a terrible business it all was; what was the world coming to? Lynn, who had heard the whole story including the contents of Rose's letter, marvelled that Swarup was here at all. "But it was my fault too," Nita had said brokenly. "It was what we both said at the Sangeet. Neither of us meant any harm. How could we have known? Rose took everything too much to heart and we let her; we thought that was how she should be. We listened too much to Bheji, perhaps . . . but if we let Bheji realise that, she will die too, of heartbreak.

398

She loved Rose. Oh, my poor Rose. She was dead when I found her in the morning."

Amrit was sitting by Rupa, motionless alike in face and body. Rupa was murmuring to her and Amrit was presumably listening but she was not responding. The waiting went on and on and Lynn began to long for the next thing to happen, for this dreadful occasion to get on its way and be over.

At the front door, the influx of mourners had slowed down. Kartar came inside. Charan had disappeared and Perry was in the hall. "The hearse will be here in a few minutes," Kartar said. "I wish all this was behind us. I am worried about Charan. The poor fellow looks ready to collapse. Where is he now?"

"He said he must go to the bathroom." Satinder Singh came out into the hall. "My poor son. I think perhaps he wanted to break down a little, in private."

"I know," Kartar said. "This is terrible for him, terrible, as bad as for Nita and me. He really cared so much for her. If I could get my hands on the man who did it, I would kill him. I think perhaps he has been caught; the police have got a man who attacked a girl last week and perhaps it is the same. But whatever happens to him it will not be enough. There would be nothing of him left to stand trial if I could get at him."

In the bathroom, Charan was sponging his face in cold water. His skin and his eyes felt too dry and too hot, the results of long, sleepless nights of grief and rage. He dried himself on a towel and stood holding it, meeting his own eyes in the mirror above the sink.

The grief and rage were still with him. They were welded together into a burning knot in his stomach.

His beard was neatly rolled as usual for when one's whole world had disintegrated, it was more necessary than ever to hold on to one's dignity. But beneath it, his jaw muscles were clenched hard.

He had come to a decision.

From the window of the front room, the ladies saw the black hearse draw to a halt outside. "She has come home," said Nita, rising to her feet. "They have brought her home." With a commanding sign, she brought Ranbir and Amrit to their feet with her and the three of them moved to stand in the doorway, looking out into the hall.

Kartar was opening the front door wider, putting a doorstop

in place to hold it there. "Perry, fetch Charan. He asked to be a bearer."

"He's here," said Perry, as Charan came down the stairs. The three of them, together with Balbir, Sunder and Charan's brother Surjit, went out to meet the hearse. A few moments later, Rose was borne back into her home on their shoulders. Lynn, who had stood up to look into the hall from behind Amrit, saw the coffin go past the door and into the kitchen and realised suddenly what the empty table was for.

There was a slight grating sound as the coffin was set down on the table. And then, horrifyingly, the sound of someone plying a screwdriver.

Lynn found Shanti beside her. "Is this very strange to you? It is our custom. It is all right. We shall just file past the coffin and pay our last respects and look on her for the last time. It is just to say goodbye."

The priest came out of the dining room and went into the kitchen. They heard his voice begin a prayer, in a calm and steady tone. He must be used to this, Lynn thought. He uses that very level voice to damp down all this feeling under the surface, to keep things dignified. The air is so tense. I'd like to scream or cry or tear my hair, myself. I wish we could have just gone straight to the crematorium.

The men were beginning to file in a slow line into the kitchen, down one side, round the table, and then gathering on the other side of the room. The undertaker's men in their long black coats were waiting with them. The ladies followed the men. There was indeed a neighbour, English, who had taken charge of the children. Lynn, leaving Tina and the cot with her, went obediently with the rest. There was the sound of slowly shuffling feet, an occasional muffled sob, a slight hardening of the priest's steady voice as the emotional temperature increased.

Rose had been laid under the red and gold veil which she should have worn on her wedding day. Her head rested on a white pillow and her face was delicately painted, her eyelids and lips glossy, and her features so dwindled and so void of expression that they were unrecognisable. Nita, pausing to look down on her daughter, suddenly put it into words. "That isn't Rose. It can't be Rose."

"Oh, the wickedness of what that man did to her," said Ranbir. "Oh, the waste."

Lynn found herself level with the coffin, looking at Rose, and then, unable to bear it, turning her head away. Her eyes suddenly met Charan's. She wanted to speak to him, to express her sorrow for him, but there were no words which seemed adequate. Coming into the house, all she had managed was a murmur. Now she could not even achieve that.

And then, taking Lynn and everyone else by surprise, Charan stepped forward.

He made a sharp, imperious sign at the priest, and the latter fell silent, although the flash of surprise in his dark eyes clearly showed that this was not a scheduled part of the ceremony.

Kartar, with alarm in his voice, said, "Charan . . . !"

Charan raised a hand for silence. Everyone was in the room now; the square kitchen was crowded and breathless. "I have something to say," declared Charan.

The silence continued. Lynn saw Kartar and Perry exchange glances but neither of them interrupted.

"I have the right," said Charan. He looked straight at Kartar. "Had Rose lived, we would have been married and her children would have been mine. I repeat: I have the right."

The silence held. Lynn's mother took her daughter's hand and on impulse Lynn reached out with her other hand and found Shanti's. Their fingers, cold with fright, gripped each other gratefully.

"I am sick," said Charan, "sick to the heart, of hearing people say what a terrible thing it was that happened to Rose, and what a waste it is that she is dead, without hearing anyone say, loud enough to be heard, that she had no need to be dead, that what happened to her was not a reason for her to die."

Kartar broke in at last. "But my dear chap, we all know that, everyone realises that. That is the very heart and core of our grief. Charan, my dear fellow, let us . . . "

"Do we all know that?" said Charan. His voice had an intonation so steely that the priest, who had opened his mouth to resume his prayer, closed it again. Satinder Singh, who had moved forward as if to check his son, also halted. "Then why," said Charan, *"didn't she know it too?"*

The silence fell again, while Charan looked from one face to the next. No one this time attempted to speak. They waited.

"I have seen her letter," Charan said at last. "Her sad, sad letter in which she said goodbye to us all, and goodbye to me. In which, for the first time, she revealed the crime which had been committed against her. Till then, she had told no one but a doctor who was a stranger and she only did that for fear of transmitting a disease to me. She loved me enough to protect me but she didn't know me well enough to trust me . . . "

"Why did she not turn to us?" Nita cried out. "Her own parents – we would not have let her life be spoiled! If only she'd told us!"

"She trusted no one," said Charan. "She thought that somehow or other she would be held to blame. Who taught her to think that because of a crime committed by someone else, she had no right to her own life? Who taught her to believe that all men are so drunk on their pride that not one of us, not even I, her Charan, is capable of reasoning from A to B?"

He paused, and they saw that he was fighting to control tears. Swarup Sharma, stupidly, broke into words. "She was such a good girl, so pure, she felt the dishonour so keenly! She died because she felt so dishonoured and she feared it would harm her family. She did not have Western values."

"Western values, Eastern values: who cares where values come from? The point is, what kind of values are they?" shouted Charan. "What sort of value is it that condemns the innocent? What is this dishonour? The man who attacked her was dishonoured, nobody else! Oh, yes, her letter talked of dishonour! She had heard other women clacking phrases like spoiled goods! Oh, God, I have lain awake at night and thought, if she had told me, would I, just for a moment, have looked at her differently, would she have seen some atavistic barbarian in my eyes, condemning her? Perhaps she would, but I swear to God I would have reached into myself and strangled that barbarian; he would have died in that moment. As for her family . . . " His angry eyes stared in turn at Kartar and Nita, flicked briefly to Ranbir and then back once more to Rose's parents. "You were the people who brought her up; it was from you she took her ideas, her beliefs. You bear much of the responsibility for her death!"

His brother Surjit gave their father a quick, reassuring glance and stepped quickly forward to take Charan's elbow. "Charan, you are in a state of shock, you are not yourself . . . "

Charan shook him off. His gaze had now transfixed Amrit. "You, her sister, she named you in the letter! She was afraid she would injure your marriage chances. Are you happy she's dead? Do you think your future, the match you hope to make, is worth your sister's whole life, our life that we should have had together? I wish you joy of your marriage when it comes, Amrit. I hope it's worth the price that was paid for it! If I had been Rose, I would have said to you, *Tough, Amrit dear, but I am the one who was violated, not you.* But she didn't have enough belief in herself and her own worth to say it to you, did she? Oh, God!" shouted Charan, turning and gripping the edge of the coffin with both hands. "I don't want talk of purity and honour; I want my Raminder Rose, alive and in my arms, dishonour and all! Rose, come back, come back!"

All but the priest and Surjit were standing as if paralysed but these two now seized hold of Charan and pulled him away.

"This must stop," said Surjit. "No, it must. You have said what you need to say, but that is enough. No more, Charan, please."

"There's one thing more!" Charan turned towards the priest. "You will give the oration at the crematorium. Listen to me. When you speak of her, say that she died untimely and need-lessly, speak of our love and our sorrow, but do not say one word, not *one word* about purity or dishonour or I will spring forward and throw you off your rostrum! Do you hear me? But if you wish, you can say that she was murdered, and you can point the finger at us, at all of us, the so-called mourners, and you can accuse us of being accessories to the crime of murder because that is what we are!"

He stopped. He shook off the priest and Surjit, leant down once to rest his lips on Rose's forehead, and strode out of the room, pushing his way past the crowd in the doorway. They heard his footsteps go out on to the front path and halt, and then, looking after him, they saw him clutch the gatepost and double over. Satinder and Surjit, without a word, hurried after him.

Those remaining in the kitchen looked at each other. "He was right," said Lynn defiantly. "He was *right*."

Nita said, "Bheji! Help me, someone, quickly!"

Ranbir, her face the colour of parchment, was fainting. Lynn and Shanti rushed to help Nita steady her. They found a chair and sat her on it with her head between her knees.

"Close the coffin." Kartar's face was almost green. He was not far off fainting himself. "Let us say farewell to her and take her to her last repose as quickly and decently as we can." He looked at the priest. "You heard what Charan said concerning your oration. I agree that there should be no talk of either purity or dishonour, if you please. The rest of what he said, you may forget."

"I am all right," Ranbir whispered. "I can stand if you support me."

"Let me," said Nita, and then she and Ranbir, holding on to each other, began to move towards the door. Lynn and Shanti followed.

Outside, Surjit and his father were getting Charan into the back of his father's car. The undertakers stepped forward to perform the mundane task (so curiously suggestive of a workshop, thought Lynn, so out of keeping with the occasion) of screwing the lid down again.

The face of Raminder Rose was hidden once more.

"Let us," said Kartar grimly, "get this over."

Chapter Thirty-Four

Dusk and Firelight
1988

"This is a new experience for you, Bheji," Perry said over his shoulder as he turned the car off the M4 motorway and plunged southwards into Wiltshire. "You've never been to this part of England before, have you? I must say I'm very curious to see Balbir's place. What do you think of the countryside here?"

"It is very green," said Ranbir, gazing out at the grassy banks which verged the narrow road down which they were now purring, and glancing upwards at the smooth slopes of a hill over which cornfields and a meadow were thrown like a coverlet. "It is nice country. But it is much like places I have seen when Kartar takes Nita and me driving, and when we went to Leeds on Amrit's marriage."

"But all that is mostly on big roads," Shanti said. "Just here, one can almost touch it. It is nice; different from India but very nice." She twisted her head to look out of the rear window and said, laughing, "There, I said that that was Lynn and Sunder we passed on the motorway; there they are behind us. Look, Bheji. Let's wave!"

"Is it very far now?" Ranbir asked.

"No, only ten minutes or so. Are you tired, Bheji?"

"No, not very. This car is so smooth," said Ranbir.

"I thought you might enjoy a ride in it," Perry said. "That's why I said to Kartar: let Bheji come with us. This car is brand new." Perry was glad that he had kept his physical fitness now that he was into his fifties. It had enabled him to keep his painting and decorating business going, with the help, now, of a partner, and he was prospering enough these days to afford a car straight from the manufacturers. It wasn't the way he had once envisaged prospering but he was satisfied. He liked what he did and there was much to be said for that.

Balbir had given precise instructions about the route. Presently, Perry swung the car left into a lane which ran through a postcard-pretty village with thatched roofs and a green with a pond and white railings. Then came another left turn into another lane. At the end of this was an open five-barred gate, beyond which was an expanse of gravel in front of a square brick house. Several cars were already parked on the gravel.

Perry drew up, and with a swish of tyres, Sunder's car pulled in alongside. Both families climbed out and exchanged greetings. Sunder and Lynn unloaded their two children and Nerin, smiling broadly, came round the house to welcome them.

Ranbir looked about her with doubtful interest. She had not been sure whether she wanted to come to this party or not. This was partly to do with always feeling tired and never quite well, but partly, too, it was to do with a feeling that . . .

That she did not want to plunge too far into the depths of this strange land England. Southall was all right, and it was all right too when they visited Amrit's new family in Leeds, because in these places, one simply mixed in Indian society and once the front door had closed behind you, you could imagine you were back in Delhi.

In Balbir's home, somehow, she was certain that the illusion would not hold. Perry and Kartar had told her that he was living in an English country village where there were no other Indian people and where the local inhabitants were steeped in their own way of life. In such a place, Ranbir had thought instinctively, the strange, off-putting atmosphere which to her was England – she saw it in her mind as something grey and cold and sharp-edged and heard it speak with an accent of maddening superiority – must surely be winning.

And yet Balbir had never, unlike his father and Sunder, for a moment abandoned the hallmarks of orthodoxy. He continued to keep his turban and his steel bangle and he and Nerin often made time on a Sunday to drive up the motorway and join the rest of the family at the Gurudwara, and their two sons had topknots and one day would wear the turban too. His wife Nerin was a dear girl, and Ranbir liked Nerin's parents very much.

No, she had been right to come, especially as this was a double celebration. Partly, it was because Balbir and Nerin had at last got their home into what they said was a fit state for a housewarming, and partly, it was for the birth of the third child, a daughter whom they had called Meena. I could not have stayed away from this, Ranbir decided.

Most of the land owned by Balbir and Nerin had been put down to crops of one kind or another but as Balbir had once said, when chatting after a Gurudwara service, "Nerin would be miserable if she had no flowers to water and no lawn at all to mow." Behind Balbir's house, therefore, was a garden.

It was already full of people, both family members and Indian friends and English people who were presumably Balbir's and Nerin's neighbours. The garden consisted of a formal lawn flanked by flower beds and bisected by a crazy paving path with rose arches. The path led to a grassy bank at the end of the lawn and up a shallow flight of steps. Nerin shepherded them up the steps and they found themselves in a more casual garden, with fruit trees dotted amid uncut grass, flowering shrubs at one side, a goldfish pond at the other, and at the far end, a sandpit where Balbir and Kartar were busy with a barbecue.

"Nearly everyone's here," said Balbir, abandoning the business of kindling the charcoal bed in order to greet his family. "Harry Sheridan hasn't arrived yet. You'll like him, Dad. I don't think you've met him before; he hasn't been here long. He's manager of the Shire horse stud that's just been started a couple of miles away. He's one of the best, sort of calm and solid and takes you as he finds you."

"What is a Shire horse?" Ranbir asked.

"Oh, a very beautiful sort of heavy horse, very massive. They used to be used for ploughing and pulling big loads and then, of course, the tractor took over and thousands of them were just slaughtered. There's a move to start breeding them again now. It's partly to do with the environment – horses provide manure instead of polluting the air – and partly because they're just plain gorgeous. Sheridan has a farm to run as well and he works it with the Shires. I was looking over a fence one day and saw him working with a team and we got talking. Next year," said Balbir, grinning, "he just might come along with a team and turn the soil on one of my fields if I let the public come and watch and be given a lecture by loudspeaker on the history of the Shire horse. He's half promised, anyway . . . Lynn, that pond isn't at all deep, but . . . "

"Oh, good heavens!" said Lynn and sped in pursuit of her daughter Tina. "She's only three and a half but I think she's got ambitions to travel the world," she said, returning with the errant Tina, protesting loudly, in her arms. "If Jonathan is as bad when he gets bigger, I don't know what I'll do. Where *is* Jonathan . . . oh, you've got him, Sunder."

"Bring them along and let them meet the guest of honour," said Balbir, brushing charcoal off his hands. "We're so delighted with her; Nerin was very keen to have a daughter, after two boys. She's going to be pretty; one can see it already. She's in her cradle over here under the Cox's Orange Pippin . . . "

Most of them would be staying the night. "We've plenty of space," Balbir had said when backing up the invitation cards with telephone calls. "Bheji can have the spare room and we've plenty of divans downstairs."

The party, therefore, could run on through the evening into the September nightfall, and because the weather was still warm, it could take place comfortably out of doors. Later, Ranbir, settled in a chair, with a small table to hold her plate and her orange juice, watched the scene in some bemusement.

It was in some ways not unlike open-air parties in India, when the coolness of the night was often the best time to choose for get-togethers and celebrations. Fairy lights and lanterns had been strung among the trees, just as they might be in Delhi. The charcoal fire glowed and there was a pleasant smell of smoke and cooking.

True, there were steaks grilling along with the kebabs and the pork sausages, and steaks wouldn't usually figure at an Indian party, but a party in Wiltshire was bound to have some differences, and she had been introduced already to several people who wouldn't usually feature at a celebration in Delhi either. Among them were the District Nurse, who had instantly whisked Meena out of her cradle and demanded to know if her parents intended having her vaccinated against whooping cough, two quietly spoken men who were apparently in some way connected with Balbir's profession and who at once fell into a technical conversation with him about pest control, and a tall woman with an incisive voice who had told her that Nerin was a popular member of the local Women's Institute (she had called it WI and Nerin had had to explain) where Nerin was apparently in the habit of giving lectures on Indian cookery. Balbir and Nerin seemed as much at ease with these people as they were with their own family. It was, thought Ranbir, quite remarkable.

There was music going, although not loudly, a tape compiled by Balbir and Nerin together, of lively light music which included popular Indian film themes as well as songs and tunes from English groups. The infant Meena, who had slept peacefully throughout the evening and was still placidly snoozing, had been placed under a lantern where she could be seen and Balbir was announcing a toast. Champagne corks popped and bubbles hissed, and there was a shout of laughter as a cork shot into the midst of the barbecue and gave off a fizz of sparks.

"Hold it!" Perry shouted just as Balbir, glass in hand, was about to take up his position. "Someone else has arrived; I heard the car."

The new arrival was large and tweed-clad and was greeted by a joyful cry from Nerin. "Oh, good, you have come. We wondered where you were."

"Harry, this is my father," said Balbir, beginning some new introductions. "Dad, this is Harry Sheridan."

"Pleased to meet you. Look, Balbir, I'm sorry I'm so late and I'm not on my own. A colt got out of his field and cut himself on a wire fence on somebody else's land. He had to be caught and calmed down and I had to get the vet to stitch him up and the whole business took hours . . ."

"Will he be all right?" said Balbir anxiously. "Look, you must need a drink."

"I do, and so does the vet. He's sitting in the car. The poor animal was so frightened, he took some handling. He knocked us both flying before we quietened him. But, yes, he ought to be sound though he'll probably be scarred. It was a ragged cut on the shoulder; a very gory mess but fairly superficial. Only, after we'd scrubbed up, I said to the vet that I was coming to this party and why didn't he come too if he hadn't another call to make. I reckoned we could both do with reviving and I didn't think you'd mind. But he won't get out of the car until he's sure it's all right."

"I'll fetch him myself!" said Balbir. "Nerin . . ."

"You can start your drink while my husband brings the vet round," said Nerin, seizing a bottle and pouring out a glass of champagne for Sheridan. "We are about to drink a toast to the baby. Come and meet Meena."

The vet was fetched and introduced. "I'm sorry to barge in like this but Harry was so insistent . . ."

"Nonsense. The whole village can come if it wants," said Balbir briskly.

"Well, I don't know you very well yet. You haven't any

animals. You haven't got into English ways quite to that extent yet."

"It may come," said Nerin, laughing. "I wouldn't be at all surprised if Harry doesn't end by selling us a team of Shire horses!"

At Ranbir's side, Shanti appeared. "Are you all right, Bheji? I've brought you some more orange juice, because we're going to drink the baby's health. Tell me if you want to go indoors. I know that you get tired these days."

"I am all right," said Ranbir.

She leant back in her chair with half-closed eyes and listened while Balbir launched into a speech about his baby daughter. It was somewhat interrupted, because Meena, perversely, chose to wake up in the middle of it and squall loudly, and Lynn had once more to retrieve her own daughter, who seemed to be fascinated by the pond. Ranbir reached out from her chair and caught the little girl's hand as she toddled rapidly past. "Here you are, Lynn."

"Thank you, Bheji. Tina loves water," said Lynn breathlessly. "I think I'll have to see she learns to swim as soon as possible."

Ranbir nodded. Suddenly she had been overwhelmed by a sense of unreality. She had been right: in this place, no illusion of an Indian gathering could hold. It was all dissolved now in the strangeness of these ringing English voices talking of Women's Institutes and Shire horses. It came home to her, with a shock as though it were quite a new discovery, that the great-grand-daughter whose little hand she had momentarily grasped, was half English and bore the name of Tina.

Long ago, back in India in the days when she and Jog were bidding farewell to their sons as Kartar and then Perry sailed for England, they could never have foreseen this as their destination.

Never for one moment had she envisaged great-grand-children like Tina and Jonathan, half-English by blood and likely to grow up all-English in their ways, she supposed, although they were both amber-skinned and Jonathan's hair at least looked as though it would turn out jet black, though Tina's had red glints; she had clear traces of her mother's ginger.

Troubled, lost, far from home now, in both body and spirit, Ranbir groped for comfort. Sunder and Lynn seemed happy, and if Lynn had far too stormy a temperament for a woman, she had produced those two healthy children. And there were the

410

children of Rupa and Surjit, who were being reared in traditional fashion, and Balbir's boys were satisfyingly orthodox, too, even here in this country place which was so very English, and where Balbir and Nerin had, clearly, already made themselves a niche. They appeared to have committed themselves to England. One could hardly commit oneself more thoroughly to a place than by buying its land. And yet, they were still good Sikhs. Somehow, they had made terms between England and themselves.

The champagne, as usual, was producing laughter. Perry was reading out a letter which he had received yesterday from his former landlord, Robert Houghton. "I would have brought him along, Balbir, but he's ninety now and too frail to travel. But he can still write a letter and we've corresponded all through the years. He's sent his congratulations. Listen . . . "

And then, when the applause for Houghton's letter had died down, came Kartar's voice, quietening the merriment, saying, "Let us have a toast in memory of those who can't be here."

There were too many of those, Ranbir thought. The tensions of life in this far land had been too much for some. Curious, she thought, looking round the firelight garden, yes, curious and somewhat shocking, that those who had been the most willing to compromise had somehow managed best.

Of the children of the easygoing Perry and Shanti, Satnam had been lost, but the other three were happy, and close to their parents still. But Mohan Lal and Leela, who were not here tonight, had remained very Indian and were not close to any of their children. Krishna wrote now and then but she never came home, while Chandra Lal, who was not here either, now lived a life almost entirely apart from his family, seeing his parents only rarely. Sita was the one who visited them most frequently, but she did not come as often as all that, and she was not, her parents admitted, comfortable company.

Kartar and Nita too had tried hard to hold on to their own values and pass them to their daughters, particularly to Rose, and Ranbir had urged them on. But Rose, who should have been here with Charan by her side, was grey ashes now, buried beneath a yellow Peace rose in a garden of remembrance, and Charan had gone back to Canada and perhaps would never marry.

There had been a horrible moment, at Rose's funeral, when Ranbir had almost felt . . . well . . . partly responsible for Rose's

411

death. The idea had come over her so strongly that she had nearly fainted. Which was absurd, of course. Rose should have come to her, or to Nita; young people should ask their elders for advice. Her Bheji would have known what was best for her to do. Ranbir would have seen that it was all hushed up! Rose had been most foolish. It was better, really, when thinking of Rose, to be a little angry with her. Anger kept grief at bay. And it was such terrible, such consuming grief . . .

They had at least found a good marriage for Amrit. Her new family in Leeds were excellent people. They knew all about Rose and had only sympathy for her. But Amrit, also absent tonight, seemed to have buried herself among them, as though Rose's tragedy – or possibly, Charan's blighting remarks – had made her turn away from her own kin, whose visits she appeared to tolerate rather than welcome.

Though admittedly, Kartar said that her husband wanted her to use her sociology degree and Perry said that his niece reminded him of the Sleeping Beauty: one of these days, she would awaken.

Ranbir wondered how she would awaken if so. Would she be an Indian Amrit, or a Western one? Who could tell?

"Bheji, you are weary, I can see." She roused herself. The toasts were over and Shanti was bending anxiously over her. Ranbir looked up and saw that Sita was there too.

Sita was a mystery. No one knew what had happened inside that marriage in the end. One day, without warning, Sita had taken to wearing bright saris and make-up, had started up a counselling service for Asian women with domestic problems, which she ran from her home without, apparently, the slightest protest from Hari, and was going about, visiting friends and attending functions, as though she did not know the meaning of the word downtrodden. Asked what had caused the change, she merely smiled and didn't answer. There had been endless speculation, but no explanations.

But it had been noticed that her smile had none of the sweetness everyone had once associated with Sita. She had changed. There was something about her now which was hard and bright and jagged, like an edge of broken glass. The old, gentle Sita was gone.

Invited to this party, she had said she might come or might not; it would depend on how busy she was. And had then arrived by train and taxi, bearing a box of sweetmeats as a gift,

412

and clad in crimson silk with a gold edging.

"If you wish, we can help you upstairs," she said now. "Nerin has shown us where you are to sleep. She is just seeing to Meena, so we said to her, shall we look after Bheji, and she sent us to you."

"Yes," said Ranbir, not unwilling to be taken in hand. "I think I will go to bed now."

She didn't like to admit how tired she felt and was glad she had some paracetamol in her toilet bag. Soon, she would have to return to the hospital. The operation and the chemotherapy had staved off disaster for a while, but her time was growing short. There would be no last visit to India as she had once hoped. The fate which had decided that she should live in England had also decided that she should die there.

They helped her upstairs, Sita taking the lead, brightly efficient, putting the bedside light on, closing the curtains, and then, with a tolerant smile, opening them again because Ranbir protested that she preferred them thus. Then Sita withdrew, leaving Shanti to settle her mother-in-law in bed.

"Thank you, dear," Ranbir said to Shanti and thought that if it was a curious destiny which had brought her to a party in a Wiltshire house, it was an equally odd fate which had decreed that she should have grown so fond of the Hindu daughter-in-law she had once so much despised, and so willing to depend upon her. Shanti was always kind. Sita, Ranbir thought, must intimidate many of the women who came to her for help.

Nerin came presently with some hot milk and she washed two paracetamol tablets down with it. Outside, she could still hear the sound of the party, and the fairy lights cast coloured gleams on her bedroom ceiling. Somewhere a baby, probably Meena, cried.

The charcoal fire was out and the fragrances which now drifted in at the window were the fresh, moist scents of grass and leaves in an English autumn. Ranbir absorbed them, remembering Indian nights when the darkness was velvet and the baked earth breathed back the heat which the sun had poured on it so fiercely throughout the day.

The tablets had settled the pain for the time being. It was possible to lie and think in peace. But the English autumn smell worried her a little and she drew the covers up to her nostrils to keep it out. She couldn't keep sound out, though. The strains of a folk singing group came up from the garden, and she

413

recognised which group it was. It was Medway River, which Perry's one-time tenant Rick Medway had founded, with marked success. Everyone in the family had some Medway River tapes.

Close to the house, she could hear the voices of the man Sheridan, and the vet who had arrived fresh from stitching up an injured Shire colt, mingling with Balbir's voice in a discussion of some local event, a horse show by the sound of it.

What would happen to them all, in time to come, her descendants who had put down roots in this strange land? There were forces at work here, of which they seemed unconscious. But Ranbir could sense them. Age and illness and approaching death, it seemed, only made that sixth sense more acute.

This land was old and strong. It had been inhabited for aeons and its earth and its people had shaped each other, creating between them an atmosphere so powerful that it was almost a force. That was true of India too and once, Ranbir had thought that only India was like that; that other places were simply negative, not-India. But, as her daughter-in-law Nita had concluded once, sitting in a pub (a place which Ranbir would never have entered), in a place called Hampton Court (which Ranbir had never visited), it was not so.

Any people who chose to move here and remain for more than a few generations would be changed by that force. Her descendants would be changed, even those who believed most firmly that they had made terms with this land and had kept their essential Indianness inviolate.

Ranbir had believed all her life in fate and the inability of mankind to change it. And on many many occasions, as though her nature and her beliefs were incompatible, she had fought with all her strength to change it.

She could fight no more. Fate would have its way. Ranbir slept.

FIONA BUCKLEY WRITING AS
VALERIE ANAND

THE PROUD VILLEINS

"VALERIE ANAND HAS BEEN
BUILDING A REMARKABLE
BODY OF WORK, A SERIES
OF HISTORICAL NOVELS
THAT HAVE RECREATED
ENGLAND'S HISTORY BOTH
ACCURATELY AND VIVIDLY."
—THE ANNISTON STAR

BOOK 1
BRIDGES
OVER TIME

Published by SpeakingVolumes

Visit: www.speakingvolumes.us

FIONA BUCKLEY WRITING AS
VALERIE ANAND

"VALERIE ANAND HAS BEEN BUILDING A REMARKABLE
BODY OF WORK, A SERIES OF HISTORICAL NOVELS
THAT HAVE RECREATED ENGLAND'S HISTORY BOTH
ACCURATELY AND VIVIDLY." —THE ANNISTON STAR

THE RUTHLESS YEOMEN
BOOK II
BRIDGES
OVER TIME

Published by SpeakingVolumes

Visit: www.speakingvolumes.us

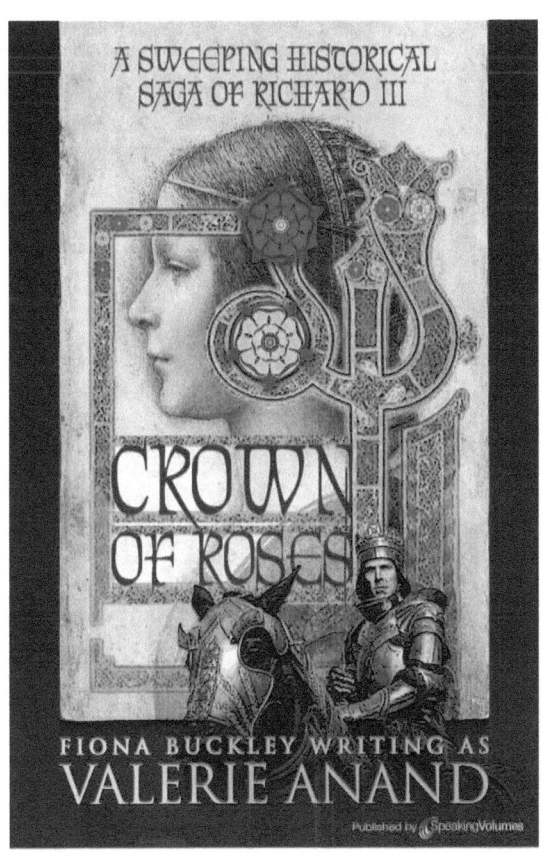

For more information
visit: www.speakingvolumes.us

Sign up for free and bargain books

Join the Speaking Volumes mailing list

Text

ILOVEBOOKS

to 22828 to get started.